D1112392

TAILSPIN

Other books by Bernard F. Conners:

DON'T EMBARRASS THE BUREAU

DANCEHALL

THE HAMPTON SISTERS

TAILSPIN

The Strange Case of Major Call

BY BERNARD F. CONNERS

BRITISH AMERICAN PUBLISHING, LTD.
LATHAM, NEW YORK

Published by British American Publishing, Ltd.
4 British American Boulevard
Latham, New York 12110
Printed in the United States of America

ISBN (cloth): 0-945167-50-4

Library of Congress Cataloging-in-Publication Data

Conners, Bernard F.
    Tailspin : the strange case of Major Call / by Bernard F. Conners
      p. cm.
    ISBN 0-945167-50-4 (alk. paper)

    1. Call, James Arlon. 2. Sheppard, Marilyn Reese. 3. Sheppard, Sam.
4. Criminals—United States—Biography. 5. Murder—Ohio—Cleveland.
6. Murder—New York (State)—Lake Placid. 7. United States. Air
Force—Biography. I. Title.
    HV6248.C125 C66 2002
    364.15'23'0977132—dc21
                              2001006368

For CCC

FOREWORD

Some months ago, Bernard Conners asked me to review his manuscript of *Major Call*. Ordinarily I am wary of such requests because experience teaches that the author is usually looking not for appraisal, but for praise. I was familiar, however, with Conners' previous books, including his two bestsellers: *Don't Embarrass the Bureau* and *Dancehall*. *Don't Embarrass the Bureau*, though wrapped in fiction, is the best book that I have ever read for an inside view of the FBI. *Dancehall* is not only a gripping story based on real life incidents, but at the same time, a brilliant treatment of capital punishment. And so, instead of ducking when Conners asked me to read his latest book, I looked forward to another tale by this eminently readable writer. Conners did not disappoint. This time, as he shifts to nonfiction, he again displays his gift for bringing a film-like "you are there" quality to his narrative, in this case a solution to an enduring mystery in the annals of American crime. Few writers come better equipped. Conners, as a former FBI agent, adds to his professional experience the instincts of a literary bloodhound. With his talent for spinning a story, he has created a nonfiction work that reads like a novel, just as his novels read like fact.

Conners' reliability is underscored by the stunning amount of documentation, forensic evidence and the fruits of many years of research. He brings his experience in law enforcement and the skills of a novelist to the presentation of a mass of factual material in an imaginative reconstruction of events, a reconstruction that sticks to what is known and what can be reasonably inferred from the evidence available. His account's meticulous description of places and personalities adds to its overall power and authenticity.

Conners unfolds the life story of an unlikely master criminal—an Air Force hero who goes into a moral tailspin culminating in a chilling crime spree that likely included a brutal crime that has haunted our memories for nearly half a century. Conners offers a convincing solution to this case after interviewing witnesses, tracking down police and trial records, consulting forensic and other experts, and fitting it all into a logical, believable chain of guilt. The reader's reward is a story that has one impatiently turning the pages and thinking, "And all this *really* happened!"

JOSEPH E. PERSICO
January 15, 2001

Joseph E. Persico is the author of several books on history and biography, including *Nuremberg: Infamy on Trial*, *My American Journey* (a collaboration with Colin Powell), and most recently *Roosevelt's Secret War: FDR and World War II Espionage.*

PREFACE

The following work is based on the life of James Arlon Call, an Air Force major whose career during its finer moments was illustrious. Brilliant, handsome, a loving husband and outstanding aviator, he appeared to personify everything that was admirable in a young man. But there was a dark side, a part of his personality which was inexplicable and led to heinous deeds that defy understanding.

To present this story of Major Call's life, the author has used a narrative technique that reasonably expresses the thoughts and actions of individuals at given times. The information on which this account is based derives from Call's own written and oral histories, interviews with relatives (next of kin and otherwise), friends and associates both civilian and military, government officials, records of police organizations throughout the country including local, state and federal agencies, files of the United States Air Force, trial records, contemporary press accounts, archival documents, and other sources (some of which remain confidential). This story of Major Call's life is a dramatized narrative supported by fact.

PROLOGUE

Lake Placid, New York
August 1954

One was shocked, the other remarkably cool. They stood virtually toe-to-toe, eyes riveted, pistols leveled. It was the briefest of confrontations but in that instant both knew death was near.

It was just past midnight in a small cabin deep in New York's Adirondack Mountains. One of the men, a police officer, had just discovered the other in the cellar hiding in a shower stall. The two were now motionless, eyes locked in a profound exchange during that infinitesimal time when synaptic gaps fuse triggering reactions. A shroud of dampness covered the fetid room. Suspended by a cord from the ceiling, a soft yellow lamp provided a glimmer of light. Then, imperceptibly, a whiff of air caused the lamp to move slightly, sending shimmering forms from the corners. One pair of eyes wavered, the other remained steady, glacial....

The eyes of the two men had viewed vastly different worlds. Dominick Valenze, Nick to his friends, of whom there were many, was an amiable, easy-going police officer; a thirty-nine-year-old family man who lived a respected and sedentary existence in the small hamlet of Lake Placid, New York. Rarely in his police work, until this moment, had Nick been on the wrong end of a firearm. Indeed, seldom had his revolver been unholstered, save for an occasional cleaning. Although minor legal infractions were part of his day, he handled them with equanimity, for Nick was first and foremost a *peace* officer.

A far different world had been witnessed by the other eyes now gripping Nick from the shower a breath away. They belonged to an Air Force major, recently decorated for flying sorties over Korea. They were eyes that had seen death many times, in many forms.

Now, in that eternal second, Nick Valenze knew he was at the brink. The trim, trenchcoated figure regarding him coolly from the shower stall had his arms folded languidly across his chest. In his right hand, held so that it pointed directly at Nick from the crook of the figure's left elbow, was a 9 mm Luger.

While the confrontation was taking place between the two men inside the cabin, waiting outside in a pouring rain was Officer Dick Pelkey, another family man. A few minutes earlier, he with Nick and two other Lake Placid policemen had come to the cabin in response to reports of suspicious activity. During recent weeks there had been burglaries in the area, including a $100,000 jewel theft at the renowned Lake Placid Club—highly unusual for a community which was virtually crime-free. Residents were uneasy. Particularly worrisome were reports that showed the perpetrator was a "hot burglar"—one who relied on weapons rather than stealth to accomplish robberies.

In view of the recent crimes, Nick and his fellow officers had reason to be apprehensive when they had rendezvoused at the cabin a short time before. Nick and another policeman, pistols drawn, had entered the premises, while Dick and the fourth officer had remained outside to cover the front and back doors. Dick had taken a post at the back near one of the large spruce trees surrounding the dwelling, from where he had watched as beams from the officers' flashlights flitted about inside.

Now, as his fellow officers moved unknowingly toward the confrontation with the stranger in the cellar, Dick was becoming increasingly uneasy. No longer could he see the flashlights. His eyes narrowed, scrutinizing the dark beyond the windows. Why are there no lights, he wondered. He stood near the towering trees, as motionless as their heavy trunks. More than the activity inside the camp, it was the surrounding blackness that made him uneasy. His position rendered him an easy target if there were something back there in the trees watching....

Suddenly, a light flashed in the cellar window. Then voices, sharp, threatening. Dick straightened, his hand loosening his pistol in its holster. All at once, a gust of wind ... a sharp fusillade of rain ricocheting off the camp roof. It startled him. Gimlet-eyed he focused on the base of the house where the cellar window glowed dimly.

The rain was severe now, rattling on the visor of his cap, stinging his cheeks, lips. Little could he know that in seconds the interior of the cabin would be ablaze in gunfire. Some fourteen bullets would rip through walls, flesh and bones. Bodies would crumple. Dick, himself, would lie mortally wounded.

Behind him, awaiting the survivor of the impending mayhem, was the vast Adirondack Forest, an arboreal kingdom of quiet natural beauty. The violent noise about to erupt in the cabin would be quickly muted in the forest, where the only sounds were the mysterious nocturnal rhythms of the alpine wilderness. Here a heroic airman turned predator would follow the dark beat of the wild.

◆ ◆ ◆

PART I

Tucson, Arizona

September 1949

1

"James Call. He's the man you want, Colonel. Brilliant young fellow. Catches on quickly. They say he can do things in the air at three times the speed of anyone else."

The two men were sitting in the posh lobby of the Conquistador Hotel in Tucson. Nearby, a young woman sat with a slender book on her lap, at which she glanced frequently but read only sporadically. At the moment Muriel John was more interested in the conversation she could not help but overhear between the two middle-aged men in military uniform a few feet away. One wore the silver eagles of a colonel, the other a captain's double-bar insignia.

"Captain Walsh was with him at Mather," the officer continued. "AOB school. Finished first in his class. Flew B-25s, C-47s."

"I've heard he's a little aggressive." It was clear from the colonel's tone the comment was not intended as a compliment.

"Well, sir, that's what we train them to be, isn't it? And from what you've told me about the assignment you sure don't want some laid-back—"

"Yes, yes," the colonel interjected, with a trace of irritation befitting a ranking officer. "But we need someone we can control and.... Well, I've talked to some people since our last conversation. From what I'm told, Lieutenant Call can be quite a handful."

"Yes, sir. I just thought since we were all here at the same hotel we could have a drink together and—"

"Excuse me, Captain," the colonel interrupted, nodding toward the entranceway. "Is that your man?"

Muriel followed their gaze across the lobby to where a trim figure in uniform emerged from the revolving door. Even from a distance the man had a commanding presence. He looked briefly about the lobby and proceeded directly toward them, walking with a casual, confident stride. Muriel pretended interest in her book, but as the man drew near she stole a quick appraising look. He exchanged the glance before she quickly averted her eyes. She saw enough to know that Lieutenant Call was indeed an attractive person. He had dark hair and strong tanned features. But it was his expression that was most striking. She was later to describe it to her mother as a no-nonsense look, as though he had a real purpose.

"Colonel, this is Lieutenant Call." The two men stood to shake hands with the younger officer.

Muriel, her eyes fixed on her book, listened as they exchanged amenities. She was immediately struck by the younger man's poise. Although respectful of the superior officers, he spoke with the relaxed fluency and self-assurance of one not easily intimidated.

"Shall we have a drink?" the colonel suggested, motioning toward a cocktail lounge beyond the lobby.

Although she dared not look again, Muriel sensed from the colonel's manner and tone that the lieutenant had made a good first impression.

"After you, sir." The lieutenant stepped back, allowing the two officers to precede him.

As they moved away, Muriel abandoned her book, staring after the young officer. Gosh, he was handsome.... Suddenly the lieutenant looked back over his shoulder, catching her gaze. His eyes lingered and a trace of a smile appeared. Embarrassed, she looked away. Too late, though. He'd caught her staring at him. Although it had been a brief exchange of glances, there was something about his confident easy manner which she found fascinating. The supercilious arch of an eyebrow, the slightly patronizing smile, a subtle expression that seemed to whisper, "We'll meet again." As he moved out of sight she chanced another look, her eyes following wistfully.

Ordinarily Muriel would not have been piqued by such an ephemeral encounter. But having arrived in Tucson a short time before, she was already experiencing an edge of loneliness. If the right person came along she would not be averse to engaging in conversation. The lieutenant, perhaps. Would she ever see him again? Probably not. Yet that look....

Muriel was used to men's admiring glances. Some were less obvious than others, but they all looked. For Muriel John was a head turner. "Absolutely gorgeous," in the words of one admirer. "Most beautiful girl in Mississippi." Although right now she wasn't entirely at her best. She had come to Tucson from her home town of Meridian, Mississippi, a few weeks before with hopes that the arid climate would relieve the asthma that had afflicted her since she was twelve. The travel and a temporary loss of appetite had left her a bit wan. Nevertheless, with auburn hair, soft inquisitive eyes shuttered by long ebony lashes, and a striking figure, she presented a definite allure. For that very reason, before she had left Meridian her father had been concerned about his only child.

"Careful who you take up with, honey." It had been one of many warnings on the eve of her departure, and when Muriel had finally protested that she was, after all, almost twenty-one years old and capable of running her own life, her father had delivered his final admonition. "All right. You're a lot smarter than I am. Been to college. Know all that poetry, just like your mother. But looks like yours attract things. All kinds of things...."

Her father would know. Although Victor John was a highly respected man with powerful political friends in Meridian, the family affluence exceeded considerably what one would normally expect from the few small businesses he owned. Indeed, there were occasional whispers about questionable enterprises—gambling, bootlegging whiskey (Mississippi was a dry state).

Otherwise the Johns' lifestyle was wholesome, with a lovely mansion on fashionable Poplar Spring Drive and membership in St. Paul's Episcopal Church, where Victor's wife Robbie enjoyed an impeccable reputation. "Robbie has absolutely nothing whatever to do with Victor's businesses," was one telling remark offered by a friend of the family. And Muriel? "Why, there isn't a more considerate, lovelier girl in all Meridian than Muriel John."

Now sitting alone some 1,500 miles from home in the lobby of a Tucson hotel, Muriel John was indeed a true Mississippi belle. But as Victor John had warned, a girl with her looks attracts things ... all kinds of things....

◆ ◆ ◆

2

"He's a plunger."

"How deep is he?"

"Coupl'a thou."

Two men in tuxedoes stood near a cashier's window in a sprawling, crowded Las Vegas casino. "Pit bosses" or "enforcers" in gambling jargon, they were observing a figure in a khaki officer's uniform standing at a nearby crap table, his back to them. One of the men, a short balding individual whose worn features reflected the late hours of his trade, held a check in his hand. "Maybe he's lost more," the man speculated. "I'm only talkin' the last hour or so."

"Lot of bread on lieutenant's pay...," mused the other. Although younger than the shorter man, it was apparent that he was the superior. "Drinking much?"

"Some. Tom says he's been in before. Drinks moderately. Avoids the broads. I told him when he asked to cash the check that he might be gettin' in a little heavy."

"What'd he say?"

"Ignored me. Said I didn't look like his chaplain, but I sure sounded like him."

"Wise fucker," allowed the taller man. "Tough lookin' hombre."

"Tom said he's got a temper. A guy grabbed his dice out of turn. Told him if he did it again he'd tear his arm off.... How 'bout you tellin' him you won't cash his check?"

"What about his ID?"

"Air Force. Looks legit."

The taller man paused, studying the broad-shouldered figure at the table. Suddenly the object of his attention turned and looked straight at him, eyes hard, unwavering. The manager avoided the exchange. "Cash it," he said, walking away.

The subordinate moved to a cashier's window, exchanged the check for chips, and proceeded to the crap table. "Here you are, Lieutenant," he said with a tight smile. "Good luck."

The lieutenant frowned as he took the chips. "That took a while. I'm running late." He turned and immediately placed the entire stack on the no-pass line. The pit boss paused, arched a brow, then backed away.

On the other side of the table the shooter, a blonde woman who looked to be in her early thirties but was probably closer to forty, observed through narrowed eyes the officer betting against her. "Thanks for the vote of confidence, Lieutenant." She extended her hand holding the dice toward him, slowly shaking her fist up and down suggestively. It was an obscene gesture, not lost on those around the table.

"Shoot him down, honey," said one.

"We're with you, doll," from another.

The officer ignored the comments, his eyes fixed on the board. The dice tumbled from the woman's hand, coming to rest at the end of the table. "Six!" the croupier announced. "The point is six," he repeated, pushing the dice back to the shooter with his crook.

"Buck sergeants," said the blonde, using the gaming term for the two threes she had just rolled. "You got me outranked, Lieutenant."

The officer, impervious to the comment, kept his attention riveted on the board. Several rolls of the dice ensued, each with supporting words from bettors around the table. And then, "Seven!" A groan from the crowd. The croupier moved his stick deftly around the table, collecting the house winnings. His assistant placed a stack of chips next to those the officer had wagered on the no-pass line.

With a quiet indifference, the lieutenant gathered his winnings and walked directly to a window, where he cashed the chips. As he moved away counting the money, the blonde woman fell in step beside him. She seemed unfazed by their encounter at the crap table. "Where you going, Lieutenant?" She smiled invitingly. "I could show you a good time with some of that."

The lieutenant continued to count the money, never looking at the woman. "Lady, my life's already about as dangerous as I want it to get." He quickened his pace, leaving her behind.

She started to respond but her words were lost in the cacophony of throbbing music, whirring slot machines, clinking glasses, and conversation that resonated through the large room. It was an exciting milieu, offering promise of fun and reward for occasional gamblers, onlookers, and vacationers out for a good time. Less visible, on the edge of the glittering casino, was the darker side of the enterprise. Here were the addicted, the mainliners, the unwary, those who lived on the edge. Here a brilliant life could be destroyed.

♦ ♦ ♦

3

Rising some 9,000 feet out of the desert, the Tucson Mountain Range was a towering citadel encircling the city of Tucson. For a young woman far from home unfamiliar with such topography, it evoked conflicting emotions. By day, the grandeur of the peaks was inspiring for a young poet, inducing feelings of well-being. At dusk, however, the range was transformed into a jagged silhouette which could be harsh and foreboding.

Muriel John was not especially fond of the view during the evening. It was then that the tugging strains of loneliness were most prevalent, when she questioned the wisdom of her quest for change. There had been a few such nights when she had considered ending her trip, only to awaken to a glorious sun-filled day that helped to stiffen her pride. An early return to Poplar Spring Drive could prove embarrassing after her assertions of independence.

On this particular day Muriel, clad in a one-piece bathing suit and sunglasses, relaxed in a chaise on a terrace beside the Conquistador Hotel swimming pool. The dry desert air and warm sun combined to make the weather exceedingly pleasant. Right now she took comfort from the broad brigade of peaks in the distance, brightly clad sentinels standing boldly in the sunshine.

On her lap was a slender volume of poetry from which she would alternately read a few lines and then reflectively rest her head back against the chaise. So absorbed was she that she failed to notice a waiter placing two large drinks on the table beside her.

"There you are, madam. Enjoy."

"What?" said Muriel, sitting up, removing her glasses. Her eyes flashed from the drinks to the waiter, who was walking away. "Oh, just a minute, please. Waiter! I didn't order these. There must be some mis—"

"I ordered them," came a voice from behind. It was a pleasant voice, deep, resonant.

She turned quickly and looked into smiling eyes and a handsome face. It was the young officer she had seen in the lobby a few days before. He was wearing a light blue shirt and jeans. Out of uniform he seemed less imposing, more youthful. Her pulse quickened.

"I'm Jim Call," he said, continuing to smile. "I think we met inside a couple of days ago."

Muriel, not easily intimidated, ordinarily would have been up to the challenge. But caught unaware, she was overwhelmed by the charming manner and the offer of drinks. "I'm sorry...." she murmured. "But ... I don't believe we've met."

"Well, I suppose we didn't actually meet in a formal sense," the man responded, leisurely drawing up a chair from a nearby table. "But, uh, we sort of exchanged looks." It was an awkward moment, but he didn't seem at all fazed. In fact later, upon reflection, she would marvel at his confidence.

"Oh, really?" Muriel said, attempting to regain her composure. She shifted and drew part of the towel on which she was resting over her thighs. "Are you sure you have the right person? I've only been here a short time."

"Oh, I'm sure," he replied with conviction. "Won't you join me for a drink?" Not waiting for an answer he took the two glasses from the table and handed her one. "Frozen daiquiris. Very refreshing on a hot day."

Muriel hesitated, then almost reluctantly accepted the glass. "Well, ... thank you," she murmured.

"I suppose you think I'm a bit forward."

She sipped the drink, her brown eyes measuring him. A combination of beauty and intelligence had enabled Muriel to achieve a level of confidence and sophistication unusual for her age. She recovered quickly. "Forward? Yes, maybe. What if I'd said 'no'? Wouldn't you be embarrassed toting these drinks off to some other table?"

The man shrugged, smiling. He looked at her for a moment, musingly, his eyes steady, penetrating ... unsettling.

"Hello!" she said, waving her fingers to regain his attention.

"Oh, sorry." He blinked, recovering. "You, uh, you remind me of someone. Sorry." He seemed genuinely contrite.

Muriel softened. Perhaps she'd overreacted. "Who's that?" A flicker of a smile.

"Actually, a movie actress."

Oh, the phony! She should've known better. "An actress?" she said skeptically, eyes narrowing.

"Honestly," he said. "You resemble her. I can't think of her name. Maybe it'll come to me."

"Is that so?" Was he being truthful? And those eyes … why did he keep staring? At least blink or something. She leaned forward to place her drink on the table and in doing so knocked the book from her lap. Several postcards and a newspaper clipping tumbled onto the ground. It was a moment that called for assistance.

"Here, let me get those." He stood quickly, retrieving the items, his eyes lingering on the clipping as he handed it to her. "Looks like someone's on vacation," he said, reclaiming his seat.

"I beg your pardon?" She'd heard him and understood the implication, but sensed an impending involvement. He certainly was charming, though. When he had been close, retrieving the cards, she had noticed the scent of shaving lotion—clean, fresh.

"Postcards," he continued, nodding at the cards. "Where's home?"

She paused. "Mississippi." She refocused on the book, not inclined to elaborate.

"I've been there," he continued. "But I guess I've been everywhere—for a day or two, anyway. Whereabouts in Mississippi?"

Another pause. "Eastern part of the state," she replied cautiously, her father's admonition in mind. But then, realizing she was being excessively unresponsive, "Meridian. Small place. Not many people know it."

"Oh, sure. I've heard of it. I'm from Chicago. My name's Jim Call."

"Yes, you mentioned that."

"And yours?"

"Oh … Muriel."

"Muriel? I like that. Three syllables. Nice name."

"Thanks." She flipped a few pages of the book.

It seemed for a moment that he might break off the conversation, but then, "Actually, I'm from Glenview, Illinois … near Chicago. But I've been flying everywhere the last six years."

"Really?" she said, trying to sound casual. "Air Force?"

"Yeah."

"Do you enjoy traveling?"

"Yes, but sometimes it's frustrating. I've been pulling duty all over the planet. From Alaska to Saudi Arabia. Never anyplace long enough to get to know anyone."

There was an awkward pause. Then, as if to make small talk to keep the conversation going, he mentioned a few of his recent trips to far-off lands. As she listened she could see how he might be lonely, anxious to talk. He spoke softly with a quiet charm and she liked his urbane manner. She felt herself softening. "Must be interesting, all those exotic places."

As if encouraged by her comment he shifted in his chair, moving closer. "Went to Florida in '43 when I was first sworn in, then to Hiram College—ever hear of Hiram? It's in Ohio. I was there '43 and '44. Flew piper cubs—concentrated flying instruction—then to San Antonio for preflight. All over the country after that." He paused, drawing a package of Lucky Strikes from his shirt pocket. After offering her one, which she declined, he lit up and continued. "VJ Day, I remember a friend doing a barrel-roll in a B-25. Unheard of then. Just this past year I've been to the North Pole on two occasions. Flew 113 hours in 10 days, never saw the sun. Saudi Arabia, Libya, the Azores ... really wears you down."

Muriel was tempted to inquire about his military status, how long he would be in Tucson, where he was stationed. Instead, she was silent, stirring her drink with a straw. It wouldn't do to appear too interested.

He was quick to note her pretended indifference. "Sorry, I shouldn't be rambling like this. I guess that's what happens when you spend time alone. You finally meet someone and you can't stop talking. I hope you'll forgive my—"

"Oh, no, not at all," she said, brightening. "It sounds fascinating." She straightened in her chair, offering a smile as if to say, "Tell me more."

"Well, that's enough of my travels," he said. Then, nodding at the book in her lap, "What are you reading?"

"*The Rubaiyat.*"

"Oh, of course, by Omar...." He paused as if trying to remember the rest of the author's name.

"Khayyám. Omar Khayyám. You're familiar with *The Rubaiyat?*"

"Well...." He hesitated, moving his hand in a qualifying gesture. "Just the pictures, really."

"The pictures?"

"You know, the drawings," he said, nodding at the book.

"Oh, the illustrations, you mean." She opened the book as she spoke, slowly turning the pages. Throughout the work were prints of miniature paintings done in the vibrant red and blue colors characteristic of ancient Persia.

"They are wonderful," said Muriel. "Quite inspiring."

"I used to sketch them when I was in high school," he said. "I like to draw. A friend of mine had a copy of the book. A paperback. Not as elaborate as yours."

"And you drew these pictures?" said Muriel, her interest mounting. "Do you still do sketches?"

"A little painting, when I have the time. Landscapes, mostly. I like the outdoors—woods, lakes—that sort of thing. Who's Mubby?" He pointed to a handwritten inscription inside the cover of the book, drawing his chair closer.

"Oh, that's just a nickname my mother gave me."

"Mubby? No kidding? May I call you Mubby?"

"Most people call me Muriel," she said, stiffening.

"Okay, whatever you say. Although I do sort of prefer Mubby."

Muriel turned to look at him. His face was very close and she drew back. "You know, you really are kind of ... well, pushy."

He shrugged. "That's what I'm trained to be. I fly combat aircraft."

"You're not flying now."

"Well, actually I am. Right now my head's sort of up in the clouds."

She looked at him curiously. "What's that supposed to mean?" she asked cautiously.

"You know, you've kind of knocked me for a loop."

"Oh, c'mon." Muriel drew back with a slight frown. "I really don't know what to make of you. I hardly know you."

"I'm doing my best to remedy that," he said smiling, stubbing out his cigarette in an ashtray. "And I figure you're only going to give me so much time. C'mon tell me about your book."

Muriel continued to regard him quizzically, reservedly. Was he really interested in the book? Or was it just a ploy? He was awfully close. She was good at sizing up people. He seemed smart. Maybe he did want to know about the book. He said he'd done the sketches. And *The Rubaiyat* was high on Muriel's list of interests. "Some people think of it as hedonistic—you know, glorifying the good life," she said, deciding to describe the book. "But actually it has great spiritual meaning. You have to study it, though. The author was a Persian mathematician."

"And poet, right?"

"Yes, of course he was a poet. He had to be a poet to write it. 'Rubai' is the Persian word for quatrain and 'yat' is the plural suffix, so it means quatrains, understand?"

"Sure. Okay, so what about—?"

"You don't even know what a quatrain is," she said challengingly.

"Of course I do. Everyone knows what a quatrain is." He leaned over and flipped a page in the book. "Okay, tell me more."

"No, no," she said, putting her palm firmly on the book. "First you tell me what a quatrain is if you're so sure you know."

He paused for a moment, then flashed a winning smile. "Four locomotives, right ... Mubby?"

She looked at him quizzically for a moment and then they both laughed. Muriel's eyes drifted toward the pool where a young couple was swimming, exchanging frivolities. Maybe they too had met recently, she thought. Here at the pool, perhaps. She felt more relaxed with her new acquaintance. Enough so that she said, "Do you meet lots of people this way? Buying them drinks? I should think it might get pretty expensive. Particularly if you get turned down."

He laughed easily. "Well, you do have to be careful. Or else you end up drinking lots of daiquiris. Say, what's that?" He pointed to the edge of the newspaper clipping showing beneath the postcards she had placed in her book.

"Just a clipping," she said, not inclined to elaborate.

"I know, I saw the title when I picked it up. It said 'Story Places First.' So what's the story?"

"Oh ... something I wrote." She covered the article with the postcards and took a sip of her drink.

"No kidding. Mind if I read it? The article, that is?"

"You know, you really are kind of bold." Muriel knit her brow. "What if it were personal?"

"Well, it couldn't be too personal if it's in the newspaper. Do you always carry your clippings with you?" he asked facetiously.

Muriel responded with a wry smile. "You know, I find you rather Rabelaisian."

"Rab ... what?" He drew his head back, perplexed.

"Rabelais," said Muriel smugly, as though regaining control of the conversation. "He was a French satirist."

"Oh, you mean Rabelais," he said, accenting the last syllable. "Of course. Your pronunciation...." He arched his brow imperiously.

Muriel regarded him for a moment, a glint of disdain in her eye, considering her response.

"C'mon, let me read your clipping," he said, not giving her time to reply. Then, adding a disarming smile, "Please ... Mubby?"

"Oh, here," she said with mock contempt. "You really are persistent."

"Of course, I am." He took the clipping. "That's what I'm trained to be—"

"I know, you fly combat aircraft," she said, teasingly. "I have the feeling all of your combat isn't just flying."

They fell silent as he shaded his eyes from the sun and began reading the clipping:

STORY PLACES FIRST

Miss Muriel John, daughter of Mr. and Mrs. Victor John of Meridian and senior at the University of Mississippi, won first place in the short story contest at 'Ole Miss'. Her story 'Jamie' placed first among the many entered in the short story contest at 'Ole Miss'. It will go to the Southern College Regional Writers Association in Memphis to be judged with winners from other states. Miss John will be graduated this spring. She is an English major.

"Impressive," said Jim, handing back the article. "I like the title. 'Jamie'—a derivation of James. I have a friend in Chicago who calls me 'Jimmy.' I'd like to see your story. I enjoy reading."

"You do?" Muriel replaced the clipping in her book. "What types of things do you read?"

"Anything I can get my hands on. Particularly military history. Romans, Greeks, Peloponnesian Wars.... But I like novels, too.

Melville, Dreiser, Remarque…. I just finished *All Quiet on the Western Front*. Great war book. I have lots of time to read with all the travel." He paused, then said, "What are you doing here in Tucson?"

"I've enrolled at the University of Arizona. Doing some graduate work in English."

"Graduate work? I thought so," he said, beaming. "When I was over there watching you with your book, I thought, 'She's not only beautiful, she's very intelligent.' I have this uncanny sixth sense about things like this."

Muriel, her wariness surfacing despite their recent joking, wasn't about to accept his compliment at face value. "Does your sixth sense tell you I don't believe a word you're saying? You know, I'm beginning to wonder if you're not a fake." Although said in jest, she regretted having used the word "fake." But Muriel John was nothing if not forthright, a trait which occasionally could offend.

"Muriel," he said evenly, "I've been called everything, but never a *fake*."

"That may be a bit strong," she said, backtracking. "But, you must admit, some of your compliments do seem, well … excessive."

Looking mildly offended, he said, "Honestly, Muriel, I haven't said a thing to you I didn't really mean."

His exuberance had brought them closer together, and as she looked into his eyes she perceived a warmth and sincerity she had not noticed previously. Although she had been with him for less than an hour, Muriel realized there was something special about her new acquaintance.

She was about to respond when he shifted in his chair, looking away. "There goes one of mine," he said, pointing to a plane. "B-29. That's what I fly."

She looked up and saw an aircraft ascending in the distance. As she watched it disappear over the mountains she noticed a slight change in the weather, a haze moving over the sun, the far-off peaks now clad in battle gray.

◆ ◆ ◆

This photo was taken in 1941, after the pool opened at the El Conquistador Hotel. The hotel opened in November 1928 and catered to the rich and famous. Fashion retailer Cele Peterson used to host fashion shows around the pool and take her children horseback riding at the stables. El Con Mall occupies the site today.

Swimming Pool, El Conquistador Hotel
(Arizona Daily Star)

4

Dear Mom,

Another beautiful day. The air is so clean and dry and the sun shines all the time. I think it's helping. Haven't had any real trouble since I've been here. Talked again to the lady who has the room. It's farther out in the suburbs but it sounds nicer than the one in town—less expensive too. I'm going to see it this week.

I met an awfully nice person at the pool today. His name is James Call. He's a lieutenant in the Air Force at Davis-Monthan, a big air base here. He's charming and very handsome. Looks a little like Gregory Peck. Even Daddy would like him. Don't mention it to him right now, though. I wish you'd try to explain to Daddy that I'm almost twenty-one. That letter he wrote to me last week, you'd think I was still in high school. He told me I should let someone at the hotel know where I'm going when I go out. Can you believe that?

I had *The Rubaiyat* with me at the pool and we read parts of it together. Jim, that is. He was really taken with it. He's very smart and seems well-read. After we left the pool we went to an ice cream parlor. He asked me to go out to dinner with him tonight. We're going to a Mexican restaurant in the old part of town. I know it probably sounds like a lot in such a short time, but I actually met him a few days ago, sort of. Anyway, he says time is everything in his life because he's always flying away somewhere and he has to make the most of it—time off, that is. He flies to England tomorrow and is coming back the end of the month.

He's very sweet and considerate. He asked me to go down to Mexico with him when he gets back from England. It's not that far. 60 miles or so. He says we can drive down in the morning and be back before dark. Before I forget, would you please send my brown suit?

The evenings can get pretty cold here. Also, my black dress with the black shoes.

Well, that's about all for now. Tell Auntie Edna that she's right about Tucson. It's really great. And getting better. I miss you all very much.

Love,
Mubby

P.S. Just read this over and I definitely wouldn't show it to Daddy.

◆ ◆ ◆

5

Muriel John saw much of the Southwest during ensuing weeks. Her days were filled with thrilling new experiences that included car racing, sporting events, gambling casinos, and a variety of restaurants. There were morning bird walks in the park, camping trips in the mountains, and late night frolics out on the mesa. The reason, of course, was her new-found friend.

It was a rapid transition from small-town campus life to the fast-paced world of James Call. Her lieutenant had made captain, and with the promotion had come new exhilarations: high-speed aircraft, frantic intervals of courting between missions, even the veiled suggestion of an engagement in the spring. For Muriel, time was literally flying; never had she been so happy.

Her health improved with her happiness. She gained ten pounds. Her comely if somewhat frail figure assumed new and curvaceous proportions. At first, this was a concern, but the admiring comments from Jim and others allayed her initial fears. Indeed, so taken had she become with her suitor—now lover—that her primary interest was to please him. If an additional ten pounds enhanced their relationship, so be it.

There were depressing moments as in any relationship, but most had to do with her beau's seemingly endless trips to far reaches of the world. Their separation was eased somewhat by a stream of letters, postcards, and hurried phone calls from places such as Alaska, Greenland, and Goosebay, Labrador. "Hush-hush" missions as Jim termed them.

Nor was her time with him completely devoid of concern. One of his friends had said to her, "Jim has a passion for speed and danger." She was quick to see these traits, and while alarming, for a young woman in love they added to the mystique, the allure, the ineffable charm of her captain.

It was an evening in April of 1950 when the voice of the landlady's daughter—a pleasant if somewhat puckish teenager—called from downstairs. "Muriel, your dreamboat's out front!"

Muriel's heart jumped, but then she caught herself. The girl was entertaining friends and was not above practical jokes. "Not so," she called blithely. "He doesn't get here 'til tomorrow."

"Well, there's some elegant dude in uniform who looks an awful lot like him getting out of a cab."

There was an earnestness to the comment that propelled Muriel breathlessly to the front window of her room. Looking out into the twilight she saw Jim standing next to a cab, paying his fare. He was wearing a tan full-dress officer's uniform, and as he turned toward the house the fading sun briefly lit his handsome features. For an instant she was gripped by an incomparable joy that held her at the window. Then, gliding to a mirror she moved long slender fingers deftly through her hair. After a final appraising glance, she floated downstairs to the front porch.

"Jim," she said, attempting without success to rein in her emotions. She had found early in their relationship that it was best not to gush over him. He seemed to prefer the somewhat cool, reserved manner reflective of his own style. "It's so good to see you, honey. I didn't expect you 'til tomorrow."

"Thought I'd surprise you," he said, mounting the steps toward her. "You are glad to see me, aren't you?"

"Oh, of course I am, darling." She kissed and embraced him amorously, foregoing the reserve of a moment before. Then, whispering in his ear, "I've missed you so much. It's awful without you."

He lifted her against his body and for a moment it appeared the reunion might give way to passion. Quickly Muriel recovered, a backward glance confirming a gathering of eyes in the front window. Disengaging, she drew him down the steps toward the side of the house. "Let's go out here in the garden. The house is filled with kids and they're all in love with you. Now that I've got you I'm not sharing you with anyone."

They stepped under the shelter of some dogwoods where they kissed long and passionately. When she sensed him becoming aroused she drew back and motioned toward some lawn chairs nearby. "Let's sit over here. I want to hear all about your trip. How did you get back so soon?"

"Change of orders this morning." He moved one of the chairs close to the other so that they were facing and sat down. "I was going to call but, well ... here I am." He spread his arms out palms up in a hapless gesture. It was an endearing mannerism.

"What a wonderful surprise." She took his hand and squeezed it. "I just can't tell you what it's like when you're gone. My life ... it just stops."

They sat for a moment in silence, looking at each other. "What are you thinking?" she asked. "I can always tell when your mind's on something else. You get that distant look."

"Oh, nothing." He shifted in his seat. "Actually, I have another surprise." He withdrew his hand from hers and started to unbutton a breast pocket on his tunic. "Close your eyes."

She felt a wave of excitement. Could it be? No, no she had to control herself. But there'd been signs: casual references to glove size; oblique discussions about jewelry preferences. Still, she mustn't let herself be carried away. Tomorrow he could be off on one of his "hush-hush" missions and it could all be over. Hushed up for good.

"Are they closed?" he asked.

"Yes."

"Real tight?"

"Real tight."

"OK, open them."

Her long dark lashes fluttered open, revealing the most precious object she had ever seen. Glistening in the fading light drifting through the trees was a beautiful solitaire diamond mounted on a platinum ring. She watched, spellbound, as he slipped it on her finger.

"Oh, Jim," she said, her eyes tearing. "It's just...." Her voice faded as she struggled for composure.

"Does this mean, 'Yes'?" he asked softly. "You'll marry a poor, wandering airman?"

"Oh, darling. Yes, yes." Rising, she moved to him, coming to rest in his lap. He turned so that he cradled her in his arms, and kissed her fervently.

From the upstairs gallery, which had moved from a front to a side window, came a prolonged sigh. And then, a teenaged voice said resignedly, "Mom, I think you're about to lose a boarder."

◆ ◆ ◆

Jim and Muriel

6

The angry roar of heavy engines reverberating from the hot tarmac at the Davis-Monthan Air Force Base reflected the mood of the
young officer who strode purposefully toward the giant B-50 being
prepared for departure. Jaws clenched, lips pursed, eyes narrowed to
dark slits, it was a formidable countenance.

The lieutenant standing near the plane, watching Jim Call
approach, knew something was wrong. "What's up?"

"Libya," Jim replied, stopping next to the man and throwing a
flight bag he was carrying to the ground. His voice was quiet, deadly,
the soft hiss of a missile before detonation. "I've got more goddamn
time over Libya than the entire Libyan Air Force."

"Man, that's tough. When's the wedding?"

"You mean when *was* the wedding." He paused and then, "Week
from Saturday."

"You sure he knows about it—the colonel, that is?"

"Of course he knows. I told him two months ago. Says he needs
me to plan the mission. At best, I won't be back 'til a week from
Wednesday. That gives me two days to get ready for the wedding."

"How big's the wedding?"

"Huge. They've got everyone in Meridian coming. You'd think she
was a maharanee." He dropped his head. "Jesus! Wait 'til I tell
Muriel."

"How about the chaplain?" the lieutenant asked sympathetically.
"Maybe he could intervene with the colonel and—"

"Are you serious?" Jim interrupted. "Can you imagine the colonel
if he heard the chaplain was involved. I can just hear the sarcastic bastard. 'Sure it's okay with me, if the chaplain can fly the mission.' He'd
send his freaking mother up there before he'd abort—"

"Oh, Christ," interrupted the lieutenant. "Here comes Asshole!"

A van came to a stop a short distance away and a tall angular captain with graying hair and a pompous bearing climbed from the vehicle. Upon emerging he straightened and began dusting and patting his tunic and trousers fastidiously, as though he had just completed a trip through the Urals in an open rig. As the van pulled away he glanced about imperiously as if expecting an honor guard. His eyes finally came to rest on the two officers. He regarded them for a moment with the sniffish look of one who had been left beside a malodorous pit.

"Where's the rest of the crew?" he asked curtly.

"We just got here, Captain," the lieutenant replied.

"Why are you standing there?" the man said. Although of comparable rank, his tone was distinctly magisterial. "Let's board. There are things I'd like to discuss."

"One minute, Captain," said Jim evenly, restraining his emotions. "The last I heard, Major Beltner was in charge of this mission."

"Yes, let's thank the gods for that," the officer said with undisguised contempt. "Otherwise, we'd probably all end up in Monte Carlo."

It was an obvious reference to Call's gambling addiction, which had been the subject of Officers' Club gossip. Jim hesitated. For an instant the scene on the Davis-Monthan tarmac teetered on the brink of a major brouhaha. Jim stared at the man with enmity. Then, without a word, he turned and walked to the plane.

After a pause the lieutenant leveled a cool look at his superior. "That was unnecessary, Captain."

"He'll get over it," the captain replied, dismissing the encounter with the airy confidence of one accustomed to confrontation. "Don't worry about him."

"Oh, I'm not worried about *him*," said the lieutenant, stooping to pick up his flight bag. And then, over his shoulder as he walked away, "You don't know Jim Call, Captain. I'm worried about *you*."

◆ ◆ ◆

7

It was July 7, 1950, and St. Paul's Episcopal Church in Meridian, Mississippi, was filled. Soft organ music drifted from the choir loft and blended with the hushed conversations of the assemblage. The interior of the church resembled a garden in springtime. There were flowers everywhere, from elaborate decorations in the chancel to bright sprays adorning each pew. Contributing further to the botanical effect were row upon row of floral print dresses and flowered hats. The subdued murmuring of Meridian's gentry was broken occasionally by whispered greetings as white kid gloves waved above the garden like small fluttering birds. It was a traditional southern wedding, the mood one of graciousness and anticipation.

Near the altar at the front of the church, attired in summer officer's uniform, ramrod straight, stood Jim Call. Next to him was his best man, a tall pleasant-looking individual named Robert Sylvester. The two were close friends, having grown up together in Chicago. While an element of tension prevailed in the first rows of pews where family members awaited the start of the ceremony, the groom appeared relaxed and confident. His dispassionate gaze followed the movements in the congregation, occasionally holding on other eyes that were disposed to exchange his glance. It was as if he found the proceedings of curious interest, his manner deferential but unintimidated.

The minister, an avuncular, middle-aged man of dignified bearing, stood on the raised altar benignly observing the congregation. Occasionally he glanced at the bridegroom. He was struck by the man's composure. Most young men awaiting such a profound moment showed some signs of anxiety. Sweating, swallowing, shifting. This young man seemed at ease, almost indifferent.

Eleven o'clock, the scheduled starting time of the ceremony, came and went, and a few heads bowed to consult watches. The minister maintained a stoic manner, but even he began to shift slightly, stretching his neck in the collar of his vestments. Then, just as unease became apparent in the congregation, a relieving peel from the organ floated from the choir loft to announce the arrival of the bride. Heads turned expectantly toward the rear of the church, from which bridesmaids in elegant dresses came at measured intervals. Muriel John, radiant in her satin bridal gown, then appeared on the arm of her father. In her left hand was what appeared to be a traditional prayer book, but in reality was a volume of Walt Whitman's poems. Her auburn hair and tanned beautiful face contrasted with the white veil. She proceeded slowly down the aisle with her father, exchanging glances with dignity and grace.

Victor John wore a firm smile, his expression a fusion of pride and nervousness. He moved carefully with the precision of an aerialist, as though one misstep might send him crashing into the bowels of St. Paul's. Now wasn't the time to trip, step on the hem of the wedding gown, sneeze. As they approached the altar his eyes caught those of his soon-to-be son-in-law. It was a brief exchange but, as always, he sensed the indifference. The strange unwavering eyes invariably induced an unsettled feeling in him. Although always gracious and respectful, the young man's look conveyed the unmistakable impression that Victor John was of little importance in the life of Jim Call.

But if the father of the bride were uncertain, the feeling did not carry over to his daughter. Muriel was poised at the verge of paradise. Although experiencing the usual bridal anxiety, her love and confidence in the man awaiting her at the altar transcended all other emotions. Soon she was with him, his reassuring smile, his hand clasping hers. Despite his restraint, she had come to know that beneath his cool exterior was a passion equal to her own.

As though aware of the unusual time constraints in the lives of the couple before him and noting, perhaps, the inadequacy of the whirring fans in the hot church, the minister conducted a proper but swift ceremony. Within minutes he was uttering the magical words, "I now pronounce you man and wife." Muriel felt Jim's hand close on hers gently. They turned, kissed. Had the choir of angels adorning the walls of St. Paul's come singing to life, the moment could not have seemed more heavenly.

Sighs, glistening eyes, dabbing handkerchiefs, glove-clad hands quickly arranging wide-brimmed flowered hats, and then, the exhilarating chimes of the wedding recessional announcing the arrival and short happy life of Captain and Mrs. James Call.

◆ ◆ ◆

A young Muriel

Portrait of Muriel

Muriel's house in Meridian

St. Paul's Episcopal Church, Meridian

8

"Congratulations, Major."

It was February 1951 and Jim Call stood in the office of his commanding officer at the Tucson Air Force base. He had just been advised of his promotion from captain to major. The colonel extended his hand across the desk. He was a tall, slender, waspish man, with thin lips and cool gray eyes that seemed to focus somewhere near Jim's navel. Not a friendly countenance. Although professing to be complimentary, the officer was unable to conceal his innate arrogance. "A well-earned promotion," he continued. "Keep up the good work."

It was a perfunctory presentation and, the civilities completed, the colonel returned to his chair. Behind him on the wall was an array of memorabilia reflecting a career of dedication to the military: emblems, plaques, commemorative ornaments, vestiges of World War II. On a credenza behind his desk, incongruous perhaps since it gave rise to the question as to when he would have had time for such frippery, was a photograph of a woman and five children.

Having read the orders of his promotion which had been handed to him moments before, Jim carefully folded the paper and put it in a pocket of his flight jacket, concern on his face.

"Is there a problem?" the superior asked. "Thought you'd be glad to see that."

"Oh, I am, sir." Jim looked at the officer and for an instant a flicker of pleasure showed. It was quickly replaced by a frown, however. "It's just ... well, it's the travel. My wife's expecting next month and I've been—"

"That's your job, Captain—Major, that is." His delivery was clipped, and impatience surfaced. "Your missions are in line with operating procedures."

"I know, sir. But my wife isn't doing that well. She's having some problems...." His voice trailed off uncomfortably.

The colonel regarded the younger man closely for a moment. Although appreciative of the officer's aeronautical brilliance, he had always considered him something of an enigma. His attitude—too independent, unpredictable. At the moment he had more pressing concerns, and was unmoved by his subordinate's personal problems. Besides, who didn't have problems? There was a war going on.

"Perhaps you should put it in a memorandum." The colonel stood abruptly extending his hand, indicating the meeting was over. "Congratulations, Major."

Jim seemed about to speak but restrained himself. Shaking hands, he turned and left the room.

Later, when he called Muriel from the Officers' Club, he was more buoyant regarding his promotion. "It just came through, honey. I'm a major."

"Oh, that's wonderful, Jim," said Muriel, exuberantly. "What great news! Will you be able to spend more time at home?"

"Well, I don't know.... The CO is a tough guy. How you feeling?"

"So, so. The asthma's acting up. The doctor says the baby's fine, though. Will you be home for awhile?"

"I can't be sure. Tomorrow I'm on a B-50 to Alaska. Could be gone for a week."

There was a pause and then Muriel said, "What if the baby comes when you're in Alaska?"

"We've still got almost a month. I should be back by—"

"No, no," she interrupted. "Anything can happen now. I'm just so afraid you won't be here. What if...." Her voice cracked slightly, trailing off.

Jim hesitated. It was an unusual response from his wife, who was normally unruffled by adversity. "I'll be there," he said, forcefully. "If I have to commandeer the bloody plane, I'll be there. Don't worry."

"I miss you so much." Her voice was subdued, barely audible. "We've been married a year and it's been all phone calls."

"You've got to hang in there, honey. Things will get better. Believe me. They want me to spend more time in the planning section—less flying. I should get more leave."

"Oh, I hope so. It's like our wedding. I didn't know until three days before if you'd even make it." There was a pause, and then her voice steadied, as if she were determined to control her emotions. "You should see me. I'm big as a house."

"Good. I want a big guy."

"What if it's a girl?" she asked. "You want a big girl? Mother thinks it's a boy. She can tell from the way I look. But really, you should see me. I look like one of your B-50s. Have you thought any more about names?"

"I like what you said. Jeff. Jeff Call. That's a great name."

"Or Edna?" Muriel said, referring to her aunt.

"Edna? Hmm...."

"Maybe."

"After the dragon lady? I don't know," he said dubiously. "Besides, it's a boy. I absolutely guarantee it. Say, listen, I've gotta go. They're waiting for me over at operations. I love you. Talk to you later."

"All right." Her voice, although plaintive, strove to be cheerful. "Come home soon ... Major. I like the sound of that. It'll be great on Jeff's birth announcement. Major and Mrs. Call."

◆ ◆ ◆

9

Looking wan but enthralled, Muriel cuddled the small bundle—nine precious pounds of baby boy. "Isn't he simply beautiful, Jim?" she beamed. "I can't believe he's ours. I keep thinking someone's going to come in and tell us it's a mistake ... take him away."

Jim, looking uncharacteristically tense, had entered the hospital room a few minutes before. After kissing his wife affectionately he had glanced down at his new son uncertainly, the look of one who had been the recipient of a blessed event but was not quite sure how to react.

But having recovered, and as though sensing more enthusiasm was in order, he echoed his wife's description. "Yes, he certainly is beautiful," and then with added emphasis, "*really* beautiful!" Gently, almost timidly, he brushed the infant's cheek with his forefinger. "Jeff," he said softly. "Welcome aboard, Jeff."

For Muriel it had been an exceedingly difficult pregnancy—particularly the last three weeks. In addition to the usual discomfort of her prenatal state she had suffered repeated asthmatic attacks which exacerbated her condition. There had been long days and nights of loneliness, broken by visits from her mother and worried phone calls from her traveling husband. It was through the intervention of her physician that Jim finally had secured emergency leave and had rejoined her before the birth. The doctor had been forthright with Jim. The last few days had been critical for both mother and child. But with the arrival of Jeff things improved markedly, and the birth was pronounced a resounding success.

As they talked, Muriel radiated happiness, unfazed even by Jim's recent disclosure of imminent travel. "Think of it," she said, eyes sparkling in a tired face full of shadows. "Two handsome men in my life. What more could a girl want?"

"What more?" replied Jim, his mood sobering. "How about a full-time husband? Right now you have a part-time husband and a part-time father. Flying is okay for a single guy. Not for a family man."

"You could look for something else. Flying isn't the only thing in life."

Jim shrugged, the hopeless gesture of one who had given the subject much thought to no avail. "It's all I know."

"But you could try another field." Muriel shifted the baby. "You have a brilliant record. You're still young."

"I suddenly feel a lot older," said Jim, nodding at the baby. "It's a new life."

"A new life with old aspirations." She lowered her head, pressing her cheek against the baby. "We're entering another phase, Jim." She was solemn for a moment, but then, brightening, she added whimsically:

> Alas that Spring should vanish with the Rose!
> That Youth's sweet scented Manuscript should close!

"I like that," said Jim, raising a brow. "*The Rubaiyat?*"

She nodded. "Yes—my treasure chest."

"Kind of sad, though."

"Not really. The spiritual interpretation is different. You really have to study *The Rubaiyat*. Khayyám was a great religious poet—a mystical philosopher. He really helped me these last few months. You should take it on your trips."

"Why don't we make some tapes of you reading it?" Jim said. "I can listen to them when I'm away. Help pass the time."

"Let's do that." Muriel again shifted the baby, her eyes beaming. "That would be fun. I'm going to teach you the spiritual significance of *The Rubaiyat*. It'll really help you. You need something to believe in."

"Don't worry, I've got two very special things to believe in. Now all I have to do is figure out how to be with them. Remember, I'm gone again next week."

"Humph," said Muriel, feigning annoyance. "Well, at least I've got Jeff now." She nuzzled the baby's ear with her nose. He smelled so good, so glorious. Her world was complete.

"I'm not even sure where I'm going yet," Jim said quietly. "Could be anywhere."

"Oh, well," Muriel said, unwilling to relinquish the joy of the moment. "That's next week." She smiled, adding a line from *The Rubaiyat:*

> The Nightingale that in the Branches sang,
> Ah, whence and whither flown again, who knows!

"What's that mean?" Jim asked curiously.

Muriel laughed, cuddling the baby. "He who knows, he knows; none else knows."

Jim as young officer   Muriel and Jeff

10

"Interphone check." The pilot's voice crackled from the interphone. It was August 1951, at an air base in Guam, and the B-29 crew was readying for a combat mission to North Korea. "Prepare for preflight. Acknowledge."

Jim reviewed the navigation charts on the station table in front of him in anticipation of the preflight checking routine. From his window he looked across the tarmac to where other B-29s were preparing for the same mission to bomb munition factories on the Yalu River, the boundary between North Korea and Manchuria. A stressful operation was expected, one that would likely encounter hostile fire from anti-aircraft batteries and enemy fighters. Because of the loss of aircraft during similar missions, the trips were termed "suicide flights" by the crews.

"Request compass check," came the voice of the bombardier.

"I'm reading one six niner," replied Jim. As he spoke, he glanced at a small picture which he had taped to the bulkhead above the console. It was a recent snapshot of Muriel, laughing, looking radiant as she held Jeff over her head. Jim was fond of the picture and planned to have it enlarged. "I'll ask the photo lab to blow it up for us," he had told Muriel. "We'll frame it for our den."

"What den?" she had asked.

"You know, when we settle down and get a house."

"A house?" She had laughed. "Here we go again. We don't even have a house and you're already furnishing it. You certainly are a romantic."

However romantic, Jim had been having just such thoughts during recent months. Although he realized the impracticality of buying a house, given his travel and susceptibility to transfer—to say nothing of the cost involved—it was still the theme of his daydreams.

At times, particularly during long flights, he would gaze out toward the horizon, envisioning all sorts of houses. His favorite reverie involved a small cabin nestled among trees in some remote unsettled area. He loved trees. They would have many of them, with long branches reaching low over the house, their leaves rustling softly. But Muriel was right, he thought. He was a hopeless romantic. His dreams of a house and home life had little more substance than the vapor trails that followed his seemingly endless flights.

"Weather at base." It was the radio operator, continuing the preflight routine on the interphone. "Scattered clouds at two thousand, wind northwest, one six, altimeter, two niner four eight. Base requests our position."

Thoughts of home life quickly evaporated, replaced by the hard reality of combat. There followed transmissions from the gunners and then the voice of the flight engineer. "Check list complete, ready to start engine."

The huge silver fuselage came throbbing to life, engines grumbling loudly, a gleaming armor-clad warrior roused for battle. Although it was a routine through which Jim had gone many times, he always found it stimulating. He reveled in the rumbling sounds, the trembling infrastructure, the redolence of high-octane fuel, the anticipatory thrill of being aloft, the impending danger. Once aroused, such instincts left little time for domestic thoughts.

As did other members of his crew, he had concerns about the Boeing B-29. The "Superfortress" had been a formidable weapon since its introduction during the later stages of World War II. It had been used in the relentless firebombing of Japanese cities, and a few years previously had dropped the atomic bombs on Hiroshima and Nagasaki, ending the war in the Pacific.

Although termed a miracle weapon when first introduced, the B-29 was not without its problems. Jim's major concern was engine fires resulting from insufficient cooling of the cylinders. Pilots and flight engineers were required to go through complicated procedures to manage the engines, and a relatively simple mistake could result in dangerous loss of power. "Flying the damn thing was a given," said one former pilot, "but controlling those engines was something else. Everything had to work perfectly or that sucker could overheat and self-destruct. Takeoffs could be hair-raising as hell. Lose an engine on takeoff at full gross weight in that baby and it's all over. Little else you could do but drop it down straight ahead—wherever that might be."

Although many of the plane's shortcomings had been remedied over time, some problems such as the engines overheating persisted. And while Jim had overall confidence in the aircraft, he was thoroughly aware of its limitations. He sat at his navigator's station watching from the window as the craft lumbered forward into position for takeoff. The pilot turned carefully onto the runway, keeping the inside wheel in motion to avoid throwing a tire. The enormous weight of the craft required that such maneuvers be executed gently.

Taxiing to a point as close as possible to the threshold of the runway so that they had maximum distance available, the pilot held the brakes and got a power check before beginning the takeoff. Shortly, the plane was thundering forward, the pilot deftly controlling the rudder to maintain direction. A speed of 100 MPH was reached quickly in a B-29, but from there on acceleration was painfully slow. Elaborate procedures were required to gain lift while at the same time preventing overheating of the cylinders.

On this day, the takeoff was without incident and soon they were airborne with a power setting that enabled a maximum climbing rate while still keeping the cylinder head temperature within the allowable limits.

As navigator, Jim was particularly concerned about the point of climb. Fuel was of paramount importance in long range bombers such as the B-29, and since fuel consumption was greatest at high altitudes the plane was kept at minimum levels for as long as possible. A climb too late in the flight to the target could be disastrous for the mission, however, since the North Korean fighters functioned better at low altitudes and were ever alert for a helpless bomber in a climb.

The hours dragged by as the plane droned high over the Pacific. When they had reached the set altitude, Jim was on the interphone reminding the pilot of his estimated time of arrival at the Korean coast, and control points to the munition plants on the Yalu. Tension mounted among the crew as they approached their target. Here one could expect the greatest concentration of anti-aircraft fire and attacks by enemy fighters.

It was shortly after the turn onto the axis of attack that they encountered anti-aircraft fire. It began with a few bright flashes and distant thumps. Soon the fire was intense. Flak of over five bursts per second in close proximity rocked the plane continuously and sent shock waves through the cabin. Later, under reporting standards, it was estimated that the shelling came from heavily defended areas in which more than twenty guns, designed to offer effective fire against high-flying bombers, were utilized. It was a "continuously pointed" type of fire where gun batteries fired individually and attempted to keep the bursts on target continuously as long as the aircraft was in range.

Suddenly, there was a wrenching, cracking sound and the plane shuddered violently. Jim knew immediately that they had been hit. Stunned, he waited anxiously, anticipating the deadly signs of a stricken aircraft. Once again a severe vibration shot through the plane. There was no question now. They were in trouble. How badly? Would there be time to bail out? A fire? Explosion? Was there smoke in the cabin? No, he had imagined it. He waited for word on the intercom from the pilot, the engineer.... But then the plane steadied, continuing on course as they neared their target. Jim again focused on his instruments. Despite heavy bursts that continued to buffet them, and the feeling that they must have sustained damage, his voice remained calm and deliberate as they commenced the bombing run:

Jim:	Pilot, three degrees right
Pilot:	Three right
Jim:	Niner degrees right
Pilot:	Niner right
Jim:	Radar switch to 30 mile range
Radar Operator:	Roger....
Jim:	.... Ready.... Mark
Radar Operator:	Coming up on 67 degrees
Jim:	.... Ready.... Mark

The process was continued until the order to release the bombs. With bombs away, the plane lurched upwards and Jim immediately turned on the aerial cameras to assess the bomb damage.

There was little time to reflect on the bombing, however. No sooner had their plane passed through the anti-aircraft fire when a small formation of Russian-built MiG-15s, presumably flown by North Korean or Chinese pilots, was observed far below. All gunners readied in anticipation of the expected assault. The nose gunner was particularly alert since experience indicated that 49 percent of enemy fighter attacks came on the nose of the plane. While other gunners were taught to commence firing at a range of 1000 yards, nose gunners were instructed to fire at the first sight of an attack. Nose attacks happened so quickly that a gunner had less than five seconds from the time an enemy fighter was sighted before accurate fire was impossible.

From his navigator's station Jim had a good view of the enemy formation and waited expectantly for their lead planes to begin the climb that would signal an attack. Instead, the fighters veered off, a covey of small birds disappearing into the cover of a large bank of cumulus clouds. It was a welcome relief to the tense crew, who had undergone several agonizing minutes of heavy flak. For Jim, however, the prospect of the aerial confrontation had induced a strange anticipative thrill, an emotion his fellow airmen would have found incomprehensible in light of the trauma they had just experienced.

As the plane turned for the long trip back to the home base the interphone was alive with crew members assessing damage to the aircraft. It was determined that a sizeable chunk of the tip of one wing was missing, but the plane seemed airworthy. The preliminary assessment could not be made with certainty, however. The mission was never complete until the plane was safely on the ground. Many crews had been relieved after completing harrowing bombing runs only to end up ditching because of mechanical failure. Recovery from the vast Pacific was always unpredictable.

As the hours passed on the long flight home, the crew settled down to its normal flight duties. The tumultuous bombing run was forgotten for the time, a dramatic event to be resurrected and discussed over drinks back at the base.

For Jim, absorbed by his navigational duties, there was little time to think about the bombing. When he did reflect on it near the conclusion of the flight his mood was exceedingly sober, a psychological letdown that often followed periods of intense excitement. It was a time when he often questioned the rationale of the missions. What had they actually accomplished? Weren't the real targets on the other side of the Yalu River in China where they were forbidden to fly?

Wasn't it from there that North Korea received the supplies that enabled it to continue the war?

And there were other questions as well. Deepening concerns about the long periods away from home and its effect on his family, his wife's health, monetary setbacks from gambling.... Now, as he gazed at the picture of his wife and child above the console, his passion for the thrills of combat had diminished, left behind with the vapor trails beyond the horizon.

♦ ♦ ♦

B-29s in-flight

(Courtesy of Squadron/Signal Publications, Inc.)

(Courtesy of Squadron/Signal Publications, Inc.)

11

"You're borderline, Major. I suggest you restrain yourself." As he sat listening to his subordinate across the desk, the colonel's expression had changed in the space of ten seconds from genial, to stern, to acerbic.

Jim trained a double-barreled look on his commanding officer. It was not the look of inferior rank. "It's been bad enough with all these trips. And now this!" He displayed a piece of paper, his voice low, defiant. "My wife's health is not good, sir. She's pregnant. We had problems with the birth of our first child. She's asthmatic. That's why she moved here to Tucson in the first place."

The summer of 1952 was particularly trying for Jim Call. He was fed up with military life and it was showing. When a few minutes previously his commanding officer had presented him with orders transferring him to McDill Air Force Base in Tampa, Florida, he had reacted with cool disdain. The colonel, although anticipating a stubborn response, was unprepared for the officer's animosity. He was on the verge of delivering a strong rebuke when Jim fell silent, gazing thoughtfully through a nearby window as though matters of more interest were unfolding on the parade ground beyond. The rather abrupt shift in Jim's attention struck the colonel as a bit odd in light of their conversation."McDill Field is a good base," said the colonel, trying a more civil tone. "I was stationed there a few years back. I'm told they have a fine base hospital. You could've done much worse. My advice is that you—"

"No, Colonel," Jim interrupted, his attention once again riveted on his CO. "Things can't get much worse. I have a son only a year old and a wife who's very sick. No one seems to be listening. That Guam assignment was terrible. I advised them repeatedly of my family situation and—"

"That's enough, Major." Sensing a serious confrontation, the colonel stiffened in his chair, gray brows and mustache bristling. It was time to take charge. "I think you and I better have an understanding. I realize you've had problems. But so have other people in this outfit. I've been hearing things...." The colonel paused, his words measured, as though uncertain how much he wanted to reveal about things he had heard. "Things that concern me," he continued. "Your attitude. And frankly, some are questioning your emotional stability."

"Who's questioning my stability? You mean that gook who passes himself off as a personnel officer?"

"Hold it, Major. Hold it right there." The colonel targeted a forefinger at his subordinate's chest. "One more comment like that and you're on report. Do you understand? If you value your future in this organization you'll get hold of yourself." The officer paused, getting hold of his own self while glancing toward his outer office where emotional stability reigned supreme. "Now, you've had an outstanding career in the Air Force. Everyone admires your talent. For that reason I'm overlooking here what has come close to insubordination. You have relatively little time left on this base. I don't want any more displays of your temper. And furthermore, I don't want to hear any more of your complaints. Do we understand each other?" The colonel paused, collecting a quivering mustache, his gray eyes all business. "That's all, Major."

Jim's breezy exit through the outer office caused papers to flutter. From the downcast eyes at the desks it was apparent that the colonel's strong rebuke had been overheard.

Once outside, Jim paused, trying to organize his thoughts. He stood, simmering in the summer heat, reflecting on the transfer. How would he break the news to Muriel? Her life had been difficult enough during recent weeks. Although Arizona's arid climate was beneficial, it was not a cure for her asthma. And now that she was pregnant, the turmoil of moving to a new base, coupled with his prolonged trips away from home, would be a heavy burden.

Yet he knew she would handle it. One of her traits that filled him with admiration was her resilience. There'd be some grumbling at first, but then she'd manage to see some redeeming features in the transfer. It was the way she reacted to all adversity. But it was her health that concerned him most. Although appearing robust, her asthmatic condition, coupled with her pregnancy, could present severe problems. Since the birth of their first child, he had harbored an abiding fear that he might somehow lose her. Such thoughts were prevalent when he was away on missions. On one such occasion he was said to have confided to an associate that if anything should happen to his wife he'd "cash out."

Now, standing by himself on the street near the CO's office, contemplating his future and what he should tell Muriel, his mind was churning. For a moment he considered returning to the colonel's office and resigning his commission. But that would be foolhardy. His wife, baby, another on the way....

Besides, Muriel would know what to do. He had to talk it through with her. She'd have some ideas. Thoughts of her resoluteness bolstered his spirits. Turning, he started walking across the parade ground toward the Officers' Club. Yes, Muriel would put it all in perspective. And if she didn't ... well, he thought with a touch of whimsy, *The Rubaiyat* most assuredly would.

◆ ◆ ◆

12

Much to Jim's relief, Muriel handled the news of the transfer with remarkable equanimity. After the initial shock, that is.

"Taipei! Jeepers! China?"

"No, no," replied Jim quickly. "Not Taipei. *Tampa!* Tampa, Florida. Boy, what kind of geography did they teach you at Ole Miss? I'm glad you're not a navigator."

"Oh, Florida. Of course, I know where Tampa is. Gulf Coast. Near Clearwater. For some reason I was thinking of Taipei. Why wouldn't I, the way you travel? Alaska, Guam, Saudi Arabia. Tampa, hmm.... Well, I suppose it's better than China. I don't care. I was getting tired of this place, anyway. Particularly those officers' wives." (The morals of some of the wives had been a frequent source of concern to Muriel.) "Besides, we'll be closer to home. We can see more of the family."

The move to Florida followed shortly and was accomplished without incident. Soon the Call family was adjusting to life at McDill Air Force Base. But things did not go well. They had no sooner settled in when Muriel became ill with a virulent infection in a fallopian tube. Her prognosis was not good. For Jim, the impact was profound.

The emotional toll was apparent to his military colleagues. His mood was the subject of discussion in the Officers' Club:

"Wife's pretty sick. She's the glue that holds him together."

"He's tough to be around. Brilliant in the air, though. I'd fly with him anywhere. But steer clear of him on the ground."

"Yeah, one of these days he's gonna lose it. Man, I hope I'm not around when it happens."

Such sentiments were of no concern to Jim. His mind was consumed by his wife's illness. In the early fall of 1952, he entered her room at the base hospital. He was surprised to see her with her head elevated, bolstered by pillows, appearing relatively comfortable.

It was in sharp contrast to the previous day when she had lain back, tired, speaking little.

"Well, my girl's looking pretty chipper. Sitting up. You look like you're about ready to come home."

She greeted him with a smile. "I'm so glad you came early. How's Jeff?"

He kissed and embraced her gently, then drew a chair close to the bed and held her hand. "You look great, honey. How are you feeling? What about the cramps? Bother you during the night?"

"Not too bad last night." She squeezed his hand. "How's Jeff?" she repeated.

"Fine. Couldn't be better. Your mom and dad have been wonderful. How's my sweetheart?" He kissed her again on the forehead. "We're going to have you out of here soon."

"Oh, I hope so. Everyone's so nice here. But I get discouraged. I miss Jeff, and you. No fun, honey...." Her voice trailed off and she closed her eyes. For a moment it seemed she was asleep. But then, the eyes blinked open. "I've been thinking of names. I think we should call the baby Grace—after your mother. Grace Butterworth Call. It would make her happy, don't you think so?"

"You're sure it's going to be a girl?"

"Yes," she said with finality. "Yes, I'm sure. Just think, a boy and girl. The perfect family. We're so lucky, darling." Again the eyes closed and she appeared to drift off. It was at moments such as these, sitting beside her, looking at the beautiful ashen face, that he was consumed by grief. It seemed that each day she was slipping further from him. The thought of losing her became unbearable. The previous night he had stayed very late, finally falling asleep after resting his head on the pillow beside her. He had been awakened by the nurse who insisted he go home to rest.

Jim noticed the red volume of *The Rubaiyat* on the bedstand where his wife kept it for ready reference. The book had become a bond between them and they regularly discussed the work's spiritual significance. Muriel had begun taping passages that Jim took with him on trips. Gently, so as not to disturb his dozing wife, he withdrew his hand from hers and picked up the slender volume. Opening it to where she had inserted a bookmark, he read the passage which apparently she had been reading:

Come, fill the Cup, and in the fire of Spring
The Winter Garment of Repentance fling:
The Bird of Time has but a little way
To fly and lo! the Bird is on the Wing.

He found the passage disturbing. He was pondering the lines when he felt her stir. Her eyes fluttered open and she gazed at him silently, a clouded distant look which at first showed no recognition.

Jim took one of her hands, holding it gently. "Well, you're awake. I thought you were going to sleep the afternoon away."

She focused on him for a moment, and then noticing the book on his lap, she knit her brow curiously. "What's that?" she murmured. "*The Rubaiyat?*"

"Yes, I was just looking at what you'd been reading."

"Read it to me," she said brightening.

"Sure," said Jim, focusing on the book.

Come, fill the Cup, and in the fire of Spring
The Winter Garment of Repentance fling....

Here he paused, quietly closing the book. "How about something to drink?"

"Read the rest of it," she said.

Jim, pretending not to have heard, reached for a small container of juice on the bedstand. "Here, have a sip of this."

"No, thanks." Muriel gazed at him, eyes leaden. "I love you so much, Jim."

She closed her eyes. Jim, thinking she was dozing, started to withdraw his hand, but she held it. Squeezing it gently, she said, "Lo! the bird is on the wing."

◆ ◆ ◆

13

Muriel Call was near death. Her condition had worsened, and the doctors transferred her from the base hospital at McDill Field to the Municipal Hospital in Tampa. But nothing would save her from the raging infection afflicting her pregnancy. Jim, seated beside her bed, could see her slipping away. Tears clouded his vision as he struggled for control. They had been married only two years. Much of the time he had been away on missions. He was plagued by anguished thoughts of the irrecoverable moments they could have spent together. It had been so unfair. A future without her seemed unbearable. Thoughts of his son weighed heavily. No mother. No father, really. Muriel's mother had performed admirably in caring for Jeff during recent weeks, but what would be done for the long term?

The pressure had begun to show, his emotional state deteriorating. He was plagued by guilt, holding himself responsible for his wife's condition. Occasional notions of suicide flitted through his mind but were repressed by thoughts of Jeff. Now, as he focused on the remnants of his wife's beauty, he was consumed by remorse. Her face, exceedingly thin and drawn, still retained its classic lines. Occasionally her lips quivered as though she might speak. And then, the dark lashes fluttered, the eyes opened, moved slowly over the ceiling and came to rest on him.

"Jim?" she whispered. "Is that you, Jim? I'm so glad. I thought you were gone. I was dreaming ... about Jeff.... Where's Jeff?"

"He's fine, darling. Just fine."

"Oh, Jim. When am I going home? I want to be home with you and Jeff. Can you take me home?"

"Yes, honey." He agonized. "We'll go home. Don't worry, we're going home."

She appeared to have drifted off, his words unheard. He pressed his cheek against her face and there followed the long inconsolable silence found only in terminal wards of hospitals. A moment later, her eyes opened again and moved over the room, coming to rest unfocused on some distant point. Then a semblance of a smile, as though life were affording some momentary final pleasure. Shortly afterward, she lapsed into a coma from which she never revived. She died four days later on October 15, 1952.

◆ ◆ ◆

PART II

Meridian, Mississippi

October 1952

14

After his wife's death in October 1952, Jim Call went into a tailspin. Following the funeral he took an extended leave from the military and visited with his in-laws, who were caring for his son in Meridian. He also spent time in Mantua, Ohio, with his sister, Mrs. Stella White*, with whom he had a close relationship.

His grief was profound. According to published reports, his mother-in-law, Robbie John, said that after her daughter's death, "James was a disillusioned bewildered boy who lost all desire to live." She went on to say that James loved his son and would spend long hours frolicking with him, but that he would lapse into periods of deep depression. Occasionally, he would display a strange grim smile for no apparent reason. Friends of the major in Meridian said that he was never the same after his wife's death. An associate stated that Jim would sit for hours listening to recordings that he and his wife had made, and had once asked: "You reckon if I die, I'd be with Muriel?"

From all available information, it seems that until his wife's death Jim Call's life had been dedicated to his family and country. His Air Force efficiency reports were filled with glowing tributes from commanding officers, from which the following are excerpted:

November 30, 1949: This officer is one of the most promising observers we have in the squadron.

July 1, 1950: He possesses an outstanding creative ability and was recently selected the outstanding Navigator of his class at the Combat Crew Standardization School.

---

*fictitious name

March 15, 1951: He possesses a keen and brilliant mind ... he has been the number one man in his class at both AOB and Combat Crew Evaluation Schools.... He is scholarly, well-read and informed on world, professional, and cultural matters. The results he obtains are unquestionably accurate and his efficient and positive indulgence insures a complete success of any mission assigned him.

May 1, 1951: Major Call is one of the more brilliant young navigators in the Air Force.... He is scholarly and devotes many off-duty hours furthering his studies.... [He] is a fine example of what is desired of an Air Force Officer.

October 25, 1952: Major Call is young in years, he is old in experience, and is recognized by many as one of the more outstanding navigators in the Air Force today. Major Call is a devoted father, a credit to the community, and promotes good relations for the Air Force by his participation in many civic functions. He spends many of his off-duty hours reading the classics and studying art.

The record would later show: Major Call distinguished himself while participating in flights in the Korean conflict.... These flights were exceptionally hazardous because of long distances over water and the number of hours spent over enemy territory during which time enemy contact was probable and expected.... Because of his courage and fortitude he was awarded a number of citations including the Air Medal.

From the record, it seems clear that until his wife's death, Jim Call had managed to suppress the darker side of his personality. Although gambling forays took place and fits of temper often surfaced, for the most part he was regarded by those close to him as a fine citizen and family man. After that time, the picture that emerges from the strange tragic life of Major Call is a profile in infamy.

◆ ◆ ◆

15

Later in the fall of 1952, the young officer approached his new commanding officer at McDill Field. Associates would say afterward that, given Jim's state of mind, it was predictable he would volunteer for "extra-hazardous duty."

The CO, a compassionate man nearing retirement, quietly studied his subordinate sitting across the desk before replying to the request. He was aware of the young man's grief since the recent death of his wife. Leaning back in his chair he said, "You sure you want to do this, Major? You've had a rough few months." He looked at him through eyes that had seen young men perish. "Why don't you take a few days and—"

"I'm sure, Colonel." Jim's voice was measured, unemotional. "I've thought it through, sir. Very carefully. Right now I need combat assignments."

The colonel nodded thoughtfully, reluctantly. "All right. It's your prerogative."

Within days Jim was airborne in a B-29 to Kadena Air Base in Okinawa. Between January and July 27, 1953, when the Korean War ended, he flew 17 combat missions: long perilous trips over vast stretches of the Pacific to enemy territory where hostile fire tested the resilience of the aircraft and crew.

Colonel Samuel Battalio, a veteran of both World War II and Korea, later recalled the bombing raids:

> They were certainly dangerous missions. I was chief of the Planning and Analysis Section at Kadena and worked closely with Major Call on a daily basis. We flew several raids together. Our daylight bombing runs encountered heavy enemy resistance, forcing us to resort to nocturnal missions.

The enemy fighters weren't equipped for night flying and were less effective. There was still great danger from enemy flak, however. The Russians helped to install and train personnel for anti-aircraft facilities. They had the latest equipment, including brilliant spotlights. We were absolutely forbidden to bomb anything on the other side of the Yalu. If we did, even though it was an accident, it was an automatic court martial. Yet, at night we could see the Russians taking off from across the Yalu, their lights heading straight for us. They weren't that effective, though. Not at night, without radar. But there was always a lot of trauma on those raids ... particularly over the targets.

Nor was the emotional strain on the crew confined to the bombing runs. It continued throughout the long return trips to Kadena with senses attuned to the possibility of damage to the aircraft from enemy fire. Any change in the plane's normal odors or in the drone of the engines was suspect, indicating a possible malfunction or a fire which could signal every airman's worst nightmare, a ditching. Surviving a crash in the Pacific was a dubious outcome, given the possibility of encounters with sharks or a slow agonizing death on a raft.

If Jim's emotional control had shown signs of weakening following his wife's death, it was not the case in the skies over Korea. "His nerves were like steel," said those who flew with him. "He was a wizard. He'd figure out in a few minutes what it would take anyone else an hour to do—and under pressure."

His list of decorations and awards was impressive: Good Conduct Medal, American Campaign Medal, World War II Victory Medal, Air Medal, Korean Service Medal with one Bronze Service Star, United Nations Service Medal, National Defense Service Medal, Distinguished Unit Citation Emblem, Aviation Badge "Aircraft Observer," Armed Forces Reserve Medal.

But there would have been no award for congeniality, a fact borne out in a conversation between two officers over coffee at the Kadena Base one morning in 1953.

"How well do you know Call?" asked one.

"I was his immediate superior, flew several raids with him," replied the other officer. "Very intelligent. Started out as a good staff officer, eager to fly missions, but because of his brains they put him in the mission planning section."

"Bet he liked that," said the other man, facetiously.

"Yeah, didn't work out. His attitude got pretty bad. They'd give him an assignment and he'd grumble like hell, do an excellent job, then grumble all over again. He wanted to mastermind a whole plan rather than coordinate with others. Very temperamental. Took his wife's death pretty hard. Douglas roomed with him. He said Call would lock himself in the room and listen to recordings he and his wife made. Some kind of poetry. They put Douglas ahead of him in the planning section and he really resented it. Colonel Carney called them both in and gave the reasons for choosing Douglas but it didn't help. Call was depressed most of the time."

"Gambles a lot?"

"Yeah, all the time off duty. They say big money too—five hundred on the throw of the dice."

"Jesus, he must have something going for him besides his officer's pay. Seems pretty straight though, from what I've heard. His morals and stuff...."

"Yeah, not bad," agreed the other man. "He's a lone wolf. I never knew him to fool around with the local women. Started drinking after his wife died. Doesn't show it, though. Actually, when he wants to, he can really turn on the charm."

"Too bad it doesn't happen more often. Strange guy."

The change in Jim Call's personality began to find its way into subsequent efficiency reports. One dated April 5, 1953, by Colonel Battalio, took note of attitudinal deficiencies:

> This particular failing can possibly be ascribed to the recent death of his wife which obviously has caused great sorrow in his life. It is believed that this bereavement affects his current attitude to a very large extent and tends to exaggerate otherwise insignificant or small disappointments or inconveniences.

When the war ended in the summer of 1953, Jim remained overseas a few months, traveling to Japan and Hong Kong, where he purchased some civilian clothes. His taste ran to the conservative.

Tweeds, loafers, soft knit ties. It was in Hong Kong that he purchased an expensive well-cut suit that he saved for special occasions. One such occasion would later turn out to be very special. The suit would become evidence in a celebrated murder case.

Though he cut a striking figure in "civies," it was in uniform that Jim was most dashing. Whether on a Hong Kong street or a New York subway, it was difficult for him to go unnoticed. "He was just too handsome for his own good," allowed one law enforcement official who later pursued him throughout the country. "He didn't blend in."

But if his outward appearance distinguished him from most people, his internal makeup was even more unusual. Beneath the colorful array of campaign ribbons on his tunic, was a heart which beat to the rhythms of a far different soul.

In October 1953, he returned to the States and was stationed at Barksdale Air Force Base at Shreveport, Louisiana. After months of combat it seemed he had earned a period of rest and rehabilitation. But the hazardous life Jim Call had chosen for himself would not stop in Korea. Rather, it would become even more perilous, certainly more bizarre.

◆ ◆ ◆

16

"You'd look mighty good in that, Major." The salesman, a round balding man in his late forties nodded toward the gleaming green Jaguar on the showroom floor.

"Why?"

"Why?" repeated the salesman, surprised by Jim's question.

"Yes. Why?"

"Well ... because you would," he replied uneasily.

"Yes, but why?" Jim persisted, focusing a bombardier's eye on the man.

"Well ... because you're a good lookin' guy and that's a good lookin' car." He eyed the rows of campaign ribbons on the major's chest. What was with this dude, anyway? Tough lookin' bastard. Those freakin' eyes!

"Well, if you think we go so well together maybe you'll take a grand off that price," said the major, gruffly.

"Listen buddy, I've already—"

"I like '*Major*,'" Jim interrupted, one eyebrow arching imperiously, eyeing the salesman as if he had just crawled from under the Jaguar.

"OK. Sorry ... *Major*," said the man, flustered. "I told you before, the price I quoted is way below retail. We don't get many of these models in."

The salesman had been with his customer for less than five minutes and already he didn't like him. But he had to go easy. Couldn't offend him. Business wasn't all that good. Besides, there was something about the guy. Odd as hell. Mean. Unnerving. And all those freakin' medals. Somebody must've got hurt somewhere along the line.

"What'll it do?" from Jim.

"Do?"

"Speed? How fast?"

"Oh. Oh, hell that thing'll ratchet up to 150 in a few seconds. Actually, it could probably do—"

"Listen, mister. Cut the bullshit." The eyes were now deadly earnest. "I fly B-50s. Thousands of pounds of thrust and even they won't do that on the ground."

The salesman rolled his eyes. "Major, look, I'm just here to sell a car, that's all. I quoted you a decent price. You either want it or you don't."

"Let me talk to your manager."

"What?"

"Your manager."

"He's out."

"Who's that guy over there behind the glass door that says 'Manager' on it?"

The man, frustrated, started to speak. Then, wearily, "Just a minute ... *Major*."

Jim was seated behind the wheel of the Jaguar when the salesman returned with his boss. As the two approached, Jim stepped from the vehicle with an outstretched hand. "How do you do. I'm Jim Call."

The manager, a portly middle-aged man with an amiable countenance, shook hands enthusiastically. "Hello, Major. I'm George Heller. Can I help you out?"

"Yes, sir," said Jim, with a callow smile. "I'm interested in this here Jag. Just back from Korea. Don't have a lot. Can you give me a break on this?" Another winning smile.

The salesman, stunned by the metamorphosis in his customer's manner, stood by suspiciously.

"Of course," said the manager, elbowing his salesman aside. What was the matter with his employee? Hardass? Nonsense. The customer was a real gentleman. And his salesman had almost let him walk out. Time to show a little salesmanship. Maybe some of it would rub off. "Spent some time overseas myself a few years back. 34th infantry. Red Bull Division. North Italy. Sure, we can help you out."

Within minutes a sale was consummated close to the price Jim had suggested earlier. Following quick calls to validate credentials, and the signing of finance documents supplied by a local branch of the Bank of America, Jim turned to leave. "I'll pick it up late this afternoon."

"*Pleasure* doing business with you," said the manager, shaking hands.

"Yes," agreed the salesman, with less enthusiasm. "Enjoy the car, Major."

"Thanks," said the major, turning to the salesman and shaking his hand cordially. "Call me Jim."

◆　◆　◆

17

"You heard the colonel." Jim's voice was remarkably calm considering the matter at hand. "Survive anywhere, anytime."

"I don't give a rolling fuck what he said. I'm not eating that thing even if you do catch it—which I'm beginning to doubt."

Jim paid the other man little attention. He was too occupied trying to corner a five-foot diamondback rattlesnake. The reptile rattled its tail ominously and seemed poised to strike at the stick Jim was using to force it against a rock embankment.

The two officers were in the Nevada desert during their third week of survival training. Jim's new Jaguar had provided thrilling moments on the road, but his compulsive need for risk and adventure was not satisfied by a mere high performance sports car. After a trip to Meridian to see his two-year-old son Jeff, and a few weeks of high altitude training in B-47s at Barksdale Air Force Base, he had applied to the Air Force's Survival, Escape and Evasion School—a renowned combat training unit whose mission was to give aircrews the means to survive "anywhere, anytime" by simulating extreme environments and conditions. His application had been accepted and in January of 1954 he had presented himself to the school's commandant at Stead Air Force Base near Reno, Nevada. After several days of intensive training he found himself with another officer in the desert, literally trying to survive. At the moment he was engaged in a fight for survival with the large highly venomous diamondback, and the man with him watching the encounter was beginning to wonder if it might not be the snake who emerged the survivor.

"Hey, Jim, watch out for that thing." The man, who under ordinary circumstances could be described as clean-cut but was now bearded and covered with days of desert grime, was becoming increasingly apprehensive about the snake. "That thing nails you, you're a goner. Don't look for me to start sucking out the venom, either."

"Will you shut up?" Jim demanded, finally cornering the snake's head against the rock embankment. "I'm trying to concentrate on this mother—okay, there, got 'im!" He had reached for the reptile, grasping it well down its girth. The head, free from his grip, was swaying in all directions.

"Jim, for chris' sake you got him by the tail. You gotta get the head—the head! Oh, Jesus, you're in trouble, man!"

"Here, grab the son-of-a-bitch," yelled Jim, moving toward his comrade. "Get him behind the head."

"What? Get the hell away. Throw it away," the officer shouted, retreating.

But Jim, now that he had the snake, was not prepared to let it go. Dropping the stick, he used his other hand to grab the snake behind the head. It was a successful, if risky, move. Taking a long knife from its sheath on his belt, he proceeded to decapitate the reptile. It was not a pleasant thing to watch, and whatever hunger pangs Jim's companion had felt were now gone.

"Well, we got dinner," said Jim, holding up the remnants of the snake. "Now all we need is some way to cook it."

His companion turned away in disgust. "I'd rather starve. I should've gone with the other guys."

The "other guys" were the rest of the twelve-man contingent who had been turned out into the elements to test their skills. The school curriculum simulated combat conditions. Should trainees be "captured" by a school cadre acting as an Asian enemy (North Korean uniforms were worn), they were taken to a prison compound where they were vigorously interrogated, then incarcerated underground in a grate-covered pit. It was harsh training under primitive conditions.

The previous day Jim and the rest of the contingent had argued about directions, and Jim and the other officer had disengaged from the group. Now his companion was having serious regrets about his decision to accompany Jim. "I'll just eat berries and stuff."

"Berries! What are you talking about?" Jim looked at the man incredulously. "Where do you see berries?"

"Well, that instructor.... He said berries have nourishment that—"

"Jesus, you scare me. There are no freaking berries. You're in the desert, man. You're eating snake for dinner."

"The hell I am," responded the officer. "How about the rations? You eat the snake. Give me what's left of the rations."

"Christ, you're a liability. The rations are almost gone. I'm gonna end up carrying you back in. I'd rather spend two days in the pit."

"You know, the fact is you don't really mind being out here in the wilderness, do you?" the man said in a hostile tone. "The truth is you like all this shit. Right up your alley, I can tell. Down deep you love this stuff."

Jim shrugged, not arguing the point. "It could be worse...."

"God almighty," said the man, lowering his head in disbelief.

Despite his earlier comments, Jim gave his comrade what was left of the rations while he ate the snake—or part of it, anyway.

It was following "dinner" that Jim, sitting next to a fire, paused while cleaning flesh from the snakeskin. "Never know when this might come in handy," he said, holding the skin at arms length admiringly. "Never throw anything away in the desert. Say, uh ... there's something I've been meaning to talk to you about. Kind of dislike bringing it up...."

Immediately, the other man was suspicious. There was something about Jim's manner, a sudden deferential tone that did not quite ring true. "What's that?" he asked, uneasily.

"Well, it's my dad. He's been taken sick. I may have to borrow 1500 bucks from you to help him out. I'll pay you back in a couple of weeks." Jim returned his interest to the snakeskin, avoiding his companion's eyes.

The other man regarded him closely for a second. "That's bullshit, Jim. Everybody in the outfit knows you're losing your ass gambling. If I gave it to you, you'd just blow it all in the casinos."

Jim did not reply. A grim look replaced the affability of the previous moment. He sat looking into the fire, jaw set, winding the snakeskin about his hands, stretching it tightly.

There was something about the movement that his companion found unsettling. "C'mon, Jim," he said, soothingly. "We'll talk about it when we get back. This isn't the time for us to—"

"Forget it," said Jim with finality.

"Take it easy, buddy." The other man looked away. He'd heard about Call's temper. Things were difficult enough without incurring the wrath of the person on whom he might have to depend for survival. "Let's get some sleep. We'll talk in the morning."

Jim did not respond. He hunched over the remnants of the fire, winding and unwinding the snakeskin, his smoldering eyes reflecting the dying embers.

♦ ♦ ♦

18

The speckled ivory cubes tumbled across the green felt surface, ricocheted off the rail at the end of the crap table, and came to rest.

"Seven!" the croupier intoned.

A gasp rose from the crowd that had gathered about the table to watch the shooter, a large balding man of middle age, who was on a roll of major proportions. It was his sixth "natural"—a winning combination of the dice on the first roll totaling seven or eleven. A spectacular piece of luck by any standard.

Not the least impressed among the onlookers was a slender dark-haired man who stood well back on the fringe of the crowd. He had watched the extraordinary run, his interest mounting with each colorful stack of chips that rose in front of the shooter. It was past midnight but the large crowd milling inside the Las Vegas casino showed no signs of thinning. Indeed, the glittering hall seemed to pulse with enthusiasm as clusters of ever-optimistic patrons eddied among the tables, smoking, drinking, eager for the score.

Jim had been gambling throughout the evening and had already lost several hundred dollars. Now, observing the man gathering his winnings at the crap table, his mind was busy contemplating a more serious form of chance, one he had pursued with increasing frequency during preceding months. What he had in mind was riskier, the stakes much higher, the thrills even greater than those he had been experiencing in the casinos.

He watched from the edge of the crowd as the winner walked purposefully toward the cashier's window. After pocketing his money, the man moved across the large hall toward the entranceway. Near the door he paused, availing himself of a cocktail from a tray carried by a slender hostess in a dark dress. Few places were more liberal with liquor than Las Vegas casinos. After downing the cocktail, the man walked out the door. At a discreet distance, Jim Call followed.

It was a pleasant night, the cool desert air having displaced the heat of the day. Jim stood in the shadows of the parking lot, watching his intended victim climb into a dark sedan. When the car pulled away, the officer moved quickly to his Jaguar and followed the vehicle out to the glittering strip that formed the main thoroughfare of Las Vegas. He proceeded slowly, threading his way through the traffic, allowing several cars to intervene between him and his target. The distinctive style of the Jaguar rendered it a poor vehicle for surveillance, requiring more discretion.

When traffic stopped for a red light, Jim reached beneath his seat and withdrew a black holster holding a German Luger. He placed the pistol on the passenger seat while he reviewed his plan. He would follow his victim until he reached his destination. When the man left his car, he would stalk him and, at a propitious moment, rob him at gunpoint. Because of its license plate and downscale style, he suspected the car he was following had been rented. This should make the job easier. His target was probably staying at a hotel; hence, the person would be less familiar with the area than a resident. He felt sure the man was carrying several thousand dollars. That had been apparent from the black and orange high-stake chips at the crap table.

Drawing closer to the car, he got a better look at his intended victim. Suddenly the man glanced in his rearview mirror. Was he becoming suspicious? Jim slowed his vehicle, dropping further behind.

Traffic thinned as they proceeded toward the outskirts of town. The lack of traffic was now a source of concern. More exposure. He continued to allow the other vehicle to draw away. There were occasions now when its tail lights were barely discernible in the darkness. An intersection brought his surveillance to an end. There was no sign of his quarry. He had little time for disappointment, however. As he drove slowly through the intersection, a sense of something coming toward him, perhaps the sound of a motor, caused him to look to his right. A flash of headlights, snake eyes barreling toward him. He braced, dropping his head toward the steering wheel. An explosion of glass and metal rocked the vehicle as the other car rammed into the passenger door of the Jaguar.

Stunned, Jim felt blood coming from his forehead where it had struck the steering wheel. Excruciating pain shot through his right knee. Recovering, he caught a glimpse of the vehicle that had struck him. It pulled back sharply and, tires screeching, shot off into the night.

Finding his car still running, Jim drove through the intersection and pulled off to the side of the road. With his handkerchief, he wiped the blood from his forehead, trying to get his bearings. It had happened quickly. He could not be certain. But from the glimpse he had of the other vehicle, he was not altogether sure that it was not the car he had been following.

◆ ◆ ◆

19

Having successfully concluded his training at Stead early in 1954, Jim had rejoined the 376th Bombardier Wing, 514th Squadron, at Barksdale Air Force Base, Louisiana. Within weeks he was once again traveling, this time on temporary duty status to Mather Field, Sacramento, California, where he attended high-speed navigation school. Here, as elsewhere, he impressed his superiors and fellow officers with his keen mind and determination to live life on the edge.

Gambling was big business in many western states and for a practitioner of Jim Call's inclination the opportunities were limitless. Those familiar with his gaming activities said he was convinced his mathematical talents—which were evident during military operations—would enable him to devise systems that would break the casino banks. His off-duty hours were consumed by the endeavor, which had reached obsessive proportions. He confided to friends that it helped to take his mind off the loss of his wife. Trips to resorts such as Reno, Carson City, Lake Tahoe, and Las Vegas had been common since his return from Korea.

The accident in Vegas had severely damaged the Jaguar and given rise to gossip among his fellow airmen. "Just a matter of time before it happened," allowed one acquaintance. Others agreed. "Fucking mad man about speed and danger" … "Gas pedal never left the floor on that car" … "Lucky he's alive."

The injury to his knee resulted in a pronounced limp which lasted months and was to become part of evidence implicating him in subsequent crimes. The head injury sustained when he hit the steering wheel was less noticeable—although conceivably more lasting in its effects.

After securing an extension of travel time to have the Jaguar repaired, he spent several nights at Las Vegas casinos and, as he later said, "went broke." Bad checks began to surface. Feeling pressure, he took his car from the garage before it was properly fixed and in early May 1954 returned to Barksdale. A few days later he drove to Meridian to see his son Jeff and to pick up summer uniforms. During his brief stay in Meridian it was apparent to Robbie John that her son-in-law's mental condition had deteriorated. Although he seemed delighted with his child, she sensed that he was deeply depressed. She continued to attribute this to the death of her daughter.

Back at Barksdale, other factors exacerbated his problems. His superiors were being confronted with letters and telephone calls regarding his bad checks. On May 11, 1954, Lieutenant Colonel O. A. Weddle, commanding officer of the 514th Squadron, called a subordinate into his office.

"Look at this, Captain." He handed the officer a sheaf of letters. "Harold's Club, Reno; Thunderbird Hotel, Las Vegas; El Rancho Hotel, Las Vegas; Officers' Club, Mather Field...." The colonel, a pleasant man with a reputation for being firm but fair, was genuinely perplexed. "I took over this squadron only a week ago and I've been besieged with letters and telephone calls about this man's finances. What's going on? His record shows him to be an outstanding officer."

"It's a complicated case, Colonel," said the captain, a short, fair-complexioned man with a receding hairline. "Call has problems. His wife died about a year-and-a-half ago. His friends say he's been in a tailspin ever since." The officer shrugged slightly, placing the sheaf of papers back on his superior's desk. "He's an inveterate gambler. Just got in over his head, I guess."

"What about these burglaries in town?" the colonel asked. "I got a letter from the Provost Marshal's office. The robberies all follow the same pattern. High-end residences, forced entry, cash, jewelry. They feel strongly that someone here at the base is involved." He paused, picking up the letters regarding Jim's bad checks and glancing through them. "Think there could be any connection here?"

"Burglaries?" The officer looked at his superior curiously, considering the implication of the man's statements. "You mean...? No I don't think so, sir. Not Jim Call."

"You never know," said the colonel. "Someone gets their back against the wall. I've seen some outstanding officers do mighty strange things. Anyway, I have to talk to him about these checks."

He glanced down at the letters, a resigned look on his face. "Better get him over here."

A short time later, Jim strode into his office. "Sit down, Major," said the colonel, motioning to one of two straight-back chairs which stood in formation before his desk. "I'll come right to the point, Major. I have here a number of letters from banks and other establishments inquiring about checks you've written." He paused, looking at him questioningly.

Jim returned his gaze but did not respond immediately. The colonel felt a moment of empathy. The officer before him was clean cut, intelligent. And his record was that of a superb airman. Had the death of his wife brought this on? If so, it was unfortunate. Also, there was something about the person that he liked. The man, while obviously in dire straits, seemed controlled, uncowed—traits the colonel admired.

But he quickly shrugged off any sympathy. There was a job to do. "What do you have to say about this, Major?"

"There's nothing I can say, sir," replied Jim simply. "I've had some checks bounce. I was in a bind, Colonel." He shifted in his chair, squeezing his flight cap, the only sign of unease. "Figured I'd have time to cover them ... got caught up in flights. No excuse, sir."

The colonel eyed him for a moment. "Guess you've had a rough year, huh?" Curiosity crept into his voice, inviting a response.

There was none. Jim sat quietly, unblinking eyes riveted on his CO. The colonel, clearing his throat, looked down at the letters. "Very well, Major. Let's put these matters in order. This office takes such derelictions very seriously. You've got too good a record to let something like this impact your career. I'm giving you three days to straighten out your affairs. Is that understood?"

Jim nodded. "Yes, sir. Thank you, Colonel."

As the man strode from the room, the commander gazed after him thoughtfully. He had seen gambling destroy lives. He turned his attention to the papers on his desk. From the pile he withdrew the recent letter from the Provost Marshal's office, a heavy frown clouding his features.

◆ ◆ ◆

20

"The only way I can come out of this is to rob a bank." Jim was describing his financial plight to Calvin Gaskins, a fellow officer at Barksdale Air Force Base.

"Cal," as he was known, had met the major when Jim returned from overseas several months previously, having socialized with him at Barksdale and "tented" with him at Stead Air Force Base. A friendship had evolved—somewhat unusual in view of Jim's introvertive tendencies—and he was now responding to an invitation to Jim's room to "discuss some problems."

Cal, a sensitive courtly gentleman with southern roots who had majored in psychology while in college, was now observing a man deeply troubled. He had considerable "affection" for Jim, as he said later, thought him "brilliant," and as he listened to him relate his problems, wondered how such a "sharp" person had allowed his personal affairs to deteriorate to such an extent. Even more alarming was the fact that, given his friend's mental state and proclivity toward derring-do, Cal could not be certain Jim would *not* rob a bank.

"I got in over my head." Jim sat on the edge of his bed, hands folded, eyes on the floor. "Out at Mather. Wrote some checks. Reno, Vegas. I can't cover them. The ol' man's given me three days to straighten it out. I need four grand." He shook his head morosely. "I've got to come up with it, one way or another," he added ominously, his face shrouded with lawless intent.

The expression was not lost on Gaskins, who was surprised at the change from his friend's usually cool demeanor. He averted his eyes to a nearby window which overlooked a patch of greenery where two trees blossomed in springtime color. A solitary bench underneath was strewn with petals from the trees, forming a soft taffeta quilt. It was a restful scene, offering momentary respite from his sense of impending involvement with his friend's problems.

"Seems it'd be easier to *borrow* the money from the bank rather than *rob* it," he said, smoothing his sandy hair. "Why don't we call your bank?"

"I don't know.... They'd want collateral." Although Jim seemed dubious, there was a touch of hope in his voice.

"It's worth a try. I'd be glad to help." Cal felt a personal guarantee looming. But his loyalty proved equal to the challenge. "C'mon, let's go talk it over with the bank."

"I don't think they'll do it, not under the circumstances." Jim hesitated, his tone conveying a mixture of doubt and embarrassment. "I suppose we could give it a try, though. I really appreciate this, Cal."

"Not at all." Cal rose extending his hand. "That's what friends are for, right?"

The visage that confronted them a few hours later at Bossier City Bank in Shreveport, Louisiana, was less sympathetic. "I'm sorry, Major. Your checking account has a number of overdrafts. Under the circumstances we're unable to act on your request." It was a brief meeting.

"It's not the end of the world," Cal said after the bank encounter, now committed to helping his friend. "I've got some money in my bank at Fort Sam Houston. I can get a thousand dollars."

Jim, deep in thought, was no longer listening. To Cal, it seemed his friend's mind was again consumed with alternative solutions.

True to his word, Cal contacted his bank. After advising Jim that he would have the money in two or three days, he flew to Wichita, Kansas, to pick up a B-47 on orders from the squadron commander, Colonel Weddle. That night in Wichita he received a call from Weddle.

"Where's Major Call?" The colonel's voice was agitated. "No one knows where he is. Better get back here and find him."

Cal returned to Barksdale immediately, deeply concerned. Based on his conversations with Jim during preceding days he believed the man had reached the end of his rope, that he "might well revert to criminal means to obtain money" and, further, "feel justified in doing same."

But efforts to locate the missing airman were to no avail. It was May 13, 1954. Major Call's military career had ended, his criminal career begun.

♦ ♦ ♦

PART III

Chicago, Illinois

June 1954

21

"Are you serious, Jimmy? I thought you were joking!"

Robert Sylvester leaned forward in his chair, his eyes narrowing in disbelief as he listened to his life-long friend. It was June 1954, and the two were sitting in a Chicago hotel room. Jim had just disclosed that he had gone AWOL from the Air Force and had embarked on a life of crime.

"I'm serious, Bob," said Jim quietly. "Look at these." He leaned over and casually opened a military bag near his chair. Resting on top of an assortment of clothing were three pistols—a Luger, a .32-caliber automatic, and a snub-nosed .38-caliber revolver. "I just robbed a guy in a hotel," he continued in a casual tone as though describing some minor occurrence. "Gives you a great rush. You know—spark, thrill."

Robert was stupefied. The two men had known each other since grammar school in Chicago, a relationship which had culminated in Robert having been chosen best man for Jim's wedding four years previously. Because of their different careers, the two had seen little of each other since the wedding, but had stayed in touch through recordings and written correspondence.

A tall pleasant-looking individual in his late twenties, Robert Sylvester could already point to an honorable life that had included military service, college and graduate studies, marriage, and a promising future in chemistry. The son of a successful physician, he had demonstrated since his early years a work ethic that augured well for the Sylvester legacy—a quality he had always presumed was shared by his life-long friend "Jimmy."

His own rather sedate life was in sharp contrast with the exciting life of his friend, and he had followed the flyer's exploits with interest and admiration. When Jim had called him earlier, announcing that he was in Chicago, Robert had invited him to his father's house with enthusiasm. Instead, at Jim's suggestion, they had met in his hotel room. What for Robert had begun as a pleasant reunion turned into a horrifying revelation as Jim calmly described his recent criminal activities.

"Why would you do this? Why go AWOL?"

"I had no choice," Jim said. "The squadron commander gave me three days to straighten out my finances. No way. I've got a lot of bread out there to cover. Five grand."

"But you can't just walk away," said Robert, now thoroughly alarmed. "That's desertion. They'll come after you. It'll ruin your career, your life!"

His admonitions seemed to have little effect. As he paused, looking at his friend's intractable countenance across the room, he was struck by his appearance. Although clean shaven, with hair neatly combed back as always, Jim seemed oddly dressed for an Air Force major—bright red T-shirt, blue trousers, and sneakers. An indication of his new lifestyle, thought Robert.

Sensing his words were doing little to change his friend's mind, Robert finally said, "Look, Jimmy, if you'll go back to your base I'll lend you the five thousand to pay off your debt. You can pay me back when—"

"No, no," Jim interrupted. "I still owe you the money from the wedding. Say, why don't you take my Jag? It's pretty banged up from the accident, but you can have it if you want to keep up the bank payments."

"I'm already making payments on my own car," said Robert, thoroughly bewildered by his friend's behavior.

"I suppose I could sell it," Jim continued. "Kind of hate to let it go, though." He lowered his eyes momentarily as though contemplating the sale of a vital organ. But then, just as quickly, his spirits seemed to brighten. "Why don't you come with me. We'll have a great time. We'd be a terrific team. Think of the jobs we could pull. It'll really turn you on. Believe me, there's no high like it." As he spoke, a glimmer came to his eyes, the usual impassive exterior giving way to animation.

Robert was incredulous. Years later in a written document which described their meeting he would say:

His [Jim's] mind seemed clear and functioning well enough, but the lack of rationality of what he was saying was alarming. Every shread [*sic*] of logic was gone.

It was not the first time Robert had noticed a change in his friend. Following the death of Jim's wife two years before, he had detected a disturbing change in his personality. He was unsure how much of Call's present imbalance derived from bereavement. In the same document, he commented on the dramatic change in his friend's behavior after Muriel's death:

> I flew to Meridian for the funeral and I recognized the change in Jim right away—beside the fact that he was grief stricken, he drank, constantly from morning to night, sipping a little now and then until he averaged almost a fifth of Scotch a day. He never exhibited drunkenness or showed intoxication in any way. I was shocked, and when I spoke to him about it, he passed it off lightly.

Robert continued to implore his friend to return to the Air Force, but to no avail. Jim left the hotel room with his three guns, apparently as committed to a future in crime as when he had arrived in Chicago.

Their meeting weighed heavily on Robert Sylvester after his friend's departure. Apprehensive, fearing for the welfare of Jim and his potential victims, as well as sensing possible complicity now that he had been informed of his friend's criminal intentions, Robert discussed the matter with family members. The next day he and his sister went to the FBI office in Chicago and reported that Jim Call was "AWOL, armed, and possibly dangerous."

Regrettably, his report to the authorities was too late.

◆ ◆ ◆

22

West of Cleveland, on the shores of Lake Erie, were several small suburbs. They were attractive communities, particularly along Lake Shore Road, a rather busy thoroughfare, where a filigree of fine houses embellished the gray bluffs. On a windy or stormy day the gigantic waves that punished the shore beneath these houses were every bit as strong as the surf of coastal waters. Many of the Lake Shore houses were inhabited by those who enjoyed socializing and showcasing their wide horizons and glorious sunsets. Dinner parties were a frequent source of entertainment.

It was a cool evening in June 1954, and a soiree was in progress on Lake Shore Road. A dozen people were gathered, and following cocktails and dinner the hosts and their guests had retired to a paneled library for relaxation with brandies, soft music, and cigars. The formality that had fostered restraint earlier in the evening had long since yielded to lively conversation and laughter. The revelry was confined to the library, however. Elsewhere in the house a more somber enterprise was underway.

As midnight approached, one of the guests excused herself to go to an upstairs bathroom. As she reached the landing at the top of the stairs, she heard the roar of the surf pounding the shore beyond the bluff. But there were other sounds—noises coming from the bedroom through which she had to pass to reach the bath.

Curious, she proceeded into the bedroom. A man was standing amid debris, emptying contents of a bureau drawer onto the floor. Stunned, she put her hand to her mouth. "Who are you?" she exclaimed. "What are you doing?"

The man paused to look at her, showing no more concern than someone interrupted in the middle of a domestic chore. She quickly realized the person must be a burglar, but the most striking aspect was the intruder's lack of stealth and, except for an occasional threatening glance, his brazen disregard for her presence. Shocked and frightened, she remained motionless.

Suddenly, from the stairwell, came the sound of someone mounting the steps. The man hesitated, listening, then walked to an open window at the rear overlooking Lake Erie. Here, he turned toward her for a moment. Then, like a lithe animal, he vaulted through the window onto an adjoining roof into the darkness.

The party ended quickly that night, but burglaries by an intruder who was seemingly unconcerned about awakening inhabitants continued in Cleveland's suburbs into early summer. The burglaries remain unsolved.

♦ ♦ ♦

23

Life was uncomplicated at the Liberty Package Store. Located at the foot of Lebanon Mountain just over the New York line near Hancock, Massachusetts, it was a peaceful rural spot where on any given summer night the loudest sounds were those of a whirring ceiling fan and the soft rhythmic breathing of an old black lab that slept on a rug at the rear of the store. Occasionally a heavy trailer rumbling past on Route 20 sent mild vibrations through the shop, causing melodious tinkling among the liquor bottles that lined the walls. For the most part, evenings here were slow and mellow.

Not far away, however, only a mile or so over the mountain, activity picked up considerably. Here, amidst a configuration of neon lights and throbbing music was the Showboat, a night club replete with burlesque shows, spirits, gambling, and all types of ancillary action—a place where a sporting man would find much to titillate his fancy. And if there were not enough to satisfy one's nocturnal interests here, there most certainly was directly across the road at another night spot called "The Ruby."

Racy though these spots were, there was even more for one who chose life in the fast lane. A few miles away was the Lebanon Valley Speedway. Built in 1953, it had a half-mile track with a grandstand that held 1200 people. Here, sports cars, including the redoubtable Hudson Hornet, provided white-knuckle thrills under large incandescent lights. For one with a passion for speed and thrills, Lebanon Valley was the place to be.

It was not unusual for habitués of these spots to find their way to the Liberty Package Store. This was quite all right with Edward Freehoffer, the genial 56-year-old proprietor. A bald man, small of stature but large of spirit, he welcomed the visitors—particularly the strippers from the Showboat, for whom he had a particular fondness.

Their arrival served to break the tedium and to provide him with stories he could relate to his neighbor, John Connors, who owned a restaurant next door called "Ida and John's."

But these visits provided only infrequent oases in the slow routine. And given Edward Freehoffer's age and disposition, that too was quite all right. He was happy with his life and there was little that detracted from his contentment in the establishment. That is, until 10:00 p.m. on Saturday, June 5, 1954, when the small bell attached to the top of the front door jingled, announcing a visitor.

"This is a stickup!"

Edward stiffened in his chair near the cash register, the color draining from his face as he looked across the counter into the muzzle of a pistol. Holding the weapon was a dark-complexioned man in a tan suit, of medium stature, his black hair combed straight back, a deadly expression on his face.

"Give me the money!" said the man, motioning toward the register. "Put it in that bag."

Rising to his feet, the proprietor took the money from the register—approximately one hundred dollars—and shoved it into one of the paper bags used to package liquor. Hands shaking, he placed the bag on the counter in front of the robber.

"Give me a couple of those." The intruder pointed to quart bottles of Corby's whiskey on the shelf behind the proprietor. "Hurry up," he said glancing toward the door.

Edward was quick to comply. From the rear of the room he heard the dog stirring. He hoped it would remain there. A friendly animal, it would do nothing but complicate matters, and Edward's main concern was to have the robber leave as quickly as possible.

Trembling, he placed the liquor on the counter. Then, from force of habit he found himself saying, "Anything else I can get you?"

"Turn around!"

"What?" croaked Edward.

"You heard me," commanded the gunman, brandishing his pistol. "Face the wall!"

"Oh, no," thought Edward. Slowly he turned, expecting the worst. It came quickly. There was the sound of something moving toward him and then a flash of light exploding in his skull. For an instant the room reeled around him before another blow from the pistol sent him to the floor unconscious. Moments later he awakened to the sensation of wet, sticky blood covering his face. Then, it seemed from far off, a jingling sound. Was it the bell attached to the door? Yes, the intruder had left.

Edward reached for the top of the counter and struggled to his feet. Blood gushed from his wound as he lurched from the shop and made his way next door to his friend's restaurant. Here he blurted out to Mrs. Connors, the shocked wife of the proprietor, the circumstances of his ordeal. She immediately called a doctor and the State Police. Later she told authorities, "Edward was in very bad shape when he staggered into the restaurant. He was covered with blood and still dazed from a blow on his head."

The robbery came as a shock to the small rural community. The armed holdup was the first in that area in many years in which someone was hurt, according to authorities.

Edward Freehoffer recovered from his injuries but was unable to recall much of the details of the holdup. "It all happened so quick, there's very little I can tell," he said. "He just came in and told me it was a stickup, conked me over the head, and that was it. I've got a couple of nice holes on top my head where he hit me with the butt of his gun. I didn't see his car. In fact, I'm not sure he even had a car. Didn't look much like a robber when he came in. Nice lookin' guy, well-dressed. Must've come from the Showboat. He was wearin' a suit."

♦ ♦ ♦

24

"It's just what it feels like." The words were measured, unnerving. "Pull over!" Jim Call had shoved his pistol against the back of the cab driver's skull. He had purchased the weapon, a .32-caliber automatic, serial number 570568, at the Springfield, Massachusetts, Arsenal in December 1945, for $29.75. His status as an Air Force officer had enabled him to make the purchase. It was one of two weapons he carried, the other being a German Luger, serial number 8782T, which he purchased the same year from a soldier at Westover Field, Massachusetts, for $50.00. John O'Connor, the cab driver, would not have been interested in the nomenclature of the guns. The cold muzzle pressed against the back of his head was enough to tell him his life was imperiled.

It was June 12, 1954, at 11:30 p.m. on a dreary stretch of road outside Springfield, Massachusetts. One month had passed since Jim went AWOL from his base at Barksdale, Louisiana. Having engaged in "many transgressions," according to his later admissions, he had left the midwest and proceeded east to avoid detection. Unable to sell his Jaguar because of the attention it would bring—payments were overdue at the bank—he had left it at the Swan Ramp Inc., 48 Swan Street, Buffalo, New York. To throw off authorities he believed would soon be pursuing him, he had told the attendant he was going to Canada for a few weeks. Reasoning correctly that it would be some time before checks were made on the car, he had continued his crime spree, traveling extensively throughout Ohio, New York, and Massachusetts via train and bus.

While staying at the Ten Eyck Hotel in Albany in early June, he had made nightly forays to nearby Massachusetts, where he attended car races, gambled at the Showboat, and engaged in other nocturnal pursuits such as the Liberty Package Store stickup. It had been in the

Ten Eyck Hotel that he had seen an advertisement for a sports car race at Westover Field, where he had been stationed several years before. Leaving his hotel, he had headed for the race. En route, he had continued with his "many transgressions," the cab driver being his latest victim.

John O'Connor, a driver for the Allied Taxi Companies, never suspected the fare he had picked up five minutes earlier would turn out to be an armed robber. "Young guy, good-lookin', real nice when he got in."

But the metamorphosis which took place in his passenger on that lonely stretch of road left no doubt in the driver's mind that the person in the back seat was dangerous.

"Pull over!" came a gruff command from the rear.

The alarmed driver slowed his 1951 black Chevrolet, easing it toward the side of the road, preparing to stop. But not quickly enough for his passenger.

"I said pull over, damn it!" The robber slapped the weapon against the side of the driver's head.

Stunned, O'Connor brought the cab to a lurching stop. Expecting the worst, he sat head down, trembling.

"Gimme your wallet, watch, rings—everything!" The voice was low, deliberate.

"Okay, just take it easy," pleaded the driver, removing his watch and handing it back. "No rings," he said, fumbling in his jacket for his wallet.

"One hand!" shouted the robber. "Keep your other hand on the wheel!"

"Okay, okay." The driver withdrew his wallet, handing it over his shoulder, avoiding looking. He sensed he was about to be shot. Maybe if he didn't look, he'd be spared. No witness. "Not much there," he mumbled.

"Better be something," came the voice. "'Else you're gonna end up in that ditch."

O'Connor, terrified, listened as the man went through his wallet. Then, "Twelve bucks! You kidding me?" exclaimed the voice. "Twelve fucking bucks! You got more stashed somewhere. Let's have it!"

"Listen, mister. I swear," the driver said, hoarsely. "It's all I—"

"Get out of the car!" interrupted the voice. "Keep your hands up!"

This was it. The man was going to carry out his threat. O'Connor, shivering, eased from the cab, both hands over his head. The robber stepped out of the back and confronted him on the side of the road. He was holding a pistol. Gone was the pleasant, good-looking man he had picked up. In his place the cab driver saw a killer.

"What you gonna do?" O'Connor said, his voice barely audible. The man regarded him in silence, his eyes black slits. O'Connor agonized. It was coming; an exploding flash from the muzzle; the bullet tearing into his chest. He closed his eyes, prayed.

But there was nothing. Then footsteps. He opened his eyes to see the robber climbing into the driver's seat. With a screech of tires and scattering gravel, the cab disappeared into the night.

◆ ◆ ◆

25

Sports car racing is not for everyone. The incessant rumble of engines, roaring crowds, screeching tires, malodorous fumes—for many, a battering of the senses. For Jim Call, however, it was a totally gratifying high.

Although Call's psychology was incomprehensible—particularly the thought processes involved in his criminal acts—his passion for sports cars was clear and dominated much of his life. His own experience on the track had been limited. Although he had appeared in a few minor races and showed promise, Air Force commitments precluded serious involvement as a driver.

As he sat among the crowd of spectators in the worn green wooden bleachers at Westover Field on June 13, 1954, he was captivated by the grinding, whirring stream of cars. So much so, that when a pretty blonde young woman sitting nearby attempted to strike up a conversation, he ignored her. Not that he intended to be rude. Under other circumstances he would have responded, would, in fact, have been quite charming. At the moment, however, his attention was riveted on the stream of cars hurtling around the track. When a driver skillfully avoided a near accident on a turn, Jim clenched his jaw and nodded appreciatively. The fact that only the night before in nearby Springfield he had assaulted, robbed, even considered killing a cab driver, affected him little. Today was complete bliss.

It wasn't until the following morning in a room at the St. Charles Hotel in downtown Springfield that he really assessed his perilous situation. The authorities had the cab by now—and a witness. Since he had abandoned the car downtown they would conclude, and rightly so, that the assailant could still be in the vicinity. It was time to leave. First, he would do as he had done in the past. Throw them off his trail. He had a low regard for police mentality, little doubt that he could outsmart any posse. To a large extent, events would prove him right. He was intrigued by the evasion process. In some ways it was like the survival camp at Stead Air Force Base, or devising systems to beat the odds at casino gaming tables. As he would say later, "My entire life was a gamble."

After slipping unnoticed from the hotel without paying his bill, he went to Gordon's Army Navy store on Main Street. Here, in a brazen move which had come to characterize his modus operandi, he took one of two blank checks he'd found in the cab driver's wallet and used O'Connor's identification to purchase a sleeping bag, knapsack, and other camping equipment, indicating that he planned to hike the nearby Appalachian Trail. Facing charges for crimes in Massachusetts, including the assault, armed robbery and kidnapping of the Springfield cab driver, it was highly improbable that a person of Call's reputed brilliance would use his victim's check and identification two days after the crime and signal his plans for a trip on the nearby camping route. More likely the contact at the Springfield store was made to provide disinformation to throw his pursuers off his trail, as he had done when leaving his Jaguar at Swan's garage in Buffalo a short time before. Rather than hiking on the trail, the evidence clearly shows that he went where he always did when in trouble, back to Mantua near Cleveland.

Later, under questioning about the period following his Springfield crimes, Jim Call would fail to furnish a single verifiable presence for the next 19 days until the night of July 5, 1954, when he mysteriously resurfaced in Lake Placid with a severely bitten finger.

◆ ◆ ◆

PART IV

Lake Placid, New York

July 1954

26

Jim Call claimed to have arrived in Lake Placid in the early morning hours of July 5, 1954, and by his own subsequent account, promptly commemorated the occasion by robbing a drive-in theatre. If he did commit the robbery—indeed, there was no specific record of it—it would have been a clumsy effort, intended more to create an alibi than for any reward. (He later would say that his only take from the job was "about enough Babe Ruth candy bars to feed most of the squirrels in the north woods.") His selection of the Sara-Placid Drive-In as a target for burglary is revealing in itself. The theatre derived its name from its position equidistant between the towns of Lake Placid and Saranac Lake, designed to draw customers from both communities. Between the two areas, some ten miles apart, lay little more than desolate mountain forest. Obviously, with no security during closing hours, the management left little of value at the remote location. But for Jim it offered a risk-free break-in that would create a police record and serve to establish his presence at that time in Lake Placid. By doing this he hoped to distance himself from a far more serious crime he had committed only the day before miles away in Ohio.

The "Candy Caper," as he termed his drive-in theft, would be the first of numerous robberies for Jim in the northern region. His appetite for burglaries proved insatiable and reflected his inexplicable addiction to the risks involved in covert undertakings. It seemed that second-story jobs provided him with thrills similar to those he derived from the gaming tables or the bombing raids in Korea. It was difficult for his associates to explain. Said one, "An adrenaline high, I suppose."

As Jim Call's one-man crime wave progressed in the Adirondacks, the police theorized that the perpetrator might be hiding out in the woods. They based this assumption on items taken during burglaries, such as blankets and cooking hardware. Crimes in Lake Placid increased, particularly at luxurious summer houses—"camps" as they were called. This had never happened before. What was particularly alarming were the "not so cat-like" methods of the burglar. He seemed to become increasingly bold. Nor were his activities confined to burglaries, as Fred Wertheim, proprietor of the Highland House, learned to his dismay.

It was a cool dark evening in July. Mr. Wertheim was taking a late night stroll near his residence at 3 Highland Avenue, enjoying the peaceful beauty of the Adirondack hamlet. A holdup on the quiet street was the last thing on the gentleman's mind. That was for places such as New York or Chicago, not crime-free Lake Placid. And so he thought it not at all unusual when a figure wearing a trenchcoat, collar turned up around his face, hands in pockets, approached from the opposite direction. Indeed, the village being as friendly as it was, Mr. Wertheim was preparing to nod and to offer a cheerful greeting.

The first words uttered on the lonely street that night, however, were far from an amenity. "This is a stickup! Gimme your wallet!"

Wertheim was flabbergasted. Here in Lake Placid? Couldn't be. His first inclination was to resist, to yell. And yell he did, as loudly as he could. "Help! Help! A holdup! Help!" His cries intensified, reverberating from the mountains that ringed Lake Placid.

The robber was the one who was now surprised. Ordinarily, it didn't work that way. He attempted to draw a pistol from his coat pocket, but the slide became entangled in the garment. Mr. Wertheim would later learn to his dismay from the State Police that had the robber been able to draw the gun quickly he would have shot his victim on the spot. Instead, as Wertheim's yells began to light up the quiet street, his assailant quickly departed.

News of the attempted holdup spread like an avalanche over the mountain community, smothering enthusiasm for the time-honored custom of evening strolls. Said one longtime resident, "Got so you weren't safe anyplace. He was robbin' ya *inside*.... He was robbin' ya *outside*."

◆ ◆ ◆

27

For the moment residents of Lake Placid, terrorized by the rash of brazen burglaries and armed robberies, were safe. Jim Call was in repose. It had been over three weeks since Jim's arrival in the North Country, and he was in seclusion at what he termed his "permanent camp" deep in the Adirondacks. It was a place to which he retreated for days at a time to recover from one-night stands in other areas of the mountains.

In spite of the primitive conditions of the site, he was not uncomfortable. Indeed, at the moment he was reclining in a lawn chair (a recent acquisition from one of the camps) smoking a cigarette while sipping cocktail sherry (another acquisition) from a tin cup. On his lap was his treasured volume of Muriel's *Rubaiyat,* which he had kept with him since her death. As he sat smoking and drinking he consulted the book meditatively.

A light rustle of nearby leaves drew his attention and his hand moved instinctively to the Luger on his belt. He watched motionlessly as a black nose and tan and white head of a doe pushed through the foliage. The animal paused, her ears quivering, her soft brown eyes regarding Jim curiously. She emerged from the heavy growth and passed no more than fifteen yards from where he sat. Soon, she was followed timorously by a russet-colored fawn. Taking a sip of his sherry, Jim watched as the animals vanished in the underbrush. The serene encounter brought him a feeling of comfort. For one ever alert to intrusive signs in the forest, Jim knew there was no better barometer of impending danger than the behavior of wildlife.

The "permanent camp" had started out with bare necessities—a green poncho and brown canvas stretched over three poplar poles attached to a crosspiece between two towering pines. It was similar to "tenting," as it was called in survival school, when a parachute was used to make a lean-to. But with successive burglaries the place had taken on a semblance of comfort. An array of canned and jarred food-stuffs was lined up neatly in a cupboard he had fashioned from boughs. Two suitcases and his B-4 bag stood nearby, serving as clos-ets for spare garments—a wardrobe which expanded with successive visits to Lake Placid residences. A portable radio rested on a stump just outside the lean-to, while inside on a canvas "rug" was a rolled sleeping bag. Hanging from the crosspiece of the lean-to was a gray blanket. Near the sleeping bag were two plastic-covered pillows, a towel, and a raincoat. Several books were neatly arranged between two small rocks serving as bookends. These included several novels, a copy of *The Prophet* by the mystic Kahlil Gibran, and a map, *Trails of the Adirondacks*.

The evening was darkening. Nearly time to prepare dinner. On a table made of tree limbs was a bottle of Old Taylor bourbon and a bot-tle of Hudson Bay scotch. Several cartons of cigarettes were strewn close by. Jim glanced toward his "oven," a small hole lined with stones carved at the base of a tree—a survival technique designed to reduce chances of detection, the smoke becoming diffused through the tree limbs overhead. Next to it was a can of coffee, a container of baking powder, and a jar of salt. A frying pan and sauce pan, both charred black on the bottom, sat nearby. As he looked at the cooking utensils he remembered the small coffeepot he had seen in a house during a recent burglary. He was sorry he had not taken it—not an unusual thought. Sometimes he would overlook something that caught his fancy, only to regret it later. Since many of his jobs were pulled in upscale residences, there was usually a large inventory from which to choose. Later he would comment that at times it was rather like shopping in a department store.

Soon he would light a fire and warm a can of Dinty Moore Stew, compliments of the Davies camp. And there was the added attraction of White Rose peaches for dessert. He took a long drag on his cigarette, which by now had been reduced to little more than a small red orb resting on his knuckle. Little remained beyond the ash by the time he discarded a cigarette—unless during a "job" when there was no time. He drained the last bit of sherry from his cup and set-tled back in the lawn chair. Patches of fading light filtered through the trees, creating gilded patterns on the forest floor. A change in the air suggested a cool night. He glanced at the sky, a clear blue with long streaks of pale orange. A break in the tree line allowed a look at a distant valley—almost an aerial view, he thought. He missed flying, the thrill of the missions. The constant travel and regimentation to which he had strenuously objected during previous months seemed in retrospect less burdensome, more appealing.

Perhaps he could return to the Air Force. It was a matter of time, letting things settle down. He would have to cover some bad checks, and he'd been AWOL several weeks, but this could be overcome. His only problem was money. What he needed was a stake, funds with which to get started at the casinos. He was confident he could beat the odds. Using his mathematical skills, he was devising a system which he believed would enable him to win enough to cover his debts and then some.

He worked on his gambling strategy regularly. Hours which otherwise might have been wearisome in the woods passed quickly, keeping at bay anxieties that might have been debilitating to someone less occupied. He had cause for anxiety: the recent violent crime that he had committed in Ohio had received national attention from the media. After his flight to Lake Placid, he had spent days and nights of uncertainty as he followed developments through radio and newspapers. There was nothing to connect him with the case, he reasoned—as long as he remained in the woods. Interest in the matter would eventually subside. In the meantime, he'd remain out of sight, build up his war chest, perfect his system for the assault on the casinos. Thoughts of the horrifying crime were put aside. Such ruminations had no place in the mind of a survivalist.

He returned his attention to *The Rubaiyat*, slowly turning the pages, finally stopping at a passage he had found of particular interest in recent days:

> Here with a loaf of Bread beneath the Bough,
> A Flask of Wine, a Book of Verse—and Thou
> Beside me singing in the Wilderness—
> And Wilderness is Paradise enow.

He recalled discussing the quatrain with Muriel, little realizing at that time the profound implications of the wilderness in his own future. For Muriel, the lines conveyed a mystical or spiritual significance which suggested more of a meditative wilderness, or inner silence free of unpleasant thoughts. Jim was content with a more prosaic interpretation to which he could relate his present situation. He believed the poet was advocating the enjoyment of life through simple things that were available to everyone: basic food, wine, and an appreciation for the beauty and serenity of nature. They were pleasures Jim had always valued and now enjoyed in spite of his fugitive status. What was missing, of course—and what would have raised his life to the status of paradise enough—was Muriel beside him in the wilderness.

On the page opposite the quatrain was a print of a miniature painting done in vibrant red and blue colors, illustrating the lines in the poem. It showed a pastoral scene in which a turbaned man was reclining beneath a tree, holding in one hand a glass and in the other an open book. An ornate wine vessel and a loaf of bread were nearby. Friendly-looking birds and animals were pictured in abundance. Lying beside the man, seeming attentive to his needs, was a beautiful woman.

The picture evoked a strange ambivalence for Jim that stretched his emotions. He found the truth in nature which the painting expressed to be inspiring, but invariably it brought memories of Muriel and overwhelming sadness. Although she had been gone a year and nine months, he was unable to shake off the despondency which had enveloped him since her death. There were moments when he felt her beside him, much like the woman in the painting. He longed for the tapes, the firm clear voice expressing her love as she read the quatrains. Many of them he had memorized and could play at the touch of a mental button.

Thoughts of his son flitted through his mind. The smile, the small eyes lighting up at the sight of his father, the squeaky laugh, frolicking on the floor. Haunting memories, irrecoverable.

He felt a crush of emotion. Shifting in his chair, he closed the book. It was important that he keep his feelings in check. He recalled the psychologist's warning to their group in survival camp: "Control your emotions. Self-pity is debilitating."

He glanced down at his bandaged forefinger, which had begun to throb painfully—a bite wound he had sustained during his recent crime before coming to Lake Placid. The injury was not healing as quickly as he had hoped and he worried about infection. He considered injecting himself with one of the morphine ampules he had in his bag, but decided against it. There were only a few left and other painful episodes could lie ahead.

Shadows lengthened, small objects grew larger in the darkness. Soon he would start the fire. A warm dinner. Then he would crawl into his sleeping bag, let his mind go ... the tapes ... the haunting lines of *The Rubaiyat*.

He glanced over his camp. Everything seemed in order. Yes, it was far from luxurious living. But for a fugitive with a deep affinity for the wilderness, it offered an acceptable alternative—at least for a while, until things cooled off elsewhere.

◆ ◆ ◆

28

By the 1950's the Lake Placid Club lacked the allure that had characterized its earlier years. The once splendid resort which had attracted luminaries from throughout the world during previous decades had lost much of its elegance. Although the main lodge and surrounding villas were not yet the tatterdemalions they would later become, they had taken on the tired look that often afflicts older properties. Also, the jet age had produced competition from far-off romantic places with all the conveniences of modern living. Affluent notables who had once braved the long hours of travel by motorcar through the Adirondacks to reach the Club were finding it propitious to rendezvous at more accessible sites. Although still retaining an aura of dignity, the Club was now an aging lady, struggling to retain the trappings of her illustrious past.

This is not to say the Club no longer attracted wealthy guests who traveled far to enjoy its old-style charm. One such person was a Texan named Mrs. Lucy Roe, a gifted amateur golfer, who with her husband Edward Jedd Roe, a prominent investment banker and rancher, occupied one of the suites in the Club's Agora Building on Mirror Lake Drive. A well-to-do person upon checking into the club in July, she was soon to be less so....

It was Monday, August 1, 1954, another cold rainy day. A figure wearing a tan trenchcoat waited patiently behind a wall of pine bordering the Agora Building. The rain bothered the man little. Although it matted his jet-black hair and ran down into his face, he accepted it with indifference. He was accustomed to the elements in all their forms. Of more interest to him were the goings-on inside the building where a certain couple would soon be leaving their suite. This he knew from recent casings of the premises. He had determined also that security at the Club was virtually non-existent, consisting of one policeman—a night watchman, really.

As minutes passed, the figure leaned nonchalantly against the trunk of one of the pines, his right hand in the pocket of his trenchcoat, fondling the wooden stock of his fully-loaded Luger—eight rounds in the magazine, one in the chamber. The sound of voices drew his attention to the entrance. Suddenly, the door opened and two people emerged. Although they were no more than one hundred feet away and possibly could have observed him had they turned and looked in his direction, he remained leaning against the tree, coolly indifferent to their presence. They had no reason to look his way, he reasoned. Soon they were gone, moving off toward Mirror Lake Drive.

They were barely out of sight before he was inside the building, walking toward their apartment. At the doorway to their suite, he inserted a plastic card behind the latch and easily gained entrance. Because of his earlier observations, he knew precisely where he was headed. From the sitting room he walked to a bedroom, where he removed a white leather suitcase from the closet. Forcing it open, he withdrew a small jewelry box. He fumbled with the container's latch for a moment before emptying the contents. A treasure of glittering jewels spilled out onto the bed—29 pieces in all. (Later they were described in police reports as: 7 bracelets, 9 rings, 3 necklaces, 1 gold and diamond Swiss watch, 1 diamond clip, a jeweled pin, and 3 pairs of earrings, many of which were studded with rubies, diamonds and sapphires.) Included in the loot, according to the victim, was an emerald-cut solitaire, in itself worth $26,000.

It was far more than the intruder expected. Methodically he gathered the gems into a large blue bandanna, twisted the corners into a knot, and stuffed it into an inside pocket of his trenchcoat. Without looking further, he walked calmly to the front door and out of the building. Within a few minutes the figure, moving rapidly despite a limp, had passed down Morningside Drive, across Main Street, up River Street, and entered the forest bordering West Valley Road. Here he found a familiar trail and followed it several hundred yards, finally emerging from the woods into a small clearing behind a tenebrous structure known as the Perkins camp. He waited here patiently for a considerable period under the cover of tall spruce trees, watching the house closely, listening to the steady rain falling overhead. After assuring himself the premises were unoccupied, he moved silently to the house, forced the latch on a window near the rear door, and crawled through the opening.

Once inside he produced a flashlight and went directly to a stairway leading to the cellar. The basement was a dingy 22' x 12' cinderblock room with a cement floor and 8' ceiling. In one corner, below a 24" x 26" window, was a white metal shower stall. A cylindrical furnace the size of a large man stood in front of the opposite wall, guarding a crawl space about two feet high with a dirt floor, which stretched cave-like under the rest of the dwelling. It was here, directly across from the shower in the southeast corner, that the man finally stopped. After resting his flashlight on the edge of the crawl space so that it shone back into the darkness beneath the house, he took the knife from his belt and placed it next to the light. Then, removing his trenchcoat, he withdrew the bandanna containing the jewels and carefully placed them next to the other two articles.

The sound of a passing car caused him to pause momentarily. Was it stopping? He stiffened, listening intently. He was relieved to hear the motor fading in the distance. The sound of the rain falling outside was comforting. There was less activity on a rainy night.

With considerable agility, he hoisted himself up into the crawl space on his stomach. Taking the flashlight, knife and jewels, he squirmed back into the interior beneath the house. Beside a large pipe near the east wall, he kneaded the earth with his fingers, and feeling a soft area, dug a hole with the knife approximately one foot deep. Here, he deposited the bandanna containing the jewels. After filling the hole and carefully smoothing the dirt, he squirmed his way back into the basement.

He stood for a moment, brushing the dirt from his clothing. After putting on his trenchcoat, he shone his flashlight back into the crawl space, marking the location of his treasure one final time. Then, turning, he mounted the stairs and returned to the forest, leaving the Perkins camp dark, but bright with future expectations.

◆ ◆ ◆

29

"Maybe he's runnin' from somethin'," said Sergeant Nick Valenze, his brown eyes gazing meditatively through a window at the falling rain. "Must not want to be seen for some reason. 'Else, why's he hidin' out in the woods?"

"Maybe he's not in the woods," Bernie Fell answered. He raised a long leg and rested his heel on the corner of the desk in front of him, prepared to discuss the proclivities of the robber who had unnerved the community.

"But look at the stuff he's stolen from the camps," Nick retorted. "Food, clothes, blankets, pots and pans. Stuff you'd need if you were campin', right? I think maybe he uses the Perkins camp on rainy nights."

"Uses lots of camps on rainy nights," Bernie said. "Look at that burglary report."

"Yeah, but the Perkins caretaker says someone's been stayin' in the place. It's close to the Jackrabbit Trail. Perfect escape route. He sees someone comin', he's out the back door, gone in the woods. The Perkins camp is really the only lead we've got."

"Wonder what he's runnin' from?"

Nick shrugged. "Who knows? Seems he knows how to handle himself in the woods."

"That's for sure." Bernie paused for a moment, looking out a window at the rain. "Bob Reiss over at Old MacDonald's Farm told the chief that every other day for the past ten days, one of their prize cows hasn't given the usual amount of milk. He thinks someone's goin' into the barn early mornin' and milkin' his cow."

"Are you kiddin' me?" Nick looked at his fellow officer incredulously. "Jesus, this thing gets weirder by the minute. You don't really think this guy is milkin' peoples' cows, do you? Anything goes wrong, everyone blames it on the robber."

Bernie shrugged. "I'm just telling you what Reiss told the chief."

The two officers were seated at a table having coffee in the offices of the Lake Placid Police Department, a busier place with the advent of the crime wave. Affable, well-liked men under normal circumstances, they had become defensive during recent weeks as pressure mounted. Rarely a day passed in the latter part of July 1954 that their organization was not the object of ridicule.

"Let's try leavin' the curtains open at the Perkins camp," said Nick. "Last time the subject was there he may have closed them, according to the caretaker. Dr. Perkins said he never closed the curtains. Nights when it rains who's ever on duty can make a few passes. Make sure we get a key from the caretaker. If the curtains are closed we'll go in and check it out."

Bernie raised his brow dubiously. He was a handsome man with dark hair, wide clear eyes, and a somber expression when warranted. It was warranted now as he reflected on the predatory nature of their subject. "We gotta be careful, Nick. No one should go in after that guy alone. He's armed. Pretty cool. Ask Fred Wertheim."

"We're not even sure he's the same person who stuck up Wertheim." Nick dropped the pad on which he had been making notes onto the table. "Probably is, though. All these burglaries and robberies all at once. Gotta be the same guy." He swallowed the remnants of his coffee and pushed his stocky form back from the desk. "We're gonna have to do somethin'. Town's scared to death. They say business is way off. Robberies ... all this rain."

"Maybe that's why we got so many break-ins. The rain's driving our guy out of the woods at night."

Nick leaned back in his chair, frowning. "The chief's gettin' pressure. People are afraid to go to bed at night. Everyone's sleepin' with a gun. Someone's gonna get shot eventually."

"He must be a nerveless character," Bernie said. "Goin' into these camps with people in there. Doesn't seem worried about wakin' people, either. Nobody's sleepin' good, that's for sure. You watch, someone's gonna put a bullet in this guy."

"That's what Art Devlin thinks," said Nick, referring to the former Olympic ski jumper and CBS commentator who operated a local motel. "Claims his business is way off. Says it's not only the lousy weather, tourists are afraid to come 'cause they hear there's a crazy man runnin' around holdin' people up, breakin' into camps."

Bernie chuckled. "Well, he's right. Maybe this guy will try to rob Art's motel. That'd be the end of our crime wave."

"Set up that Perkins camp," Nick said grimly, failing to see the humor. "Maybe we'll get a break."

"Break-*in*," corrected Bernie, dryly.

♦ ♦ ♦

30

Approximately four miles as the crow flies from where the police officers were talking, the subject of their discussion was relaxing in a camp chair considering his plans for the evening of August 5, 1954. The rain falling on the poncho overhead beat a steady rhythm distinct from other sounds in the deep forest. It was a soft rain and for Jim, accustomed to alfresco living, it was of little concern.

A visit to the Perkins camp—he thought of it as the "doctor's camp," having seen evidence in the house of the dentist's profession—had been on his mind that day. The trip would not be made to escape the rain, as suggested by Officers Valenze and Fell. Rather, it was to wash, shave, and otherwise make himself presentable for one of his "social visits" to town. Such trips were undertaken with due regard for the risks involved in exposure to populated areas. No matter how careful he was, there was always the possibility of provoking unwanted attention. But the chances of this were slim. Lake Placid was a tourist town and provided a degree of anonymity lacking in most communities its size. As one town official lamented when questioned by the press about the lack of suspects in the crime spree, "This time of year the town swells ten times its normal size. Everyone's a stranger. Everyone's a suspect."

Unlike burglaries and holdups, social visits to town could have posed sartorial problems for one living in the woods. Not so with Jim. He had considerable clothing with him when he first arrived in Lake Placid and, using the alias of F. A. Corbett, had arranged to have the garments freshly laundered and dry-cleaned at the Troy Laundry and the Berkley Dry Cleaners in Saranac Lake. Included had been the expensive tan suit he had purchased the previous year in Hong Kong.

One respected investigative journalist would later describe the considerable extent of Jim's social activities, as well as a certain romantic interest Call developed at the Lake Placid Club:

> Major Call had burglarized at least two suits of his size, complete with white shirts and ties. He was ever mindful of proper footwear for survival purposes. But, he also managed to appropriate a pair of black dress-shoes and socks to coordinate with the suits and ties. According to one source, [New York State Police investigator Harry Blaisdell] Call would make occasional trips into Lake Placid to purchase supplies. During these visits he would sometimes visit the Arena Grill, Ruth's Diner, and the Majestic Restaurant for meals and even, at least once, attended the Palace Theatre to watch a movie.

In the 1950's, the Lake Placid Club was known throughout the country as a summer home to the rich. To gain social access to the Club, Call knew he had to play a role. It was first important to dress the part. Sportswear by day; appropriate suits (and sport jackets) for social functions in the main building at night. That an intellect and an imaginative background story could place an outsider on the inside during an era that paid minimum attention to security at the Club was quite possible.

Call made day visits to the Club, wandering the grounds, walking through the main clubhouse, chatting with Club members and staff. Then, dressed in appropriate suit and tie, he started to sample the nightlife; drinks in the lounge and events in the main ballroom. One evening, he met an attractive brunette, the daughter of a wealthy industrialist who was vacationing at the Club. While accompanied by the young woman, Call carefully picked his target: a Texas millionaire, the wife of whom was nightly bedecked in glittering jewelry.

Major Call's young companion found him to be a fascinating, though somewhat mysterious summertime acquaintance. Though nothing is known as to how Call lent legitimacy to his presence at the Club, it was obviously good enough to interest the young lady. Later information suggested that he became sexually intimate with her.

The journalist went on to cite other sources and evidence supporting his comments. Major Call himself would later acknowledge gate-crashing Lake Placid Club functions.

Although unquestionably bold, such incursions were considered by Jim to be relatively benign compared to some of his other endeavors. Now, as he sat in his camp chair in the woods, it was the Lake Placid Club that he had in mind for the evening. On one of his previous visits he had, indeed, met a strikingly beautiful young woman named Greta Brown* from New York City who was vacationing at the Club with her parents. He had introduced himself as an engineer for an aircraft manufacturer on Long Island. Several meetings had followed, some of which had led to late night walks culminating in lovemaking on a remote dock overlooking Lake Placid. He had returned to his camp each time feeling a degree of remorse. Most of it derived from a vague sense of infidelity toward Muriel. But he was also concerned about the young woman's age. She claimed to be twenty-three, yet he had wondered. Twenty would probably have been closer to the truth. And in the throes of passion he had certainly misrepresented himself and his intentions.

Now, alone under his poncho listening to the rain and considering his options for the evening, he felt the emotional and biological urge to be with the woman. Her warmth, beauty, laugh.... It was her laugh that lingered in his thoughts. An unusual, exciting laugh of surprisingly low register that tumbled forth unexpectedly, inviting a cheerful response. They had, in fact, laughed much of the time they had been together—rare moments for a man undergoing a traumatic period of his life.

Despite his better judgment, he felt himself drawn to the Club. There was no hurry, though. He'd wait until after dinner before making a decision. But from somewhere in his mind came the laugh—rich, beguiling—and he knew the final decision had already been made.

The rain which had fallen most of the day was tapering off. He noticed that the trench he had dug on one side of his camp to divert the water was filling up, threatening to spill over. He'd have to widen the drain a bit at the base. A mist settled over the rolling green landscape. In the distance he saw that small pockets of vapor were

*fictitious name

forming in the valley. Fog was an aspect of life in the mountains he found nettlesome. Always threatening to a flyer, it had a suffocating quality in the forest. Unlike the rain, which he could keep out, fog drifted in, enveloping everything. And excessive moisture was a source of concern. Not only because of food and camping gear, but because of its effect on important survival equipment such as pistols, ammunition.

As he watched the expanding gray drifts engulf the alpine landscape he began to firm up his plans for the evening. Images flickered through his mind: dark hair ... soft eyes ... lips ... long beautiful legs ... the resonant laugh.... Yes, a good night to visit the doctor's camp.

◆ ◆ ◆

Dr. Perkins' Camp—1954

31

The Perkins camp, although more modest in design and structure, had features similar to those of a house near Cleveland, Ohio, in which Jim Call had committed a crime shortly before coming to Lake Placid. Both houses were relatively secluded but had public roads passing in front with similar names: West Lake Road in Cleveland, West Valley Road in Lake Placid. Each house had trees nearby from where the dwelling could be discreetly observed. To the rear of both premises was a vast uninhabited region—behind one, a great lake; behind the other, a great forest. In short, both possessed features that made them inviting targets for burglars. But what neither place provided was an escape route if the intruder were cornered inside. In such instances, tragedies may occur. This is what happened just before Jim Call fled to Lake Placid, and was about to happen one month later. The date was August 5, 1954....

———————

Jim stopped at the edge of the woods and peered into the clearing behind the Perkins camp. He waited several minutes, concealed by the underbrush, patiently studying the dim outline of the one-story house. The weather had taken a turn for the worse. It was colder and raining harder, a steady downpour that moments before had caused him to rethink his earlier plans for visiting the Lake Placid Club. It was not a night for long walks and romantic interludes. He stood motionlessly, watching, listening, his senses honed by weeks of solitude in the forest. The only sounds were the murmuring breeze and the soft patter of rain on leaves.

He continued to wait, wary about emerging from the woods. There was something about the dark camp at the moment that gave him a vague feeling of uneasiness. This acute sensitivity—described by

Jim as a "most uncanny sixth sense"—had enabled him to survive the many robberies and to endure in the wilderness during preceding weeks. Now this "sixth sense" was telling him to wait, and he found himself reluctant to leave the comforting concealment of the trees. His affinity for the woods had increased during recent weeks. He often thought of the forest in mystical terms, the trees his friends offering shelter and solace, communicating with him at night in their enthralling hushed tones.

Finally, thoughts of hot coffee and other comforts that awaited him inside the camp overcame the tugging misgivings. Adjusting his Luger on his belt, he stepped out into the naked clearing and moved silently toward the house, leaving behind the whispered warnings of the forest.

"It was approximately midnight, raining," he would later relate in an extraordinary statement describing the event—comments corroborated by those who survived the ensuing mayhem:

> At this time I was dressed in a wool shirt, pair of Levi's, a tan cloth raincoat made in England, and I believe I was wearing black and white gym shoes. I was carrying a green canvas backpack and a 9-mm Luger pistol which was loaded with a clip containing eight cartridges and one in the chamber. I was determined never to be taken alive. I knew I had committed many transgressions and that if I were ever in danger of being captured I was determined to shoot my way out and if unable to do so I would save one round for myself. I carried the Luger in a P-38 holster on my belt....

As he neared the rear of the camp, once again he hesitated, listening. Then, very quietly, he entered the building by using a knife on the catch of the window to the right of the rear door. It was a technique he often used to burglarize residences. For more forceful entries he carried a 12" Atha crowbar, which although relatively small, was sufficient to open most windows and doors. It had other more deadly purposes, as well. Indeed, prior to his flight to Lake Placid, it had been used as a lethal weapon.

Inside, he placed water on a gas stove to prepare coffee. After dropping his knapsack on the floor near the stairs leading to the basement, he drew the curtains on the front windows. It was a momentous mistake which he would forever regret. He then collapsed in a nearby chair, tired. It felt good, the first time he'd been off his feet since leaving his camp. He was warm, relaxed.

But he would have less than a half-hour to enjoy the comfort. At 12:30 a.m., officers Bernie Fell, Richard Pelkey and John Fagan, following up on their theory that the camp had been used on rainy nights by the marauder, pulled their prowl car into the driveway of the Perkins camp for a routine check. Parking so that the headlights played on the rear of the house and down an opening through the trees leading to the thick forest, they quickly noted that the curtains in the front window had been drawn. Someone was in the camp. Their trap had been sprung.

"Bernie, you cover the front door," Dick Pelkey said. "I'll watch the back. John, get on the car radio and have them get Nick. He's probably home. Tell him to bring the key to the camp."

Sensing they were on to something big, the officers took positions around the camp and nervously awaited the arrival of the other officer. Sergeant Nick Valenze, reached at home, rushed to the camp with the key. Having been roused from bed, he was in civilian clothes—loafers, no socks, a nightshirt, pants, and a suede jacket. The other officers were wearing their uniforms, complete with caps.

"What'll we do, Nick?" Bernie asked when the sergeant arrived on the scene.

Nick's eyes, which only minutes before had been closed in sleep, now traveled over the camp, searching for the answer. "We'll go in," was the decision. "Bernie, you and Dick watch the rear door. John, you and I'll go in the front."

It was a plucky decision, considering that the officers had reason to believe their subject was armed and dangerous. Less determined individuals might have seen the advantages of waiting for reinforcements—more firepower, tear gas. But the four were up to the challenge. Cautiously, they approached the house.

Inside the camp, though his tranquility had been shattered by the arriving police, Jim remained remarkably composed, his mind keen and deliberate. He made instant plans for escape. When the car had pulled into the driveway, at first he thought it was the owner. But someone had run to the rear of the camp and he had heard a voice

128

shout, "You sure he's in there?" and then, "Nick's on his way with the key." He realized they must be the police. Later, in written comments he would state:

> I thought of every conceivable way of getting out of the camp. I picked up a chair with the idea of throwing it through the front window as a diversion so I could go out the back, but just then another car pulled up. I heard a voice say, "Have you got the machine gun set up?" The other voice said "Yep" or "Yeah." However, I gained the impression from their comments that they were not positive someone was in the house. Then, those in the back hollered to those in front "Are you ready?"

Once the men stated they were entering the house, Jim's options were limited. Since there was no second floor, there was but one way for him to go.

> After hearing indications that the men were going to enter the camp, I went to the basement. I thought of going out a basement window but I saw flashlight beams in the windows and knew there were persons outside. I heard persons enter the camp and conduct a search on the first floor. Then the light came on in the cellar....

Jim realized that in seconds they would come down. He gripped the Luger on his belt as his options began to slip away. He looked furtively about the room. There was no logical place to hide in the 12' x 22' cellar. The crawl space provided concealment, but he would be easily trapped if discovered. The shower stall in the northwest corner of the room offered the only hiding place from which he could maneuver. He hesitated, realizing they would probably look inside. Again, there was no choice. He moved rapidly across the room and squeezed into a corner of the stall.

> I heard footsteps on the cellar stairs. Whispering that indicated there was more than one person. I believe the persons stopped at the bottom of the stairs and I heard conversations regarding their searching the cellar and the crawl space under

the front of the camp. I saw the beams of flashlights searching same. I do not recall just when I drew my pistol, but I had my Luger in my right hand and my right arm was bent upwards at the elbow and the gun was held close to the front of my body with the muzzle pointing upwards. My mind was churning....

Realizing there was little time left, Jim considered stepping from the shower and shooting his way out. He would have the advantage of surprise. Footsteps moved cautiously about the room. Little conversation now from those searching as their senses concentrated on unknown danger. Jim heard steps approaching the shower. His mind raced. Once again, he pressed the safety to ensure it was off. He was prepared to go down shooting. Within seconds he could be killed. But there was no alternative. Once captured, background checks would connect him with the other far more serious crime a month before. No, they'd never take him alive. Not as long as there was a round left in the chamber. Footsteps, now directly next to the shower. Jim stiffened, took a deep breath, exhaled.

I saw a man come to a point where he looked into the shower stall opening. We both looked at each other. It appeared to me that he had on some type of hunting shirt. Up to this time I had expected to see policemen and on seeing this person I hugged the shower walls. Upon seeing me, this man jumped back towards the direction of the stairway. I then heard a short conversation between the men but I cannot recall what was said....

Having seen the civilian clothes, Jim held his fire. No one had announced they were police. If they were civilians, it changed everything. Possibly he could talk his way out. A breath of hope—but it would be short-lived.

Nick Valenze, who only seconds before had found himself staring into the muzzle of a Luger, conferred excitedly with Bernie Fell, "He's got a gun." Then, raising his voice, "Throw out your gun!" he commanded. When there was no compliance, he hesitated, then made a fateful decision. Stepping to his right and without further warning,

Valenze fired his .41-caliber Colt revolver five times into the north side of the shower wall. The shower stall rocked back and forth from the force of the bullets. Nick would later tell State Police investigators that he believed the subject had been hit and lay dead or wounded.

In the shower, Jim was stunned. He felt the power of the bullets smashing into the wall beside him and was convinced he had been shot.

I believe I saw and heard five shots come through the shower stall wall. I thought that the shots had gone right through me but I could feel no pain or any feeling of a physical nature to indicate that I had been hit. But I did assume that I had been seriously hit, that I was dying....

Having faced death repeatedly, Jim knew his time would come. Yet now that it was at hand, he felt strangely detached. Unlike most persons who would have been overcome by the firepower and in a state of shock, he calmly stepped out of the shower and returned the fire.

I then stepped out of the shower and I saw two men, one to the left about 6 feet in front of me and the second to the right, 12 to 14 feet away. Their guns were pointed at me. I pointed my pistol towards the man [Nick Valenze] to the left and reactively fired. I moved the gun towards the man [Bernie Fell] to the right and reactively fired. I then observed a third man [Dick Pelkey] on the stairs and I moved my pistol towards him and fired. I fired so fast I don't remember how many shots. I shot from the hip without aiming and just automatically pulled the trigger. I later discovered on reloading my pistol that I had fired seven shots.

Remarkably, under the circumstances, five of the seven rounds he fired within four seconds found their target. Officers Valenze, Fell, and Pelkey were all critically wounded, Pelkey fatally.

Nick Valenze later stated he saw Fell grab his stomach and go down and then he himself was struck twice and driven against the stairs. "I was hit in the right arm and my gun fell to the floor. I picked it up with my left hand and went up the stairs. At the top of the stairs I saw Pelkey on his haunches. I told him that both Fell and I had been hit and that if he had the chance, to 'shoot the son of a bitch.' " There was no response from Pelkey. Nick managed to struggle from the house and go to the car radio where he called for an ambulance.

Back in the cellar, which only seconds before had been the scene of a wild exchange of gunfire, it was now strangely silent. A pungent odor of exploding powder, and a smoky blue haze pervaded the room. Jim stood in the middle of the cellar evaluating his situation. "It was amazing," Fell would later report. "He just stood there surveying things like he didn't have a care in the world."

For Jim, it was a moment of cool assessment.

An oppressive silence then reigned in the basement. I looked at my front to see where I had been hit but I could see no holes or blood. I saw the policeman that was to the right of me [Fell] on the floor in between a prone and stand-ing position, and his gun was on the floor in front of him. We looked at each other. He reached for his gun and I said, "Don't pick it up" or "Leave it alone." He said "Oh, my leg," or something....

Having seen the uniforms on the other men, Jim was now aware that his adversaries were policemen and that those who awaited him upstairs were prepared to shoot to kill. They had given him little chance to surrender in the shower. Now that he had taken down some of their buddies, he'd have no chance at all.

I believed that the other policemen were upstairs, and I knew the only way out of the camp was for me to walk this man [Fell] up the stairs and out of the house. I picked up his gun and got him on his feet. I then hollered to the policemen upstairs and also told this man to holler up to his buddies in words or substance—that they were not to fire as I was com-ing up with their buddy. He yelled, "Nick! Nick! Don't shoot!" He was scared to death. I had one gun in each hand and I then walked this policeman up the cellar stairs. At the top of the stairs I heard someone moaning and groaning but I could not see who it was as it was dark. I then marched this policeman out the back door of the camp and down the back stairs. I remember that as we got to the head of the cellar stairs and hearing the moaning, the officer with me said, "Is that you Nick?"

The moaning sounds were actually from Richard Pelkey who, having struggled up the stairs, now lay mortally wounded. It was at this point, while attempting to keep Fell on his feet by holding him up with his free hand, that the bandage from Jim's left forefinger fell off. (It was later recovered by State Police investigators.) Realizing his hostage could go no farther, Jim decided to take the officers' car.

When this officer and I reached the ground in the back of the camp, he slumped against the wall. I then saw the headlights of the car in the driveway and I told this officer that I wanted to get the car. On seeing a man standing at the side of the car, I told the officer with me to tell the man to get away from the car and go across the street. I do not recall whether or not I hollered to him. The officer with me told me that he could go no further. I then saw a car with a flashing red light drive up behind the first car and I believe this was either an ambulance or a police car. I then abandoned the hope of stealing the car and turned and ran into the woods at the rear of the camp, taking my Luger and the officer's gun with me. I knew the path and had a flashlight. I ran blind using the flashlight at intervals. I ran full speed, came to a bridge, crossed it. I fell down over a rock and skinned my left shin. I finally made it back to my camp. I was cold and wet and crawled in my sleeping bag.

Despite his exhaustion, Jim did not sleep. Shivering, his mind racing, he tried to sort out preceding events. The shootout had raised the stakes enormously. He sensed the officers had been badly wounded, some maybe dead. Repercussions would be swift and deadly. He lay very still, listening to the unrelenting rain. From the tall darkness of the forest came reproving whispers.

◆ ◆ ◆

Lake Placid Police Department—circa 1954
P. McKeown, J. B. Fell, R. Borden, L. MacDonald
N. Valenze, H. Pratt, N. Pratt, J. Fagan
(Lake Placid Police Department Archives)

32

While Jim Call lay wrapped in his sleeping bag, the once peaceful cabin nestled among the tall spruce on West Valley Road was now in chaos. Groaning police officers lay near the camp, blood from their wounds forming scarlet rivulets in the pouring rain. Lights blinked on throughout the village as wailing sirens reverberated down the narrow streets, lamenting the loss of nearly half the police force.

It was approximately 1:00 a.m. Responding to calls for assistance from the Lake Placid Police Department, Reginald Clark, an ambulance paramedic, raced to the scene, where he saw John Fagan, revolver drawn, standing next to a police car outside the camp. Suddenly, a man in a bent position holding his hands across his stomach stumbled from the police car and staggered to the ambulance. It was Nick Valenze.

"What happened, Nick?" exclaimed the astounded Clark.

"He got me, Reg," groaned Valenze, who was bleeding profusely. "He got me good. Get me to the hospital." He collapsed into the driver's lap.

Clark, aware that the officer could be mortally wounded, hastily backed the ambulance from the drive and headed for the hospital. "Shall I call the State Police?" he asked anxiously.

"Yes. Call the chief, too," Nick gasped.

Within minutes they arrived at the hospital. As attendants were removing Valenze, Clark received a call instructing him to return as quickly as possible to the scene of the shooting as there were other officers wounded. Siren blaring, Clark rushed back to the camp. As he pulled up front he saw a man lying on the ground beside a car. Turning the ambulance spotlight on the form, he recognized Richard Pelkey. Jumping from his seat he rushed to the man and knelt beside him. "Dick, Dick, it's Reggie," he said, placing his hand on the man's chest. "How bad is it, Dick?"

"It's pretty bad," Pelkey replied, grimacing.

"Can you walk?"

"Maybe. I think so."

But then, noting blood streaming from Pelkey's chest and right leg, Clark thought better of it. "Better not move, Dick."

At that moment groans came from the woods at the rear of the camp.

"That's Bernie back there," Pelkey said. "You better get him. He's hurt worse then I am. He can't walk. I know he can't."

Clark, desperate for assistance to help with the gravely wounded officers, admonished Pelkey to stay put, and raced to find his assistant Charles Stephan who lived nearby. As they returned, they observed Arthur Adams, another ambulance driver, pulling up in front of the camp.

"Art!" Clark shouted. "You take Dick, over there by the car. He's pretty bad. We'll get Bernie. He's back in the woods."

Clark and Stephan jumped from the cab, pulling a stretcher from the ambulance. Uncertain what awaited them—the assailant could still be there—but determined to help the wounded officer, they rushed behind the camp. Here, they found Bernie Fell lying among some rocks near the southwest corner of the building. Fell, moaning, was in great pain. Clark and Stephan gently placed him on the stretcher and maneuvered their way over the difficult terrain back to the ambulance.

While this was happening, Arthur Adams and one of his colleagues had found Dick Pelkey, who was now leaning against the left front fender of Sergeant Valenze's car. They went to him quickly, attempting to put him on a stretcher, but Pelkey would have none of it.

"Never mind me," Pelkey said, speaking with difficulty. "Go get Bernie. He's lying back there near the cabin."

"It's okay, Dick," Adams reassured him. "Reggie's got him. C'mon, lie down here. We gotta get you to the hospital."

Dick Pelkey finally acquiesced. With the help of the two paramedics he eased himself down onto the stretcher. "Call my wife. She'll be worried." Shivering, with pain and shock, he closed his eyes. It had been a tough night for a tough police officer.

◆ ◆ ◆

DESPERADO'S HIDEWAY — This secluded cabin near Lake Placid is the scene of the brutal shooting of three policemen by an armed robber. The aerial photo was taken by John Lonergan while pilot Morris Broderick of Plattsburgh swooped low over the scene of the crime. State police took the cabin over and directed their search from it. Truck contains food for the possees. Suburban holds police radio equipment.

Aerial view of Dr. Perkins' camp—August 6, 1954
(The Press-Republican)

THEY MISSED DEATH BY INCHES—Sgt. Dominick Valenze of the Lake Placid police, left, shows where a bullet smashed two ribs in a gun battle, July 5, with an unknown killer. Patrolman J. Bernard Fell, right, who was in the same battle, was shot in the stomach and is scheduled for another operation next month. Both were released from Lake Placid Memorial Hospital and are shown recuperating at their homes.

Nick Valenze and Bernard Fell—August 22, 1954
(The Post-Standard)

33

Captain Harold T. Muller was six feet plus of seasoned, demanding, troop commander. And what else to expect from the top law enforcement officer in the desolate woods of northern New York State? "Dutch" as he was called, but rarely to his face—certainly never by subordinates—was an all-business professional who evoked respect and high performance from those he commanded in his Troop B State Police command post in Malone, New York.

From the moment he took charge of the case involving the Lake Placid shootout, Captain Muller was confident he would get his man. No bastard was going to take down three police officers on his watch and leave the territory, unless it was on a one-way trip to Sing Sing's death house. Most experienced law enforcement officers would agree that if anyone could find and apprehend the fugitive who had terrorized the North Country during preceding weeks, it was Dutch Muller.

Within minutes of his arrival at West Valley Road, the camp was transformed into an efficient command post, crackling with sharp orders and terse directives. Troopers with emergency equipment had been dispatched immediately to mount a comprehensive dragnet throughout the region. Road blocks, search parties, and roving patrols were systematically employed to seal off logical avenues of escape. At the scene of the shooting, in the cellar, technical personnel were combing the area for evidence. A blunt communication was sent to all New York State Police stations:

REF 3618 FILE SP MALONE NY—ASSAULT ON POLICE OFFICERS—FOLLOWING DESCRIPTION OBTAINED FROM VICTIMS STILL IN CRITICAL CONDITION DUE TO WOUNDS AND OPERATIONS— ASSAILANT 35-5-10-180—BLACK HAIR—AVERAGE

GROWTH—MEDIUM WIDTH—MEDIUM TO BARI-
TONE VOICE—NO HAT—BELIEVED WEARING TAN
TRENCH COAT WITH BELT KNOTTED IN FRONT—
MEDIUM TO DARK COLORED WRINKLED
TROUSERS

ASSAILANT BURGLARIZED CAMP AND CON-
CEALED HIMSELF IN SHOWER STALL LOCATED
IN BASEMENT AS OFFICERS ENTERED CAMP AND
CELLAR—IN THE EXCHANGE OF 14 SHOTS—SEVEN
BEING FIRED BY ASSAILANT—9 MM—POSSIBLE
LUGER—THREE OFFICERS WERE WOUNDED IN
BASEMENT—ASSAILANT THEN ESCAPED BY REAR
DOOR OF CAMP—USING ONE OF OFFICERS AS
SHIELD AND TAKING OFFICERS 38 CAL S & W 5
INCH BARREL REVOLVER—SERIAL NUMBER NOT
AVAILABLE AT THIS TIME

INVESTIGATION REVEALS THAT ASSAILANT WAS
NOTICEABLY CALM AND COLLECTED AND FOR
THIS REASON USE EXTREME CAUTION AS NOW
ARMED WITH TWO GUNS

AUTH CAPT H T MULLER   MANSION 2223

ADDED SP ALBANY NY TO ALL STATE POLICE
STATIONS—REBROADCAST THIS DESCRIPTION
FREQUENTLY TO ALL PATROLS AND KEEP
REBROADCASTING UNTIL FURTHER NOTICE

Sitting with a subordinate in the kitchen of the Perkins camp,
Harold Muller glanced at the communication which had been handed
to him moments before. "Cool son-of-a-bitch," he said focusing on the
last paragraph of the order bearing his name. "Talk about composure
under fire. Three officers blasting away at him and he walks through
the whole thing like it's a training exercise."

He flipped the paper onto the table and raised a large hand to his
thinning dark hair, his gray eyes lost in momentary meditation.

Deep lines etched on the sides of his face anchored the corners of a thin mouth. A square jaw fairly radiated belligerence. It was a strong, mirthless countenance, almost handsome in its distinctiveness.

"This guy's no mere indigent, Harry," he said, once again focusing on Harry Blaisdell, sitting across the table.

Blaisdell, a sergeant in the State Police Bureau of Criminal Investigation, or "BCI" as it was called, had a relationship bordering on friendship with his superior. The captain, who had great respect for the sergeant—a man renowned for his investigative abilities—had sent for him immediately upon learning of the confrontation on West Valley Road.

"He's been living in the woods, robbing camps for food and things to subsist on. He's hiding out from something, Harry. Or why engage in an all-out gun battle with four police officers? All he had to do was give up. What's he get for breaking into a camp? Nothing. Maybe a month or so in jail."

"Yeah," agreed Harry. "And you'd think he'd find a little jail time pretty good compared to those woods." He adjusted his horn-rimmed glasses and peered thoughtfully at a pad on which he had been making notes. In his late thirties, Harry had an avuncular appearance more like a university professor than a police officer. He was tall, with grayish thinning hair, regular features, and a congenial manner. In addition to his investigative talents, he possessed a persuasive personality that enabled him to communicate with the most obstinate criminals.

At the moment, Harry was as puzzled as his superior about the circumstances that had led to the tragedy on West Valley Road. "No," he mused, "no ordinary bum. He steps out of the shower and, according to witnesses, matter-of-factly drops three police officers, firing from the hip, probably with a Luger. Sounds to me like a professional."

"What'd they get out of the cellar so far?" Muller asked.

"Shells, casings. Blood all over." Harry displayed his notes and a detailed drawing he'd made of the cellar. "One of the officers thought the subject fired from inside the shower, but the shell casings from the Luger were all out here." He pointed to an area on his drawing well away from the opening of the shower stall, where marks and measurements indicated the locations of the recovered casings. "The officers were firing revolvers, so the ejected casings had to have come from the assailant's weapon. He must have come out of the shower before he started shooting. A fingertip bandage, apparently belonging to the subject—wasn't from the officers—was found at the top of the stairs. A knapsack, nothing in it except some food. We're photographing everything. Von Schaick and Robinson are dusting for latent prints and collecting blood samples. Soon's we finish the preliminary we'll get the stuff to the lab and establish liaison with the FBI and RCMP [Royal Canadian Mounted Police]."

The captain was only half-listening now, once again the gray eyes unblinking, reflective. Suddenly he slapped the table with a heavy palm, interrupting the subordinate's commentary on the evidence. "This guy wasn't gonna be taken alive, Harry. Else why shoot it out with four armed police officers only a few feet away? Most guys would've surrendered. And these men weren't pushovers. Look at their records. One a former Marine. Yet he outgunned them. This guy is something different. He's on the lam from something, and it's something *big*."

◆ ◆ ◆

Bullet-riddled shower stall
(NYSP Archives)

Aerial photo of NYSP roadblock
(NYSP Archives)

34

Word traveled fast in Lake Placid. Residents were now in a state of intense anxiety with news that almost half the police force was gone, shot down by the mad robber. Rumors flew almost as fast as bullets, and in no time the community was on the verge of panic.

"Good God, it was bad enough when we *had* a police force!"

"Yeah, this guy's gonna take over the whole town!"

Security was uppermost on people's minds. The tourist trade took another precipitous dip. Visitors already there began weighing their options. Art Devlin, owner of the Olympic Motel, expressed what most of the tradesmen were thinking: "Why vacation someplace where it rains everyday and a madman's running loose shooting people?"

A few miles away, however, in Jim Call's permanent camp, the mood was one of relative tranquility. The precipitator of the unrest in town lounged in his chair, watching the rain fall in the valley below. It had been three days since the shooting, and the excitement had worn off. Remarkably, he felt only mild emotion about the encounter, reverting to his usual fatalistic attitude. They opened fire, he returned fire. For him it had been purely reactionary. He only did what he'd been trained to do. They would have killed him had they been able. He still couldn't understand how the bullets had missed him. They appeared to have come right through the shower stall into him. Perhaps they had, he mused in one of his more philosophical moments. Maybe he'd been killed and was now floating about in some ethereal after life. It seemed he'd already lived several mini-lives, all tragic. Perhaps there was no real end to life, no final expiration. Just a recurring nightmare that went on forever. He'd discussed such philosophical observations with Muriel and she had drawn comparisons with the fatalism expressed in *The Rubaiyat*.

The radio, one of several he had stolen, kept him informed of developments following the shooting: Three officers critically wounded, vague descriptions of the gunman, the assailant's extraordinary self-control throughout the engagement, ensuing posses, bloodhounds, roadblocks, helicopters.

Although it was his intention not to stray far from his camp, he had made a few scouting trips up Scarface Mountain. From there he had observed troopers far below on patrol, setting up roadblocks, stopping motorists. Based on what he had seen and heard on the radio, it was a comprehensive, well-planned dragnet, which they were tightening by the hour. His own experience planning tactical military missions gave him a grudging admiration for the skill and efficiency of the New York State Police. He would later admit that he underestimated the commitment and resources of this organization.

But for the moment, he was not excessively concerned. Events of recent years had taught him to take the gravest crisis in stride, a trait often noted by fellow airmen who had marveled at his coolness under fire. He didn't understand it himself, actually. Perhaps, he thought, he simply didn't value life as highly as others ... even his own.

He watched a nearby pool of water expanding in the rain, which was now a downpour that struck the water in long vertical lines. In one square patch over 300 drops fell per second. He estimated the number based on a mathematical formula he'd devised—one of many diversions to pass time.

He was glad of the rain. The harder the better. Everything hunkered down in the rain. Bloodhounds were useless with scents washed away. The choppers had poor visibility. It was hard enough to see from the air when visibility was good. Rain slowed things down. For the time being, he was safe. That is, as long as he stayed put. They'd expect him to try to leave the area. But he would be like an animal in the forest whose first reaction to danger was to remain still, blending with the surroundings. Movement drew attention.

Yes, he'd remain where he was until things cooled off. He had sufficient provisions, if he were careful. The police would burn out eventually, assume he'd made his way out of the area. For the moment he was just another tree in a landscape of millions. Let them find that one tree. The odds were in his favor, and he knew odds. Besides, what if they did find him? They'd never bring him in. Not with that one round left in the chamber.

He stared at the pool of water, its surface heavily pockmarked by the driving rain. It reminded him of strafing passes over water, .50-caliber bullets kicking up spray. He thought of Korea ... the raids ... the people killed.... But the dead were not confined to Korea. Inevitably, more recent memories began creeping in. The cries ... the blows ... bloody images. He resisted the thoughts, trying to focus instead on the rain, Muriel.... Instinctively he reached for *The Rubaiyat*.

Soon, the rain let up. With dusk came a sunset, glimmering beyond the clouds. He put the book aside and, standing, moved to one of his "cupboards" at the rear of the lean-to. Here he rummaged among several bottles of whiskey, withdrawing a half-filled bottle of Old Grandad bourbon. It had been almost full the night before. As with other supplies, he had to ration his liquor. Replenishing things would now be more difficult. He unscrewed the cap and the heady aroma filled his nostrils. He held the bottle up to the fading light, admiring the amber-colored liquid. After a moderate swig he replaced the bottle among the boughs.

Returning to his chair, he looked out over the valley to the horizon, where a profusion of clouds filamented with long crimson strands stretched above the peaks. The mountains had turned dark in the fading light, but patches of blue sky were now visible. Bundles of clouds formed images: A large elephant overhead. A B-29 trailing a long clean line of vapor. And yes, over there with the baby.... Feeling the rising emotion, he picked up a nearby stick and began making random marks in the soggy ground.

He thought again of the shooting. The rapid exchange of gun-shots reverberating through the cellar, the smell of gun powder, the falling officers.... Probably good guys. A different time they might've had a beer together. But last night they were the enemy, no different than the gooks in Korea where if they found you, they'd bring you back to the cage ... execution.... The alternative wasn't that bad if you liked solitude, a shot of bourbon, the sunset. Welcome reprieves.

The sky was now an inferno of billowing red and black clouds. No place like the Adirondacks. He could die here, probably would. Each sunset he treated as his last. He had done the same in Korea.

That's what made them precious. Made anything precious. The uncertainty, the risk....

The sun was fading now. Almost gone. He leaned back in his chair, closed his eyes. The bourbon was still warm in his throat. He'd made it through another day. Just like survival school—only easier.

◆ ◆ ◆

35

"The job at the Club? The jewel robbery?" Dutch Muller drew his head back sharply, his chin tucked well into the folds of his neck. His expression was one of skepticism yet profound interest, as though he had just observed a two-headed fly on his desk. He had been sitting in his office with Harry Blaisdell reviewing progress reports on the manhunt, when his subordinate had drawn a connection between the jewel robbery at the Lake Placid Club and the camp assailant. "We can't try to pin every goddamn crime around here the past twenty years on this guy."

"Actually, until this guy showed up, there hasn't been that much crime around here the past twenty years." Harry spoke lightly, concealing his tenacity. Although not wanting to challenge his boss, he was not one to abandon a premise easily. "And the jewel robbery was only three days before the shootout. The location, the time frame, the method of entry—it all fits our man. Look at some of these other jobs," the sergeant continued, drawing a sheaf of paper from a folder. "July 13th and 20th the Davies camp. July 11th the Wertheim stickup. July 27th the Tyler and Brewster burglaries. August 3rd the Grand View Cottages. The list goes on. And all within a three-week period."

Dutch shook his head dubiously. "He's hiding out from something. He's stealing stuff he needs to survive—food, clothing. Jewels don't fit the pattern. What's he gonna do with jewelry in the woods?"

"He won't be in the woods forever. He's probably—"

"Geez-chris," said Dutch irritably. "Let's *hope* he's not gonna be in the woods forever. I hope we're gonna drag his ass out of there one of these days. Although the way things are going I wouldn't bet on it."

Harry waited a moment for his chief's ire to subside and then said, "He could have pulled off the job at the Club very easily. He's had access to most of the establishments in town. He's a suspect in an armed robbery very close to the Club. A hundred grand worth of jewelry? That's not bad. And you're right, Harold, he doesn't need it in the woods. He's too smart to keep it with him. He stashes it somewhere. Comes back and gets it later on."

Dutch listened. Unlike many authoritative people, he was not averse to changing his mind when presented with a convincing argument. This Harry knew.

"Well, we'll certainly talk to him about it when we bring him in," Dutch said. "Although this guy's gonna have more to worry about than a jewel heist. The doctors don't think its good to interview Pelkey. Doesn't look like he's gonna make it. If Pelkey goes, this guy's facing murder one. The chair, for sure."

"We're doing a composite drawing of the subject," Harry said. "A local artist named Arturo Monaco is working with the witnesses. We should have that soon."

Dutch stood, stretched, then walked to a window. He looked out to the mountains in the distance, where a steady rain fell on a bleak and foreboding landscape. "He's gotta be out there somewhere," he mused. "I don't care what kind of woodsman he is. He's gotta be damned uncomfortable."

◆ ◆ ◆

36

It was time to move. Several days had elapsed since the shootout on West Valley Road and, after taking inventory of his diminishing supplies, Jim had concluded he would break camp. With topographical maps that showed the trails in the region (stolen from camps during preceding weeks) and his navigational skills, he was confident he could avoid the roads and populated areas where the State Police were concentrating their resources. He would head south, his goal New York City. Canada had occurred to him as an alternative, but he reasoned that the authorities would expect this and would have increased coverage on the border. Besides, he was comfortable in the metropolitan areas. His extensive travel with the Air Force had taken him to many of the large cities of the world. Manhattan with its concentration of people and diverse interests should be a good place to hole up for a while. Restaurants, art galleries, shows—and rich neighborhoods....

He had been following news reports on his portable radio. Officer Pelkey had succumbed. The death of the popular family man had elevated the search for his killer to that of a crusade. The populace of the northern region had been saturated with accounts of the shooting and wild speculation followed regarding the nature of the killer. That he was a gifted survivalist was unquestioned by the many woodsmen enlisted to help in the manhunt. But the fact that he was also a gunslinger who fired from the hip with the accuracy of a Wyatt Earp propelled him to a level of notoriety unheard of in the North Country. Although concerned about the public reaction, Jim took it in stride, convinced that he could outwit his pursuers. He'd have to do something stupid to be caught, and that wasn't going to happen. His plan was to move by night, sleeping and coordinating his points during the day.

Having made the decision to move, he spent the remainder of the day with his maps, studying the trails and selecting supplies for the trip. As nightfall approached, he sat in his chair looking out at the valley, contemplating his travel. Although he did not realize it at the moment, the trip on which he would set forth would take him through the heart of the Adirondack wilderness—one of the most extraordinary escape and evasion treks ever undertaken.

The days that followed saw Jim traveling in a southerly direction through thick underbrush that at times defied passage. A severe storm in 1950 had caused great destruction in the region, leaving behind deadfall and nearly jungle-like conditions, with some areas virtually impenetrable. He adhered to his plan, however, traveling over Scarface Mountain and following the Johns Brook Trail, hoping to emerge in Keene Valley. En route, he managed to rob farms and several remote logging camps for food and additional clothing. Change of clothing was essential, not only for comfort and to ward off the elements, but to confuse the bloodhounds which had been deployed in the manhunt.

Nor were his burglaries confined to clothing, food, and beverages. He had his eye open for treasures. Cash would be important when he reached the city. "I planned to rob other places like the Adirondack Lodge on Hart Lake, but the opportunities did not present themselves," he would say later. Amazingly, in view of repeated warnings from the media about anticipated robberies, his string of burglaries during the trip went unopposed. This was fortunate for the area's inhabitants. As Jim later commented, "I was prepared to shoot anyone who stood in my way."

As he proceeded toward Keene Valley, trooper patrols were being increased. Captain Muller and his staff had anticipated that the fugitive would use a variety of escape routes. Having analyzed the evidence, they had noted which trail and topographical maps had been stolen from the camps and possibly would be followed by the subject. With the help of experienced woodsmen, they had delineated certain areas for increased coverage. Men with vehicles were stationed on trails leading from Lake Placid to intercept the fugitive. It was sound strategy, but it would bring two troopers squarely in the gun sights of Major Call's deadly Luger.

◆ ◆ ◆

Ira Rosenberg

Troopers, on road-block duty, stopping traffic at dusk at an intersection on Route 28N at Newcomb, N. Y., in the uing hunt for the man who shot three Lake Placid policemen during a burglary Aug. 5. This community is -five miles south of Lake Placid by road and the trails leading south come out of the woods in the area.

NYSP at roadblock—September 2, 1954
(*New York Herald-Tribune*, Photo by Ira Rosenberg)

37

September is glorious in the Adirondacks. The alpine landscape becomes a patchwork of brilliant tones as summer verdure gives way to the spectacular orange, yellow, and crimson shades of autumn. Among the natives it is referred to as "the season of flaming leaves." With the brilliant foliage comes the first signs of winter—in the Adirondacks a season to be reckoned with. This fact was not lost on Jim. The nights were becoming colder. Soon the leaves would start to fall. Less camouflage meant increased visibility from the skies. It was some of these considerations that prompted Jim to pick up his pace—to move by day rather than to undergo the slower more laborious travel by night.

It was late morning and he was proceeding through the woods parallel to the trail—he would never walk the trail itself—that led to Keene. Suddenly, there was a crackling sound. Jim stopped abruptly, listening, attempting to determine its source. What was it? The wind? An animal? A bird? No, it had been different—not a natural sound of the forest. After weeks in the mountains his senses were well attuned to the wilderness. He remained motionless for several seconds, his tan jacket and dark trousers blending in with the woods. Then cautiously he moved ahead, stepping carefully to avoid objects that would break the silence.

He had advanced several steps when again he heard the sound. Louder, no more than thirty yards down the trail. Immediately, he was on his stomach, flattening his body against the ground, his Luger in his right hand. This time it was clear, unmistakable—a car radio. But how? In the woods? He lay motionless, listening. The sound continued at irregular intervals. Voices—radio transmissions, he thought.

Unlike most who would have fled, Jim hesitated. Flight would compound his problem. He would spend hours wondering what he had encountered, what threat might have awaited him. Instead, with remarkable temerity, he wriggled several yards forward to a point where, no more than twenty yards away in a small clearing, he observed two troopers leaning against a radio car. The two, assigned to surveillance in that location, had somehow managed to drive their car through an open area to a point in the woods that enabled them to surveil the trail.

Jim lay watching the men, his Luger trained on the head of the trooper who was farthest away. Suddenly, the man turned, looking in his direction. Had he noticed something? Jim steadied, his sights locked on the officer's forehead. Should the man show any awareness of his presence, he was prepared to squeeze the trigger. The trooper turned away and then moved toward the car, apparently unaware. After a few moments, Jim withdrew. Asked later what he would have done had they discovered him lying in the underbrush, he replied with characteristic assurance, "Well, then you would have had two dead troopers."

This near encounter, plus his additional sightings of State Police, finally convinced him that "because of the continuous trooper patrols, I realized I could not get out that way." Reluctantly, he made the decision to reverse direction and return to his main camp in the woods near Lake Placid. It was the last thing they would expect him to do, he reasoned. Therefore, the right decision.

After several days and nights, he finally made it back to his camp. The trek had been made with severe hardships. Burglaries during his trip south had heightened awareness of his presence, and robberies for supplies were becoming exceedingly risky. Hence, he'd had little food. But another problem developed of even greater concern. The dampness and continuous travel were taking their toll on his feet. Jim was acutely aware from survival training that this part of the anatomy required great care. His concern for his feet had been evident to his pursuers from the quantities of socks and foot powder he had stolen. Therefore, upon arriving at his main camp, one of the first things he did was retrieve a can of foot powder and some dry socks from one of his suitcases.

There followed a few days' rest, during which time he listened to news reports and tended to personal hygiene. Throughout his journey he had shaved and cut his hair regularly, using a mirror and scissors, to avoid the scraggly woodsman-like appearance the populace had come to expect. It was a discipline that would serve him well in unexpected confrontations during coming days.

As he listened to reports of the "tightening dragnet" throughout the Adirondacks, he devised a new plan for his escape. Once again, it was simple. He would proceed north and west through the woods, aligning himself with the New York Central Railroad tracks as a guide, travel to Ray Brook, Saranac Lake, and on to Lake Clear Junction and Tupper Lake.

After a brief respite he started out once more, following the tracks but usually remaining "from 100 to 500 feet back in the woods." Although he began moving by both day and night, after several sightings of trooper patrols he once more reverted to travel by night. During his trek he survived on edible plants and an abundance of blueberries. When available, he scavenged garbage from remote country estates. "In a camp near Floodwood I ate bread and garbage and drank vinegar."

Finally, he arrived at Tupper Lake. It was here that he encountered three armed policemen looking for the "Lake Placid cop killer." Once again, under intense pressure, he would demonstrate his intelligence and extraordinary composure.

◆ ◆ ◆

A LONELY VIGIL.—Two state troopers, taking part in the manhunt for the gunman who shot three Lake Placid policemen on Aug. 5, find comfort in a roadside fire as they keep an all-night watch on Highway 10, south of Tupper Lake, where the search has been concentrated since the killer was sighted there on Sept. 13. Left is Trooper R. E. Shanahan, Clarence sub-station, and Trooper W. A. Gesswein of Clarkson sub-station.

NYSP at roadside fire—September 26, 1954
(The Post-Standard)

38

It was not a prudent course of action. But blueberries will carry a man just so far. An empty stomach was something to be reckoned with. It was near a school in Tupper Lake that Jim decided to enter the town in quest of food. He had prepared for the occasion: clean shirt, trousers, trenchcoat, loafers, freshly shaved, hair trimmed. The image he presented was hardly that of a fugitive who'd been living in the mountains for weeks.

He had no sooner stepped from the woods and started walking down a street, however, when he was dismayed to see a police car headed in his direction. He realized that every law enforcement officer in the North Country was looking for him now. And the officers in the Perkins camp had provided a reasonable description of him. It had been a mistake to leave his cover. Quickly he assessed his options. Should he turn, try to avoid them? Or make a break for the woods? There was still time.

But that was not the Call style. Suppressing the flight instinct, he maintained his stride, concealing the limp that his victims had described in news articles. Maybe they had not noticed him. But if they had and he changed direction, it might well provoke a confrontation. And then? Well, then it was anyone's guess.

He continued walking—a rather slow easy saunter that displayed a military bearing. As the distance closed he felt the eyes from the cruiser. They were going to stop him. Having made his decision, however, he was unwavering. His hand in his pocket closed on the Luger.

Suddenly there were sounds of voices—pre-teen youngsters playing baseball behind the school. Without hesitation, as though it were his destination, he walked deliberately across the street onto the ball field. With purposeful strides, he crossed the infield toward the pitchers mound.

"Let me show you how to throw that," he said, approaching the young pitcher, his hand out for the ball.

The boy, surprised, but agreeably impressed by the affable, good-looking man, handed over the ball. "Sure, mister."

"Here's how you get more speed on a pitch," said Jim, taking the ball. "See, hold the seams with your fingers like this. And when you throw, let it slide off your middle finger. It sends the ball up and in on a right-hander. Handcuffs him."

The other boys, their interest mounting, drifted in from the infield. They were not alone in their curiosity, however. The police cruiser drew slowly up to the curb next to the ball field and stopped.

Jim continued his instruction, acutely aware of the cruiser. Two policemen sat in the front seat, watching. Little else was the focus of North Country police these days besides the frantic search for the killer of a fellow officer. Every stranger, whether good-looking and well-dressed or not, was subject to scrutiny. A tense minute or two passed and then, after observing the comfortable rapport between the man and the boys, the officers moved slowly away. Jim closed his eyes for a second, feeling the relief and exhilaration he invariably experienced after a brush with danger. Then, quick to sense that he had stumbled onto valuable assets, he went about cultivating the friendship of his new young acquaintances. It was not difficult, given the threshold of boredom in twelve-year-olds. Anything new and interesting was welcome. Within minutes, displaying an easy manner, Jim was one of the group, regaling them with stories of airplanes and far away places.

Jim's dalliance with the young boys at such a critical time would have been understandable to Robert Sylvester, his closest friend. Later he would write about Jim's affection for children:

> Jim was always extremely fond of children, always finding time to play ball or teach them football, or build things with them—this was at a time when the average high school kid didn't know younger kids existed. I remember many times having to wait for him to finish playing baseball with a bunch of little kids, and how it always rankled me....

No doubt this affection for children kept Jim at the ballpark this particular day. Having survived the encounter with the police, it would have been better for him to move on. But starved for companionship, and foreseeing some advantages in his newfound friends, he lingered.

As noon approached and the boys talked of going home for lunch, Jim allowed as how he was a trifle hungry himself. Perhaps one of them could pick up a couple of hamburgers for him on their way back, he said, handing one boy a dollar bill. He'd wait around and they could play some more ball in the afternoon. It seemed a good idea—except that Jim had not foreseen the entrepreneurial qualities of the boy to whom he gave the money. Instead of going to the hamburger stand, the boy decided to pocket the cash and go to his mother for the food. Upon hearing about the "terrific man," Aldona Oberlander packed some sandwiches and sent them with her son back to the ball field. But then came second thoughts. A call to the police followed.

The result was Reg Cormier, an easy-going young man with five months on the force, tooling up to the ball field on his motorcycle. Jim was standing on the mound pitching at the time. When he saw the officer coming, he nonchalantly picked up his trenchcoat lying nearby, his hand sliding into a pocket. His concern was quickly allayed by the officer's friendly smile as he dismounted from his cycle and approached.

"How ya' doing?" the officer said. "We got a call at the station about some stranger. Everybody's uptight since that officer got killed over in Placid. Live around here?"

"I've been working up at the Saranac Inn," Jim replied, convincingly. "Just quit a couple of days ago. I'm leaving for Watertown tonight. Waiting around for the bus."

"What you gonna do in Watertown?"

"Visiting my sisters."

"Got some ID?"

"Sure." Jim reached into his pocket and withdrew the wallet that he had stolen from John O'Connor, the Springfield cab driver. He displayed the credentials to the patrolman, who seemed satisfied.

"Sorry to bother you," said the officer, mounting his cycle. "But we're checkin' all strangers. People are pretty uptight," he repeated. With a kick of his foot he started the machine. He was about to leave only to find the rear wheel of his cycle spinning ineffectively in the sand. The officer gunned the engine but the wheel deepened.

"Need a push?" Jim asked. Without waiting for an answer, he moved quickly behind the motorcycle, lifting and shoving it forward out of the sand. Never was assistance rendered with more brio.

"Hey, thanks, buddy," the officer said, the eyes behind the dark glasses showing surprise and admiration for the display of strength. In an explosion of dust and noise, he was gone. It had been a cordial meeting.

But this was not the case with a confrontation a short time later. Jim had donned his trenchcoat preparing to leave his newfound friends when a police cruiser eased to the side of the road near the field. Inside were two officers. This was serious. Two men were far more of a problem. And the fact that they had come back was significant. Maybe the headquarters had checked out his Saranac Inn story.

He continued to watch the police car from the corner of his eye, tension mounting. Perhaps they'd move on. But no. Car doors opened and two uniformed officers emerged. They stood for a moment near the car, conferring, and then started walking toward him. Is this the way it would end? On a ball field ... with kids? He continued to talk with the boys, but his right hand moved imperceptibly into the pocket of his trenchcoat, closing on the Luger. With a finger he pushed the safety, releasing the trigger. He watched every step as they approached. Should either make the slightest move toward the service pistol on his belt he was prepared to shoot it out, even if necessary to grab one of the boys as a hostage, as he had done with Bernie Fell.

As they came closer, however, he was somewhat relieved. Their body movements were not hostile. In fact, one officer's face bore the semblance of a smile.

"Mornin'," said one as they came to a stop on the fringe of the group. "We're makin' routine checks. Police officer was killed a few weeks back. You stayin' in town?"

Jim, feigning slight frustration, pulled out the identification, explaining how he had been interrogated by a motorcycle cop only moments before.

"He check out your ID?" one asked.

"Apparently," Jim said with a shade of annoyance. "I gave it to him."

Satisfied, the officers returned to their car and drove off. Asked later what he would have done had the officers required he go with them for further questioning, he replied, once again unhesitatingly, "I would have shot them."

But he'd had enough of the ball field. After a hasty farewell to his new young friends he departed, happy to leave Tupper Lake.

Unfortunately for the motorcyclist, Reg Cormier, Tupper Lake was home. Later, when it was learned from the report in the local paper that Reg had confronted the cop killer and that the fugitive had actually helped push Reg out of the sand, life was hard at the station house. But Reg, a good-natured fellow, took it well. "I got a little bit of ribbin', that's about all," he would say later. "I just laughed about it. That's about all I could do. Anyway, how the hell could I know? We were lookin' for some crazy, bushy-haired guy who'd been in the woods for weeks. This guy was clean, good-lookin', acted real intelligent. And he didn't seem to be scairt of anythin'. He was real cool!"

Who could blame Reg? Well, his boss maybe ... a little. What did he have to say to Reg?

"Chief Timmons?" said Reg when asked the question by a reporter. "Well, when they found out it was the killer—I was workin' night duty then—the Chief, he came and woke me up at two o'clock in the afternoon. He called me outside, and I sat in the police car with him. He was kinda' mad. But there was nothin' I could do about it. Coulda' happened to anybody. He told me, he says, 'You know that guy you talked to down at the ballpark? The guy who pushed you outa' the sand?' I says, 'Yeah, what about it?' 'Well,' he says, 'that was the Lake Placid killer!' "

"I told the chief," Reg continued, "that the poster picture and the guy in the playground didn't look anything like the same guy to me."

" 'Well,' the chief says, 'that was the cop killer.' I says, 'Okay.' That was all that was said and I went back in the house."

◆ ◆ ◆

39

The confrontations with police in Tupper Lake cured Jim of any delusions that he could venture into populated areas of the North Country. There was simply too much publicity. Once again he retreated to the wilderness. In accordance with his plan he continued northwest. It was near Moody, west of Tupper Lake that he found himself again the focus of attention, this time literally, inasmuch as a hunter had him in the cross hairs of his 300 Savage rifle. After burglarizing several houses and establishments in the area, including the Tupper Lake Golf and Country Club and the Terrace Restaurant, Jim had taken refuge in a small barn behind an unoccupied camp owned by Ray Brunette, the local town highway superintendent.

It was dusk, another rainy evening, and Ray was making a rare check on his camp. Upon entering his barn he was surprised and alarmed at what he saw. Afterwards, he spoke of the event in detail:

> There was the throw-away mattress, right there on the damned floor. A sleepin' bag was stretched out on top of the mattress ... and the bag was open as if somebody had been sleepin' in it. Then I saw a green army duffel bag settin' right there, and there's this German Luger sittin' on top of it. I knew it was a German Luger because I brought three of them home from the service. I'm sayin' to myself, Jesus Christ, what's goin' on here? Maybe, somebody comin' through is sleepin' in the barn tonight. It could have happened. You know, kids travellin' the way they do, a tramp or somebody. But, *the German Luger*.... [emphasis added]
>
> Don't forget, all this time I've got this 300 Savage. This guy [the fugitive] don't know that I come up there to hunt deer. He probably thinks I'm lookin' for him because he's a

wanted man, right? These are things I think about after. So, I started to walk back to the road, and as I said, it's a rainy night and it's gettin' late. It's not dark and it's not light. Dusk. As I get back near the car, I see this silhouette in the brush. I can't say it's a man, I can't say it's a deer, I can't say it's a bear. I don't know what it is, but there's somethin' runnin'. When it gets to the barn, it's still in the brush. Then, it comes to me.... It's a person, and whoever that son-of-a-bitch is, he wants that gun. Prior to that, I had lifted up my gun tryin' to make out what the object was through the scope. With a scope, you can see pretty well after dusk, don't 'ya know. Anyway, I was tryin' to figure out what the object was through the scope. I had no intention of shootin'. I just wanted to see what the Christ that was. Then I figured out it must be a man, and whoever it is is tryin' to get back to the barn and get the gun. Now I'm sayin', why in hell didn' I take the gun. It was too late. What I gotta do now is pray that somebody comes down from the Tupper Lake Country Club.

And there was no other way he could get into the barn 'cept through that big door, and it was probably only a hundred feet away, and I was directly in front of it. I had the door covered simply because I was lookin' through my scope, and had the gun pointed in his general direction. Hell, if I'd known it was Call, and if I'd known he was carryin' a gun, I'd probably still be runnin' over that son-of-a-bitchin' mountain. See what I mean, I'd still be goin'.

Ray Brunette's concern was understandable. The hype surrounding the "cop killer" bordered on hysteria, and the description of the fugitive's shooting and survival skills had achieved legendary proportions. For Ray to be able to fend off a killer who'd just blown away three police officers was not in the cards.

Anyway, I don't know this. He don't even enter my mind. All at once I hear a car comin'. It's a milk truck. I can't think of the guy's name whose drivin' it. I stopped him. He'd been to a weddin', a McCauley got married. So I told him, "There's somethin' funny goin' on here. There's been a fella' around here, and he's got a gun in the barn. I'm goin' to stay here. Drag your ass down and get a trooper—get somebody here." Okay, he took off. After he left, I says to myself, the son-of-a-bitch is half-corked. He looked drunk, you know. He'd been to a weddin'. I'm thinkin' suppose he forgets. It's gettin' dark. Well, Jesus Christ, wouldn't 'ya know, 10 or 15 minutes go by. *Then I hear a siren a comin', then I see a trooper a comin'.*... [emphasis added]

The arriving trooper was Harold Osborne, a tall handsome individual highly regarded both as trooper and family man in the upstate communities. Brunette was exceedingly grateful for his arrival.

He pulled in and, of course, I'm still standin' there. I run up to the car and tell him there's a man stayin' in the barn. There's a German Luger in there, and there's candles. Jesus Christ, he run down to the barn with his gun out. Don't forget, he's got his pistol out. And I was right tight to his ass. When he saw that German Luger, he said, "Watch this door, we've got something hot here." So I watched the door. Like I said, he went back to his car and got on his radio. *Good Lord a lovin' Christ sirens, and everythin' was goin' wild.* [emphasis added] Jesus, Jesus another 15 minutes. It sounded crazy, you know what I mean? And up and down the road.

Brunette was convinced he had seen Major Call even before the barn incident. Later, upon viewing Jim's picture, he identified him as a person he had seen occasionally at the local country club.

Now I knew I seen the killer before. A couple times. Directly across from my camp. On the other side of the road from my camp, there was a tee. I had seen this man, white shirt, just sittin' there in the mornin', lookin' around, ya know. There really didn't seem to be anything unusual about it. He was well dressed. He was gettin' white shirts and stuff outa' the Country Club. Ya' see, it was the old Country Club that burnt. The old one was a log building. It was a beautiful building. On the side was the locker room, and the door was never locked. So he went in there and got white shirts. Times I saw him he was sittin' on a bench, just lookin' around. I even waved to him once. It was not uncommon to see someone sittin' there. Anyway, through all this horseshit, I don't know that the killer's in this country. I don't know where he is. He don't even enter my mind. Like I told you, I'd still be goin' over that son-of-a-bitchin' mountain if I'd a' figured it was him. A trooper I talked to later said the killer was asked, "If you had your gun, what would you have done to Mr. Brunette?" He said, "I'd have shot him and taken his car."

According to Ray Brunette, the anxiety caused by the manhunt was not limited to fellow humans. The deer population suffered as well:

Huntin' season opens here sometime around the 25th of October. Same day I found the killer in my camp. The fire sirens all blow. When the firemen arrive at the station they're told "There's no fire, the cop killer is up around Brunette's camp. Get your rifles loaded, and we're goin' lookin' for him!"

Well anyway, Mike—I forget his last name—lived right across from the fire station, and he told 'em, "You damned fools, we're goin' into the woods with guns and we'll be shootin' each other." Made a hell of a lot of sense, ya know. Anyway, all the outlaws of Tupper Lake, there ain't a one of 'em that would lift a hand to help the state police, but that night, they were out in force. They were jackin' deer in the best jackin' country in the world at Whitney Park, and at Litchfield Park. If anybody checked, they were just lookin' for the killer. There they were, ridin' the roads with flashlights, searchlights, pickin' up eyes. Bang! Down go the deer. I'm tellin' you facts.

For example, I had a search light in my truck. You'd be goin' up the road shinin' your light in the woods. The troopers didn't bother you, you were lookin' for the killer. Hell, they weren't lookin' for the killer, they were lookin' for deer, they were trying to spot deer eyes. The huntin' season didn't start until a month later. Actually, the deer season opened a month earlier that year. It started when I found the cop killer. Every outlaw in Tupper Lake took out his gun,

5 cell flashlight. Well, everybody was interested in gettin' a deer, they didn't care about that killer. You'd meet a man in the woods and ask "What are you doin'?" He'd answer, "Lookin' for that cop killer."

♦ ♦ ♦

ADSIDE CAMPSITE.—An improvised shelter, a bonfire and some hotdogs offer e troopers relief from cold, rainy weather as they stand a 12-hour-a-day guard on highway near Long Lake. The post was set up two weeks ago when the report of tolen jacket indicated the Lake Placid cop-killer might be in that area. Troopers , left to right: R. J. Brownell, Watervliet, Troop G; S. A. Chieco, Binghamton, op C, and R. A. Wolf, Malone, Troop B. In the background are two forest rangers, J. Parker, left, and B. W. Stanton, both of Long Lake. Boys in photo are not ntified.

NYSP at shelter—September 26, 1954
(The Post-Standard)

40

"It's the Luger that killed Pelkey." Harry Blaisdell handed the report from the crime laboratory to his boss. "He's our man."

Dutch Muller studied the report for a moment, dropped it on his desk, and leaned back in his chair, a deep frown creasing his rugged features. "Now all we gotta do is find him. He can't be far."

The two were sitting in an office of the State Police substation at Tupper Lake which had been set up as a command post following the discovery at the Brunette barn. More than a month had passed since the gun battle at the Perkins camp. It had been a period of unrelenting pressure for those managing the manhunt. Countless reports of burglaries, robberies, strange encounters, even shootings, had been attributed to the Lake Placid fugitive. To its credit, the New York State Police responded to virtually every credible report. It was an impressive performance and Dutch Muller was inclined to comment about it when addressing the news media.

"Some people don't seem to understand what we've got here, Harry."

Harry understood. He suspected that his boss used him on occasion to try out his press releases.

"What we've got here is an experienced woodsman who's hiding out in the Adirondack wilderness, an area of over six million acres. You know how much that is, Harry? That's over nine thousand square miles—nearly three times the size of Yellowstone National Park."

Harry knew. He'd already read the same information in the Adirondack Mountain Club's *Guide to Adirondack Trails*, a copy of which lay on a credenza behind his boss' desk.

"And we know that unless our man stole a helicopter somewhere," Dutch continued, "he's located right here in the High Peaks Region where winter temperatures above the tree line are roughly the same as you get at the Arctic Circle. So what does it mean? It means our guy has to get out of here in the next few weeks or he's gonna freeze his ass off. I don't give a damn how good a woodsman he is, no one's gonna stay alive out there in those mountains. If we don't find him soon, we'll never find him 'cause no one's gonna find a goddamn skeleton in nine thousand square miles of wilderness. You read me, Harry?"

Harry read. He saw little merit in making the point that it was only a three to four hour drive out of the wilderness if their fugitive stole a car and somehow made it past their road blocks. "We've got another contingent of troopers coming in from Albany this afternoon," Harry said softly. "Everything's covered. Roads, trails. He'll be feeling the heat."

"He won't be feeling much heat at night, that's for sure," Dutch shot back, unwilling to let go of his weather observations. "Not in those mountains. Getting damn cold around here at night." The captain paused, picking up a sheaf of papers listing the items discovered in the Brunette barn that were presumed to belong to the fugitive. "How the hell did he carry all this stuff? Gotta be over a hundred different things here. He must have a lot more out there, too, judging from the stuff he's stolen. Maybe he's operating out of different campsites." He flipped the report across the desk to his subordinate.

Harry had studied the list earlier, but out of deference to his boss glanced over the items again. "Looks like a reader. *The Rubaiyat, The Prophet*. Heavy stuff."

"I talked to one of the woodsmen who's been helping us," Dutch said. After he saw that list he's more convinced than ever the guy's a trained survivalist. Everything points to it. He thinks he might have been in the service. Olive-colored gear, aviator boots, wooden matches.... He says they always carry wooden matches."

"Could be," mused Harry, continuing to look at the list. "Interesting. He had a meerschaum pipe. I asked a pipe smoker, he said they're pretty rare. Pipe bag has initials LHS."

"Probably most of it's stolen," said the captain.

"Eleven condoms." Harry shook his head, bewildered. "What the hell would he be doing with rubbers in the woods?"

"Well, maybe he hasn't been in the woods all the time," Dutch said with a deepening frown. "Look at those toilet articles. Deodorant, Vitalis hair oil, plus the rubbers. Seems like the guy was doing more than burglaries. Could be he's right under our nose. I'm beginning to wonder about those composites. Probably don't look anything like him."

"Possibly," allowed Harry, shrugging. "Monaco, the artist, got most of it from the officers. Could be kinda' tough gettin' a good physical description when the guy's blastin' away at you with a 9 mm Luger."

"Yeah, I s'pose so," Dutch said, turning toward a window and swinging a leg over the arm of his chair. "I don't think that guy's goin' far. Not without his sleeping bag and all his gear. Goddamn cold last night."

◆ ◆ ◆

41

Beyond the timberline a wolf moon glided among the peaks in a black sky. In the treetops a stiff cool breeze moaned of impending winter. Although the autumn days were still warm and sunny, the night temperatures in the forest could easily dip below freezing. Nowhere was the cold more evident than in low-lying areas where the moisture crystallized and formed a wafer-thin coating of ice on fallen leaves. For one traveling quickly at night, the footing became treacherous. And Jim Call had been traveling quickly.

At the moment, however, he was resting, huddled at the base of a large spruce where he had started a small fire to stay warm. Once again, in keeping with his evasion training, he had made the fire in a small hollow at the base of the tree so that the smoke would be diffused through the leaves.

Flushed from the Brunette barn a short time before, he had only the clothes he was wearing and his .32 automatic, which he had been carrying in his belt at the time. Pinned to a pocket on his jacket was a compass. When first discovered at the camp by Brunette, he had considered a bold attempt to recover his equipment. But believing Brunette was guarding the door to the barn with a shotgun, he had elected to flee.

His options had narrowed precipitously. Without supplies he faced a daunting trek through the mountains. His plan was to proceed south as rapidly as possible, raiding houses for food and clothing as he went. Pressure would intensify. Burglaries were increasingly dangerous. Articles left in the barn would provide authorities with valuable clues. The Luger was his greatest loss. Not only was it the weapon on which he had come to rely, they now had the gun which killed the police officer—critical evidence which could send him to the electric chair. Other articles such as his Air Force boots and the crowbar were traceable. And his fingerprints were on everything. In short order, they would identify him.

But for the moment, his main concern was to stay warm. He had been running and walking continuously since being driven from the barn; his underclothes were soaked with perspiration. Hypothermia, a severe drop in body temperature, could be fatal if not remedied, and was much on his mind. Exhausted, he fed the glowing embers with small sticks of wood, first licking off the ice crystals to quench his growing thirst. As he lay huddled near the fire he experienced the first signs of a deadly chill. He curled himself even closer around the dying embers, overcome by an intense drowsiness. He knew what was happening, but felt his will to survive slipping away. The short tragic life of James Call might well have ended at that point had it not been for his pursuers.

Suddenly, from far back in the woods a persistent sound permeated his subconscious. At first, it was vague, distant. But then, yelping, a whistle—bloodhounds! Had they set them loose? The clothing he'd abandoned in the barn ... a fresh scent. The thought of being attacked by dogs drove him to his feet. He stood, clearing the cobwebs, then started throwing dirt on the fire. Sticking his automatic in his belt he started off again into the forest. He lunged ahead rapidly, aided by the moonlight, the yelping dogs now fading in the distance. Revitalized, his mind focused on survival. He needed a change of clothes, food, blankets, red pepper to throw off the dogs, supplies ... a house!

The opportunity would come soon. Shortly after daybreak he stumbled into a clearing and looked out over a great valley. It was an enthralling view for one emerging from a nightmare in the forest. As the edge of the solar sphere rose above the distant peaks, he made out what appeared to be a stately mansion far down in the valley. His spirits lifted. A source of supply. With renewed vigor he headed toward the house, unaware that awaiting him would be yet another close call with troopers.

◆ ◆ ◆

Bloodhounds involved in Call manhunt

TRACKING THE KILLER.—State police bloodhound, "Holly," one of three used in the all-out effort to capture the phantom killer of the Adirondacks, leads state troopers

August 5, 1954
(The Adirondack Daily Enterprise)

"HOLLY" A BLOODHOUND of the Malone Barracks of the New York State Police, that was used this morning in the woodland search for the desperado who shot the three Lake Placid policemen. The State Trooper shown above with "Holly" Cpl. Eber O'Donnell, the dog's trainer. Another State Trooper had the bloodhound in charge during the search.

November 14, 1954
(The Post-Standard)

42

Expectations were high in the trooper command post at Tupper Lake. In a later interview, Harry Blaisdell described what took place:

We felt that finally, after two months of unrelenting pressure from politicians and the media, we were close to getting our man. In checking the equipment [the subject] had left behind in the Brunette barn we found many things that had been stolen in recent burglaries. We immediately dispatched cars to the area, and the various zone-uniformed lieutenants in charge of the road patrols set up roadblocks on the highway between Tupper Lake and Long Lake. There were many estates and large homes in that area which we started searching. However, that's a big area. We knew he was out of clothes, blankets, food and that he'd have to immediately start burglarizing houses for supplies. Later he told us that after hearing the bloodhounds he started sprinkling red pepper behind him to lose the dogs, to kill the scent. But we never heard any complaints from our men handling the dogs that they suspected red pepper was being used. They claimed that Call was just too smart about changing clothes and using streams.

We came very close to getting him between Tupper and Long Lake, though. That was right after the Brunette raid. Like I said, we knew he'd have to burglarize places to get what he needed so we were searching these large homes which had been vacated with the passing of the summer season. It was late in the day when two troopers drove up to this estate....

Jim, relaxing on a chaise longue in an upstairs bedroom, was jolted to attention by the sound of wheels crunching on gravel. Having entered the house early that morning, he had planned to spend the night and leave before daybreak. Looking cautiously from a front window he was dismayed to see a troop car coming up the drive. The car stopped at the entrance, the doors opened simultaneously, and two troopers emerged. They were imposing-looking in their gray uniforms, knee-high black boots, and tan Stetsons with the familiar purple band. From their cartridge belts, which were lined with copper-colored .38-caliber bullets, hung black holsters bearing Smith and Wesson revolvers. Each carried a flashlight. One trooper approached the front door while the other moved to the side of the house, presumably to watch the rear. Their manner was serious, confident.

Jim moved swiftly across the room and waited behind the bedroom door, alarmed but composed. His .32 automatic was cradled in its usual ready position in the crook of his left arm, the safety off. He listened as the troopers entered the house and began silently searching the rooms on the first floor. Their lack of conversation added to Jim's concern. He sensed the two were not rookies covering frivolous leads. Rather, they seemed mature, methodical, professional—not to be taken by surprise as were the officers at the Perkins camp.

Then, the sound of boots coming up the stairs slowly, deliberately. He glanced quickly around the bedroom for concealment. Behind the draperies? The closet? As the footsteps neared the top of the stairs, he dropped to the floor and crawled under a bed next to the wall. From this position he could see the black boots up to the knees, and the beams from the flashlights playing on the walls in the hallway beyond the bedroom door. He lay on his stomach, arms stretched in front of him, his automatic trained on the troopers' legs.

They paused. Still no conversation. Had they observed some telltale sign? The smell of a cigarette? A cigarette butt? Shoe marks? Their silence left him at a disadvantage. Then one pair of boots moved slowly into the bedroom and stopped. Seconds passed, the boots firmly planted. Had the trooper become suspicious? Why no movement? Was he motioning to the other man in the hall? ... He knew they had their pistols at the ready, that they'd open fire at the slightest provocation. A "cop killer" had few rights.

The other trooper entered the room. Beams flitted about from their flashlights. At this point Jim was certain they would look under the bed. They were less than three feet away. He lay motionless, his pistol trained on the legs of the closest figure. When the man bent over to look, he would shoot, assuring that one trooper would be taken out. (One of the troopers, Fred Wright of Rouses Point, New York, later recalled that he believed at this point he had actually sat down on the bed.)

To Jim's amazement, the troopers did not check under the bed. After looking in the closet, the two left the room. He heard them checking the other bedrooms, and finally their boots treading down the stairs. In a few seconds, the front door opened and closed. Then came the relieving sound of crunching gravel as the car departed. Jim relaxed, feeling the "rush," the euphoria that followed such moments of stress.

Later on, Harry Blaisdell would ask Jim, "What would you have done if they'd spotted you under the bed?"

Jim replied with his usual off-handed candor, "Well, I reckon I would've shot them. I had my .32 automatic right on 'em. Yeah, I think you would've had two dead troopers."

Some years later, asked for his opinion on Call's remark, Blaisdell was less convinced. "Two dead troopers? Well, I don't know. Remember, those troopers were not like the four Lake Placid policemen caught by surprise. I know those two men. They were seasoned troopers, crack shots. They knew what they were looking for, and the risks involved in entering those houses. Two dead troopers? From that position under the bed? I don't know—one, maybe. Not two."

◆ ◆ ◆

TYPICAL MANHUNT SCENE.—Picture shows a typical scene in the Adirondack as three state troopers search a wooded area for a gunman who wounded three Placid policemen—one of them fatally—Aug. 5. The arrest of a suspect in Reno, is the first big break in the longest police manhunt on the North American conti state police said in a surprise news conference yesterday. **(Stories on Page 1).**

November 16, 1954
(The Post-Standard)

43

Jim awakened to the sound of rain beating against the windowpane above his head. He lay motionless for several seconds, eyes evaluating his surroundings. A survivalist learned early the wisdom of remaining still upon awakening, never knowing what strange bedfellows his body warmth may have attracted during the night. But quickly realizing he was not in the woods, he sat up and swung his legs from the chaise on which he had been sleeping. He sat rubbing his eyes, reflecting on his brush with the troopers the previous evening. It had been another exceedingly close call and once again affirmed the necessity of leaving a house immediately upon completion of a burglary. At the moment, however, he felt secure in the knowledge that the premises, having already been checked by the troopers, were reasonably safe.

He glanced down at his forefinger and inspected the wound. It was healing quickly, allowing him to discard the bandage several days before. There was a momentary recollection of the biting ... the yells ... the struggle ... the crunching sound of the crowbar..., thoughts he dismissed quickly.

He looked across the room to a large Palladian window where the rain ran down the panes, attracted by the symmetry of the opening with its arched top and tall slender openings on the sides. With the diffusion of light through the crystals of water, the window shimmered like a jewel-encrusted mosaic. Extraordinary, he mused. What a wonderful subject for a mural. For a moment he savored the memory of his painting endeavor. A relative of Muriel's, an accomplished portrait artist, had looked at some of Jim's work and had been encouraging. But there had been relatively little chance to improve his technique. Before the shootout in the camp he'd done some sketches in the woods, even considered painting to pass the time. He might have done more if not for the clash with the policemen.

He stood and walked to a nearby window which looked out at what appeared to be a teahouse. The rain poured down the cone-shaped roof, spilling over the full drains. On one side, the roof joined a portico, forming a concave or chute-like surface, where the water cascaded down like a small waterfall.

For most people, it would have been a morning best spent in bed. But for a fugitive hounded by helicopters, roving patrols, and blood-hounds, it was a splendid day to travel. Patrols hunkered down under trees. Bloodhounds had nothing to sniff but themselves, and who knew better than Jim the futility and danger of putting aircraft aloft in zero visibility? After equipping himself with as much food, blankets and clothing (including foul weather gear) as he could carry without hampering his travel, he left the house and once more headed south through the forest.

Several days passed as he performed a rash of burglaries at remote camps to replenish dwindling supplies. In Long Lake he stole from the MacCormack and Parenteau properties, as well as from parked cars. From one car he took a wallet belonging to Patrick J. Evans of New York City, which would surface in a future crime. Having observed a trooper roadblock at Long Lake, "I decided I had to cross the lake by boat," Call said later. After burglarizing the Endian camp, he stole a canoe and paddled across the lake to Deerland.

Continuing south, he passed through Blue Mountain Lake, Indian Lake, Wells, and Speculator, finally arriving in Northville in early October. It had been a journey that would have tested the most expert survivalist. Days were shorter now, the air brisk with impending winter. Autumn colors, brilliant by day, faded into the invisible withering frost of night.

In Northville, he stole a 1950 Ford and drove to Gloversville. Asked later why he had not stolen a car sooner, he replied, "I did not want a car. The roads in the North Country were so clogged with troopers I wouldn't have had a chance."

Abandoning the car in Gloversville, he proceeded southeast across the Mohawk River at Indian Mounds, arriving at Sloansville around the middle of October. It was here that Fred and Irene Montayne, a couple who raised foxhounds for a living, themselves fell prey to a foxy predator of the forest.

◆ ◆ ◆

44

Irene Montayne was a conscientious housewife whose commitment to domestic matters was evident in her neat, orderly, well-stocked household in Sloansville. Few complaints were heard from her husband Fred, the beneficiary of his wife's workaday efforts. Meals were on time, disagreements relatively few, and for the most part life at the Montayne household in Sloansville was regular and uneventful; that is, until one day in the fall of 1954. Mrs. Montayne remembered it well:

Fred did a lot of hunting. He'd normally have quite a bunch of dogs along with him. He'd turn the dogs loose and they'd go yelpin' after a scent. If they found one they'd run it—bring the fox to bay. We had the dog pens at our house. They were way out back, chained to their coop. Well, one day I noticed a lot of food seemed missin' from my pantry. Same time my husband noticed that the meat supply for the dogs was goin' down. We couldn't figure out why. We had a big grove of pines way out back. The meat was in a big metal container sittin' under the trees to keep the feed cool. A little later, I began to notice that canned goods were missin' from the pantry—cans of tuna, maybe some salmon, pineapple … stuff like that, missin'. I was pretty well supplied and suddenly I wasn't.

So, you can see what was happening. The dogs, they'd bark. They'd make an awful lot of noise if a stranger approached. What happened was the robber saw my husband feedin' the animals a few times. He could easily see Fred go through the routine without ever bein' spotted. Then he just fed the dogs to keep 'em from barkin' so he could come in and steal. Really somethin'. Can you imagine anyone that bold?

Well, if that wasn't bad enough, one morning I came downstairs, started cookin' breakfast. Then, I happened to look out the window and the car, my 1950 Ford, was ... well, it was simply gone. I let out a yell an' Fred comes runnin' down the stairs and right away calls the troopers. Well, they finally found it. Abandoned in New York City. We had to go down to Harlem to pick it up. After we got it back, they found a camp back in the woods where someone had been stayin'.

"It was just a little camp in the woods," according to Harry Blaisdell. "Nothing like Call had in Lake Placid. Just a few evergreen branches piled up so he could crawl under and spend the night. Some blankets, clothing, odds and ends...."

Mrs. Montayne was skeptical when informed of the robber's modest inventory:

Well, I don't know 'bout that. We found he'd been robbin' other places nearby. The Carters, one of our neighbors, they lost two cameras and some other stuff. To top it all off, I get a summons from the New York City Police that I'd parked my car illegally and never paid the ticket, and they was gonna revoke my license.

♦ ♦ ♦

PART V

Manhattan, New York

October 1954

45

"I'll take Manhattan, the Bronx, and Staten Island...."
(Frank Sinatra's "Manhattan," by Lorenz Hart)

Jim, a Lucky Strike between his lips, sat at a bar in a small café near New York's Penn Station, listening to the strains of the song he had just selected from a jukebox. The lyrics seemed to fit with his plans. He had every intention of "taking Manhattan," or at least as much of it as he could carry away. It was just a question of where to start.

Occasionally he removed the cigarette to take a leisurely sip from a bottle of beer. An effort by the female bartender to strike up a conversation—"Been in here before?"—was met with a firm negative shake of the head, not designed to encourage discourse.

From his position at the end of the bar, he looked out through a plate glass window adorned with serpentine neon tubing that blared out the name of the establishment with inelegant blue lettering. Beyond the window was a tumultuous mass of people, cars, and trucks that constituted 8th Avenue. It was not aesthetically pleasing. Here, snarling vehicles competed with snarling pedestrians in a raging affray that gave no quarter. The cacophony of braying horns and revving engines had the one redeeming value of drowning out obscenities. People jostled other people, their brows collapsed into deep frowns as though they had just suffered a dreadful experience and were rushing to yet another. If there were any semblance of civility at all, it was with the panhandlers who sat on the sidewalk soliciting the passing horde.

Having arrived in the city a few days before, Jim had abandoned the Montayne car at 276 St. Nicholas Avenue in the Bronx. Here he had taken the subway to Penn Station and from there had gone to a nearby hotel for a bath and haircut. He had then proceeded to the

Camera Exchange shop near Radio City Music Hall and sold two cameras and an exposure meter, all stolen from the Carter residence in Sloansville. A trip to a men's store followed, where he purchased some stylish clothes, including a jacket, trousers, shirts, ties, and shoes. Rather than the wild killer of the Adirondacks portrayed in the press during recent months, it was a handsome, genteel Jim Call who lounged at the bar, smoking and sipping beer.

His thoughts at the moment were of Greta Brown. She had come to mind repeatedly during recent days. Recollections of her beauty and contagious laugh evoked a variety of feelings: passion, tenderness, hopelessness. Was she with her parents? Traveling? Another man? She had mentioned that she lived in New York City. He assumed she meant Manhattan. Perhaps he should call her. But she'd be difficult to locate. Lots of Browns in the Manhattan directory. Besides, she'd told him she was going to be in Placid with her parents during October to see the foliage. Just as well, he finally concluded. Now wasn't the time for diversions.

Although he'd been in the city only a few days, he already had begun to feel a faint but gnawing wanderlust. His ultimate destination was Reno, Nevada, where he was familiar with the casinos and where he believed his latest mathematical formula for beating the house would prove successful. Perhaps he could talk Greta into coming out for a few days. She'd expressed an interest in the casinos. A whimsical thought he quickly abandoned—impractical, too risky.

But to be successful in Reno, he needed more cash, lots of it. His plan, extraordinary for its temerity, was to travel to one of the more affluent areas of New York—probably Long Island—and once there, utilize his methodical system for robbing the homes of wealthy people. He would use the element of surprise, pulling jobs quickly before the local police had time to react. It had worked elsewhere, why not here?

Given his restless nature, it did not take him long to implement his plan. The following day he was on a train to Long Island. There followed a succession of burglaries that unnerved the normally blasé detectives of Suffolk and Nassau counties. The jobs followed the usual Jim Call mode: casing the property, a nocturnal entry through a window or basement door, a direct trip to the bedroom where valuables were usually available.

Detectives in such wealthy suburban areas were accustomed to an occasional outbreak of burglaries, but in this case it was the nature of the intruder that bothered them. Whoever was committing the crimes seemed unconcerned about awakening inhabitants. One such victim was Elbridge T. Gerry, a noted polo enthusiast, who resided in a luxurious estate in Old Westbury, Long Island. It was October 19, 1954....

———

The elegant two-and-one-half-story wood-frame dwelling was nestled behind a profusion of trees and shrubbery which represented the finest in landscape architecture. To the dark-haired figure standing in the shadows, the structure reeked with riches. It was well past midnight. A faint island breeze whispered in a grove of trees, respectful of distinguished neighbors sleeping in nearby mansions. The figure stood, leaning against a tree trunk, casually smoking a cigarette. He had been observing the house closely for well over an hour. Through the large windows he had watched as uniformed staff, after performing evening chores, moved on to the servants' quarters at one end of the house. A man who from his deportment appeared to be the head of the household had retired earlier to an upstairs bedroom. By midnight most of the lights, with the exception of one in the servants' wing, had been extinguished.

The figure continued to wait patiently, his eyes fixed on what he assumed to be the master bedroom. After abruptly dropping his cigarette and grinding it beneath his foot, he stepped from the shadows of the trees and approached a sun-porch on the west side of the house. Here he tried the door and was surprised to find it unlocked. Cautiously, he moved inside and quickly found the stairs leading to the bedrooms. Within seconds he had mounted the steps and was in the master bedroom.

The sound of steady breathing greeted him inside the door. With the aid of a pencil flashlight, he moved quickly about the room. Caught up in his quest for valuables, he displayed only moderate concern for stealth. On a dresser, he discovered an expensive blue morocco leather billfold with gold metal edges. Inside he found $350. Continuing his search, he noticed trousers hanging from a closet door. In one of the pockets he discovered a gold money clip holding $15.

Suddenly there were shifting sounds from the nearby bed, interrupted breathing. The intruder's hand slid into his pocket and closed on a .32-caliber Colt automatic pistol. Thoughts of another night a few months before flitted through his mind ... a person awakening ... the violence that followed.... He stood motionless, adrenaline rushing. But then, once again came the sound of heavy breathing. It was fortunate. Given the competitive nature of Elbridge Gerry, it is likely a confrontation would have taken place had he awakened. If so, it is probable the polo ponies in Old Westbury would have been minus one rider.

Now provided with invaluable identification and $365 richer, the robber left the premises. He stopped across the road just long enough to obtain transportation to his next job. Since he was in a classy neighborhood, why not a classy car? From the driveway of Elbridge Gerry's neighbor, he appropriated a sleek 1953 Buick Roadmaster. Old Westbury residents awakening the following morning to lament their losses would be unaware of how lucky they had been. It could have been far worse.

For Jim, the trip to the island had been rewarding. A few days later, loaded with treasures that included countless wallets containing identification and credit cards, he was on a bus to Chicago. Here, he called his old friend Robert Sylvester to see if they could meet. "He said he had a lot to tell," Robert recalled later. But Robert was extremely busy that day and they were unable to get together.

From Chicago, Jim went on to St. Louis, then to Cheyenne, Wyoming, finally arriving in Reno, Nevada, on or about October 26, 1954. It would be here in Reno—where he had envisioned his greatest conquests—that he would suffer his greatest defeat.

◆ ◆ ◆

46

SQUEAKY SHOES BURGLAR STRIKES AGAIN

The Reno daily newspaper, unbeknownst to its editorial staff, was heralding the arrival of Jim Call. To feed his gambling compulsion and, perhaps more importantly, his adrenaline high—to which he was now totally addicted—Jim was once again at work burglarizing luxurious houses. His disregard for his victims' sleep had earned him the name "the Squeaky Shoes Burglar." Mrs. George Thatcher of 7 Elm Court vividly recalled her experience with the burglar. "He woke me from a sound sleep. Why, when I sat up, he simply ignored me. Walked right over and started going through the bed stand next to me."

Another victim, Mrs. Gladys Mapes of 1501 Arlington Avenue, stated she was awakened at 1:33 a.m. by a small flashlight beam to find a man going through her purse. She said the man, who seemed young, slim, and "quite agile," fled from the scene taking her purse with him.

Other victims, including Mr. E. F. Loomis of 600 Island Avenue and Otto Linnecke of 585 Marsh Avenue, reported that the burglar seemed unconcerned by their presence. Mr. Linnecke stated that he was awakened when he heard the floor creaking, and looked up to find a man in his bedroom. He said when the intruder left the room, he followed him to the back door where the burglar turned and smiled at him boldly. Mr. Linnecke said that the thief then picked up some books and "walked out the driveway over the grass in an unknown direction." The victim returned to the bedroom to find that his wallet with ID cards and $135 had been stolen. All of the burglaries were committed within a few days of each other. (Jim would later readily confess to the crimes after the victims' personal property was found in his possession.)

Understandably, the fathers of the city were upset by the brazen raids on the citizenry. No one was more sensitive to the problem than

Detective Sergeant William Gregory, a veteran of the Reno Police Department's burglary detail. His squad had meticulously recorded property stolen from the residences and circulated lists to all city pawnshops. When a call came through on November 9, 1954, from the Reno Bonded Loan and Jewelry Company reporting someone trying to pawn a $500 wrist watch, Gregory was quickly on his feet. "Stall him. We're on our way."

Within minutes, detectives were approaching a handsome, well-dressed young man standing inside the pawnshop. Gregory would later say, "The man was very relaxed, almost as though he'd expected us."

"Gregory, Reno Police Department," the detective said, displaying his credentials. "This is Detective Waller. We'd like to see some—"

"It figures," interrupted the man with a shrug. "The watch, right? I found it back there on the street. I didn't know what to do with it so I saw this pawnshop and decided to turn it into cash."

"What's your name?"

"Morgan."

"Full name," Gregory demanded, taking a notebook and pencil from a breast pocket. "Full name and address."

"James Morgan," Jim said without batting an eye. "1066 Christopher Lane, Lakewood, Ohio."

"What are you doing here in Reno?"

"I'm on vacation," Jim replied calmly. "Doing the casinos. Am I gonna be in trouble over this?"

The detective studied his charge for a moment without answering. Because of the man's appearance and ingenuousness, Gregory was inclined to believe he was telling the truth. But when he asked the man where he was staying, he sensed something that might have gone unnoticed by someone with less experience—a certain flinty look, a hardness in the eyes that didn't seem to go with the rest of the man's air of bland naiveté. He returned his pencil and notebook to a breast pocket, leaving his right hand on his lapel where it was closer to his shoulder holster.

"The El Cortez Hotel," replied the man. "I hope I'm not going to get in trouble. The watch was just lying back there in the street— actually the sidewalk. I didn't know what else to do with it."

It sounded convincing, particularly when delivered with wide eyes professing innocence. Perhaps he had overreacted, thought Gregory.

"Well, you'll have to come to the station. You got stolen property here. We'll have to check you out, check the hotel."

If the eyes had professed innocence before, this was no longer the case. They were now evaluating options. Fortunately for the detectives, Jim Call's .32 automatic was in his bag back at the hotel. He would later say that if he had his pistol, at that point he would have shot both officers.

At the police station Jim's fortunes took a further turn for the worse. The police retrieved his bag from the hotel. It contained his Air Force identity card bearing his fingerprints, numerous wallets from his East Coast burglary spree, including that of Elbridge T. Gerry, as well as loot from his recent robberies in Reno. In addition, there was the matter of the fully loaded automatic in his bag. But the most damning of all the items was an Associated Press clipping detailing the killing of the Lake Placid police officer. Jim immediately developed amnesia.

As they were booking Jim, William A. Gold, a cub reporter from Reno's *Evening Gazette* who frequented the station house looking for stories, noticed the handsome well-dressed man. When Jim's personal possessions were placed on the desk the reporter asked if he could have a look at the newspaper clipping. The duty sergeant acquiesced, and the reporter made notes from the clipping and went to a nearby Western Union office. He dispatched a telegram to Lake Placid authorities advising them of the arrest of a man suspected of burglaries who had the AP clipping in his possession.

Muller and Blaisdell, who were in New York City checking on the car stolen in Sloansville, responded promptly. A call was made to the Reno authorities asking them to forward the suspect's fingerprints. Within a short period the Reno police responded, not only with fingerprints, but with a report stating the suspect had been identified by the FBI from his fingerprints as James Arlon Call, an Air Force major who was AWOL. Fingerprint experts with the New York State Police compared the prints with the latent prints lifted from the Perkins camp and quickly identified seven of Call's ten fingers. Muller and Blaisdell were on the next plane to Reno. They had their man.

◆ ◆ ◆

Call mugshots, Reno Police Department—November 1954

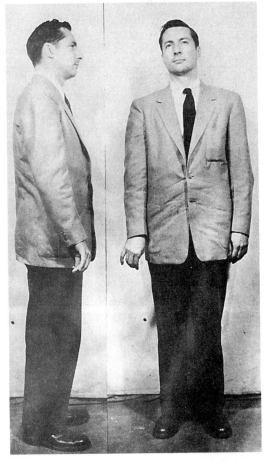

47

RENO'S "SQUEAKY" BURGLAR
CHARGED WITH NY MURDER

The headline appeared in the *Nevada State Journal*, a Reno daily newspaper, on Tuesday, November 16, 1954. The story related how James Arlon Call was apprehended by the Reno Police Department while attempting to sell a $500 watch stolen during one of the area's recent estate burglaries. It said that New York State Police had identified Call through his fingerprints as the man suspected of killing a Lake Placid police officer, and were on their way to Reno with an indictment charging him with the murder. Although it was a dramatic announcement, it was nothing compared to the bombshell that followed. The *Journal* went on to state:

> As if Call's definite linkage with the New York murder were not enough, last night there were persistent reports that he would be questioned as the "bushy-haired burglar" who Dr. Samuel Sheppard is claiming at his trial in Cleveland, Ohio, killed his pretty wife Marilyn. When Call was booked as James Chandler Morgan he gave his home address as Lakewood, Ohio. Lakewood is near Bay Village where Mrs. Sheppard was killed in the bedroom of her lakefront home.
>
> Call told police he came to Reno October 27 [1954] by bus and made his residence at the El Cortez, a fashionable downtown hotel. He said the air force [sic] identity card and stolen wallets which crammed his suitcase were given to him by a man in St. Louis. He said he can't remember anything he might have done "east of St. Louis," alleging that he is subject to "lapses of memory."

The recipient of the explosion of media attention sat in his cell at the Reno police station, calm as always, considering his options. They were few. He had been undergoing relentless questioning by the Reno detectives about the Sheppard homicide. It was of far more interest to them than the residential crimes. Had he committed burglaries in Bay Village? What was the significance of his Lakewood identification? Had he committed a Lakewood burglary? What did he know about the Sheppard murder? His answer to all questions was the same. "I don't know what you're talking about."

But Jim Call knew precisely what they were talking about. How could he ever forget that horrific mid-summer night in Bay Village four months previously? He was there.

♦ ♦ ♦

PART VI

Four Months Previously

Bay Village, Ohio

July 1954

The Sheppard family: Marilyn, Chip and Sam—circa 1949
(Sheppard family archives)

The Sheppard residence
28924 West Lake Road
Bay Village, Ohio—circa 1954

Marilyn and Sam Sheppard waterskiing
(Cleveland Public Library)

48

It was an attractive white Dutch colonial house at 28924 West Lake Road in the small suburb of Cleveland called Bay Village. At the front of the house was a large lawn where old elm and maple trees shielded the residence from a moderately traveled thoroughfare. The rear of the house looked down from a steep bluff covered with tall grass and heavy brush to a bathhouse and narrow beach on Lake Erie.

By day, it was a warm, cheerful house where laughter mixed with the sounds of children playing, a dog barking. Occasionally a screen door slammed following the exit of an exuberant seven-year-old, running to join friends beneath a basketball hoop over the garage. They were the domestic sounds of happy family life. By night, however, the residence assumed a different character. Often, the sounds were of rattling wind and pounding surf from the darkness beyond the bluff. Nights here could induce strange feelings in the timid.

The elements were not the only disquieting aspect of the residence. For one knowledgeable about crimes involving breaking and entering, the house was vulnerable, easily "cased" by would-be intruders. Just beyond a neighboring house to the east was a wooded stretch bordering Huntington Park, a popular recreation area open to the public. Here, concealed by trees, one could easily observe the dwelling and its residents with little risk of exposure. To the west were two houses and then a small cemetery—another haven for someone with ulterior motives. The lake at the rear provided freedom from observation, while the pounding surf drowned out noise. The road, of course, offered means of immediate flight. In short, it was a residence accessible to the public, readily observable from the road, and offering sanctuaries on each side. One might say number 28924 West Lake Road was, in fact, a residence awaiting a predator.

On July 3, 1954, the wait was over. A comely young woman stood at a rear bedroom window of the house, looking out at the broad expanse of water. In the black sky, a pale lunar disk sailed amid scattered clouds auguring pleasant, if windy, weather for the following day. And tomorrow's weather was important to Marilyn Sheppard, a pretty auburn-haired women of thirty-one with a winsome smile and attractive figure—"that California look," observed one admirer. For tomorrow was Marilyn's Fourth of July cookout. Marilyn's husband Sam, a handsome thirty-year-old surgeon who practiced with his father and two brothers at the nearby family-controlled Bay View Hospital, had invited several couples, mostly interns and resident physicians, for a hot dog roast.

Anticipating a busy schedule, Marilyn was anxious to retire. Don and Nancy Ahern, a couple who lived five houses to the west, had departed a few minutes earlier after a dinner of cottage ham, potatoes, string beans, tossed salad, and applesauce, followed by a blueberry pie that Marilyn had baked that afternoon—her husband's favorite dessert. Sam had fallen asleep earlier on a daybed downstairs. This was not unusual given his stressful and uncertain working hours. Just a few hours previously he had tried unsuccessfully to save a young boy's life during an operation following an auto accident.

As she stood in the window in her pajamas looking out at the battering surf, Marilyn was in good spirits. Four months pregnant, her healthy seven-year-old son Chip in the next bedroom, a successful husband sleeping downstairs—her life was full of promise.

And for the solitary bushy-haired form in the white shirt and dark trousers who stood smoking a cigarette in the darkness, looking up at her from the beach below, so too, things seemed promising....

♦ 1:00 AM* ♦

It was early morning on July 4, 1954, and the inhabitants of the Dutch colonial on Lake Road were asleep. Sounds were those of restful breathing. Dr. Sheppard lay on the daybed just inside the living room door at the foot of the stairs. Chip, his son, was upstairs in his room, lost in the deep sleep of a seven-year-old. Kokie, their dog of

*the times listed as headings in this section are approximate.

pointer-setter origin, was elsewhere in the house, presumably also sleeping. Never a watchdog, she would not be heard from on this terrifying night.

According to the Aherns, who had left shortly before midnight, "Marilyn could hardly keep her eyes open." She now lay upstairs in her bed sleeping soundly, brown curls and pretty girlish face resting on a pillow, the surface of which would soon be imprinted with horrifying scarlet images. It was a peaceful, unstirring house.

Not so outside on the bluff. According to Fred Drenkhan, a personable Bay Village police officer who was patrolling West Lake Road, the wind was blowing hard that night. John Tronti, a fisherman who was at Huntington Beach around midnight, said the lake was extremely rough. "It was so bad you couldn't fish. The wind was coming in from the northwest and the waves must have been coming up thirty to forty feet on the beach. That's how bad it was."

The festive crowd that had gathered at nearby Huntington Park earlier to watch a fireworks display had departed, leaving a few stragglers unwilling to relinquish the pleasures of the day. With darkness, a more somber mood had settled over the Sheppard property. Gone were the laughter and exuberance that had drifted from the park. The light breeze which sang in nearby trees during the day had been replaced with a cheerless wind that moaned beyond the bluff. The small, thin moon cast a grayish light, providing just enough illumination to highlight brighter tones in the darkness: foaming whitecaps, the silver spray of waves breaking on the beach, and the sheen of an occasional car creeping along Lake Road, headlights winking through the trees. Also, though briefly, the lunar glow caught the outline of a white shirt moving among the shadows on the ridge.

The wearer of the shirt preferred the darkness. Bright moons were inimical to his nightly forays. And he needed little light to see his way. He had meticulously scouted his target a few hours previously. Earlier in the evening, unnoticed among the crowd at Huntington Park, he had observed the comings and goings at 28924 West Lake Road. He'd watched, calmly smoking a cigarette, as the attractive young woman had stood alone at the door bidding goodnight to her guests. Picking up a suitcase, he had then moved to the rear of the house. Lurking in the shadows of trees, he had watched the upstairs bedrooms. Because of Marilyn's practice of leaving the shades only partially drawn, teen-aged voyeurs had been known to assemble here to see her prepare for bed. It is probable that a person casing the residence on this night would have done the same. If so, he would have seen no sign of Sam Sheppard, still asleep on the daybed downstairs. With the rest of the house in darkness, an observer might well have concluded that the attractive young woman was alone.

Now, as he stood watching from the bluff, the figure wondered about a dim light that had remained on upstairs after the bedroom light had been extinguished. A nightlight he reasoned. Suddenly, from beyond the bluff, came the sound of voices. He moved back into the shadows as a couple on the beach below the bluff strolled by hand-in-hand. He watched as they continued walking, finally sitting down some distance away. No problem, he thought. They were quite far off and from their amorous behavior he reasoned that their interest lay very much with each other. He glanced toward Huntington Park. Frugally placed light poles cast dim images over the deserted parking lot. At the far end a few cars remained facing the bluff—still gray shapes in the shadows.

He withdrew a Lucky Strike cigarette from his pocket, lighting it with a wooden match, one of several wrapped in aluminum foil. Relaxing, he took a long drag from the cigarette, his eyes surveying the beach. He would have to wait awhile. It was still early for his type of work. With his left hand he smoothed back his straight black hair which had become disheveled in the wind. Hair tonic he had applied earlier was ineffective in the strong breeze and his hair now stood up stiffly like a long brush cut.

Bending over, he picked up his suitcase, an Air Force B-4 bag, 24" x 18" x 4", made of duck with external pockets on each side. It was ideal luggage for one engaged in his type of endeavor; relatively small, but easily expanded to accommodate whatever booty might be available. After concealing the bag in nearby bushes, he straightened and glanced up once again at the bedroom window, his excitement building. From the surf came long rumbling sounds as Lake Erie surged forward in its timeless assault on the beach. The figure looked out over the bluff at the black water. For an instant there was the feeling of ascending in a plane, the thrill of impending danger. But it was still too early. After a final drag, he dropped the cigarette and turned, making his way toward the lights in Huntington Park. He would be back.

♦ 2:00 AM ♦

"Pretty windy out there." Donald Tripp, an amiable young man in his twenties, peered through the windshield of his 1948 Dodge sedan, a concerned look on his face.

Alfred Adams, who was sitting next to him in the passenger seat, did not reply immediately. Although not a taciturn man, Alfred was not disposed to idle conversation. He glanced through the side window at the passing trees swaying in the wind in Huntington Park, and allowed as to how it might be a little rough out on the lake. "Should calm down by the time we get the boat out, though."

The two men, Akron, Ohio, residents, had traveled to Cleveland to watch a baseball game earlier in the evening, and after a few beers at a local bar were now en route to Sheffield Lake west of Cleveland to do some fishing. They intended to reach their destination in time to catch a few hours' sleep in the car before renting a boat at 5:00 a.m.

Alfred, some ten years older than Donald, was the acknowledged leader of their trip. Having seen action as a captain and tank commander in Italy during World War II, he was described by associates as "an observant person who remembered everything; a no-nonsense guy, confident of his views and not inclined to much bullshit." To his younger companion Don, these were admirable traits that provided strong direction when needed.

For this reason, Don was quick to react when his friend pointed out a narrow bridge taking shape in the darkness beyond the windshield. "Better slow down. There's a guy standing there on the bridge."

The object of Al's attention was a figure leaning against a concrete partition which acted as a guardrail. Lights mounted on the corners of the bridge provided a good view of the person, who was thirty-ish, of medium height, wearing a white shirt. The two in the car were struck by the man's hair, which was dark, bushy, and standing up in the wind. Both men were immediately suspicious.

"What the hell's that fellow doin' out there this time of the morning?" said Al, perplexed. "In this weather? No jacket?"

Don echoed his friend's sentiments as they passed the figure, adding, "Doesn't look like he has a car broken down or anything. Wonder what he's up to?"

"Kind of odd," continued the former tank commander, skeptically. "That guy should be home screwin' his wife."

They grew silent as their car regained speed. Unnoticed, a stone's throw past the bridge, was the quiet Dutch colonial, where upstairs a soft light glimmered.

◆ 2:15 AM ◆

It was but a short distance from the bridge to the small lair he had created earlier in the thicket behind the Sheppard house. The dark-haired figure slipped from the trees bordering the west side of Huntington Park and stealthily approached the bushes where he had concealed his suitcase. From the bluff he scanned the shore below. In the distance, now lying down, was the couple he thought he had seen earlier.

Locating his bag, he unzipped one of the side pouches and, in the manner of one who performed the chore routinely, removed a black holster containing a Luger, which he strapped to his belt. Next, he took out a twelve-inch crowbar, a red and white tool also called a prybar. Finally, he withdrew a small flashlight and a pair of thin, high-quality leather gloves. Air Force B-3 gloves, they were standard issue for all flying personnel. After stuffing the items in his pockets, he zipped up the bag and concealed it in the nearby bushes. Slowly he approached the house, soft loafers moving silently through the grass. From nearby came a rustling sound, a small creature, perhaps scurrying from a nocturnal enemy. Nearing the house he observed the structure carefully, evaluating points of entry. A formation of bristling shrubs stood guard near the base of the dwelling, while overhead long winding vines clung protectively to its sides.

It was darker now. A timid moon had withdrawn behind a barricade of clouds, from where it peeked out uncertainly. A few last firecrackers popped in the distance, remnants of a festive day. The figure paused, adjusting the Luger on his belt, then looked up toward the bedroom window. It was time.

◆ 2:25 AM ◆

Somewhere west of Bay Village on their way to Sheffield Lake, Donald Tripp and Alfred Adams may well have passed three other fishermen coming from the opposite direction on West Lake Road. If so, the occupants of the two vehicles would have more in common than their fishing interests on this ill-starred night, for those in the other car were about to have a similar look at a suspicious figure near the Sheppard residence.

Leo Stawicki, a steelworker who lived in Cuyahoga Heights southeast of Cleveland, was driving home from a Port Clinton fishing expedition with his two brothers, Charles and Joseph. They were proceeding carefully, towing a boat on a trailer behind their car, when they passed the Sheppard house and noticed a "bushy-haired man" wearing a white shirt (either T-shirt, polo shirt, or sweat shirt) and dark trousers standing in the driveway. Their view of the man was enhanced by a street light directly in front of the Sheppard property.

"I thought he was a hitchhiker," Charles would later say. "But Leo pointed out he was too far back from the road, standing under the trees. He just stared at us."

Leo Stawicki would report the incident to the Bay Village Police Department and later testified in court about what he had seen:

> It was sometime between two-fifteen and two-thirty in the morning. When I ride I take a pretty good look. I have my windows down and my bright lights on. When I first seen him, I seen him about a hundred feet ahead of me. I was looking right at him. He looked kind of suspicious to me. That's what kind of got me. I mentioned it to one of my brothers. I passed him on the side of the road, 12 or 15 feet from my car. I had the road to myself. I couldn't forget the place on account of the trees there. I know trees. I worked in a lumber camp. There were some hemlocks and some soft maples. I drove along at about 30 or 35 miles an hour. He was about 6 feet tall and his hair was standing up. He had kind of a long face with bushy hair. That's what made his face look long, with that hair just standing right up on his head.

Others would come forth to report a sinister person near the Sheppard residence that infamous night. All would furnish similar descriptions, particularly regarding the figure's hair: "Bushy, standing up." Prophetic, perhaps, considering the hair-raising events about to unfold.

VIEW LOOKING WEST FROM 300 FEET ABOVE FIRST FLOOR

Aerial view of Sheppard residence, looking west

Sheppard residence with stairs to beachhouse

♦ 2:30 AM ♦

There was no question they had seen him. They'd looked right at him. Three figures in a car. He had just come around the garage to the front of the house by the trees when they had driven by slowly, towing a boat. They'd been suspicious of him. It was obvious from their manner and the way they had stared. They'd had a good look at him, too. He watched discreetly as they drove on, waiting to see if the brake lights brightened, signaling they were stopping. It was his second encounter with a car on the road. The contacts had heightened the excitement of the venture.

After the car disappeared, he continued around to the rear of the house, where he saw a bulkhead angling against the side of the building. He had noticed it earlier and assumed it was an entrance to the basement. Located in a recessed area east of a screened-in porch, it offered a way into the house not visible from the road or from neighboring houses. As he studied the situation he withdrew a Lucky Strike and casually lit up. From the relaxed way he stood contemplating his entrance to the house, one might have thought he was surveying some yard job rather than a break-in. If there were a difference, it was in the way he discreetly concealed the burning end of the cigarette in the palm of his hand. After a few long drags he flicked it away.

Bending over, he slowly lifted the hatch and after a brief inspection proceeded down six steps to a cellar door. Carefully, he turned the knob and entered. Once inside the cellar, he withdrew a pencil-like flashlight from a pocket and surveyed the room. After assuring himself there were no windows through which light could be seen from outside, he turned on a ceiling light. He noticed a small wooden door on an adjacent wall and tried to open it. It was locked. But the lock would prove to be only a momentary obstacle. From his pocket he withdrew the crowbar. Drop-forged from high-grade hexagon tool steel, it was a lethal-looking instrument—a viperous gray with glossy red and white paint. One end, bearing chipped red lacquer, curled into two large crescent-shaped prongs. Fang-like in appearance, they would leave deadly marks that night. For the moment, however, the other end of the bar, the straight-bladed side, was more appropriate for the job. Slipping the edge between the door and the wooden frame, he easily pried the door open. It led to a crawl space which proved of little interest.

Nearby wooden steps led up to the main floor. Slowly he climbed the stairs. At the top, a door opened into a medium-sized kitchen. He stood for a moment listening. On the other side of the room he saw three steps to a landing from which stairs rose to the second floor. He moved across the kitchen, pausing before the landing to consider his options. Like most burglars, his focus was on the bedrooms, where the greatest rewards were usually found.

He looked up the stairs to where a small 50-watt bulb in a dressing room off the second-floor hall provided soft lighting. Holding the flashlight, he inched his way up the steps, favoring his injured knee, remaining close to the wall where the stairs were less likely to squeak. Adrenaline was flowing now. He was in his element. Nothing provided the thrill of a burglary. The stakeout, entry, risk, promise of reward—it was the consummate high.

At the top of the stairs he paused, listening to the soulful moaning of the wind and the rushing surf beyond the bluff. He would have no difficulty locating the mistress of the household. She slept less than eight feet away, in the bedroom off the hall just to the left of the stairs. He looked around the hallway. Another bedroom farther to his left. He glanced inside. It was unoccupied. Then, to his right, a bath, a dressing room, light on.

He entered the woman's bedroom, senses sharply honed. The sound of breathing, steady, regular. Like all second-story men, he knew sounds. Nothing was more reassuring than rhythmic breathing. He pocketed the flashlight. The glow from the light in the adjoining dressing room was sufficient for his purposes. He observed the woman in bed, her face turned toward him. Even in the soft light it was evident she was attractive.

Quickly, he surveyed the room. It was relatively small, with two windows on the north wall overlooking the lake. The windows were slightly open with shades pulled down three-quarters of the way. On the south wall opposite the windows were twin beds, the woman occupying the one on the east side near the door. He noticed the covers on the other bed had been turned down. It did not register with him as significant. A telephone rested on a nightstand between the two beds—no sign of money or jewels. On the wall to his right— the east side—were closets and in the corner near a window a rocking chair with what appeared to be a woman's shorts and undergarments.

A pair of shoes lay nearby. His attention was caught by a dresser on the opposite wall, the west side. As he moved across the carpeted room the woman's breathing was interrupted. She stirred, turning in bed. He froze, at the same time realizing he was probably silhouetted against the window.

"Sam?" she said, her voice heavy with sleep.

He waited, then believing she had dozed, moved again toward the dresser.

"Sam?" This time there was concern in the voice, that of a person awakening to strange events.

After glancing at the top of the dresser and seeing nothing of value, he turned, drew his Luger, and moved toward the door. Had the women remained quiet, the encounter would have ended without violence, as it had with so many of his other nightly forays. But it was not to be.

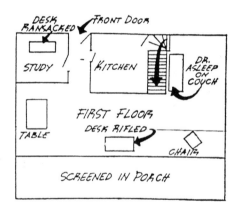

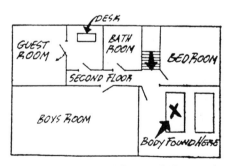

Sketches of first and second floors of Sheppard residence
(*The Plain Dealer*)

♦ 3:00 AM ♦

Sam Sheppard lay motionless on a daybed in his living room, lost in an impenetrable sleep. It had been an exhausting day. Earlier, at the Bay View Hospital, he had been confronted with the life and death trauma of a young boy. Dr. Sam, as he was affectionately called to differentiate him from his father and two brothers who also practiced at the hospital, had completed his rounds with his patients. He was preparing to leave for home when a frantic father appeared in the emergency room carrying his son, who had just been involved in an accident. Sheppard had rushed the boy to the operating room and struggled to save the dying child. But his efforts had been to no avail. Having a son of similar age, Dr. Sam was well aware of the emotional toll on the father when he had to tell him his child had died.

Despondent, Sheppard returned home. Dr. Lester Hoversten, a visiting friend of Sam's, had left for Kent, Ohio, several hours before. A social evening had been planned—cocktails at the neighboring Aherns, followed by dinner at the Sheppards. No sooner had he and Marilyn arrived at the Aherns when another emergency recalled him to the hospital; this time, a child with a broken leg sustained in an auto accident. After attending to the patient, he had climbed back into his car and returned to the Aherns. There followed some playfulness with his son Chip and the Ahern children, and finally dinner at the Sheppards. After dinner, the four adults had settled in the living room to watch a TV movie, *Strange Holiday*. Dr. Sam did not make it through the movie. Exhausted both physically and mentally, he had collapsed on the daybed in the living room and fallen into a profound sleep. He had been unaware of the Aherns departure around midnight.

Now, approximately three hours later, as he slept on the daybed, vague distant sounds jarred him back to consciousness. Sam! ... Sam! They persisted, an unremitting call. Struggling from sleep, he sat up. It was Marilyn, he thought. She must be having convulsions, as she had during her first pregnancy. Struggling to his feet, he started for the nearby stairs, his mind grasping for remedies he would need for his wife. The cries from upstairs were louder now. Still trying to clear his head, he mounted the stairs.

Sheppard daybed

♦ 3:10 AM ♦

Upstairs in bed, Marilyn Sheppard was experiencing life's final moments—a terrifying nightmare from which there would be no awakening. Only minutes before, she had been partially aroused by a vague disturbance. A slight noise? Sam retiring? The baby in her womb? Given her condition, she awakened often. Whatever the cause, it had passed and she was again dozing, perhaps lost in a reverie of whimsical thoughts: her son ... baby ... husband ... the impending cookout for the hospital staff.... But then, once again, there was a distraction of some kind. This time, her long lashes had fluttered open, revealing a dark form. It moved slowly across the room. Her husband, she reasoned, finally coming to bed.

"Sam," she murmured, closing her eyes.

She waited for the familiar sound of him slipping beneath the bedcovers she had turned down earlier. Hearing nothing, she glanced curiously toward the form now hovering over the dresser. Groggy with sleep, she tried to focus on the figure. What in the world was he doing?

212

"Sam?" Silence. "Sam!" This time louder.

When there was no reply, an uneasiness took root and began to grow as sleep gave way to awareness.

"Sam!"

The form turned slowly in her direction. Then, the shocking realization. It was not her husband. Menacing eyes ... wild dark hair ... a gun. The figure moved toward her....

Now, wide awake, she sat straight up, calling loudly for her husband. "Sam! Sam!"

It was a fatal mistake.

♦ 3:15 AM ♦

Her eyes—wide, terrified, uncomprehending. She was sitting up in bed now, calling for someone. He raised his Luger, the muzzle pointed at her face, his finger on the trigger. A slight squeeze and the 9 mm cartridge would explode in the chamber. But he chose not to shoot. The shot could alert neighbors, or someone in the house. She'd cried out as though calling for someone nearby. He had to quiet her quickly ... cover her face ... a pillow....

Reaching over a crossbar at the foot of the bed, he grasped her left leg and yanked her from her sitting position toward him. The movement pulled up her pajama top, exposing her breasts. Athletic and strong, the woman proved capable of resistance—more than he'd expected. As she thrashed about, he pinned her legs beneath the bed rail, her left pajama leg coming off in the process. Holding his Luger, he moved quickly to the east side of her bed and thrust his free hand over her mouth in an effort to stifle her cries. In desperation, she clamped her teeth on his left forefinger, biting him to the bone. It would be her final mistake.

Reflexively, he yanked his gloved finger from her mouth, pulling with it chips from her front teeth as well as a porcelain restoration from a right lateral incisor. Now, maddened with pain and believing she had bitten off the end of his finger, he struck her twice on the forehead with the Luger. The blows were not enough to subdue the hysterical woman. Pinning her against the bed with the hand holding the Luger, he used his left hand to withdraw the crowbar from his belt and to strike her with it repeatedly. Because of the relative lightness of the weapon and the fact that he was using his wounded left hand, none of the blows penetrated the skull, but instead inflicted long crescent-shaped wounds. When she continued to struggle, he dropped the Luger on the bed, transferred the crowbar to his right hand, and pummeled her into unconsciousness.

Suddenly, there were sounds of footsteps mounting the stairs. He stood quickly and pressed against the wall near the door. When a tall form appeared in the doorway, he delivered a crushing blow with the crowbar to the back of the neck. The figure crumpled to the floor.

Breathing heavily, he stood for a moment surveying the mayhem. From the bed he retrieved his Luger where it lay in a pool of blood beneath a pillow. Then, withdrawing a cigarette from his breast pocket, he lit it with a match from a wrapping of aluminum foil. Hindered by his wounded finger, he inadvertently dropped a piece of the foil to the floor. Inhaling deeply, he looked at his victims, one on the bed, the other nearby on the floor. Both appeared dead. The realization of what he had done slowly took hold. He was shaken by the violence, particularly the attack on the woman. But there'd been no alternative. They had stood in his way.

It was quiet in the house. But from outside on the bluff came the relentless moaning of the wind and the pounding of the surf. They were disturbing sounds that could not be blocked out. Particularly the repeated roar and withdrawal of the surf—crescendos of rushing water, followed by silence, sounding like a succession of rumbling jet planes taking off one by one.

Inhaling deeply, he turned and walked to the bathroom close by, where he removed his glove and examined his injured finger. It was a deep wound but his finger was intact. He noticed that a small piece of the leather glove had been torn off. Although the injury was severe the pain was less than before, his finger having numbed.

He looked at his reflection in the mirror, hardly recognizing the image. The horror of the preceding events was all too evident. His face, arms, torso, even his shoes, were covered with blood. He drew heavily on his cigarette, flipped it into the commode, and returned to the bedroom.

The scene was ghastly. Blood had spattered everywhere. The woman lay in a deep crimson pool. In spite of what he'd been through, he had nothing to show for it. Taking a deep breath, he set about trying to salvage what he could from a burglary that had gone terribly wrong. Quickly, he yanked the watch from the woman's wrist. He tried unsuccessfully to take off her rings, pulling them to the knuckles. Turning to the man, he yanked off his wrist watch and removed a wallet from his pocket. There was little inside other than small bills. He noticed a key chain attached to the man's pants and ripped it off, tearing the trousers. Standing, he gave a final look at the scene. It was a dramatic change from the orderly room he had entered moments before. Turning abruptly, he went out the door. As he descended the stairs, blood continued to flow from his finger, dropping onto the left side of the steps, some possibly thrown back to the vertical part of the risers from the backswing of his hand during the descent.

Once downstairs he quickly surveyed the premises. He rifled through a desk finding trivia of little value, including a green bag containing boating tools. Dumping the tools, he placed the man's watch, a fraternity ring, key chain, and sundry small items in the bag. On a shelf in the kitchen next to a breadbox, he found a woman's wallet containing a few dollars. Moving quickly down a hallway, he entered a small room which appeared to be a den or study. He noticed a rack containing several pipes, from which he selected an expensive meerschaum. There appeared to be little else of value.

The futility of his venture began to take hold. He'd undergone considerable risk, probably killed two people, and had nothing whatever to show for it. His finger was now throbbing painfully. Observing some sports trophies against a wall, in an outburst of anger he knocked them from their mountings. It was near the doorway leading from the den on his way back to the kitchen that he saw the doctor's bag. Expectations growing, he emptied its contents onto the floor and found a bottle of Demerol. Then, with even greater satisfaction, he discovered a box of ampins (emergency morphine ampules with needles which can be broken and injected rapidly for emergency medication—a standard issue on Air Force planes.) He was about to administer one of the ampins when he was alarmed to hear footsteps upstairs in the hall. The man must have survived. Surprising—he had thought it a lethal blow. It was time to leave.

Shoving the ampins and Demerol into his pocket, he took the green bag in which he had put the valuables and moved quickly toward the screened-in porch overlooking the beach. He heard footsteps descending the stairs, and feeling his pursuer close behind, raced from the house toward the bluff. Once outside, he headed for a line of shrubs next to wooden stairs which led to the beach. Here in tall grass, he threw away the green bag containing the valuables that could link him to the house—a common practice of burglars in danger of apprehension.

Somewhat hampered by his injured knee, he made his way down the slope of the bluff to the beach. He thought he had eluded his pursuer but suddenly, a figure rushed down the steps, tackling him at the water's edge. A struggle ensued and for an instant he considered shooting the man but hesitated, quickly realizing that the person, perhaps weakened from the previous blow to his neck in the bedroom, had little strength. Certainly he was no match for a combat-trained veteran. With a deft survival tactic often practiced in the military, he grabbed the man by the head, wrenching it sharply. He heard a cracking sound and sensed immediately that his opponent was disabled. Releasing his head, he let him slide to the ground.

Breathing heavily, shaken by his pursuer's attack, he glanced to the east toward Huntington Park where he had concealed his B-4 bag. Several people—perhaps fishermen—were on the pier jutting out from the park in the distance. Afraid of being seen, he decided to head west down the beach in the opposite direction. He could always double back to retrieve his bag—he'd be less suspicious up on the road and there would be less reason to connect him with the house.

Hastily he removed his bloodstained shirt, stuffing it under his belt and replacing it with the white T-shirt from his adversary. He had started down the beach when in the distance he saw what appeared to be the couple he had observed earlier, lying on a blanket. Unwilling to pass them, he climbed the bluff to the small cemetery located three lots west of the Sheppard house. Here he rested for a moment.

Though he was outwardly cool, his mind was scrambling. Flight dominated his thoughts: No lights in adjoining houses, a good sign … lucky not to have fired his pistol … risky going back for his bag. But he had little choice. There was enough in the bag to identify him. As he regained his composure he attempted to formulate a plan. He'd return to the park, doubling back through the trees to recover his bag.

Then he'd grab a bus, pick up his gear from his quarters in Mantua, and head east for some remote place. If only she hadn't bitten him.... God, he needed a cigarette.

After brushing sand from his trousers, he tried to smooth back his hair, which was now standing straight up in the wind. Looking cautiously in both directions, he stepped out onto Lake Road. He had walked only a few yards when a car drove by slowly. The couple inside looked at him suspiciously and he thought at first that they might stop. But the man appeared to make a comment to the woman and they drove on. Immediately, he thought of his two previous encounters with people in cars on the road. Had the robbery gone as planned they would have been of little consequence. Now, there were three sets of witnesses.

Crossing Lake Road he walked quickly back toward Huntington Park. As he passed the scene of his crime he scrutinized the premises. The house was quiet ... no sign of life.

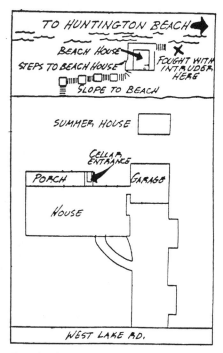

Sketch of exterior of Sheppard residence
(*The Plain Dealer*)

◆ 3:45 AM ◆

"Did you see that?"

"See what?"

"Down there." Jack Rogers* pointed in an easterly direction toward Huntington Park, from where he and his female companion had come earlier. "Some guy ran up the bluff toward the cemetery."

"So?" The young woman glanced up at her lover. "What do you care?"

"I don't know. Seems unusual, that guy running up toward the road ... this time of night. Maybe he wanted to avoid us."

Jack returned his attention to the woman, but his thoughts lingered on what he had seen. He had reason to be nervous. A married man with children, it would be shattering for him to be caught in a tryst on the beach.

"Relax," said his companion, unconcerned.

Jack, back in the arms of his paramour, quickly dismissed the incident from his mind. But during ensuing weeks as he followed events in the wake of the Sheppard murder he became haunted by what he had seen that night. Many years afterward, a year before he died, he felt compelled to tell his Cleveland lawyer William Lawko about the incident. Mr. Lawko later recalled what his client had said:

> He saw a man running behind the Sheppard house around the time of the murder. Dark hair, standing up, just like the description in the paper. He couldn't be sure what it was ... if the person had anything to do with it. The authorities would've wanted to know everything—why he was there, who he was with, what he was doing. You know how it would've been, all the publicity. He didn't know if that person had anything to do with the murder or not. Chances are he didn't. But he was damn sure of one thing. It wasn't worth ruining his marriage.

---

*fictitious name

♦ 3:50 AM ♦

The individuals in the car who had observed the bushy-haired man after he had stepped from the cemetery were Mr. and Mrs. Richard Knitter of Sheffield Lake. Mr. Knitter later testified in court that he was returning with his wife and niece from a late movie in Cleveland when they saw a suspicious-looking man with his hair standing up, walking east along Lake Road near the cemetery a few yards west of the Sheppard property. When asked during his testimony to describe the man, he stated, "I mean crewcut hair growing in. Large eyes, large nose, and his eyes appeared to be bulging like. He wore a light-colored shirt, dark trousers, and was about five-foot-eight and one hundred seventy-five pounds."

"How long was his hair?" a prosecutor asked.

"I would judge maybe about three inches long," Knitter replied.

"Three inches?" said the prosecutor.

"Three or four," said Knitter.

"You mean his hair was standing up three or four inches?"

"The front where we could see," answered Knitter.

The description furnished by these witnesses was very specific, enabling a police artist to render a composite picture which the Knitters believed bore a valid resemblance to the man they had seen.

The Knitters stated there was no one else on Lake Road that night, and that the man was only "about a foot from our car." Mr. Knitter said that he would never forget the look on the man's face. He described it as a "look of horror, bewilderment and panic." For a moment he considered stopping to determine if the individual needed help, but frightened by the man's appearance, he pulled away. Mr. Knitter said he remarked to his wife, "How would you like to meet that guy in the dark?"

The Knitter car rolled on, the "bushy-haired man in the light shirt" temporarily put out of mind. Had the Knitters known what they witnessed on this infamous night their blood would have chilled. Because to the great misfortune of Marilyn Sheppard, she did indeed "meet that guy in the dark."

POLICE ARTIST SKETCHES
SUSPECT. Top: Patrolman
Richard B. Adler of Lakewood
sketches the likeness of a new
suspect in the murder of
Marilyn R. Sheppard as Robert
Knitter gives a verbal de-
scription of the man. Bottom

Richard Knitter gives verbal description to police
(The Plain Dealer)

SHEFFIELD LAKE RESIDENTS, Mr. and Mrs. Richard Knitter were called by Dr. Sam Sheppard's attorneys to testify about report they saw suspicious person near home in which Marilyn Sheppard was killed on morning of July 4.

(The Cleveland News)

♦ 5:00 AM ♦

Not long after the Knitters saw the suspicious figure near the Sheppard house, Mrs. Beatrice Wolfe of Elberta Beach, a small town west of Bay Village, boarded an early bus for Cleveland. It was the first leg of a trip that promised to be wearying. Not only was travel on a holiday difficult, her ultimate destination was Union City, Pennsylvania, where she was to attend a funeral.

Though in a somber mood, she took comfort from the emerging day, which promised sunshine and pleasing vistas. As the bus rolled smoothly along the highway she succumbed to the relaxing rhythm of the engine and the soft, steady vibration of the heavy tires. Soon she was dozing. It wasn't until they had passed Sheffield Lake that she awakened.

A short time later, "somewhere near Bay Village," the bus stopped for a passenger. The figure who boarded caught her attention immediately. He was unkempt, his hair disheveled. He seemed hurried and fumbled out a bill of large denomination to pay his fare. When she left the bus in Cleveland, the man remained on board heading eastward.

Mrs. Wolfe thought little more about the incident until she read the account of the Sheppard murder. Then she immediately contacted the Cleveland police and related her sighting of a tall, bushy-haired man wearing a white shirt, carrying a suitcase.

♦ 9:00 AM ♦

Mrs. John Lesnak, a forty-one-year-old housewife was described by family members and associates as an intelligent woman of considerable presence who was "well aware of things going on around her." This alertness was at no time more manifest than the July morning she stood in Colliers General Store in Mantua Corners, Ohio, looking curiously toward a dark-haired man who stood outside the door waiting for a bus. There was something about the man's manner that aroused her suspicions. He was smoking, his hair blowing in the wind, and seemed to be impatient for the arrival of the bus. Later, upon hearing about the Sheppard murder she contacted John Eaton, chief of the Bay Village Police Department, to relate what she had seen.

Chief Eaton was overwhelmed by the attention focused on his department following the Sheppard murder. His small force lacked the resources to cope with such a notorious event. It is significant, therefore, that out of all the communications that flooded his office, he would see fit to concentrate on a report from such an obscure place as Mantua, Ohio (population 900), and to write the following letter:

Police Department
Mantua, Ohio

Gentlemen:

Mrs. John Lesnak, Wayne Road, Mantua, Ohio, claims she has knowledge of a stranger around the Sheppard home in Bay Village, Ohio, July 4, 1954, prior to the murder of Marilyn Sheppard. Will you please contact her and relay to us any information you may secure from her.

Thanking you for your attention in this matter, I remain

Yours very truly,

John P. Eaton,
Chief of Police

JPE:ea

Mrs. Lesnak's daughter, Mrs. Joyce Nichols, later stated that her mother had called her in Hawaii at the time and was quite adamant about having seen the man at the Colliers bus stop. Mrs. Nichols stated that her mother had great credibility and would not have pursued the issue with authorities unless she was confident of her information. She said that family members had teased her mother a bit at the time, but that whenever asked about the incident her mother would reply adamantly, "*I saw that man!*"

The object of Mrs. Lesnak's attention that morning at the bus stop was unaware of her interest. His mind was consumed by urgent matters, uppermost being the realization that he must flee the Cleveland area as quickly as possible. Following the murder, he had returned to gather his belongings from his quarters in Mantua.

Here, he had cleaned up and hurriedly packed his B-4 bag with personal effects, including dress clothes such as the suit he had purchased in Hong Kong and sports clothes acquired in Tucson.

Now, standing in the breeze at the bus stop at Colliers Store, intently smoking a cigarette, his mind was churning. He realized the furor the homicide would cause and decided to lay low in the mountains of northern New York State. Having just traveled across the state a few weeks previously, he was familiar with the terrain and the Adirondacks offered the sanctuary and obscurity for which he had been trained.

His intent was to proceed north from Mantua on Route 44 to Route 20, the main arterial road leading to New York. Then, by whatever means available, including bus and hitchhiking, he would make his way up to the mountains. It was pursuant to this plan that a short time later, while hitchhiking eastward on Route 20 east of Cleveland, his path crossed with that of a bright premed student from Colgate University....

Colliers Store and Bus Stop, Mantua, Ohio—circa 1958
(Location where Mrs. Lesnak observed subject)

♦ 12:00 NOON ♦

From the moment the hitchhiker settled into the car, Gervase Flick realized he was strange. When he had slowed to pick him up moments before, his impression of the person had been quite good. The man was nice looking, about thirty years old, with straight black hair combed back. He was wearing a short coat, dark blue trousers, "darker than jeans," and carrying a suitcase. He had not at all appeared "to be a bum or itinerant," but when entering the car had seemed "pleasant and well-spoken." Now, Gerry, as he was called, was having second thoughts.

Gerry had planned that day to visit his girlfriend in Brockton, New York, and earlier that morning had asked his father if he could borrow one of the family cars.

"Take mine," his father had said. "Just remember, it's brand new."

"Thanks, Dad. I'll be careful. I really appreciate it."

Gerry had left his house in Cleveland some time after 11:00 a.m. and headed east. It was a pleasant day, although a trifle cool for the Fourth of July. A short time later on Route 20 east of Cleveland near Ashtabula, he had stopped for the hitchhiker.

"I didn't think you were going to stop," the man had said with a smile, throwing his suitcase in the back seat. He had seemed genial, appreciative.

Now, with the man on board, Gerry realized it had not been a good idea. Not only was the man's suitcase soiled, his shoes, which looked like brown loafers, were covered with—"well ... *something.*"

"I'd appreciate it if you could watch your feet," Gerry said, concerned about the carpeting on his father's new car and eyeing the man's shoes curiously.

"Yeah, sorry," said the man. "I'll be careful." And then, apparently noting Gerry's continuing inquisitive glances at his feet and feeling some explanation was in order, he said. "Dog's blood. My previous ride, we hit a dog. I kicked it off the side of the road and got blood on my shoes."

"Geez, be careful," said Gerry, rolling his eyes. "All I need are bloodstains on this thing. Where you heading?"

"Erie, Pennsylvania. I'm catching a train there for New York City."

Seemingly intelligent, the man made small talk for a few minutes and then fell silent, directing his attention to the passing countryside. Gerry didn't press the conversation. That is, until the man brought out a cigarette. He watched uneasily as his passenger produced a wooden match, lighting it with a casual flick of his thumb. When the smoke started filling the car Gerry decided to speak up. "I'm sorry, but I'd appreciate it if you didn't smoke," he said sheepishly. "My dad, he doesn't go for smoking. Particularly in his car ... if you know what I mean."

The man extinguished the cigarette without comment. They rode in silence for awhile before the passenger said, "Mind if I turn on the radio?"

"No, not at all."

The man turned the dial to different stations, finding only country and western music. He seemed agitated and flipped the radio off with a cursory, "Nothing interesting."

Cool character, thought Gerry. Pretty damn sure of himself for someone hitching a ride.

At a roadside restaurant Gerry suggested they stop for some coffee. Upon alighting from the vehicle and walking toward the establishment he noticed the man limping. "Hurt your leg?"

There was no immediate response and Gerry thought perhaps the hitchhiker had not heard him or that he was preoccupied. But then the man said, "I hurt my ankle ... kicking the dog off the road." There was a brusqueness to his manner which seemed to discourage conversation on the subject.

Inside, they ordered coffee at a counter. As the man raised the cup to his lips he inadvertently bumped Gerry, spilling coffee, the liquid running down onto Gerry's trousers.

"Sorry," he said, taking a napkin and casually mopping the coffee from the counter. He seemed unconcerned.

What's with this guy? Gerry leaned away slightly, brushing his pants.

Back in the car they continued their ride with little talk, his passenger appearing lost in thought. Finally, the man broke the silence with a few offhand comments. Then, "What do you think about that murder in Cleveland this morning?"

"Yeah, Mrs. Sheppard," replied Gerry. "My father mentioned it before I left. Pretty bad."

"We were listening to the news reports on the radio during my last ride," said the man. "Apparently it was a burglary. They said she was killed with a wrench."

"Really?"

"Yeah.... What did your father say about it?"

"Not much. My father's a doctor at the Bay View Hospital, but the people he talked to hadn't heard much about it. I guess it only happened early this morning."

Again silence with few interruptions until they reached a filling station near Erie, Pennsylvania. "Anyplace along here," the man said with the authoritative air of a commander directing a young subordinate. After a perfunctory "thanks," the man was gone, leaving Gerry Flick with mixed emotions. He looked on the floor of the passenger's side for bloodstains and was relieved not to find any.

It wasn't until a few weeks later when Gerry came home from college and his mother showed him the clippings and composite picture from the newspaper that he connected the hitchhiker with the Sheppard murder. The man certainly looked like the intruder. And how did the hitchhiker know about the crime? Had he really heard about it on the radio?

Although reluctant to become involved, Gerry's conscience compelled him to report the incident to the authorities. Ironically, the Cleveland Police Department rewarded his civic-mindedness by making him a suspect and forcing him to undergo a polygraph test. He was cleared, of course, but only after providing an airtight alibi and suffering much embarrassment. Notwithstanding the lack of follow-through by the police department, one knowledgeable person closely involved with the case would later state, "Dr. Flick is a well-respected individual. He would be a very credible witness."

Several years later, after viewing photographs and studying detailed descriptions and background material regarding Major Call, Gervase Flick, who had become a highly-regarded doctor, lawyer, and author, stated he was certain the hitchhiker and Major Call were one and the same.

◆ AFTERMATH ◆

Following the murder, things heated up in Bay Village. The Sheppard case received nationwide attention. *The Cleveland Press*, led by editor Louie Seltzer, a seventh-grade dropout who had clawed his way to the top position, launched a vitriolic campaign designed to force officials to indict Sam Sheppard for the murder of his wife. Rarely in the annals of journalism had a newspaper editor managed to manipulate the outcome of a criminal case to the degree that Seltzer did in the Sheppard case.

Having made up his mind that Sheppard was guilty, Louie initiated his demand for justice. (Critics contended he really saw the case as a chance to sell papers and save his fading empire; there were those who foresaw a diminishing role for afternoon papers such as the *Press*.) "SOMEBODY IS GETTING AWAY WITH MURDER" screamed Louie in one headline. "WHY DON'T POLICE QUIZ TOP SUSPECT?" said another. Yet another, "WHY ISN'T SAM SHEPPARD IN JAIL?" Finally, an unbelievable command headline: "QUIT STALLING—BRING HIM IN."

Other newspapers in Cleveland of higher quality and integrity such as the *Plain Dealer*, were more restrained but ultimately would follow the *Press'* lead. Within days public opinion was so poisoned against Dr. Sheppard that he had no reasonable chance to defend himself. Later, US Supreme Court Justice Thomas Campbell Clark, in writing the court's opinion of the case, would chastise the proceedings for its "carnival atmosphere" and cite "massive, pervasive, and prejudicial publicity that attended his [Sheppard's] prosecution." Justice Clark would conclude that "Sheppard did not receive a fair trial consistent with the due process clause of the fourteenth amendment...."

Sharing with Seltzer much of the blame for this ludicrous spectacle was Seltzer's friend, Samuel Gerber, the Cuyahoga County coroner. Similar in both demeanor and style to Seltzer, Gerber played the press card to the hilt. Responding to a Seltzer headline "WHY NO INQUEST? DO IT NOW, DR. GERBER," the very next day the coroner hauled Dr. Sheppard and his family into a high school auditorium in front of neighbors and the press corps, where he humiliated them in an extraordinary inquisition under the guise of an inquest. It was a wretched charade which made a mockery of due process.

Unwilling to stand against Seltzer's relentless campaign, the other elements of the Cleveland justice system fell in line. Soon, Sam Sheppard was indicted. The resulting trial would be regarded later as one of the great travesties in the history of American jurisprudence. Edward J. Blythin, former mayor of Cleveland, was the presiding judge and a candidate for reelection to another six-year term. Since he was the chief jurist in the criminal division, he decided to assign the highly publicized case to himself. The lead prosecutor, John J. Mahon, was also facing reelection. Obviously, a conviction was important for Mahon's political ambition. It was not a propitious time for aspiring public servants to frustrate the wishes of a news brute such as Seltzer. A powerful kingmaker (he was widely credited with getting one man elected governor of Ohio), Louie Seltzer could also be a formidable enemy, particularly for those holding public office. Louie had already passed judgment on Sheppard. It was now the job of aspiring politicians to implement the verdict.

Not one piece of credible evidence would be presented at the trial to show that Sam Sheppard had murdered his wife. In fact, information developed by investigators showed that the accused was innocent—for example, signs of a forced door in the basement, and unidentified blood samples at the crime scene indicating the presence of a third party. All of this evidence would be suppressed by the prosecution and never made available to the defense.

Typical of the prosecution's overreaching would be the celebrated bloody pillowcase introduced by Gerber, who claimed it showed the outline of the murder weapon—"some type of surgical instrument," he asserted. "An unmistakable blood signature." Inasmuch as the defendant was a doctor, the pronouncement would have a profound impact on the jury, perhaps serving as the pivotal "evidence" that would swing reluctant jurors to a guilty verdict. This despite the fact that Sam Gerber was never able to identify the so-called surgical instrument.

Gerber's motivation for prosecuting Dr. Sheppard was not solely Seltzer's campaign. Evidence showed that animosity had existed between the coroner and the Sheppard family for several years because of professional differences deriving from the osteopathic practice of Sam's father and brother. Bay View physician Horace Don would testify at a later trial concerning the Sheppard case that in a conversation with Gerber one month prior to the Sheppard murder, Gerber had said to him, "I'm going to get them [the Sheppards] some day."

And so with a case bereft of evidence, but strong on the presumption that the accused must have done it because there was no information presented that anyone else could have done it, Dr. Samuel Sheppard was convicted and sent to the Ohio State Penitentiary. Jack Pollack, who covered the trial for the *Chicago Tribune*, after exhaustive research would sum up the debacle with the words, "It was a damn shame!"

Later, in 1962, Louie Seltzer would state in his self-serving autobiography, *The Years Were Good*, that he had decided Sheppard was guilty, and since the authorities were dragging their feet, he elected to do something about it. Because he thought the paper's liability was so great in such an unusual campaign he chose to accept the responsibility and "write the editorials myself," a highly dubious claim according to some of his peers who had little regard for Louie's writing abilities.

F. Lee Bailey, the renowned lawyer who successfully defended Sheppard at his second trial, would write Seltzer a letter at the conclusion of the trial in 1966, in which he would hold the editor principally responsible for the arrest and conviction of Sheppard. An excerpt from the letter states:

> You took a man who was immersed in the greatest personal grief and smothered him in your brand of muck.... By your callous and ruthless acts you robbed Dr. Sheppard and his entire family of each ounce of dignity you could slice away.... You caused brutally the deaths of both his parents....

Many individuals with the benefit of hindsight will concede their errors and show compassion for injury inflicted on others as a result of their mistakes. Not Louie. In his autobiography, while commenting on his actions which wreaked havoc on an innocent American family, Seltzer would state in a boorish postscript to a tragedy of epic proportions, "I would do the same thing over again...." He probably would have. No shrinking violet, Louie. He appeared to revel in life's brutal dramas. Reportedly, he willingly attended the executions of many individuals in Ohio's electric chair.

As one knowledgeable person who did extensive research on the Sheppard case later said, "It is regrettable that Gerber and Seltzer were never held accountable for their despicable conduct in this affair."

Jim Call, who had followed developments in the Sheppard murder through newspapers and radio from his Adirondack hideout, had been fascinated by the fraudulent representation of events by the coroner and the editor. His own sense of vulnerability to the homicide had continued to lessen as the inexorable Cleveland judicial proceedings moved Sam Sheppard ever closer to the Ohio State Penitentiary. He could not have wished for more than these twins in infamy, Seltzer and Gerber.

But now, a few months later, in November 1954, sitting in his cell at the Reno jail, he felt the inquisitive eye of justice turning in his direction.

◆ ◆ ◆

Major Call
November 1954

Major Call
circa 1950

Composite drawing by
Sheppard witnesses
July 1954

Major Call
November 1954

Major Call
circa 1952

PART VII

Reno, Nevada
November 1954

49

It was one week after his apprehension that Call was taken into the interrogation room at the Reno police station. He was familiar with the room, having spent several hours there the previous week during interrogation by the Reno detectives. What was not familiar were the two austere-looking men sitting at a table just past the door. He sensed immediately that they were police officers. Probably from Cleveland, following up on the Sheppard murder. Using the Lakewood identification had been a terrible mistake. The Cleveland crime posed a much greater threat then the Lake Placid matter. If he were connected to the shootout in Placid, he at least had a chance. There the police had opened fire first; he had returned their fire in self-defense; the only officer he had seen when it started was in civilian clothes. The newspapers had said as much. But the murder of a defenseless woman was something else. He had read about the crime scene evidence such as the torn fragment of leather found near the victim's bed, her broken teeth, the composite picture from witnesses who had seen him outside the house at the time of the murder. As he entered the interrogation room, adrenaline was flowing.

"Sit down James," said the older of the two men, nodding toward a chair, his craggy face serious but not threatening. "I'm Captain Muller of the New York State Police. This is Sergeant Blaisdell."

Jim dropped into a chair, surprised, but greatly relieved.

◆ ◆ ◆

Call Maintains Silence
Due from Reno Tonigh

**Suspect in Co
Killing Will I
Taken to Plac**

AF Major Age
Quizzed, Clai
Mind Still Fu

Special to The Post-Standa
RENO, Nev. Nov. 17.
absent-minded Air Forc
jor accused of fatally w
ing a Lake Placid poli
in a gun duel on Aug.
arrive in New York ci
morrow night from Ren

Maj. James A. Call, lis
the Air Force as a desert
refused to talk as police
questioned him a second c
fore their departure.

"I don't feel I can say a
until my mind clears," h
Capt. Harold T. Muller
New York state police, w
rived here yesterday after
quiz the 29-year-old a
Call previously told pol
couldn't remember anythin
past activities, except for t
month.

SLAYING SUSPECT QUESTIONED.—Flanked by New York state police, Air Force
Maj. James A. Call, 29, accused of fatally wounding a Lake Placid policeman Aug. 5,
stares ahead as picture was taken yesterday in Reno, Nev., during a brief respite from
questioning. At left is Capt. Harold T. Muller and at right, Sgt. H. E. Blaisdell. (AP
Wirephoto).

Call, Muller and Blaisdell in Reno, Nevada—November 18, 1954
(The Post-Standard)

50

Harold Muller and Harry Blaisdell sat at a long rectangular metal table in the interrogation room, eyes locked on the slender young man who had just been escorted in by two police officers. Blaisdell would later describe the event as one of the greatest surprises of his life:

> When they brought Call in, Muller and I were completely astonished at the way he looked, his features—very handsome—and so forth, compared to our composite.... We talked to him for an hour about the Lake Placid homicide. He would say nothing. At no time did he ask for an attorney, and he would continually say that he knew nothing about it. His exact words were, "I don't know what you're talking about."
>
> By that time we had a warrant. It charged him with first-degree murder. We asked him if he would waive extradition back to the State of New York. He said, "I don't know, I'll have to think about that. If I waive extradition back to the State of New York, I'm going to be tried on *that* [emphasis added] murder charge, right?" We said "Yes." He said, "If I fight extradition, I'm going to have to hire an attorney and fight it here in Reno, right?" We answered "Yes." He waited a few minutes. Then he said he would waive extradition back to the State of New York. He thought about the extradition issue for several minutes before he answered. *It seemed very important to him.* [emphasis added] This man was very smart.

It was indeed an important issue for Jim. Since he believed the New York shooting was far more defensible than the Sheppard murder, his main objective was to place as much distance as possible between himself and those forces trying to connect him with the Sheppard case.

Following the interrogation of Call, Harold Muller expressed some ambivalence about his subject in a telephone interview with the *Adirondack Daily Enterprise*, a North Country newspaper:

> Capt. Muller said Call would admit nothing under questioning except that he had committed robbery in several Reno homes.
>
> "He apparently never thought of being hooked up with the Lake Placid shootings," Capt. Muller said, "When we first walked into his cell yesterday we introduced ourselves and he seemed surprised. In the back of his mind he apparently figured he'd get off here on a burglary charge. But he would admit nothing to us, although we questioned him yesterday afternoon for nearly five hours."
>
> "Does he look like a killer? Is he what people call a tough guy? A gunman?" asked The Enterprise.
>
> "No, I wouldn't say that," Capt. Muller replied. "He seems to be a deep thinker; calm most of the time but he's apparently sort of mixed up now. He's soft spoken, and thinks carefully before he says anything. We sort of hit him between the eyes with our statement that we wanted him for the Lake Placid shootings. He seemed surprised, but I wouldn't say he was startled. He's sort of a calm guy—at least outwardly."
>
> "Is he married, captain? Got a family?" The Enterprise asked.
>
> "He won't say. He doesn't want to discuss anything like that—or much of anything else—with us. He won't even tell us what part of the country he came from."
>
> Capt. Muller said he was convinced that his prisoner Call had been hiding out in the Adirondacks before the shootings.
>
> "I'll find out if it's the last thing I do," he said. "It was something big he was hiding from."

Finally, after three months of one of the most grueling manhunts in the annals of law enforcement, Muller and Blaisdell had their man. Few would begrudge the two a measure of pride and satisfaction at their accomplishment as they prepared for a triumphant return to New York. Much to their chagrin they would find the trip more complicated than expected. Harry Blaisdell later related what happened:

> After the interrogation we made plane reservations. The next morning we went down and got Call handcuffed and flew to San Francisco. There, we had to change planes for our New York connection. We went up to the United Airlines booth to check our tickets. An airline employee came over and said, "I'm sorry, but the company will not transport you back to New York with this prisoner...."
>
> So, we decided to try TWA. They said that they would transport us to New York City if no passenger objected. Well, no one objected. It was a night flight. By that time we had his [Call's] Air Force background. Knew more about him. From there until we got to New York City, never once did I mention the homicide. We did sleep some. Call was very talkative, very cooperative. I talked to him about his childhood, his schooling, his marriage, his son, and I concluded that Call was madly in love with his son, that the boy was Call's weak point, and that was the place to start.
>
> So, I talked to him about the Air Force, about the war. I believe he flew 17 or 18 missions. His plane received a shot through the wing one time. Had it been a foot closer, he'd have got it. He loved to gamble. He always wanted to outsmart the other fellow. He told me, "I know I can devise a system to beat that roulette wheel. It's the only thing in my life that I set out to do and didn't accomplish."

Call's return received much attention from the New York City press corps, including a full-page photo on the front page of the *New York Daily Mirror*. Most of the coverage was unusually complimentary to the fugitive, considering he was charged with a variety of serious crimes. Some articles went so far as to extol the charm, intellect, and survival and shooting skills of the handsome young aviator. Blaisdell later commented about what happened when they returned:

We arrived back and went to the Hawthorne barracks with the troopers who met our plane at Idlewild. [now JFK Airport] We were all pretty bushed. We got up early the next morning and Muller and I talked to him again, starting right from the beginning. We went through all the crimes he'd committed. All Call did was sit and stare ... sit and stare.

Finally, I said to Muller, "Let me talk to him for awhile." I wanted to try something. So, Muller left the room. There was another trooper in the room sitting off in a corner for security reasons. Then I started talking to him. I said, "James, we've identified seven of your ten fingers. If you never said a word, I'm convinced that you committed those burglaries and the homicide, and if you don't say anything, you're gonna be tried up in Essex County on a first degree murder charge. You told me that the sun sets and rises on your son Jeffrey, that he looks up to you, *and* that you believe you have been a good father. If you're tried for murder first degree and get life in prison or the electric chair, or if you get a lesser sentence, it will take years before you're out of prison. You're making your son Jeff carry your cross!..."

I threw more stuff at that man for about 15 to 20 minutes without stopping, pounding away all the time on the thought that he was making his infant son carry his cross through life....

Blaisdell stated that he finally tired and was about to conclude the interview, feeling he was not accomplishing anything, when as so often happens during criminal interrogations, the break finally came. The officer was totally surprised:

All of a sudden, he said, "Wait a minute." He turned away from me and started to cry. I sent the trooper out of the room to get a towel. He was perspiring, the tears were running down his cheeks. After cleaning himself up with the towel, he turned back to me and said, "OK, I'm ready." He turned the crying on, click, and turned it off, click, just like that. A very controlled man. Then Muller came back and Call gave us a detailed confession about the shooting and burglaries.

From that point on, he just opened up and was the most cooperative man you'd ever want to know. I don't believe he ever would've tried to escape.

Later on I went to see him several times at the Elizabethtown Jail, where he made a map showing dates and places of his various burglaries. This guy had a marvelous mind. He mentioned every burglary by date. His dates varied by no more than one day with mine. That was over a three month span, and to remember all of that takes a pretty good mind.

Although impressive with his recollection of dates and events subsequent to July 4, 1954, Blaisdell's prisoner was much less so when it came to the preceding period—the days leading up to the Sheppard murder. But Blaisdell had little reason to concentrate on this period. There simply were no crimes reported during that time in the areas where the subject claimed to have been.

♦ ♦ ♦

Troopers Fly Lake Placid Murder Suspe
To New York, To Drive Him Upstate Tod

Spends Night in Westchester Jail

NEW YORK, (AP).—An Air Force major who flew 18 Korean combat missions and later deserted was brought here from the west coast yesterday for allegedly slaying a Lake Placid, N. Y., policeman.

The hero turned prisoner, James A. Call, 29, formerly of Chicago, was slated to spend the night in the Westchester County jail at Eastview. He will be taken by automobile today to Lake Placid for arraignment.

Police gave no hint whether he had made any statement in connection with their accusation that he shot and fatally wounded Patrolman Richard Pelkey, 32, last Aug. 5 when surprised in an unoccupied Summer home. Two other policemen were wounded.

APPEARS CALM

Call appeared calm and collected when he stepped from an airliner at Idlewild Airport under custody of two State Troopers.

Dark-haired and handsome, he was neatly dressed in civilian clothes—suit, white shirt, knit tie and topcoat. He wore no handcuffs, but he stuffed his hands into his topcoat pockets. Call was arrested last week in

MURDER SUSPECT REACHES N. Y.—Maj. James A. Call, left, arrested Reno as a suspect in the slaying of Patrolman Richard A. Pelkey at Lak Placid Aug. 5, is shown as he arrived in New York's International Airpo yesterday morning. He was in custody of Capt. Harold T. Muller, from and Sgt. S. F. Blaisdell of the State Police.

Call, Muller and Blaisdell arrive in New York

(source unknown)

51

"Click!" said Blaisdell. "Just like that the tears were gone."
Harry knew Jim Call had great control of his emotions. What Harry
didn't know was that replacing the tears in his prisoner's mindset were
cool, calculating thoughts evaluating his chances for escape.

Jim had been quick to see through Blaisdell's ploy in talking
about his son Jeff. He finessed his response convincingly. He then
furnished a statement of some twenty pages in which he confessed to
numerous crimes of which he knew they were already aware. The statement contained many references to his military career, marriage,
penchant for gambling, and other aspects of his life that he realized
they would soon develop through rudimentary background checks.

He impressed his captors with an uncanny ability to furnish precise
dates of events, exclusive, of course, of the days immediately preceding
the Sheppard homicide. For this period his answers were vague in the
extreme. Although he claimed to have been camping by himself
along the Appalachian Trail, he was unable to explain how he subsisted
or to supply dates, witnesses, or events to substantiate his story—not
even burglaries or armed robberies, which by that time were endemic
to his life.

Indeed, evidence shows that rather than a camping expedition, Jim
had returned to the Cleveland area where family members lived. A
string of burglaries in the suburbs of Cleveland during this time bore
markings of his method of operation. In one instance, Bay Village
police saw "similarities" between the Sheppard break-in, which was
characteristic of Jim's MO, and a burglary committed about a mile
from the Sheppard residence.

Jim was quick to take credit for the purported break-in at the Lake
Placid Drive-In Theatre on July 5th. Unlike the other felonies he
acknowledged, in which authorities already had evidence linking

him to the crimes, Jim furnished this information gratuitously in order to establish his presence away from Bay Village.

Did Muller and Blaisdell suspect this? To some degree. Both were convinced he was hiding out after some big crime, and they were quoted in newspapers talking about his possible connection to the Sheppard affair. They interrogated him extensively on three separate occasions about the Sheppard homicide, and in each instance he had refused to answer, brushing off questions with surprisingly noncommital replies such as "We can't talk about that" or "I have no comment on that," as well as the familiar refrain, "I don't know what you're talking about."

The Cleveland authorities were of little help in this regard. They were less than enthusiastic about leads from other police agencies, since prosecutors were already in court trying Dr. Sheppard for the murder. The case had been solved as far as they were concerned, and nothing would complicate their prosecution quite like the surfacing of another suspect. Under the circumstances, Muller and Blaisdell could hardly be blamed for not challenging Jim's denials, or questioning him more aggressively about his whereabouts at the time of the Sheppard murder.

Although they had no way of knowing it at the time, their prisoner was a master at dissembling, a talent enhanced by his incredible coolness and steady eyes—qualities further strengthened in the Air Force survival school. The school curriculum was rich in experience developed from American fliers who had been shot down and taken prisoner during World War II. A code of conduct consistent with survival techniques had been devised to prepare pilots should they be captured by enemy forces. They were trained in methods of misinforming their captors, as well as subtle techniques for furnishing the enemy with harmless data it already had. Few mastered the art of disinformation better than Jim Call.

After his apprehension in Reno, when authorities discovered he was AWOL, he realized his captors would soon have his entire life story available to them from his military records. When Muller and Blaisdell arrived he had already devised his strategy. In a spirit of professed cooperation, he would freely tell his captors everything they already knew about his life until the time he went AWOL in May 1954. After that, he would have to be more selective.

They were aware of much of his criminal activities, having confiscated his suitcase with the wallets and other evidence implicating him in many burglaries and armed robberies. And they would have no difficulty connecting him to the Lake Placid shootout. Fingerprints, witnesses—they even had the Luger with which he had shot the police officers. His best chance was to pretend to cooperate. There was room for a plea.

But the Bay Village matter was far different. Once implicated, there would be little defense. And Ohio, like New York, had the electric chair. From their questions, he sensed Muller and Blaisdell had little evidence connecting him with the Sheppard case. And he quickly realized that they were far more interested in the capital murder charge they had against him in their own state. Although he could still end up in New York's electric chair, it had seemed to him at the time that Muller and Blaisdell offered his best chance for survival. They would be traveling to New York; he'd be out of the "tank" (cell block), from which escape was extremely difficult. Besides, as time passed he'd been evaluating the New York officers constantly. He had sensed they'd become more comfortable with him. More relaxed, less vigilant.

◆ ◆ ◆

52

"Would Call have tried to escape?" Blaisdell said, repeating the question asked later by a journalist. "I don't believe it. No, I don't believe it. I believe that man right at that point in time was saying to himself, 'It's time to atone for what I've done.' "

As skilled an investigator as he was, Harry Blaisdell severely underestimated Jim Call's desire to regain his freedom. The officer's comments reflected thinking which might well have cost him his life had the right opportunity presented itself to his prisoner—an example worth remembering for all police officers involved in travel with a man facing the loss of his own life. Call would freely admit later that throughout their trip back from Reno he was constantly measuring his chances to escape.

Just such an opportunity had come in the San Francisco terminal where they had been delayed following the refusal of United Airlines to grant them passage to New York. They had been standing near the ticket counter with two police officers assigned to assist them during their stopover, remonstrating about their loss of transportation. Several people, including airline personnel, had gathered nearby, watching them curiously....

"So, now what the hell do we do?" said Dutch Muller, his frustrated voice crunching out the words. He pushed his gray fedora back from his forehead, revealing his tired rugged features. "What a state of affairs. After we chase this man halfway across the continent they refuse to let us on a plane. What a state of affairs!" he repeated emphatically.

"I'm sure we can hold the prisoner downtown, Captain," said one of the officers, a lieutenant in his late thirties. "Until you make some other arrangements."

"Why don't I check with one of the other airlines?" asked Harry Blaisdell, who stood next to Muller, one wrist handcuffed to Jim. "I could try TWA. I can explain the situation. Maybe they're a little more flexible."

As the officers conversed, Jim stood encircled by the others, seemingly indifferent to the problem he was creating with transportation. Now and then he glanced off in the distance, one eyebrow arched in a supercilious fashion that seemed to suggest, "What in the world am I doing here with these people?" A pretty, well-dressed, young woman passed, her eyes lingering on him curiously. Their eyes met and she looked quickly away. A flickering image of Greta flashed in his mind. Occasionally he exchanged glances with other pedestrians, dismissing them with a certain preoccupied haughtiness. He appeared relaxed, even bored.

In reality, adrenaline was flowing, every nerve in his body attuned to the moment. The emotion had been triggered a few minutes before when the four officers' attention was diverted to the United Airlines counter. The lieutenant was standing no more than two feet away and Jim's eyes had come to rest on the .38-caliber revolver lodged in the black holster on his garrison belt. "It was just hanging there," said Jim later. "Just waiting to be taken at the right moment."

Jim listened for a pause in the conversation and then quietly said, "Would it be possible to go to the head?"

"Here, I'll take him," Muller said, producing a key for the handcuffs. "See what you can do with TWA."

The captain unlocked the handcuff from Blaisdell's wrist and prepared to secure himself to the prisoner. For an instant Jim was unshackled, his eyes riveted on the revolver on the officer's belt. For one facing a capital crime, it was a rare chance. Once incarcerated, it would be all over—particularly on death row.

He shifted slightly, a move ostensibly to facilitate his cuffing to Muller, but actually designed to bring him closer to the lieutenant. The pistol was no more than a foot from his hand. The officers were preoccupied talking with one another. He'd yank the pistol from the holster and step quickly back among the pedestrians. If need be, he'd grab a hostage.

He was a split second away from grabbing the revolver when he glanced up, his eyes catching those of the other police officer, who was standing a few feet away. Unlike the other men, whose attention seemed distracted, the officer's eyes were locked on him. Had the man sensed his intentions? Was he ready to leap forward, preventing Jim from grabbing the pistol? There was something about the figure—large, imposing, legs spread apart, thumbs crooked under his cartridge belt—that gave Jim pause. In that fraction of a second the opportunity was gone, his wrist shackled to the captain's.

Would Jim have been successful in his escape attempt? His captors would have been inhibited from returning fire in the crowded terminal. Considering the coolness with which he had dispatched the three policemen in Lake Placid, the answer might well have been "yes." But the moment passed without incident, and like other officers who had encountered Jim Call, none realized how close had been their brush with disaster.

However, more opportunities lay ahead. Roger Tubby, a reporter with the *Adirondack Daily Enterprise* who covered the Major Call case, wrote of a similar incident where Jim considered grabbing an officer's pistol and shooting his way to freedom:

Major Call and the troopers

"Dutch" Mueller [Muller], commander of Troop B of the New York State Police, invited me to accompany him and three or four other troopers and recently captured murderer Major Call of the Air Force into the woods near the Saranac Lake Club golf course....

The Troopers, Call and I went out along the railroad track from Lake Placid. To get to his lean-to ... we had to cross a small stream on a log. Call's wrists were unshackled so he could balance himself on the log, a Trooper walking before him, another behind.

On the other side Call said calmly to the Trooper who had been ahead of him: "I wouldn't do that again, your revolver sticking out of its holster right in front of me. I was tempted to grab it and let you all have it."

The true extent to which Jim could use his charm and intellect to create opportunities for escape would later become even more evident.

Invariably it involved beguiling his captors. He was soon to be regarded as a literary person, more interested in poetry than escape. "Jim?" one of his jailers would later say when responding to reporters' questions. "Quiet, intelligent, friendly—a real gentlemanly fellow."

♦ ♦ ♦

Call at New York Airport—November 20, 1954
(*The New York Daily Mirror*, Photo by Dan McElle)

53

Over 500 people had gathered in the darkness outside the North Elba Town Hall—a sizeable crowd by Lake Placid standards. They waited quietly, ignoring a cold rain that occasionally changed to wet snow. An air of expectation prevailed in anticipation of the arrival of the cop killer, the "phantom" who had unnerved the community during preceding months.

At 7:10 p.m. a ripple of excitement spread through the congregation. Headlights pierced the mist, and a cavalcade of State Police cars followed by media vehicles rolled down the narrow main street, coming to a stop in front of the town hall. The crowd edged forward as troopers emerged from cars and formed a phalanx, their distinctive tan Stetsons catching wet snow and their black garrison belts and high boots glistening in the media spotlights. Exhibiting the confident, friendly style typical of North Country troopers, they gently but firmly parted the crowd as Jim Call stepped from a car and made his way slowly up the steps toward the entrance to the building.

A murmur of wonderment spread through the ranks of spectators at the sight of the prisoner. Was this really the killer? This pleasant-looking young man? Kenneth Fee, a staff correspondent with a regional newspaper, captured the mood of the moment with a revealing description:

IS THIS THE MAN?

Is this the nerveless gunman who chose to shoot it out with four armed policemen? Whose deadly accuracy with a pistol was pointed up in the neat distribution of the seven shots he fired in five seconds, two shots hitting each of the three policemen? Is this the man who with the cunning of a fox eluded the best bloodhounds ... and like a will-o-the wisp flickered from cabin to cabin, slipping through dozens of traps set for him?

Seeing him in person made him no more real than the imaginary "phantom" who terrorized the Adirondacks for weeks. I saw a handsome, poised, clean cut, intelligent-looking person. His brown eyes steady, his movements smooth and sure. He walked between guards as though leading a military review. He smoked a cigarette like a movie star, raising his chin and blowing a thin cloud upwards. Only the handcuffs on his wrists, which showed as he smoked, revealed he was the prisoner.

With such media coverage it was inevitable that Jim was soon to become something of a folk hero in the North Country. As if his good looks and bearing were not enough, his military background further enhanced the image. This was evident once he was inside the Justice Court where his arraignment was to take place. He was assigned a seat in front of a large mural honoring American soldiers, sailors, marines, and *airmen*. The size and location of the mural said it all. Make no mistake, Lake Placid was a conservative patriotic town mindful of the contributions made by its servicemen during the hard war years of the forties and fifties. It induced mixed emotions among those present to see a young major, indeed a war hero, sitting under the mural, being charged with murder.

Justice Clarence Eccleston, a courtly, round-faced, middle-aged gentleman with glasses, seemed aware of the wonderment in his courtroom as he opened the arraignment. His manner was courteous as he leaned forward and told the District Attorney to begin.

Essex County District Attorney Daniel Manning rose, adjusted his horn-rimmed glasses, and proceeded to read the charges. A balding, neat-appearing man in his forties, Manning's congenial manner was apparent even while reciting the grim facts of a first-degree murder charge. Indeed, his considerate disposition had manifested itself only moments before. Manning recalled the incident years later:

> It was obvious Major Call was not used to this kind of procedure. His mouth seemed to be very dry. I thought I should be decent to him. So I reached in my pocket for a lifesaver,

and slid it across the table to him. Well, he grabbed it and he just brightened right up. He said, 'Thank you very, very much.' The court asked him if he wanted an attorney. Then the judge asked that since he didn't want to be represented by an attorney, if he'd be willing to waive an examination, which he did. So then I as District Attorney moved that the case be presented to the next session of the Essex County grand jury. The judge granted the order and also directed that Major Call be confined to the Essex County jail until the next grand jury met. That was the first time I had seen Major Call. Incidentally, I was very much impressed with him. He was a very fine-looking young man. He was a bit reserved ... quiet.

Dan Manning would later learn that, although quiet, the ostensibly gentle young man sitting across from him had a propensity for violence and plans for escape that would curl the fringe of hair on the affable DA's head.

Following the arraignment, the prisoner and his guards moved outside where much of the original crowd and media remained. With people pressing closer, anxious for a last look, Jim and the entourage made their way amid flashing cameras to the waiting troop cars. Conversations were animated. "Isn't he a dream?" one young woman exclaimed. An older man next to her, perhaps her father, frowned. "Why don't you ask Mrs. Pelkey?" he said, referring to the slain officer's widow.

On the fringe of the crowd, stylishly attired in a wool coat with fur collar and fur-lined boots, stood a young woman. A wool scarf drawn up under a firm chin and a matching cloche hat pulled low over dark eyes did not conceal her beauty. Wisps of dark hair curled from under the hat, brushing against dimples on skin tanned from leisurely days in the sun.

A chilling breeze brushed over the crowd. It was much colder now, the earlier rain having turned completely to snow. White filigree collected on the woman's cloche and formed small epaulets on her shoulders, giving the appearance of a uniform of sorts. With a gloved hand she drew the scarf up further over a small nose. Upon closer look one might have suspected that the movement was caused by a desire for anonymity, rather than the inclement weather.

Her eyes, wide and glistening, locked on the prisoner as he moved past to a waiting car, then blinked and wavered as the vehicle vanished behind a curtain of snow. Although emotion was etched on her face, the chin remained tilted, resolute. She stood for several seconds as the crowd dispersed. Then, turning, she walked in the direction of the Lake Placid Club, face now buried deeply in the scarf.

◆ ◆ ◆

54

Where the wandering water gushes
From the hills above Glen-Car,
In pools among the rushes
That scarce could bathe a star,
. . . .
Come away, O human child!
To the waters and the wild
With a faery, hand in hand,
For the world's more full of weeping than you can understand.
(William Butler Yeats, The Stolen Child)

Jim reread the winsome lines from *The Stolen Child*, then closed
the book reflectively, resting it on his knee. The poem saddened him,
evoking thoughts of his own child. How wonderful it would be to
take Jeff into the wild, to expose him to the marvels of nature, to
teach him secrets of the forest, to escape with him from the weeping
world of which Yeats spoke. The poet must have spent a good deal
of time in the wilderness, he thought. He wondered if the writer had
ever been in jail. Doing time certainly gave one an appreciation for
the wild.

He rested his head against the wall and closed his eyes, conjuring
images: Green mountains ... sparkling streams ... the profound
silence of the forest.... All gone. Perhaps forever. Except for the sky.
Through an architectural quirk, a bit of sky was visible from his cell.
By craning his neck he could see a small patch of blue above the red
brick wall of the county courthouse, which rose just a few feet beyond
his small barred window. Ironic, he mused, that after years of flying
with broad views of the horizon he should now be restricted to this
tiny patch of blue.

He lay back on his cot, looking up at the ceiling. His quarters consisted of a 5' x 10' beige-colored cell containing only a thin mattress on a metal cot, a washbasin, commode, one aluminum drinking cup, and one tin cup for an ashtray. It was enough, he thought. For the time being.

He thought of Greta repeatedly. By now, she would have learned his true identity. The press coverage had been extraordinary. Newspaper, television, radio. Even the New York City press had given it preferred attention. What a shock it must have been for her. Would she have told anyone about him? Her parents, perhaps? Probably not.

Following his arraignment he had been transported over the mountains to the Essex County Jail in Elizabethtown, a quaint, picturesque village where the county civic buildings were located. These consisted of an attractive cluster of red brick structures of traditional design, with arched white doors and long narrow windows trimmed in white. In the center was the county courthouse, its white portico supported by four tall pillars and crowned by a towering white steeple. A nearby building of similar design housed the fifty-year-old county jail. Tall shade trees and wide, carefully trimmed lawns surrounded the structures, creating a sedate campus-like setting. In fact, the graceful buildings clustered in the small Adirondack community had often been mistaken for a college campus.

Here Jim had been greeted by Sheriff John P. Crowley, a tall, courtly man who displayed more the manner of a university dean of admissions than a jailer. After an admittance procedure consisting of little more than a small amount of paperwork and a perfunctory search, Jim had been taken to his cell. His arrival at the jail was described in an article in the *Post-Standard*:

ACCUSED KILLER OF COP NOW PRISONER 13

Elizabethtown, Nov. 21—"Prisoner No. 13," James Arlon Call, 29-year-old confessed killer of a Lake Placid policeman, appeared to have settled down to the dull routine of jail life today. Lodged with 12 other prisoners in the small, red-brick Essex County jail building here, the AWOL Air Force major slept "very well" last night, according to Essex County Sheriff, John P. Crowley. Call, who signed a confession

Friday night admitting the fatal shooting of Lake Placid Patrolman Richard E. Pelkey, 32, seems very pleasant and not at all worried, the sheriff explained.

Call is lodged in a 5-foot by 10-foot cell which looks out on a wall but permits a small view of the sky. His window, barred with a special type of hard steel and a screen, is 20 feet from the ground in the 50-year-old building next to the Essex County courthouse. To a newsman who visited him in the jail, Call expressed a desire for reading matter, particularly poetry. Since Call's arrival two guards have been added to the jailhouse staff, thus providing an around-the-clock vigil at the airman's cell, each guard working a 12-hour shift. Three barred doors separate Call from the front door of the jail, the sheriff said.

Many such articles appeared describing the subdued nature of the prisoner and his daily ritual, including his interest in poetry and classical literature. What was not indicated in the articles, however, were other things of interest to the Major—the routine of the jail and the habits and personalities of the guards....

"He's a very agreeable and very gentlemanly fellow," said Sheriff Crowley. "He reads the newspapers every day after the deputies finish them. Also, magazines like *Look* and *Time* that I bring over from my house. He's fond of poetry and has several books on it. The wife got him some books from the library."

"Yes, they've been real nice to me here," said their gentle, poetry-reading prisoner in one of his many compliments about his jailers. "Under the circumstances, I couldn't ask for anything more."

He was truthful. For a military officer facing death in the electric chair, who had been trained in the best techniques of escape and survival, who *could* ask for anything more?

◆ ◆ ◆

55

"It's your mother-in-law," said the deputy, an angular man in his late thirties. "Come up from Mississippi."

Jim lowered his eyes momentarily, feeling sudden tugs of emotion. He had expected her, having talked to her on a prison phone a few days before. His attempts to dissuade her from coming had been to no avail. Now, with the moment at hand, he had misgivings. He had great respect for Robbie John, a feeling that had grown since Muriel's death and her mother's subsequent role caring for his son. But he anguished at the thought of her seeing him in his present state. From the time he was a boy, he had taken pride in how he looked and dressed. During visits to Meridian to visit his son after Muriel's death he had been careful to present a good appearance. Invariably he arrived to warm greetings from Robbie John and comments about how "dashing" he looked in his uniform, how "absolutely handsome" he was. The impending meeting would be a shock for her. The undignified surroundings ... facing a murder charge.... How would she react? How would *he* react?

His sister Stella and her husband Tom White,* had come to visit him from Mantua, Ohio, on the Monday and Tuesday before Thanksgiving. He and his sister had always been close, and it had been a difficult reunion. During their visit he had wondered again how much she suspected of his involvement in the Sheppard murder: the composite drawing in the paper, descriptions of a bushy-haired intruder, his hurried departure from Mantua. But the meeting would be worse with his mother-in-law, particularly when they talked about Muriel and his son....

---

*fictitious name

As the deputy swung the cell door open Jim smoothed his hair back with his hands, took a deep breath to compose himself, and followed the jailer out of the cell and down a narrow corridor.

"Hello, James." He heard the voice before he saw her. She was sitting near a deputy in the visitor's area. It was a light musical voice, reminiscent of his wife's. Immediately he felt a rush of emotion.

"It's so good to see you, James," she said, standing, moving forward and embracing him. "My poor boy. I've been so worried about you."

Jim's plans for restraint deserted him. He took her into his arms, hugging her tightly, struggling to keep his feelings in check.

"Please sit over here, ma'am," said one of the deputies, not unkindly, motioning to the chair in which she had been sitting.

Jim sat down nearby, started to speak but then swallowed with difficulty, looking down at the floor.

Robbie John, as though sensing he might lose control, averted her eyes but continued to talk, her voice strained but determined. "Jeff's wonderful, a real joy. I can see you in him already." She pressed on, speaking of people at home, Jeff's schooling, her sister Edna, her husband Victor who had been having heart problems— topics designed, it seemed, to pull them through the initial emotional challenge of their reunion.

She was an attractive woman, described by newspapers covering pretrial proceedings as a "tall, pretty, well-dressed person" with an "aristocratic but gracious bearing." She had retained much of her earlier beauty, and her daughter's features and mannerisms were evident. Her blonde hair was drawn back into a bun, and stylish tinted glasses covered what must have been weary eyes.

Although caught up in his own emotions, Jim realized what an ordeal the trip must be for his mother-in-law. She had always displayed tremendous grit, even as her daughter lay dying. Jim, by contrast, had been unable to cope at that time. Grief stricken, he had collapsed on Muriel's bed. Robbie John had pulled him through his anguish. It was the same now—a thousand miles from her home, in jail in a strange part of the country, her husband ill, her grandson being cared for by a babysitter while his father faced a possible death sentence. These were circumstances that would have tested the mettle of any woman. As Jim sat listening to her speak in a soft but firm voice, admiration welled up in him. He glanced at the guard, who had remained in the room but at a respectful distance, allowing them a measure of privacy.

As though sensing Jim had regained control, and aware that they were running out of time, Mrs. John pressed on to more immediate issues. "I've talked to Mr. Jones. Mr. Stewart Jones. He's a lawyer who practices in Troy, New York. The Attorney General's office referred me to him. Everyone says he's an outstanding person. I liked him very much on the phone. He's considering taking your case, but first he—"

"I don't want a lawyer," Jim said, interrupting, his eyes once more focused on the floor. He had considered an attorney during the preceding weeks and concluded that it would only drag things out. He wanted a quick resolution of his case. Prolonged exposure might somehow pull him into the Sheppard affair.

"Please, James." Her brow contracted, showing concern. For the first time her voice quavered. "We must act intelligently, courageously. Your situation is ... well, it's perilous. If not for yourself, you must think of Jeff."

Jim placed his hand over his eyes, unable to respond.

"We have no choice, James," the woman continued, her voice now firm. "We must do everything in our power for that child. That means retaining the best attorney we can possibly find. As far as I can determine, that man is Stewart Jones."

As she spoke, Jim noticed the sheriff appear at the entranceway, glancing at his watch. "I'm afraid we're running out of time now, Mrs. John." His voice was genial, even friendly.

"Yes, yes, thank you, Mr. Crowley," she said, standing. Then turning to her son-in-law, she embraced him warmly. "We must be brave, James." Again, the hitch in her voice. Avoiding his eyes, she squeezed his hand and preceded the sheriff through the door.

Jim watched her leave, wetting his lips, a tightness in his throat. Noticing the deputy by the door watching him closely, waiting to escort him back to his cell, his demeanor stiffened. Avoiding the guard's eyes, he walked from the room.

Once back in his cell, he sat on his cot, back against the wall, knees drawn up against his chest, reflecting on the meeting. Although it had been an emotional ordeal he felt strengthened, infused with Robbie John's resilience. She was right, of course. It was a time for courage, certainly not self-pity. And she was probably right about a lawyer. The court would appoint one if he didn't retain one himself.

Thoughts of Muriel floated through his mind. She would be appalled at his present situation ... the type of father he'd become ... his irresponsibility. He had to think of Jeff. And he would be no help to his son dead. He would keep his options open, both legal and otherwise. Of one thing he was certain: there was no way he was going to the electric chair.

◆ ◆ ◆

56

If Robbie John felt her world collapsing, she concealed it. Despite the sorrow she had endured for the previous two years, her manner was friendly, spirited. Nowhere was this more evident than in the relationship with her son-in-law. Her support for him, unwavering and unequivocal, had been apparent during interviews with reporters in Meridian prior to leaving for Elizabethtown to visit Jim.

"James was shattered by the death of Muriel and never recovered," she was reported to have said. "He had a very brilliant mind and with one who thought things so deeply, it wouldn't be hard for a shock to disturb the balance. He liked things orderly. He was so well-reserved and had so much dignity. If James is guilty of all the horrible things that have been said about him it's the result of a shattered mind, and he needs all the help and mercy a very sick boy requires."

She had done her best to convey these sentiments upon reaching Elizabethtown and, to a degree, had been successful. The reception from both the authorities and the media had been gracious.

However, from her perspective the meeting with Jim in the jail had not gone well, adding to her burden. His appearance itself had shocked her. Having been accustomed to a tanned, good-looking young major in crisp Air Force uniforms, she had been taken aback by the thin, sallow-faced man in prison clothes. Not only was she distressed by his appearance, his professed indifference to the outcome of his case was a source of even greater concern. If they were to weather this ordeal, and she was determined they would, she would have to instill in James the will to defend himself, to believe in something above himself, to think of his young son. Right now, it seemed as if he were prepared to accept whatever verdict the court rendered.

Later, with customary candor, she had related her feelings to members of the media at a small press conference:

James was on the verge of breaking down and was beyond speaking about his present situation during our two visits.... I saw him break down before when Muriel died and I didn't want it to happen again. He did ask many questions about his son. He is a person with great strength of character. He loves to read and asked me to get him some good books.

She concluded the interview with reporters by stating that she would remain in Elizabethtown for a few more days, but then had to return to her family in Meridian. She said that she and her husband would come back for the court proceedings. "I do not want to leave without expressing my appreciation to Sheriff Crowley and his staff," she said. "They have all been very kind to me during my two visits."

♦ ♦ ♦

57

E. Stewart Jones was not only an able attorney, he was a charming man with ivy-league good looks and a gracious sensitivity not particularly prevalent in his profession. Even his adversaries had kind words for him. "Now, Stewart Jones, he was a very astute lawyer," said prosecutor Dan Manning, in describing his opponent years later. "A fine gentleman." It was a portrayal which prevailed both within and outside of the legal trade.

A graduate of Williams College and Albany Law School, Jones had joined his father's law firm in 1935. He was described in one news article as "tall, heavy-set, calm and suave, with closely cropped wiry hair. He dresses quietly and looks more like a prosperous banker than a hard-hitting courtroom strategist who has been known to shed a tear in pleading for a client."

At the time he was retained to defend Jim Call, Jones had lost only one case in twenty years. He had represented just six defendants in criminal cases, but all of those had ended in acquittals. His father, Abbott Jones, had been an equally successful attorney, having secured an acquittal for the notorious "Legs" Diamond on assault and kidnapping charges in 1930.

Robbie John had been impressed by Stewart Jones' intellect and personal qualities from the beginning. "He is a wonderful, compassionate person," she said to reporters. "We have great faith in him." She was to retain this confidence in the lawyer to the very end.

About thirty witnesses were in the courtroom on Saturday, January 15, 1955, when the Essex County Grand Jury foreman handed up the indictments to presiding Justice Andrew Ryan. James A. Call was charged with first-degree murder and six other felonies, including attempted first-degree robbery and burglary. Jim, impressively dressed in a light gray suit, white shirt, and maroon tie, was brought before the bench. Few in the courtroom were impervious to his dignified bearing and suave manner. "He simply towered over everyone," said one veteran reporter. "He was the last man in the courtroom you'd pick out as the prisoner."

At this point, Jones stepped forward and interposed a plea of innocent to each indictment. He then said, "Your Honor, my client has been indicted for the most serious of crimes under our law, punishable by death. A life is at stake. I cannot hope to adequately defend him unless given sufficient time in which to prepare a defense."

He proceeded to relate how he had become involved in the case, stating, "It wasn't until late November that I was contacted by the defendant's family, and I didn't talk to the defendant until early December. Actually, it wasn't until last Sunday that I decided to take the case. The magnitude of the preparation is enormous. It will be necessary to obtain depositions from persons all over the country—indeed, all over the world. Europe, Korea.... It will all take time."

Justice Ryan, a balding, bespectacled man of judicial bearing, deliberated momentarily, nodding his head in a way that suggested he was favorably disposed to the request. He turned to District Attorney Manning, looking for a response.

"Under the circumstances, the request for a delay seems justifiable Your Honor," said Manning without hesitation. "We have no objections."

"Very well," said the judge. "Request granted. The trial date will be set for Saturday, April 16, 1955, at 10:00 a.m., for hearing motions and to start selections for a jury." He then remanded Jim to the custody of the Essex County Sheriff, without bail.

In an interview with the news media following the courtroom proceedings, Jones professed his belief in Call's innocence. "I've taken only six so-called criminal cases in twenty years," he said. "In each instance, I took the case because in my mind and heart I thought that the defendant was not guilty of the crimes for which he was indicted. I would not have accepted this case unless I felt James Call was innocent."

Although the statement was brief—perhaps even platitudinous by some standards—it was offered with the quiet charm and dignity that had captivated jurors over two decades. The subdued, almost docile reaction from the reporters augured well for Jim Call's chances. Said one journalist, "Unlike most lawyers you actually believed Jones."

◆ ◆ ◆

58

Stewart Jones was soon to become less sanguine about the Call case than he had been when interviewed by the press at the time of the arraignment. During succeeding weeks, as he spent many hours with Jim in preparation for the trial, a sense of his client had emerged indicating a personality far more complicated than he had originally thought. In a recorded interview with a TV newscaster years later, he described the experience:

INTERVIEWER

Do you remember how you first became involved with the Call case?

JONES

Yes, I recall quite clearly. I received a call from Major Call's mother-in-law and was retained by her. After going through the necessary legal channels, I went to the Elizabethtown jail and met Call. I was most impressed by him. He was a very handsome young man, very articulate, with the charisma of a Kennedy, and very well-schooled. He could quote Shakespeare endlessly. From that time on I was with him for many days.

INTERVIEWER

How did such a talented individual end up this way?

JONES

He was a fascinating person. He had this experience in the Korean War when his wife, whom he loved very dearly, died. He then volunteered for additional service—so-called suicide flights. It took him away from the tragedy of losing his wife. He had a tremendous war record, and then something snapped. While he was still in the service, he enjoyed high living and fast cars. He finally went AWOL. When I talked with him, it turned out he had gone into Massachusetts and robbed a taxi driver. That's what led him to New York State, the North Country. As I recall, he then foraged his way through the North Country ... broke into these summer homes.... While he was in one of those summer homes, Lake Placid officers found him inside. Apparently, this house was available to the police and it's where they would meet. They would either play cards or spend some time there. Maybe they used it to get warm too, I don't know. Anyway, Call was in there and heard someone coming so he went down in the cellar and hid in a portable shower. The policemen went downstairs, and shot into the shower, and then, Call, of course, shot back, went up the stairs and escaped. That became the famous 106-day manhunt, the longest concentrated manhunt in U.S. history.

INTERVIEWER
Right, the longest concentrated manhunt.

JONES
Call told me these fascinating tales. He had an amazing ability to survive. He had taken survival courses in the service, knew how to live on berries, how to kill rabbits and chickens. He lived in a lean-to, stayed there for quite a few days, heard people searching for him on numerous occasions. When he'd hear them, he'd climb up these heavy, thick trees. On one occasion, he was up there, probably twenty feet above them hidden by the leaves and branches, when they were below, examining the lean-to. Many times he was only 30 or 40 feet from the officers. He'd dig a hole in the ground, crawl in, and cover himself with leaves while the officers were searching all around him.

INTERVIEWER

His military associates, superiors, everyone, said he was extraordinarily bright.

JONES

No question. He had a brilliant mind. Well, now he's brought back from Reno. I go up to see him on many occasions. When he's arraigned, for instance, he suddenly has the charisma of a movie actor. High school bobby soxers would come from the local Elizabethtown high school, some from the local grammar school as well. They'd be outside the court-room, inside the courtroom, asking for his autograph. He simply charmed everyone. I never saw such an exhibition.

INTERVIEWER

He sure could turn it on when he needed it. The charm, that is. All those stories about him being so gentle. Yet, look at his record. Murder, armed robberies. He was something of a Jekyll and Hyde, wasn't he?

JONES

Precisely. Although more Dr. Jekyll, I think. These crimes.... Well, I just think he found himself in these impossible sit-uations and then just reacted as best he could. He'd been trained in combat since he was eighteen. And remember, when I came on the scene he was facing the electric chair.

For the very reasons he mentioned, Stewart Jones should have known that Jim Call, finding himself in an "impossible situation" and "facing the electric chair," would have reacted "as best he could." But as Jones would soon learn, his client's reaction would be far more than Jekyllian.

◆ ◆ ◆

iller Was Trained to Survive

(Special to the Mirror)

ARANAC LAKE, N. Y. Nov. 21—Rigorous training in the Air Force's survival
made Maj. James A. Call, confessed killer of an Upstate policeman, one of the
est wanted-men ever sought by the State Police, it was revealed Sunday.

CRIBED AS a highly in- nt prisoner—one who read baiyat and deep philosoph- orks even while evading e in the dense woods—Call us a rough time" because survival training, one po- ficer disclosed.

could tell where he was e stars and he sure knew to take care of himself," ource declared.

, Harold Muller said he iestion the handsome de- on his hiding-out tech- Muller expressed satisfac- th the showing made by ate Police in hunting the ained killer. He quoted Call itting that the force kept ttled up for many weeks "every time I stuck my nose out of a hideout I'd see a state trooper some place."

LODGED IN THE Essex County jail at Elizabethtown, Call showed no remorse for the slaying of Patrolman Richard Pelkey of the Lake Placid police force—a killing which touched off a 104-day State Police man-hunt through the Adirondacks. But Muller told THE MIRROR he felt Call "was relieved to get the killing off his chest."

Call, nabbed on a burglary charge in Reno, was described as "very cooperative." He denied other crimes committed in the Adirondacks last Summer, when Pelkey was slain, including the shooting of a fisherman.

November 21, 1954
(*The New York Daily Mirror*)

59

"No autopsy!"

"What?"

"You heard me. No autopsy was taken on the dead officer."

Dan Manning sat in his office, a dejected look on his face, talking to Harold Soden, the former District Attorney whom he had asked to assist him with the Call case.

"There must have been an autopsy," countered Soden, surprised.

"Well, there wasn't. I called Captain Muller, told him we were getting ready to present the case to the grand jury, that we needed to talk to the doctor who performed the autopsy. Muller said he couldn't recall the person, but that Inspector McDowell could tell me. So, I called McDowell and Mack says 'Well, I think you'd better talk to the captain about that,' meaning Muller. 'He knows all about it.' Well, as it turns out, they simply didn't do any autopsy."

A silence ensued as the two reflected on the consequences of attempting to prove a first-degree murder charge without proof of how the victim had died.

Finally, Soden cleared his throat and said, "Well, we got Doctor Merkel from Saranac Lake. He took care of Pelkey right from the time he was shot. He can testify as to the cause of death."

"Yes, but if we had the autopsy it would eliminate any kind of problem whatsoever," said Manning, his frown firmly entrenched. He flipped his pencil onto the desk. "I guess we'll just have to rely on Merkel. With Merkel in there as the doctor who saw him daily, saw him go down and down, and who performed the operation on him to recover the bullet, there's no break in the chain of events as far as the medical testimony is concerned. It's all we can do."

"What about Stew?" the assistant asked.

"Stewart Jones? Well, maybe he won't ask for the autopsy."

"Oh, I don't know about that." Soden shook his head dubiously. "You're talking about one of the finest trial lawyers in New York—anywhere, for that matter. He's head and shoulders over anyone else. First-degree murder? I can't imagine Stew won't ask for that autopsy. If it isn't produced he'll do everything he can to create doubts in the mind of the jury whether Pelkey actually did die from gunshot wounds."

"No question it's a weakness in our case," said Manning with a shrug. "Still, you never know. Maybe he'll just assume it was done. Not bring it up."

Soden arched his brow skeptically. "I don't know.... Besides, I still don't think there's a murder-one case here. Too many questions. The officer who opened fire was wearing civilian clothes. They never actually did identify themselves as police officers. All kinds of rumors about the officers using the camp to play cards before the shooting took—"

"You don't believe that stuff, do you?" interrupted Manning. "Rumors. That's all it is. Maybe the officers did use the camp to warm up on some occasion, but so what? Most of it's a lot of crap."

"Sure, but you know damn well how stuff gets around in a small town. Things will show up in the papers. Stew's already suggesting to the reporters that the defense will have some surprises."

"Well, we have to deal with the facts. And the facts are that the village police fired the first shots. Then Call had a chance to make up his mind on whether to shoot somebody in order to get out. That, of course, is a question of fact. That's the premeditation we need for murder one. He'd broken into the camp, was burglarizing it, right? He committed the crime of homicide during the process of committing another crime. That's felony murder. You have a situation here where the press is making a hero out of a defendant who killed a police officer. The families of those officers are outraged. They—"

"Dan," Soden interrupted quietly. "Dan, let's look at the defense. You're dealing with a war hero who'll claim he was acting in self-defense against some type of vigilantes. I hear Stew is making inquiries about having him wearing his uniform during the trial. Even though he's AWOL, Call is technically still in the service."

Manning placed his glasses on his desk and raised a hand to his forehead. It was apparent the case was weighing on him. "How are we doing with the camp layout?" he asked, referring to a miniature model of the Perkins camp which the prosecution planned to use as evidence at the trial.

"Pretty good. The final price is $3,200," Soden replied.

"Good lord," said Manning. "The cost of this trial could bankrupt Essex County."

"We need the camp model. It's essential. We have to show the pattern of gunfire to the jury. The defense is already suggesting a ricochet theory. Half of Lake Placid thinks the officers shot Pelkey."

"This trial will cost a fortune," Manning reiterated, rolling his eyes.

"Well, maybe it won't go to trial. Stew may want to negotiate."

"I doubt it," said Manning. "Not Stewart Jones."

◆ ◆ ◆

60

"C'mon Jim," said the guard impatiently. "Christ, it takes you forever to move. No wonder you win."

The deputy sat at a table containing a checkerboard in the holding room outside Jim's cell. The table was positioned so Jim could reach through the bars to play.

"What's your hurry?" replied Jim, easily. "Relax, I'm not going anywhere. And if I'm not going anywhere, you're not going anywhere, right?"

Jim was sitting on the end of his cot, chin resting in his hand, staring at the checkers as though pondering his next move. His mind, however, was on far more serious matters. After the guard's first few moves Jim knew he had already won and he was just going through the motions. The deputy invariably made the same mistakes. For Jim, the checkers and card games were boring, played more for his guard's enjoyment than his own.

Unaware of the prosecution's dilemma over the insufficiency of their case, he had spent hours of solitude contemplating his chances of a jury sending him to the death house at Sing Sing. His mind was constantly evaluating opportunities for escape and evasion. As the weeks passed, a plan had evolved and the young guard sitting across the table from him figured prominently in his scheme. The deputy was his way out. He liked the man personally. In fact, he had found most of his jailers quite friendly and courteous, given the circumstances. Some of them had even called him "Major" at first—a practice soon discontinued apparently on instructions from above. He was now called "Jim" by most of the prison staff.

But for a man with escape on his mind, personal amenities were of no more interest than the cards or checkers. He was involved in a far greater game of survival. An hour rarely passed that he did not focus on his plan. For several weeks he had been saving all metal objects, discreetly removing staples from magazines and pamphlets, retaining paperclips from legal documents whenever possible. Once, he had even kept his lawyer's pen after signing a paper. From these he had fashioned an extraordinary lethal shiv almost six inches long which he concealed in his mattress.

For weeks he had been carefully observing and evaluating his guards so that he knew the prison routine better than they did. Between him and freedom were three barred metal doors: one on his cell, another leading from the holding room outside his cell—in which a guard was stationed 24 hours a day—and the third at the foot of the stairs leading to the first floor and the entrance to the reception area. Beyond that was the Adirondack wilderness. Once he was there, as history had shown, they would never catch him.

The greatest obstacle confronting him was gaining access to the pass keys held by the deputy beyond the holding room. It was this guard who controlled ingress and egress not only to the holding room, but also to Jim's cell. Jim's plan was to incapacitate the deputy in the holding room outside his cell in a manner that was sufficient to control him, and to use the man as a hostage as he had done with Bernie Fell. In exchange for the man's safety he would demand weapons, sufficient provisions, and a car. Chances were best, he thought, during the evening when they opened the holding room door to bring him dinner.

What concerned him was the wiry stature of the man sitting at the table outside his cell. Given his training, he believed he could overcome the guard, if necessary, by stabbing him with the shiv in a non-lethal area such as the lower abdomen. But such a move involved great risk. Anything could happen. Nevertheless, he was prepared to chance it, however dangerous, should the impending trial indicate that a death sentence was possible. He'd been gambling most of his life. Certainly his chances of surviving a breakout from the county jail in Elizabethtown were far better than they would be in the death house at Sing Sing. And if he failed? Well, there was always the shiv.

◆ ◆ ◆

61

"But, Jim, how could you consider such a thing?"

Stewart Jones was sitting with his client in the Essex County Jail, agonizing over information he had received earlier in the day from Robbie John.

Jim sat on his cot, head in his hands, looking at the floor. "So, she told you about the letter, huh?"

"But why would you even think of escaping?" said the lawyer. "Our case is proceeding well. The prosecution knows they don't have a murder-one case. They'll have to negotiate. You can't jeopardize everything with such foolhardy schemes."

The foolhardy schemes to which Jones was alluding were later described by Jones in an interview with a journalist:

INTERVIEWER
You were aware of some of these plans Call had for breaking out?

JONES
Oh, yes. One thing happened that I'll never forget. An example of this man's state of mind. He would give me letters and ask me to mail them for him. Those letters would go to his mother-in-law, a friend, or whatever. And so, I mailed one to his mother-in-law one time, and she called me. She said, "Did you know that in that letter was another letter? He's getting some wrong ideas. That other letter was addressed to a very close friend of his who would do anything for him. I opened it and I want to read it to you...." Well, the letter to so-and-so was that he was confined to a small town jail. The deputy sheriffs were very friendly, and they were not of the

highest level of intelligence. He said that he felt, if so-and-so could arrange to bake a cake and send it to him, they [the deputies] would not even bother to test the cake. And in the cake, they should place a .38 caliber revolver ... loaded. *He said he could shoot his way out of that jail in no time.* He tried this on *two* separate occasions. [emphasis added]

INTERVIEWER
I think it was a relative who received that letter.

JONES
Yes, I think you're right about that. Then of course, I went up to the jail and said, "Don't get into any more trouble than you're in right now."

INTERVIEWER
Do you recall that the State Police failed to have an autopsy performed?

JONES
Yes, that's true. One of the great failures was neglecting to do an autopsy. How else can you determine, beyond a doubt, the cause of death?

INTERVIEWER
What were some of the other obstacles that the prosecution faced?

JONES
Well, of course, there was the charge of premeditated murder in the first degree. I doubt if they could have successfully gotten by a motion at the end of the prosecution's case to reduce the charge from first to second-degree murder. And I don't think that they could prove sufficient grounds to justify summation of the jury on a first-degree murder charge.

INTERVIEWER

Was there any possibility at all that you could have gotten him off altogether?

JONES

Well, the problem was that there were so many other circumstances he was facing in these charges that were fairly indefensible. If he had gotten off, he'd've had to go to Massachusetts to face some other very serious charges. In New York, he was still charged in other indictments with the wounding of the two other officers and several assault charges. The culmination of the death of one officer and the wounding of two other officers, plus the circumstances of the pending charges in the State of Massachusetts led to what we term today as a plea-bargaining situation.

INTERVIEWER

One thing I'd like to go over again with you has to do with the Lake Placid police officers and their practice of playing poker at the Perkins camp. Do you recall how you found that out?

JONES

Yes, as part of the overall investigation supplied to me by my own investigator. It was common knowledge that they used the Perkins camp and other locations as meeting places. I'm not saying that there was anything clandestine about it. They may have used the camps to warm up or to socialize.

INTERVIEWER

There was a $100,000 jewel robbery one day before the shooting at the Perkins camp.

JONES

Yes, but I'm certain he had nothing to do with that. Do you have any indication that he did?

INTERVIEWER
Yes, I have information that indicates that he pulled that burglary.

JONES
But what would he have done with the jewels?

INTERVIEWER
That seems to be the big question, doesn't it?

JONES
Well, as his attorney, he wasn't required to tell me everything.

No one was more aware than Jim Call how little he was required to tell his attorney. Had Jones had any idea of how much his client actually withheld from him, he might well have reconsidered his role as defense attorney. A day did not pass that Jim was not considering some scheme for "busting out." His letter to his friend Robert Sylvester expressed as much. During an interview years later Sylvester described the communications:

SYLVESTER
Jimmy sent me a letter from prison asking for a piece of wood with a razor blade hidden inside.

INTERVIEWER
What did he want to do with it?

SYLVESTER
I don't know and I didn't want to know. This was before the trial and before they were monitoring his letters.

INTERVIEWER
What did you do with the letter?

SYLVESTER

I was disgusted so I threw it out. But there were others. Once he sent me a letter with a message underneath the stamp. Jimmy was always able to write really small.... He licked only the corners of the stamp so that by the time it made it to me, the stamp had come off and his message was visible. I couldn't believe it. He asked me to send chloral hydrate, which is known as a "knock-out drug." I was surprised that Jimmy knew what it was. Chloral hydrate is dangerous. He wanted to take care of the guard that he played checkers with so that he could escape. He came up with all these crazy ideas. Once he asked me to send him a doctored can of fruit juice. He told me to empty the can, put scotch inside, and solder the edge shut. I did send him food, paper, cartons of cigarettes, and a bunch of stuff, but never what he really wanted.

◆ ◆ ◆

62

"I knew Jim at Okinawa." Lieutenant R.L. Kaiser, Chaplain at Barksdale Air Force Base, was sitting in his office talking to Harry Blaisdell and a fellow trooper. Blaisdell and his colleague had been dispatched to Mississippi at the request of Dan Manning to conduct a background investigation of Call in anticipation of the trial.

"I saw quite a bit of him from February to October 1953," said Father Kaiser. "I thought he was a rather strange individual. I learned that he was a fallen-away Catholic, and I tried to get him to return to the church. But he had no interest. He was a firm agnostic—said that religion had been forced on him when he was young. Whenever we discussed it, he'd argue against the existence of God. Wanted no part of the Catholic religion."

"How did you get to know him?" Harry asked.

"Some of the other officers suggested that I talk to him. He was having some problems. His wife had passed away and he was taking it very hard. He was a lone wolf—terrific compulsion for gambling."

"How about his other morals? Women, drinking?"

"They were okay, as far as I know. He never consorted with the local women, to my knowledge. I met him in Itazuke, Japan, and tried to be helpful, but he wasn't receptive. Wouldn't share his problems with anyone. He suffered extreme egotism, in my opinion. At first I thought his problems derived from the death of his wife, but after several months I concluded that it wasn't just his wife. Maybe her death exacerbated his problems, but I think there was more to it than that."

"You mentioned that you've been in touch with him since he's been in jail?"

"Yes. Some of the officers in the squadron asked me to try to help him so I wrote to Father Kelly."

"Father Kelly?" Blaisdell asked.

"Yes, Donald M. Kelly. He's a priest in Westport, New York, near Elizabethtown. I asked him to visit Call and try to get him back in the church. That he needed God's help."

"He's the priest who's been visiting Call?"

"Yes. Father Kelly told me he's talked a great deal with him, but that he has no hope whatever of helping him along religious lines. Father Kelly said that Jim wanted to be remembered to me, that things weren't as black as they were painted to be, that I shouldn't worry."

"Well, I don't know about that, Father." Harry Blaisdell stroked his chin thoughtfully. "I'd say that at this stage Major Call could probably use all the prayers he can get."

♦ ♦ ♦

63

"It's your decision, Jim. No one can make it for you."

Stewart Jones gathered up his papers, tapping the edges on his knee, then placing them in a manila folder. He had spent the last two hours with his client in the Essex County Jail, summarizing their case and outlining options.

"I've explained the legal issues. But you're the only one who can decide where we go from here. Frankly, I was surprised the meeting in Judge Ryan's chambers went as well as it did. Particularly Manning's reaction. I think the prosecution may come under some heavy criticism from the press and community if they accept a plea to murder two."

"Twenty years to life," Jim said, grimacing. "I don't think I can handle that."

"It's really less than fifteen, with good behavior."

"But even that. I'd be over forty before I'm even eligible for parole. Living in a cage—"

"Jim," interrupted the lawyer. He opened his mouth as though to speak then paused, a weary expression on his face. "Jim, you're facing first-degree murder, a possible death sentence. I don't think they could get it. But with a jury, anything can happen. And even if they acquitted you, there are all these other charges."

"But what about manslaughter? You mentioned earlier that—"

"Judge Ryan won't accept a manslaughter plea. I tried hard. The judge was very firm. It's either murder two or we go to trial."

"Tough decision," Jim murmured. He sat, looking past his lawyer, his dark eyes focused, as though answers to his problem might somehow appear on the cement-block wall several feet away. It was, in fact, a more complicated decision for him than his lawyer realized. There were other considerations. If he rejected the plea bargain and went to trial there would be continuous publicity, an important consideration for Jim. He was surprised they had not pressed him for details regarding his activities before coming to Lake Placid. Maybe they'd focus on it during the trial. Would the Sheppard murder resurface? He'd been following the investigation closely in the newspapers. The crime scene evidence ... witnesses who had seen him outside the Sheppard residence around the time of the murder.... He'd have no chance at all. There were people who knew he'd been in Mantua at that time. Probably better to plead to murder two. Prison at least offered obscurity. Interest in the Sheppard case would fade.

"Of course it's a tough decision," continued Jones. "But we're in a difficult situation. Take your time. Talk it over with your family, your mother-in-law, your sister. They'll all be here tomorrow." The lawyer rose, preparing to leave. "A young woman spoke to me briefly as I was coming back from lunch. Wanted to know if you were all right."

"A young woman?" Jim said.

"Yes, I was coming out of the Deershead across the street. Ordinarily I avoid these situations. You've got a lot of female fans out there asking about you. But she ... well, there was something different about her. Dark hair, very attractive and well-spoken. Said she knew you but declined to give her name."

"Dark hair?" said Jim, with mounting interest. "I think I know who it was. What did she say?"

"I didn't really stop. So many of them.... Can't get involved there on the street."

The lawyer lingered, looking at his client closely. "Anything I should be aware of?"

"No. Not really." Jim glanced away, suggesting he was not interested in elaborating.

"Okay, I understand," said Jones. "I'm your attorney, but you're not obligated to tell me everything." Then with a smile, "Unless it has to do with the case, right?"

Back in his cell, Jim sat down on his cot, staring pensively at the floor. He knew who the person was his lawyer had seen. There was no question. The description of the woman, the way she spoke.... For several minutes he was gripped by thoughts of Greta Brown, reliving the nights on the shores of Lake Placid, romantic interludes when plans were conceived and promises made.

He closed his eyes, consumed by thoughts. Twenty years. He'd be middle-aged by the time he was released, his life gone. He could never do twenty years. Better to die breaking out. Leaning back on his cot, he turned so that he was facing the wall, arms covering his head.

◆ ◆ ◆

64

Supreme Court Justice Andrew W. Ryan gazed from the bench in the Essex County Courthouse, his expression exceedingly grave. From his somber countenance one might well have assumed that he was about to intone the death sentence. Indeed, the judge's demeanor reflected the tense session underway as the officers of the court prepared to debate issues of life and death.

It was 11:15 a.m. on May 6, 1955, and the principals of the Call case had gathered before Judge Ryan for the third and final hearing before the trial, which was to commence on June 6th. Although it was a sunny spring morning, little of the brightness managed to filter through the long narrow windows of the cavernous building. The interior was similar to most of the old county courthouses in upstate New York, with the judge's bench, jury box, and tables and chairs for the prosecution and defense located behind a guardrail at the front of the chamber. Rows of traditional wooden benches, as well as an upstairs gallery, were provided for the public. On the walls were oil portraits of past county court justices—austere men in high square collars—dating back to the nineteenth century. It was a quaint, impeccably neat room, reflecting the spirit of an orderly rural community.

Jim sat in the back row of the jury box, his left wrist handcuffed to a deputy sheriff. Although he had appeared relaxed when he first entered, his face had now taken on the strain which prevailed in the room. Matters of grave importance to his future were about to unfold and the uncertainty of the outcome was evident not only in Jim, but in all of those participating.

Among the spectators sitting in the front row behind the guardrail were Jim's relatives, whom Ann Breen of the *Press-Republican* described in a news article on May 9, 1955 as "very nervous":

One was Mrs. Victor John, an attractive blonde, who is Call's mother-in-law. It is she who has been bringing up Call's four-year-old son since her daughter Muriel died in childbirth. [*sic*]

Beside Mrs. John sat [...] Call's sister and brother-in-law. [...] is a Cleveland, Ohio contractor. [...] is a pretty woman, apparently older than Call, with short black hair with some gray in it.

All three declined to speak to reporters, both before and after the hearing. Said Mrs. John: "I'm sorry, I just can't possibly talk about anything now. I have nothing to say."

All three sat tensely in their seats throughout the hearing. Call never once glanced at them.

As the session began at the instruction of Judge Ryan, Dan Manning rose at the prosecution table and briefly reviewed the facts of the case. He was followed by Stewart Jones.

"Your Honor," Jones said, rising and moving toward the bench. "The defense would like to withdraw its former plea of not guilty to the charge of first-degree murder. We would like to offer a move that the defendant enter a plea of guilty to the crime of second-degree murder."

Judge Ryan inched forward in his chair and looked toward Jim. "Does the defendant understand he is pleading guilty to second-degree murder?" he asked.

Jim, his jaw firmly set, responded briskly, "Yes, Your Honor, I do."

Turning to the prosecution table the judge said, "Mr. Manning?"

The courtroom became quiet as a crypt as eyes focused on the prosecution's table. Jim sat stiffly, head up, his attention seemingly riveted on a distant horizon.

"I have given much consideration to this matter, Your Honor." The prosecutor removed his horn-rimmed glasses as he rose from his chair, his manner deliberate and serious. "The enormity of the crime was so great that I have given intense thought in anticipation of this plea, before making my decision. The fact that the defendant returned from Nevada voluntarily, cooperated fully, and gave a full confession has been taken into consideration. Also, it is the prosecution's opinion that had this case gone to trial the jury would have returned a verdict of second-degree murder. In addition, although I must emphasize that this reason is secondary, the trial would of necessity have been a very costly matter to the people. In view of these facts, after much reflection, I will consent to a plea of murder second degree. I honestly and truly feel that it is in the best interests of all that I accept this plea."

An undertone of surprise filled the courtroom. A sharp rap of the judge's gavel brought order and an expectant hush as Jim was brought before the bench to be sentenced. The only sound in the cavernous hall was the monotonous whirring of two large rotating fans which peered from the front of the courtroom like a pair of enormous roving eyes. Stern visages in high collars looked down from the frames on the wall, silent forebears who brooked no interference with the administration of Essex County justice.

Judge Ryan, his slight frame amplified by judicial robes, moved quickly to impose sentence. After eliciting from Jim a series of answers to background questions mandated by the court, including an admission that he knew of no legal reason why sentence should not be pronounced, and that he had received no promises from the court with respect to the charges, the judge sentenced him to twenty years to life at Clinton Prison in Dannemora, New York.

Although Jim had anticipated the sentence, the judge's words gripped him deeply. Despite his lawyer's grimly realistic prediction, he had harbored the hope of a lighter sentence. But now it was final: twenty long years, an eternity for a young man. He straightened, showing no sign of emotion other than a glimpse of a smile at his family as he was led from the courtroom.

Following the hearing, statements by Jones and Manning commenting on the plea were reported in the press:

> E. Stewart Jones, Call's attorney, said after the hearing that the prisoner had made his decision to plead guilty only a few minutes before the court session started. "We had been thinking about it for some time," Jones told the press. "I must be frank in saying that I did advise him, but it was his decision to make. His relatives were all merely there to guide him."
>
> Manning also affirmed that the agreement not to go to trial was a momentary one. "I had anticipated that a second degree plea might be made, and I had given it a great deal of

thought," Manning said. "But none of them actually approached me about it until this morning. However, I had already made up my mind to accept it if they asked."

As the court proceedings came to a close the relief in the front row of the spectators' gallery was palpable. Robbie John leaned forward, her face in her hands. Her grandson would still have a father.

◆ ◆ ◆

CONFERENCE—E. Stewart Jones, defense attorney for confessed cop-killer, James A. Call, talks outside the Essex County Jail with Mrs. Victor Johns, Call's mother-in-law in Elizabethtown after Call was sentenced Saturday to serve from 20 years to life in the Aug. 5 slaying of Lake Placid Patrolman Richard Pelkey. Call was permitted to plead guilty to a reduced charge of second-degree murder.

Jones and Mrs. John outside jail, Elizabethtown—May 7, 1955
(The Post-Standard)

65

Thoughts of Greta were with Jim constantly. Ever since his lawyer had mentioned the dark-haired girl who had approached him outside the jail, Jim had harbored the thought that Greta might attempt to visit him. He longed to be with her; just the thought of her coming to visit caused his heart to quicken. But it was out of the question. He could envision the headlines: *Beautiful Mystery Woman Visits Cop Killer*. The press would descend on the jail, Sheriff Crowley, and the guards. They would be unrelenting until they had uncovered and revealed everything there was to know about the woman. But Greta realized this, he thought. She was too smart to subject herself and her family to such embarassing scrutiny. Still, she had come to Elizabethtown....

Leaning back on his cot he gazed through the window at the small patch of blue sky. He thought of Greta, reliving the nights they had spent together on the shores of Lake Placid. The last night had been the most memorable. The weather had been clear, a bright moon hanging above the peaks. A warm night. They had taken a dip in the lake to cool off....

"What if they ever came?" Greta asked nervously.

"What's that?"

"The people who own the camp." Greta, who was drying herself with a large beach towel, paused and looked up to the crest of a hill some fifty yards away where the outline of the main dwelling could be seen in the darkness. "If they ever came it would be pretty embarrassing. I mean, here we are in our underwear, using their boathouse, their towels. What would we ever say to them? 'Oh, hi.' " She turned in mimicking fashion as though greeting someone who had just arrived. "We just happened by and thought we'd take a midnight dip." She took a few steps toward the lake, one hand on her waist, wiggling her hips in exaggerated nonchalance.

It was an alluring performance which Jim found stimulating. "Don't worry, nobody will come," he said, spreading a towel on the dock and sitting down. "There hasn't been anyone here for some time."

"How do you know? Have you been here before? With someone else? Hmm...." She smiled at him wryly.

"Hardly," he laughed. "But I can tell. This place hasn't been used for days. The people who own these camps come and go for weeks at a time. Besides, if anyone ever did come we'd see their headlights the second they turned off the road. Then we'd just walk up the hill over there by that line of trees, on out to the road. They'd never even know we were here."

"You seem to have it all figured out." She resumed drying her hair, rubbing it vigorously with the towel. "Well, I guess I'm not worried if you're not."

Jim loved her hair. When wet, it tightened into jet-black ringlets that glistened in the moonlight. He took the moment while her face was covered by the towel to gaze at her body. It was a lithe figure, slender and athletic, breasts that filled out her brassiere, narrow waist, long beautiful legs. Her wet undergarments clung tightly, and in the dim light he was able to see the nipples on her breasts, the outline of pubic hair beneath her panties. He knew they would make love shortly and his heart throbbed in anticipation.

But unlike many young men who would have had difficulty restraining themselves at the threshold of lovemaking, Jim controlled his emotions. During their previous meetings he had been careful to allow the passions to evolve in a natural, ingenuous fashion. Greta had mentioned how taken she was with his restraint, his consideration.

Spreading her towel next to him, she sat down, taking his hand. "Isn't this glorious? It's our own little Shangri-La. I don't think the people who own the camp would mind if they knew how happy we were, do you?"

"Well.... I don't know," Jim replied. "People can get miffed about someone using their camps."

He glanced out over the black water to the mountains silhouetted in the distance. In a few hours he would be back at his camp. For an instant he was consumed by loneliness. Would he ever lead a normal life? In fact, had he ever lived a normal life? How wonderful it would be to take Greta with him back to his camp. Quickly, he dismissed the thought.

Drawing her close to him, he lay back on the dock, gazing at the heavens. An abundance of stars jeweled the black sky. "The Great Bear," he said, quietly.

"The what?" she said, cuddling beside him.

"The Great Bear," he repeated. "Ursa Major, the most prominent northern constellation. See, the seven stars. They form the Big Dipper."

"Oh, sure. The Big Dipper. How do you know so much about the stars? Have you spent lots of time with other women looking at the stars?" she chided.

"No," he said, smiling. "There was only one. I used to travel quite a bit. She and I sometimes used the stars as reference points. It's a long story," he said, dismissing the subject.

"Your job requires a lot of traveling?"

He emitted a short unintentional laugh. "Yeah, I guess you might say that." Turning, he moved so that his face was close to hers. Her eyes focused on him, expectant, confident. It was her confidence that impressed him. Unusual for her age. Much like Muriel.

"How would you like to go camping with me sometime?" he asked.

"Camping? Where? You mean out in the woods?"

"Sure. We could climb one of the mountains. Cook dinner. Pitch a tent. We'd be together ... like this."

"You mean overnight?"

"Why not?"

"Hmm ... ," the dark lashes fluttered as she considered the proposal. "Well, I suppose it'd be better than trespassing on people's property. Let me think about it." Then drawing back she looked at him, her eyes narrowing with a hint of skepticism. "You know, I really don't know what to think of you."

"Why's that?"

"Well, I'm not really sure. It's kind of strange—it seems we're always avoiding people. We never go into town. You never ask me to go on a real date—you know, like a movie, or dinner. Now you ask me if I want to go camping up in the mountains. What are you, some kind of hermit?"

He laughed, drawing her close to his chest. She moved against him, raising her lips toward his, her eyes steady, receptive.

"No, I don't really think I'm a hermit," he said. "Hermits are reclusive. They like to be alone, by themselves." He kissed her long and passionately.

After a moment she drew back. "Well, I guess you can tell," she said, her eyes laughing in the dark, "I'm certainly no hermitess."

♦ ♦ ♦

66

It was springtime in the Adirondacks. The verdure of new growth struggled to cover the ravages of winter in the alpine landscape. Rugged peaks, some still bearing white caps of snow, rose high in the northern blue sky, while far below smooth lakes reflected inverted shorelines of pine, cedar, birch, and hemlock. Spectacular waterfalls, some dropping hundreds of feet, and rocky streams gushing with newly melted snow were visible from the police cruiser as it wound its way through the mountain passes on its two-hour trip to Dannemora.

Inside the vehicle, in a rear seat next to a deputy, hands cuffed, sat Jim. Facing many years in prison, he sensed his future in sharp contrast to the fresh start and new life reflected in the springtime countryside. Although it might well be the last view he would have of the mountains where he had evaded his captors for over 100 days, he showed little interest. His mind was on the Clinton State Prison, about which he had heard much from the deputies during preceding days.

"You're gonna miss Elizabethtown, Jim," one had said. "Dannemora's the Siberia of the state prison system, believe me."

"I believe you," Jim had answered. "What's the difference? Can't be any worse than this place. Besides, maybe there'll be someone there who can play checkers ... beyond the kindergarten level," he had added wryly.

"Checkers. Hah! You seen your last checker game, Jim. Only time they let you outta' your cell up there is when the pipes freeze up and bust. I heard one inmate was sittin' on the can in his cell for two hours until one of the guards finally checked on him. Turns out he froze to death."

Jim, accustomed to the gallows humor, had smiled. "I've had enough of this place, anyway," he'd said as he left. "Maybe in this next zoo the gorillas will be *inside* the cages."

Even Sheriff Crowley had laughed. They all had been sorry to see him go. The charismatic, good-natured major had brought a sense of drama and excitement that would be missed in the tedium of prison life. A waitress from the Deershead Inn across the street from the jail who had come out to watch Jim's departure summed it up for most of the inhabitants of Elizabethtown, "We hated to see him leave. He was so charming. Just having him here was the biggest thing that ever happened to this town." Another unidentified Elizabethtown woman was quoted in the *Warrensburg—Lake George News* as she watched Call escorted from the prison. "He's so handsome I feel like crying when I see him like that."

Now, as he sat in the police cruiser, eyes closed, soberly contemplating his future, one might have thought Jim was dozing. In reality he was wide awake, his mind as always on opportunities for escape. He was acutely aware that in less than two hours he would be confined in a maximum security prison. His chances for freedom diminished with each passing mile.

While awaiting the trip to Dannemora, Jim had abandoned his plans to break out of the Essex County Jail. Too risky in the tank; no longer the threat of the electric chair. Still, he was not about to do twenty years if the right chance came along. And as everyone who has done time realizes, the best opportunities for escape are on the road while being transported. Once in Clinton, there'd be few trips.

He had correctly assessed the mode and circumstances of his travel to Dannemora. It would be a two-hour trip by car with three guards. He'd be in the back seat with one of them, handcuffed. He'd managed permission to take a book with him when they left the jail. In the binding was his shiv. "The guy loves books," said a deputy when asked about it by a newsperson. "Carried two books of poetry with him throughout the manhunt, didn't he?"

As Jim now saw it, the only thing separating him from the Adirondack wilderness flashing past his windows was a locked door and a large beefy-looking deputy who himself seemed on the verge of dozing. He later stated that if the two men in the front seat had left him alone with the deputy in the rear, he might have tried to use his stiletto to incapacitate the man, take his pistol, and use him as a hostage to reach the woods.

Sheriff Crowley, sitting in front next to the driver, could not have suspected such strange machinations from his soft-spoken prisoner in the back seat. He had come to like the young man and had publicly expressed as much many times. It was inconceivable that, having been spared the death penalty and now possibly facing less than twenty years, the man would attempt to escape. He was too "gentle," too "intelligent."

But the sheriff, a capable man with experience, was ever mindful of what had brought Jim to his jail in the first place. When his prisoner allowed that the cuffs were uncomfortable, the comment went unheeded. Another time, when Jim wondered aloud if they were going to stop at a bathroom, he was reminded that the sheriff had expressly warned them all that it was to be a non-stop trip. Thoughts of recriminations should Major Call be loose in the woods again were enough to stifle even the slightest deviation from security.

With such precautionary measures, the miles raced by without incident. Soon, through the windshield appeared the gray outlines of the great wall encircling Clinton State Prison. A somber mood enveloped the deputies as they approached the grim entrance, as though mindful of the dispiriting impact the place must have on their prisoner. A cool northern breeze buffeted them as they alighted from the car.

Jim was the first to break the heavy silence as they walked toward the building. "Feels a little cold, doesn't it?" When there was no reply, he smiled and said, "Oh, well, I reckon I'd rather freeze my ass off up here than have it burned off down in Sing Sing."

They all laughed, one deputy patting Jim on the back appreciatively as they guided him toward the entranceway. They seemed a convivial lot for men entering a maximum security prison.

◆ ◆ ◆

PART VIII

Dannemora, New York
November 1955

67

Mrs. Thomas F. White*
Route One
Mantua, Ohio

Box B
Dannemora, NY
7 November [1955]

Dear Doddy,

Thanks very much for the cigarettes you sent—appreciated them very much. Hope that everything is going well with everyone there.

Things are getting more difficult here for me all the time. They just won't leave me alone! I have continually refused to divulge any information to them—but they are determined. They want that information badly—but you can assure the proper people in Washington that I will not betray my sacred trust—no matter what!

Their agents are everywhere and they are insidious and persevering. I am indeed thankful that my training has enabled me to recognize their methods! If anything should happen to me—insist upon an autopsy!!

I hope I have not upset you—but I did want you to realize what is taking place.

I hope to see you again. Regards to Tom.

Love,
Jim

James A. Call
#33008

---

*fictitious name

John Cain, Head Clerk of the Clinton Prison, hunched over his desk, his expression one of perplexity and annoyance. The letter he had just read had been intercepted by prison officials and the original returned to the inmate bearing a prison stamp which stated that the communication did not conform to prison regulations and therefore was not mailed.

Turning to his intercom he flipped the switch. "Ask Lieutenant Mancusi to come to my office, please." Then, settling back in his chair, he glanced over a memo he had just dictated regarding inmate number 33008:

STATE OF
NEW YORK

DEPARTMENT
OF CORRECTION

CLINTON PRISON
Interdepartmental Communication

Date: November 9, 1955

FROM: John R. Cain, Head Clerk
TO: Dr. H. Freedman
SUBJECT: James A. Call, #33008

The attached letter came to my attention yesterday morning; as yesterday was a holiday I interviewed this prisoner. After a lengthy interview, he stuck to the following story: That prior to his arrest, he was cleared for access to top-secret atomic secrets and that he has flown very new and secret devices; that there exists in this institution a plot to get information from him; that failing in securing these secrets from him, the persons in on this plot will cause his death in order to prevent his exposing them. He mentions Lt. Mancusi and Gene Beaubriand as being in on this plot; that they took a map away from him several weeks ago and since have been attempting to extract information from him. He also mentioned the night men in his cell block and accuses them of awakening him at night for several weeks in order to get information from him.

Following the interview Call was placed in a hospital room under observation in accordance with the directive of the Principal Keeper. It does appear that because of the nature of his case and sentence, Call has been under very close observation for security custodial reasons. Lt. Mancusi did take a map from this inmate but the thought was that it might have had something to do with escape or some other crimes with which this inmate has been charged.

J.R.C.
Head Clerk

JRC:r
CC: Principal Keeper

Cain's review of the correspondence was interrupted by a voice on the intercom announcing the arrival of Lieutenant Mancusi.

"Have a seat," said Cain, motioning to a straight-backed chair near his desk. "I've been reviewing this Call matter. How's he doing?"

"Hard to say," replied the lieutenant, shrugging. "Dr. Freedman wants to keep him under observation for awhile. At first he thought he was suffering from paranoia. Now, he's not so sure. He says the inmate is very intelligent—that he may be malingering. Frankly, I'm worried about security. Block officers are hearing that all Call thinks about is busting out. They think he's faking his condition so he can get into the hospital—that it'd be easier to escape from there."

"That's all we'd need," said Cain. "With the publicity this case has generated." He returned his attention to the file on his desk. "What do you make of this?" He leaned forward, handing the lieutenant a typewritten page which bore a notation in block letters:

COPY OF NOTE FOUND IN CELL OCCUPIED BY #33008 JAMES ARLON CALL

"He wrote that on toilet paper," added Cain.

"Yeah, Huestis told me about it," said the lieutenant, taking the paper and glancing over the contents:

SPECIAL OPERATIONS—SECTION 3

CIA—Pentagon
Washington 22, D.C.

Attention Lt. Colonel J.L. Francis

In compliance with sp. oprat. order 125-4 12 July 1954, following report is submitted:

1. Map containing info requested will be transmitted via alternate channel at earliest date.
2. List of suspected individ. and associates will also be forwarded upon completion.
3. Contact has been established with CATO and joint action has expedited complete operation.
4. Prel. Invest. has confirmed existence of joint conditions as suspected. Greatest period of danger appears to be in early spring, possibly by March 5th.
5. Am awaiting report of special equipment and latest directive "Christmas".
6. I have complete trust in courier—appears completely reliable and close mouthed.
7. There is no indication that security of this operation has been penetrated.
8. Sure could use a bottle of H&M and a nice juicy steak!

C-5412

"He's planting these things." The lieutenant handed the paper back to Cain, a look of concern on his strong features. "Expecting us to find them. Huestis found some odd-looking maps that he'd drawn in his cell—aerial maps. He's looking for us to transfer him to the hospital. This guy's no dummy."

"I'm sure of that," Cain replied with a touch of impatience. Collecting the papers, he straightened them meticulously, tapping the edges against his desk as though trying to bring order to a disorderly situation. "Just make sure we don't end up the dummies!"

♦ ♦ ♦

68

Conditions at Clinton Prison had improved markedly following the notorious inmate riot of 1929, and by the time Jim Call arrived on May 11, 1955, the institution had abandoned the primitive practices of earlier years. Many changes had been made, such as plumbing in the cells to replace the slop buckets previously used to dispose of human waste, and the humanization of disciplinary procedures. Prisoners were now granted rights unheard of in prior decades.

But if conditions had improved, when it came to inmate #33008, Jim was determined to improve them even more. One of the best ways to achieve this—a fact well known to prisoners and administrative personnel alike—was to effect a transfer to the adjoining Dannemora State Hospital, or DSH as it was known. The DSH, a sprawling Gothic structure of gray native stone, was annexed to the prison. Its architecture was in sharp contrast to the grim fortress next to it. The exteriors of the two complexes reflected the nature of each one's function: the emphasis was on security in the prison, of course, whereas the DSH was oriented toward medical as well as custodial functions. Rather than galleries of cells where inmates were locked up most of the time, the DSH had open wards, dayrooms of sorts, some of which even had television. According to one source knowledgeable about the facilities, a wave of illness often swept over the prison population during the World Series, as inmates vied for beds in the hospital. Malingering was a common diagnosis.

But if physicians at the establishment were alert to those feigning illness, they had met their match in the brilliant young inmate who was determined to join them at the hospital. On November 10, 1955, six months almost to the day after his arrival at the prison, Jim was moved to the DSH. The transfer did not occur before doctors and prison officials conducted lengthy periods of observation and discussion.

The decision once made, was accompanied by many caveats reflecting concerns for security.

From Jim's standpoint the transfer was long overdue. He was barely in the hospital before he began to make up for lost time, fashioning his plan. As always, his first objective was to charm the hospital staff, to convince them that he was a gentle, innocent person and that his case was a miscarriage of justice.

A later interview with Jack LaGree, a veteran of the hospital staff, reflected the extraordinary power Jim was able to wield over seasoned prison personnel:

INTERVIEWER

You worked at the Clinton Correctional Facility in Dannemora for how many years?

LAGREE

Twenty-eight years. Starting in 1949—October 1st, 1949.

INTERVIEWER

Did you know an inmate by the name of Call?

LAGREE

Yes. Major James A. Call. He came into Building II, my floor. He was a very quiet guy, very intelligent. Of course, I remember the manhunt and the news stories and all. He made an impression on me because he was intelligent and didn't act like a criminal.

INTERVIEWER

Call was in the main part of the prison, behind the big wall. Why did he end up over at the hospital?

LAGREE

He'd had problems. He was a bomber pilot in Korea. Flew a lot of missions—more than he had to. When he came home from the war there was a problem, either his wife had left him or died.

INTERVIEWER

Did he ever talk to you about the Lake Placid shooting?

LAGREE

Yes, he talked to me about it every day. The story he gave me—which I believed—was that he was around Lake Placid quite a bit. He ended up at a camp up there ... started playing cards with some cops. He was sitting there one night playing cards, the door opened, and someone walked in shooting. He got behind a partition, he had a service revolver, and he said, as a reflex he'd learned in survival school, he shot back.

INTERVIEWER

Did he ever say that he had played cards with the police officers before?

LAGREE

Yes, he said he had played cards with the officers a number of times before. The cops weren't the only ones there. Call told me there were civilians present as well, playing cards.

INTERVIEWER

Did you believe Call's story? Did you think he was innocent?

LAGREE

Yes, I believed it. So did quite a few officers up here at Dannemora. We thought he was totally innocent.

INTERVIEWER

What you're saying is that in 28 years as a prison guard, you knew only one man you felt was completely innocent.

LAGREE

Yes, that's right. Call was the only guy I felt was innocent. Course, you have to remember that we'd hear it every day. Everybody was innocent. But he was the only guy we all believed in.

INTERVIEWER

Did Major Call ever talk to you about the manhunt?

LAGREE

Yes, he talked to me about the manhunt often. I remember there was a story about him in the newspapers, playing ball with some kids. I asked him if the story was true, and he said it was. And he also said he walked up and down the street while the manhunt was going on, buying papers. One thing I could never understand. If he'd been playing cards with the cops, how he could walk around and no one knew him.

INTERVIEWER

So there were lots of people who sympathized with Call and thought he was innocent?

LAGREE

Oh yes, sure. After he came into Building II, most of the officers, the majority of the officers who had any contact with him, thought he was innocent, and that there was a cover-up with the cops up there. That there was something going on.

INTERVIEWER

So, feeling that an inmate is innocent is a very unusual feeling for a guard.

LAGREE

It's rare for a corrections officer to feel that way about an inmate. We always felt that the courts were good, that those who came into the prison were guilty.

INTERVIEWER

You develop a sixth sense about an inmate?

LAGREE

Oh sure. When they come in there, you recognize people that are going to cause trouble, and those that are going to work.

You can tell the good and intelligent people. You can tell the troublemakers.

This consensus among the guards regarding Jim's innocence was not shared by the top officials at Clinton, who had less contact with him. They were influenced more by an inmate's record. And everything they knew about inmate 33008—his past escape and survival training, and information from prison informants ("Man, that dude's just waitin' to blow!")—made them very uneasy. They were receptive, therefore, when Jim appealed for a transfer to a facility closer to where his family lived in Ohio.

"My sister would like to visit me more but she lives in Mantua, near Cleveland," read Jim's petition. "It's a real hardship for her to drive all the way up here to Dannemora."

Both prison and hospital officials were quick to agree. On September 20, 1956, he was brought back to Clinton Prison from the DSH, and two weeks later—with what must have been a measure of relief from the top staff—he was transferred to Attica, near Buffalo.

But not everyone was glad to see Jim leave the North Country. His extraordinary charm had endeared him to many both inside and outside the prison walls. Women in particular had found him captivating, as was demonstrated by one of the many letters sent to prison officials:

Maxine Smith*

7-16-55

Dear Mr. Jackson:

I am writing to ask for permission to correspond again with Jim Call #33008. While he was in Essex Co Jail at Elizabethtown, we wrote each other every week. Sheriff Crowley said that if I wrote to you that you might grant me permission to write to Jim, as he doesn't have many relatives alive.

*fictitious name

I sent him cigars, magazines and cigarettes at Easter and Christmas, and I do wish to at least be able to write to him. No matter what he has done, I love him very much and I wish to write him and do anything else I can to make him happy. I receive letters from his sister, Mrs. [White] in Ohio in regard to him and also from Sheriff Crowley ...

Sincerely,

Maxine Smith

P.S. I promise not to write anything to upset him or cause you or him any trouble.

Jim welcomed such letters. They helped to break the prison tedium. But such communications meant little to him in emotional terms. The one letter for which he constantly yearned never came.

♦ ♦ ♦

69

It was impressive, the distinctive Call style which manifested itself during threatening times: a remarkable composure which suggested a casual indifference to the outcome of events, however perilous. It was present now as Jim stood, arms akimbo, one shoulder against the wall, thumbs looped over his belt, right eyebrow arched imperiously. One would hardly have known that he had just challenged another inmate to a no-holds-barred fight to the finish.

"What's that, baby?" asked the other prisoner, a large man with bulging arms and a rippling ebony torso. He dropped a heavy barbell he was holding waist high, and it bounced to the mat at his feet with a loud thud. "I don't think I heard right, man."

"No, you probably don't hear right," Jim said evenly. "Must be all those dicks you take in the ear. You wanna fuck with me, let's settle it. Just you and me. No one here to stop it. One of us walks out, the other...." Jim shrugged indifferently. "One more killing won't bother me a bit."

It was Attica, July 1957. Although he had been there less than a year, Jim had already established himself in the prison population as "one tough dude," as hard and unyielding as the steel strands that lined the galleries on the cellblocks. His reputation of having taken out three police officers in a gun battle and, it was rumored, "probably a lot more along the way," had preceded him. Because of this, and his quiet confidence, he enjoyed a measure of respect from other inmates.

An exception was the large weightlifter who now glared at him menacingly from the other side of the exercise room. The man, a recent transfer into Jim's cellblock, had already made sexual overtures, the most blatant of which had happened in the shower the previous week. At the time, because of the presence of a guard beyond the shower room, Jim had ignored the incident and avoided a confrontation. But when the man had entered the weight room moments before and had begun eyeing him, Jim had expected trouble. After the inmate had then suggested that he was going to show him some wrestling holds, Jim had made the challenge. Since arriving at the prison he had heard stories about the victims of sexual predators at the facility. The fact that he had been singled out for attention himself left him no choice but to confront the man. He thought ruefully of the shiv another inmate had offered to barter a few days before. Jim had declined. Too bad. He needed a weapon badly. Maybe one of the small barbells at his feet. He'd stun the bastard, put a survival hold on his neck. It'd be over quickly. Now, in a situation which would have had many men shivering in their shoes, he calmly awaited a response.

Surprised by Jim's defiance, the man hesitated, but then, stepping over the weights he had dropped, came slowly across the room. "Guess I gotta teach you some respect, sonny. Good lookin' guy like you's gonna need protection in this joint. I'm gonna show you what protection is, man."

As the inmate strode toward him, Jim stooped and picked up the barbell, removing the weight from one end. Then, again leaning against the wall, he said evenly, "How's it gonna feel to have this pipe rammed up your black ass. 'Course you won't feel it. You'll be dead!"

Whether it was his adversary's incredible coolness, or passing footsteps in the outside corridor, the man paused, glancing first toward the door and then staring back at Jim belligerently. Finally, he turned and walked toward the door. "I'm gonna getcha," he said, sighting Jim along a large forefinger as he left. "You got a bad attitude, man. One way or other, I'm gonna getcha. You gonna need protection, man."

But Jim would need no protection. As his son Jeff said years later in commenting on his father's confinement, "Jim could hold his own with anyone. 'Course his looks made him a real target up there. But he was one tough road warrior. Pumped a lot of iron. Stayed in great shape. He told me that he had to make sure those bulls up there in Attica knew he wasn't a heifer."

◆ ◆ ◆

70

While Major Call was serving his final years in Attica, confident that his connection to the Sheppard homicide had been buried with the passage of time, another Air Force major was busy resurrecting evidence that linked him to the crime. This was Major George Warburton, called "Mickey" by his many friends. He was an easy-going gentleman with thinning strawberry hair tending toward gray, and round pleasant features which folded easily into a smile. It was a countenance that invited conversation and would serve him well in his quest for evidence in the Sheppard case. Compact of stature, he looked as if he would fit well into the ball turret of an Air Force bomber. Like Major Call he was a navigator. He would later retire with twenty-one years of service.

Major Warburton's interest in Major Call was piqued in the fall of 1954, when Warburton was a junior at Colgate University in upstate New York. During a hunting expedition with fellow students in the Adirondack Mountains, he saw posters bearing the artist's sketch of the Lake Placid cop killer who was the subject of an intensive manhunt at the time. Like many others, he was caught up in the drama. Unlike others, however, he discerned what he believed was a resemblance between the poster picture of Call and the composite drawing appearing in newspapers of the "bushy-haired man" observed loitering near the Sheppard house.

His interest aroused, Warburton continued to follow the two cases. Later, in 1966, while living in Washington, D.C., he had access to the microfiche at the Library of Congress and perused back issues of Ohio and New York newspapers to learn of developments. When a former marine fighter pilot named F. Lee Bailey, fresh out of law school, persuaded the United States Supreme Court in 1966 to set aside Sheppard's conviction, Warburton became reinterested.

"In July 1966, I traveled to Lake Placid," said Warburton. "I spoke to anyone who would talk to me about Major Call. Most everyone was pretty nice, ready to answer my questions. From members of the prosecution team I learned that some efforts had been made at the time to connect Call with the Sheppard homicide, but that Cleveland authorities had already indicted Sheppard, convinced of his guilt. According to Dan Manning, little investigation of Call's activities prior to the Lake Placid shootout was required since he had already confessed to the shooting of the officers. However, my interviews with New York State Police officials, particularly Harold Muller and Harry Blaisdell, yielded significant information."

———————————

Harold Muller lounged in an easy chair in his house, where Warburton had tracked him down. He had been retired for a few years and perhaps had mellowed somewhat from his earlier days as troop commander. Warburton found him far less gruff than he had been led to expect.

"We had Call's confession, fingerprints, Luger, and matching ballistics, as well as eyewitnesses," Muller said. "So we knew we had our man."

"What about the Sheppard homicide?" Warburton asked. "I understand you questioned him about that."

"Yes, but the Cleveland courts were already trying Sheppard and were sure he was guilty. We had our own murder case completed against Call. There was neither the need nor the time to investigate him for all the other charges we had against him—burglaries, holdups, and the like. We had him for the maximum offense—a capital crime. But I have to tell you, that man was hiding out from something when he came to Lake Placid. I'm absolutely certain of it, and it was something very significant. Call acted very surprised in Reno when we arrested him for the Lake Placid killing. In retrospect, I believe he thought we were there for something else."

Muller found Warburton's theory connecting Call with the Sheppard homicide intriguing and plausible, and encouraged Warburton to continue his investigation.

Warburton's interview with Harry Blaisdell a short time later was encouraging as well. Warburton located the former BCI investigator at his residence in Oneida, New York. Blaisdell, also now in retirement, had lost none of his congeniality and sharpness. He was keenly interested and enthusiastically supportive of Warburton's theory.

"I did an extensive investigation of Call down south at the instruction of the District Attorney, preparatory to the trial," Blaisdell said. "I talked to people who knew Call and his family in Meridian, Mississippi, and to his superiors and fellow officers at Barksdale AFB in Louisiana. Everyone thought he was brilliant. The man was well-liked. The officers on the base kind of rallied 'round him. When I told his commanding officer we were going to send Call to the chair, he got his back up. He said they'd heard the police officers opened fire on Call and never gave him a chance to surrender. 'Naturally Call would return their fire,' he said. 'That's what we train these young officers to do.' "

"What about the Sheppard case?" Warburton asked. "Did you think he was involved?"

"I remember questioning him on three separate occasions about it. His responses were rather vague, as I recall. Very strange.... It had to make you wonder, but what could we do? You must remember, we believed we had a prima facie case for the murder of a police officer here in New York. Obviously we were more concerned about our own case. But yes, we were all convinced that Call came to Placid to hide out from some other crime."

"Where had he been before he came to Placid?"

"He claims he was on the Appalachian Trail. No proof, though. That was another strange thing. He knew precisely where he'd been after he arrived in Placid. Gave us a day-to-day account. Burglaries, everything. But his answers about his whereabouts during the previous days were very general. Nothing that could be verified."

As did Muller, Blaisdell saw considerable merit in Warburton's theory, and encouraged him to pursue his investigation into the Sheppard homicide. Heartened by his discussions with the principals involved in the Call prosecution, Warburton traveled to Cleveland, where he sought and was finally granted an interview with F. Lee Bailey and Sam Sheppard's brother Richard, who were preparing their defense for Sheppard's second trial. For over two hours, Bailey and Richard Sheppard listened intently to Warburton's working hypothesis. They then stated that their trial was imminent, and that they had developed their own theory showing someone close to the family had committed the murder. They explained how they had neither the time nor the money to investigate another set of facts.

"We thank you very much for all your efforts," Bailey told him at the conclusion of their meeting. "We'd appreciate it if you could keep your theory private until the conclusion of our trial."

Undeterred and showing the persistence and competitive characteristics of his football days at Choate and Colgate, Warburton moved on to nearby Mantua, where he went to see Call's sister Stella White.

"I was not greeted warmly by Mrs. White," Warburton recalled, "and she was disinclined to discuss her brother's activities. The most I could elicit was that her brother did stay with her sometime between mid-June and early July 1954. 'Yes, he was here,' she said. 'I don't remember exactly when. He came and went as he pleased.' "

Summing up the meeting, Warburton said, "For some reason, she really didn't want to talk to me."

Mrs. White's reluctance to discuss her brother's activities while he was in Mantua heightened Warburton's suspicions. Was she aware of her brother's burglaries? Did she suspect him of other crimes? The Sheppard murder? Her unwillingness to talk about her brother would continue. When contacted years later by telephone in 1999, she would decline to discuss the matter stating that "my back is against the wall." In a subsequent rather lengthy telephone interview conducted by the author on April 20, 2001, she graciously discussed her brother's life in general terms, but was unable to furnish specific information regarding his activities because of the passage of time.

Warburton continued with his trip in 1966, moving on to Reno, Nevada, where police officials discussed with him the circumstances of Call's arrest and permitted him to review their copious records on the case. They had, in fact, suspected Call's involvement in the Bay Village homicide, but had encountered the same lack of interest from Cleveland authorities, who were then in court attempting to convict Sam Sheppard of his wife's murder. The surfacing of another suspect and the harmful impact it would have on their own case was apparent to the prosecution team in Cleveland.

Warburton then headed east, this time to Albany, New York. Here, he received what he termed "terrific cooperation" from the New York State Police. "Under the circumstances, I didn't think they'd have that much in their files," Warburton said. "After all, the case was twelve years old, long since closed, Call in jail. They had no reason to extend themselves for me. But it was just the opposite. They were very courteous and professional."

As the years passed and George Warburton continued his sporadic interest in the case, a solitary figure passed the time in his cell painting, drawing, reading books, unaware that another Air Force major was helping to prepare the final chapter on Major Call.

◆ ◆ ◆

Captain George Warburton (bottom center)
Vietnam, Tet Offensive—January 1968

2nd Lieutenant George Warburton—1956

71

"Pulling time" is a common expression of inmates to describe their plight. It is an apt description, considering how time regulates a prisoner's life. There is a time to sleep, a time to eat, a time to work, a time to exercise. There is good time, bad time, added time, time off for good behavior. Most important is *time served*. Five, ten, fifteen, twenty to life.... The latter is indisputably hard time. For younger inmates, of whom most of the population is comprised, it is often a withering experience. Time inches by, day by day, week by week, month by month, year by year. It is hard time that ages a prisoner. The psychological effects may be devastating. Frustration yields to helplessness, then to hopelessness, and finally to abject despair. Often a profound change takes place in the inmate's personality.

Jim Call was no exception. In his case, the change manifested itself in an intense desire to withdraw. He shunned most activities not mandated by prison rules and regulations and spent his free time reading, mostly poetry and classical literature. On a few occasions, he resurrected his interest and moderate talent in oil painting. Contacts with life outside the walls consisted mostly of correspondence and visits from family members, primarily his sister. Elaborate plans for escape had dominated his thoughts during the early years of his sentence (for example, the Attica Warden Record Card reflects a terse statement on January 3, 1958, that he "associated with Higgins 12925 in plot to escape from Attica Prison"), but these dwindled in the face of the ironclad security.

Built in 1931, Attica Prison adhered to a basic plan of security within security, from the thirty-foot wall that encircled its fifty-five acres down to the cellblocks and the individual cells. There were four separate blocks of cells, designated as A, B, C and D, each with its own exercise yard. In effect, Attica was four prisons within one prison.

At the center was a check point referred to by inmates as "Times Square."

Control and monitoring of the 2,000 inmates was intense. Even for an inmate of Jim Call's indomitable escape aspirations, a breakout seemed virtually impossible—that is, until the day he met another prisoner whose life had revolved around banks and prisons—breaking *in* and breaking *out*.

"Willie Sutton? Really?"

Jim was impressed. He had just asked a fellow worker about an inmate who had recently joined them in the prison laundry. "You sure? *The* Willie Sutton?"

"*The* Willie Sutton," the man said firmly. "Everybody knows Willie. Amazing character. Busted out of some of the toughest joints in America. Sing Sing, Holmesburg.... Holmesburg was built in the late 1800's. No one ever made it out alive before or after Willie."

"Yeah ... ," Jim said, his interest aroused. "Wonder how he'll get out of this joint."

"The Dep [Deputy Warden] told Willie when he first got here that both him and the Warden would lose their jobs if Willie ever busted out of Attica. You can imagine how they watch him. There's a standard rule, Willie never goes through a locked gate unless there's a screw [guard] with him. The screw has to call the Warden's office before they let him through Times Square. And forget about yardout [recreation periods in the prison yard]. When it comes to Willie, even the word 'yardout' just scares the hell out of the Dep."

Jim watched the new arrival with great curiosity. Although years of hard time were carved in the man's craggy face, Willie's good-natured expression was that of a man who never bore a grudge, even against his captors. Growing up, Jim had read about the desperado's remarkable career robbing banks. Like the rest of the country, he had marveled at Sutton's ability to escape. Now, to find himself actually working next to the man—well naturally, for someone of Jim's inclinations, it provoked all manner of thoughts.

The prison laundry was a maximum security facility operated mostly by long-term inmates. Jim, assigned to A Block, as was Sutton, operated the laundry pressing machine. It was only natural that he would push for a relationship with Willie. Within a few days, they had become fast friends.

The two had much in common. Both reveled in their criminal endeavors. Later, Willie would author a book in which he described the thrill he derived from his bank robberies. His comments reflected to a remarkable degree the emotions experienced by Jim Call during his own gambling and criminal activities:

> Why did I rob banks? Because I enjoyed it. I loved it. I was more alive when I was inside a bank, robbing it, than at any other time in my life. I enjoyed everything about it so much that one or two weeks later I'd be out looking for the next job. But to me, the money was the chips, that's all. The winnings. I kept robbing banks when, by all logic, it was foolish. When it could cost me far more than I could possibly gain.
>
> (Willie Sutton with Edward Linn, *Where the Money Was*)

With such similar escape and survival backgrounds, it was inevitable that Willie and Jim would discuss the possibilities at Attica. But a close relationship between two men who had caused law enforcement so much anguish could hardly be tolerated by prison officials. As Willie would later write in his book, "I got along with Jimmy so well that the next thing I knew he was transferred to another job."

Although Jim would occasionally run into Willie in the cell-block, and hear stories about his activities (Willie was very popular with both inmates and prison staff), their direct contact was henceforth limited by the skittish prison officials. This was particularly disappointing for Jim, whose aspirations for freedom had mounted during their brief association.

As the years passed, Jim began to focus almost obsessively on a specific point in time: May 15, 1968, the date he would first be eligible for parole. The promise of this day dominated his thoughts. To enhance his chances for parole he often engaged in cunning manipulation of persons both inside and outside Attica, including communication with the man who had prosecuted him, Dan Manning. Years later the Essex County DA reflected on these overtures:

Call was a very bright person, very well educated. Each Christmas I'd get a card from him and I used to send one back. But I have an idea that each time he came up for parole, he figured that if he kept in with me that I would maybe recommend him for parole. When he finally got out of prison, I never got another Christmas card from him. [Manning shrugged and laughed.] But you know, there was something very pleasant about the man—except for his terrible crimes, of course. You couldn't help but like him.

Dan Manning's favorable opinion of his former defendant was shared by others in the justice system. It extended even to the New York State Board of Parole, and on July 30, 1968, after serving thirteen years and nine months of his life sentence, Jim Call was released from Attica.

◆ ◆ ◆

72

The subdued article tucked inside a northern New York newspaper contrasted sharply with the roaring headlines that had attended Jim's incarceration many years before:

Manhunt Figure Free on Parole

James Arlon Call, convicted of murder in 1955 and the subject of one of the state's longest manhunts, is free on parole after serving 13 years, 9 months and 12 days of a life sentence, Warden Charles R. Mancusi of Attica State Prison said yesterday. Warden Mancusi said the 43-year-old prisoner, whose parole began last Tuesday, was turned over to the Ohio State Parole Board and will spend the rest of his life sentence on parole. At the time of his conviction Call had a sister and brother-in-law living in Mantua, Ohio.

Having read the article, Jim rested the newspaper on his lap and gazed through the bus window at the passing landscape. It was raining and he was struck by the fresh green countryside, in marked contrast with the gray prison walls. Things that in years past would have seemed commonplace were now of interest: a dilapidated farmhouse, a line of clothing strung across its porch like flagging ensigns on a foundering ship; a woman and child beneath an umbrella; a cornfield and an old tractor; a winding dirt road, narrowing off over a hill on the horizon.

The exhilaration he had felt when first leaving Attica several hours previously had subsided somewhat. Disconnected thoughts drifted through his mind ... his son, Jeff, now seventeen ... the job awaiting him at the White family construction company in Mantua, Ohio.

And there were romantic thoughts ... female companionship ... Greta. He'd thought of her constantly, even considered writing. He'd refrained—wisely, he now thought. She must be married with children. Contacting her was out of the question. Her social status ... he an ex-con. Still, he wondered.

Recollections of his marriage were less vivid, eroded by years of prison tedium. But the memories were still there, waiting to be burnished: romantic dinners in Tucson restaurants, evenings on the mesa, the southwestern sky, the engagement, wedding, honeymoon....

There were other memories, these unforgettable. The recurring nightmare of Marilyn Sheppard. Horrific ... bewildering....

To repel thoughts of Bay Village, he reread the article regarding his release, then carefully tore it from the paper. As he folded it neatly and placed it in his wallet, once again he thought of Greta. Her laugh, nights at Lake Placid. Did she still vacation there? Probably. Once experienced, the charm of the mountain resort was never forgotten. His own plans called for him to return to Lake Placid. Yes indeed, important unfinished business there. But he must wait. His return must be handled with discretion. This time there would be no mistakes.

◆ ◆ ◆

73

It was late November, 1968. A cold, hard rain drummed on the windshield as Jim followed the dampened beams of his headlights up through the bending mountain pass toward Lake Placid. Out of prison less than four months, he was already violating the conditions of his parole. Under supervision of the Ohio State Parole Board, it was required that he secure permission to travel out of state. Obviously, such notification was impractical for one returning to the scene of his crime. Hence, Jim drove carefully, ever mindful that a mistake—even a minor traffic infraction or accident—might well land him back in Attica.

Fortunately, traffic was light due to the inclement weather and the lateness of the hour. As he made his way higher into the mountains the temperature dropped and the rain turned to a driving snow that impeded his vision. It took him longer than he had anticipated to reach Lake Placid. On the outskirts of the village he saw the small refreshment stand where he and Greta had shared a twelve-inch hot dog one night. It was closed for the winter, but the sight reopened memories....

"I'm not that hungry," Greta said, sitting down on one of the stools at the stand. "You get one. I'll have a bite of yours."

"I'll get one of those foot-long ones. We'll share it," Jim said, ordering a hot dog.

"I'm kind of an inexpensive date, don't you think?" Greta teased. "I mean, sharing a hot dog?"

"Well, I wouldn't say that," replied Jim. "I could've ordered the smaller size."

"Yes, I can tell you're a big spender," she said, dryly. "Aeronautical engineers must make lots of money."

"Not really. I do it for the fun," he said briskly, disinclined to elaborate on his purported occupation.

"Where do you spend most of your time?" she asked. "Do you travel much in your job?"

Jim sensed she was honing in, looking for information. She'd done it before. "Just the Northeast, mostly. Here, have a bite," he said, changing the subject and offering her some of the hot dog which had just arrived.

As she opened her mouth he moved the hot dog forward, causing her to take a larger bite than she had anticipated. "Oh," she mumbled. "Too much."

"Boy," said Jim with mock surprise. "I'm glad you're not hungry."

"You did that on purpose," she remonstrated after swallowing the food. "I didn't even want any. I just took a bite to be a good sport."

"Would you like to walk over by the lake?" asked Jim, controlling the conversation lest she return to the subject of his employment. "We could sit and talk on the dock awhile. It's close to the Club."

"Sure, why not." Before he realized what she was doing, Greta had taken his hand playfully and bitten a large piece out of the hot dog. "There!" she mumbled. "Now that's a real bite."

"Jesus," muttered Jim. "You almost got my finger."

"Almost," she agreed. "What happened to that?" she nodded toward his bandaged forefinger.

"That?" said Jim, momentarily startled by her question. "Oh, nothing ... just a scratch."

For an instant he was gripped by the horror of Marilyn Sheppard ... his finger being bitten ... the excruciating pain ... his rage....

"What's the matter?" asked Greta. "You okay?"

"Sure," he replied quickly. "I'm fine. Just fine."

She continued to look at him curiously. "C'mon, let's go for our walk." She rose from her seat, taking his arm and squeezing it affectionately. "You have a moody side, you know that?"

His preoccupation with the thoughts of Greta, coupled with the poor visibility, almost caused him to miss his turn onto West Valley Road. As he proceeded down the street he noted that the newly fallen snow was free of tire tracks—a good sign.

Perhaps it was the fourteen years since he had been there, or the white shroud of snow covering the trees and houses, but the road which he had traveled so often in the past now seemed unfamiliar. But there was nothing unfamiliar about the dark ominous dwelling crouched beneath the tall spruce trees at the dead end of Oneida Street. With the sight of the Perkins camp came a rush of memories: loud commands from the police, bullets ripping through the shower stall, the fiery exchange, groans of wounded men, dashing for the woods, long days of privation.

The camp was dark. No traces of activity marked the snow covering the parking area near the entrance. It appeared uninhabited, as he expected it would be at that time of year. He drove slowly past, inspecting the woods on both sides of the house. Everything was still, except for a breeze overhead in the treetops.

He continued down West Valley Road to a dead end at River Street, where he parked his car among others at the side of the road. Then, taking a flashlight from the glove compartment, he slipped from the vehicle and walked back to the woods that extended along the west side of West Valley Road. Once in the heavy growth, he turned on the flashlight and soon found the path leading to the Jack Rabbit Trail which passed behind the Perkins camp—a route he had taken many times in past years.

As he proceeded deeper into the darkness he felt the peace and contentment he always experienced in the woods. He paused for a moment, enveloped by the profound silence of the forest. Then, pushing ahead, he saw a small trail branching to the right. This would take him directly behind the Perkins camp—the same trail on which he had made his dash from the house following the shooting. From the distance came the faint sound of rushing water—the stream where that night he had stumbled on rocks and scraped his shin. He slowed momentarily, listening to the soft sounds. A line from *The Stolen Child* flashed through his mind: "Where the wandering water rushes...."

He moved down the path toward the camp, now focused totally on what awaited him inside. Would it still be there after all these years? Had it been discovered? A contractor, perhaps, performing some type of work? He shivered slightly, partly from the cold, partly from anticipation.

At the edge of the clearing he stopped and extinguished his flashlight, his eyes focused on the back door. It was a bold move— breaking into the place where he'd shot the officers. If he were caught, it would be back to Attica. There was little choice, however. For years he'd sat in his cell, contemplating this moment. But even for a risk-taker of high order, it was an audacious venture. There had been no way of checking out the camp. It might well be occupied. Someone inside asleep, perhaps armed.

He waited in the falling snow, watching and listening. It was very quiet, except for the rustling in the trees far overhead. Excitement coursed through his body. It was exhilarating. Like old times. The challenge, the incredible thrill.

His right hand slid into his pocket, closing over the cold handle of his automatic. He stepped into the clearing and quietly approached the house.

◆ ◆ ◆

74

Doctor James J. Perkins, owner of the camp on West Valley Road, was well aware of what took place that snowy night in November 1968. He, along with many investigators, was convinced that James Call had committed the Lake Placid Club jewel robbery. Later Dr. Perkins recalled the event and described what he believed happened to the jewels:

INTERVIEWER
You believe the break-in of your camp in 1968 was tied to the jewel robbery.

DR. PERKINS
I'm certain of it, as are many others. I knew the family that was robbed. They were very wealthy.

INTERVIEWER
How hard would it have been for a man like Call, dressed fairly well, to associate with people of the Club, to have spotted where the big money was?

DR. PERKINS
Not difficult at all. I worked there all my way through college. Caddied, ran the golf house, bellhopped. I could have walked into any one of those rooms anytime.

INTERVIEWER
You talked about something strange that happened after Call got out of prison. Something at your cabin.

DR. PERKINS

Well, after the robbery, and after they found out that Call was there, the insurance people came to look for the diamonds. You see, they were sure that he was the man who burglarized the Lake Placid Club. So they searched the camp. Like the insurance people, I always believed that the loot from the robbery was in the camp. And, after Call had been out of prison a few months, somebody came to the camp—it was in the winter—and broke the back door. The caretaker went into the camp for something and found the back door broken and snow on the floor where they'd come in. Well, whoever came in—it must have been at night—apparently didn't use a flashlight, but knew where he was going. Now, they didn't stay. They went down cellar and that's all. I believe that in the dirt down there in the cellar, that crawl space, the jewels were buried there. I believe Call came back to that camp, and got the jewels.

INTERVIEWER

It took Call 13 years to serve his prison term before he was released. During that time, did you ever have any break-ins at the camp?

DR. PERKINS

No, nothing at all. When the caretaker went into the camp that day he didn't realize the place had been broken into because there were no tracks leading into the camp from the road. Whoever came into the camp took the same path that Call took when he was making his escape into the woods after the shooting.

INTERVIEWER

Another thing, when the caretaker went into the camp, after the break-in, did he see footprints inside the camp?

DR. PERKINS

He first noticed the tracks in the snow and then found the tracks leading to the basement door inside the cabin. There'd be no reason for a man to come there; no reason to break in, walk down stairs, take nothing, and walk right out. It had to be Call.

INTERVIEWER
And you said the caretaker was an expert woodsman, he would know if the tracks were made by an adult who walked down to the cellar.

DR. PERKINS
Yes, of course. You have to remember, back in those days, there was very little stealing up there in Lake Placid. The Call affair was something that just didn't happen.

Dr. Perkins' sentiments were shared by others. In one of his many statements about the Major Call case, Harry Blaisdell commented on the Lake Placid Club jewel robbery:

There is one thing that was always in the back of our mind, and that's the Lake Placid Club jewel robbery. I asked Call if he'd ever been on the Lake Placid Club grounds. He said that he had. The fact that he did have some good dress clothes, like those taken to the cleaners in Saranac Lake.... It was during that time that there was a jewel robbery at the Lake Placid Club just a few days before the shootout in the Perkins camp. I have a very strong opinion that Call committed that jewel robbery.

Muller felt the same way, very strongly. We both thought Call was in the Adirondacks because he was on the run from some crime he'd committed. We thought it was something very significant. I interrogated him three times about the Sheppard murder and he was very evasive. However, that jewel robbery ... I think he did it. I think something happened forcing him to stash those jewels somewhere. They may have been 25 feet from that lean-to of his, just buried in the ground. He couldn't get out with them, or decided not to chance going out with them. He decided to just play it cool and stay around.

Then he was surprised in the Perkins camp by the officers. Who knows? Maybe he stashed them somewhere in the Perkins camp.

◆ ◆ ◆

PART IX

Mantua, Ohio
Summer 1970

75

Blonde, beautiful, vivacious. There was every reason Jim should have been attracted to her. She was standing across the lawn with a friend near a refreshment table, laughing, animated. It was a lawn party, a *fête champêtre* Mantua style.

Blanche Klose Jenkins was accustomed to attention, so when she noticed the slender man several yards away glancing in her direction, she did not find it at all unusual. What was different, however, was that this man was notably handsome with romantic eyes and dimples, and a certain élan that set him apart from other men she'd known in Portage County.

He was older, she thought. Probably late thirties, maybe early forties even—which to a twenty-five-year-old was "getting up there." But despite his maturity, she was interested. Enough so that she prodded her friend, who lived in Mantua and was knowledgeable about other residents, with questions about the stranger.

"Stella White's brother, you say? ... Major? ... Air Force? ... Single? You're kidding. Wow! ... Prison? Oh...." With a population of less than a thousand, news traveled fast in Mantua. Still, when her friend moved on and the man walked over to the refreshment table near her, she lingered.

"Nice day," Jim said, sipping coffee he had taken from the table.

"Yes. Nice." A slight smile. Cordial but restrained.

"I'm Jim Call."

It was a quick no-nonsense introduction. She liked it. "I'm Blanche Jenkins."

"From around here?" An easy smile. Great teeth.

"Of course," she shrugged. "Where else is there around here but here?"

Self-assured, Jim thought. But then, why not? There probably wasn't a better-looking woman in Mantua. Hell, in all of Portage County.

"Care for some coffee?" he asked.

"I'd rather have a beer," she said, without batting an eye.

Jim laughed. "Well...." He started to reply—something to the effect that perhaps they could go somewhere to have a drink—but then, looking at the other guests nearby, thought better of it. His background was known in the community, or certainly would be eventually. It was important that he maintain a low profile. A flurry of inhibiting thoughts followed. He sensed discreet glances from the assemblage—curious, appraising. How much did they know? What would they think, seeing him conversing with a younger woman? He had to be careful not to embarrass his sister and her husband. So, with a smile and a few amenities, "Nice meeting you, Blanche. See you in church," he withdrew to a bench under a large tree.

For Jim, the encounter with Blanche Jenkins would have ended—at least for that day—were it not for her reappearance several minutes later, bouncing nonchalantly down beside him with a force that caused the bench to rock slightly. "Remember me?" she said insouciantly.

Jim looked up, startled. "Well...," he said, taken aback. "Why don't you sit down?" He made the comment facetiously, but it conveyed a tinge of unintended sarcasm.

It stopped her momentarily, until her irrepressible ebullience once again asserted itself. "You like it here in Mantua?" Then, without waiting for an answer, "Probably better than some other places, right?"

Jim's smile froze and he gazed squarely at the woman. "Perhaps," he replied, his right eyebrow arching slightly.

"Say, that's cool," she said.

"What is?" Jim asked, cautious now, not sure what was coming. She clearly had a way of putting one on the defensive. It was an uncomfortable feeling he had not often experienced with women.

"Your eyebrow," she said, moving her face closer and mimicking his brow movement. "How in the world do you do that?"

"Oh," said Jim, relieved to be off the subject of "other places." "I don't know. Just a mannerism, I guess."

"It's kinda neat," she said, eyes smiling.

Jim knew she was toying with him, but he didn't care. Her presence had lifted his libido to a level he had not experienced recently. As the conversation continued he marveled at her roughish manner. The fact that he had not been that close to a beautiful woman in over thirteen years was certainly a contributing factor, but in any case, as time passed he felt himself succumbing.

Blanche Jenkins was an uncomplicated person and just about as direct as one could be. Jim found her candor contagious and within minutes their respective backgrounds were tumbling forth. Blanche was married, but estranged, divorce pending, living with a four-year-old daughter, Teresa. She liked a good time, a drink now and then—"Maybe more *now* than then."

Jim? Yes, he worked at his brother-in-law's construction company—for just a short time. And before that? Well ... , he had lived in a small rural community outside Buffalo, New York. Only about 2,000 people ... not too well-known. A place called Attica! They both laughed. No matter. She already knew.

A chord had been struck and Jim sensed a future with his new-found acquaintance. But there were other considerations—Blanche's divorce, his sister, small-town gossip.... Still, Cupid's missile had been launched. A rapid courtship would follow and then, as Blanche would later say, "The Klose-Call" connection.

◆ ◆ ◆

76

"They don't have to know I'm your parole officer, Jim. I could be anybody, a friend, an insurance salesman."

Harold Crew was assigned to the Ohio State Parole Board's District Office in Akron. A sensitive, pleasant man who liked his job, he projected a calm sincerity that enabled him to communicate well with the former convicts under his supervision. This talent was evident now as he sat with Jim drinking coffee in a booth at a Mantua restaurant.

"Well, whatever you say," said Jim, dubiously, his eyes flitting between his parole officer and the waitress who was regarding them curiously from behind the counter. "I don't think we'll be fooling people much around here, though. Pretty small town."

"Why don't we see how things go, okay?" said Harold softly. "If it's a problem, I suppose I could see you at your house. They'd be unannounced visits, you understand."

"The house would be better." Jim focused on the remnants of his coffee, now cold, in the bottom of his cup. "I'd like to keep it, you know, as quiet as possible. It's kind of tough on my sister and her family. But I understand," he added, resignedly. "You have to do your job."

The parole officer regarded him thoughtfully for a moment. He liked Jim, and having supervised him for several months had found him to be a model parolee who conformed to the conditions of his parole in all respects. Like others who had come in contact with Call after he had embarked on his criminal career, he wondered how someone with such a brilliant background could have sunk to the level of ex-convict.

"Well, let me think about it," said Harold. "How's your son doing? Been in touch with him?"

"No, not really." Jim's eyes drifted away, as though he were momentarily lost in thought. "Jeff has his own life down in Meridian.

I've caused him enough embarrassment. He's made it without me all these years. I don't want to lay this ex-con thing on him."

Harold expected the answer, having heard it before. He was unsure of Jim's feelings. Was he genuinely concerned that his prison background would burden his son, or was he just not interested in the young man? Harold had come to expect such ambivalence from his charges when it came to family matters.

"Well, I better be going," said the officer rising and extending his hand. "I'll be in touch."

"I'm sure," said Jim with a wan smile. He stood, shaking hands. "Anything you do is okay with me. Thanks for your help."

Harold Crew left Mantua that day with mixed emotions. Although the parole officer was a young man, he had learned already the dangers of becoming emotionally involved with parolees. Yet he found himself drawn to Jim Call. He was such a *decent* person. Years later, he would recall his feelings:

Yes, I remember Jim well. He was very smart, knew all the parole rules and appeared to avoid any situations in which his conduct could be questioned. Wanted to avoid any contact with the law. His first year on parole he never socialized, kept a very low profile. I had difficulty checking on him because he was such a loner. His neighbors knew very little about him or his activities.

He was a good-looking man, neat, always clean-shaven. And there was something about his manner ... not your average person. Very suave, gracious. Even in work clothes, he didn't look like your usual working man.

I felt I had a good rapport with him—although I did think at times that he was capable of deception, and I am not certain he always told me the truth about his activities. I sensed he had something going toward the end of his parole. Late evening hours ... might have been gambling, I'm not sure.

He had no interest in his son, Jeff. No contact with him at all that I know of. Occasionally he'd say something to the effect that he didn't want to lay his criminal background on his son, or something like that, but I always thought he was just trying to act compassionately—that he didn't really mean it. Actually, I found him to be quite cold toward his son.

No, I never knew of anything that would connect him with the Sheppard case. Do I think he could have done it? Well, like I said, Jim was certainly a very unusual man. I suppose he was capable of most anything. You'd never know it to look at him, but his record clearly showed that he had the temperament and ability to take out anyone who was in his way.

◆ ◆ ◆

77

"When's Mommy coming home?"

"Won't be long," answered Jim.

"But you said that before."

"I know. Don't worry, honey. It won't be long."

Jim, sitting in an easy chair watching television, was only half-listening to his stepdaughter, Teresa, who stood at a nearby table playing with a doll. With the persistence of a child, she had asked the same question several times in the last few minutes, but Jim did not mind. Nor was he concerned that his wife Blanche was out at a tavern drinking beer with her girl friends. It was an arrangement which might have proved awkward for some marriages, but for a man who had spent much of his previous years sitting alone in a cell, the role of babysitter was perfectly acceptable.

Hollis Dye, Blanche's brother-in-law, described the relationship as one that worked well. "Jim was a good guy. Well-liked. Good worker. Took good care of Blanche and her daughter Teresa. Blanche was kinda wild. Jim, he'd often baby-sit while she went out drinkin' with her girlfriends."

It had been a rapid transition for Jim from inmate to family man. Following his initial meeting with Blanche, there had been a series of dates and then on August 17, 1970, Blanche's divorce from her husband Furman Jenkins had been finalized. She and Jim had been married on October 2nd, six weeks later. Quick, yes, but given Jim's penchant for speed, it was natural for him to want to make up for lost time. There had followed the purchase of a house in a Mantua development at 12723 Samuel Drive. It was a modest one-story dwelling consisting of six rooms, valued at $16,900, $1,500 of which had been paid in cash. The balance was secured by a mortgage which was to be paid in full on May 1, 1974, less than six months after Jim was to be released from parole under Section 220 of New York State's penal law—perhaps a coincidence but curious timing, nevertheless. As it turned out Jim not only discharged the mortgage after his parole terminated on November 12, 1973, but also came home with a new Lotus Europa, an elegant racing car valued at approximately $8,500. Inasmuch as Jim was working for a modest salary at the construction company, the logical question was, "From where did this hit of cash come?" There were some who concluded that once he was released from parole and the umbilical cord severed with New York State, he was no longer concerned about authorities monitoring his activities. Hence, he had the freedom to indulge without having to disclose information about his finances.

Regardless of the source of Jim's income, life was good on Samuel Drive. His position as dispatcher at the company, although not intellectually stimulating, was pleasant enough and kept him busy. Yes, things were looking up for the Call family. Therefore, when Blanche returned home one night a bit later than anticipated, Jim was not concerned.

"How's my lover?" she said, bouncing into the room.

"You woke me up," answered Jim from an easy chair.

"It's only 10:30." She dropped into his lap. "Time for fun."

Jim smelled the alcohol. "I'm glad you didn't get pulled over. You're gonna end up in the slammer one of these nights."

"So what," she said, blithely. "One more con in the family. That reminds me, George said you have a prison mentality."

"George?"

"George White.* He said everyone likes you at work, but you always look at the ground, step aside to let people pass—that kind of thing. He said it's a prison mentality."

"It's called being courteous," said Jim, annoyance creeping into his voice.

"Oh, c'mon, can't you take a little kidding. You old guys lose your sense of humor." She ruffled his graying hair and kissed him on the cheek. "Doris said Hollis thinks you're a great guy, that everyone likes you. They just think you got a bad break with those cops

---

*fictitious name

up there in Lake Placid. I still don't understand it all. Why were you up there, anyway?"

Jim stiffened, sensing she was about to launch into one of her inquisitions. Her curiosity about his past life was insatiable and asserted itself often when she'd been drinking. At first he had declined to discuss it, following his sister's advice. "What's over is over," Stella had admonished, "Don't tell anybody anything. It's nobody's business."

That may have worked all right with Stella's friends, but a bright, independent-minded, twenty-five-year-old wife was something else. Her youthful inquisitiveness and exuberance had finally worn him down so that now when prodded he responded, if somewhat guardedly, about his past—that is, about most things. There were some matters that would never be discussed.

"Why was I up there?" said Jim, musingly. "I wish the hell I knew...."

There was a pause in the conversation. Suddenly Blanche sat up, looking him squarely in the eye. "I've been thinking...."

"Oh, boy," Jim said, shifting in the chair. "That's bad."

"I'm serious, Jim. Where are we getting all this money from? The house, the new car?"

"I told you. They're letting me do the books at work. It's all tax money ... family money."

Blanche settled back against him. "I'm not complaining," she said with a chuckle.

"Let's go, baby." Jim moved, preparing to rise from the chair. "Time for bed."

"Bed?" groaned Blanche. "It's early. You're gonna sleep your life away. How about a nightcap? We'll have some fun. What more do you want?"

"What more do I want? Nothing more, honey." He gathered her into his arms, burying his face in her hair, her fragrance filling his nostrils. She was soft, receptive. "It's been a long time, but I've got everything I want. Everything!"

Jim, in fact, did have all he wanted. After a turbulent life of aerial combat, horrendous crimes, and confinement in maximum security prisons, he had finally achieved the things about which he had dreamed. A normal job, a house near some woods, money stashed away, a beautiful wife, and in the driveway, what constituted for Jim the quintessence of luxury, a gleaming new sports car.

♦ ♦ ♦

78

"What about the car? It must be ruined."

Blanche Call gazed up from the hospital bed, her pretty face clouded with remorse. Although her leg was fractured and her body bruised, her main concern at the moment was the new Fiat Spider sports car, recently purchased by her husband.

"Forget the car," said the nurse, a middle-aged woman with a strong temperament and wiry auburn hair. "You're lucky to be alive, young lady. The police said you rolled over an embankment into a ravine. That leg, a few scratches.... I'd say you came out of it pretty good."

"My husband will be terribly upset," said Blanche, closing her eyes as if to block out disturbing thoughts. "He just loved that car."

"I'm sure he loves you more than the car." The nurse adjusted a pillow behind Blanche so that her head was slightly elevated, then moved toward the door. "Push that button if you need anything."

As the nurse was about to leave, Jim appeared in the doorway. In one hand he carried a bouquet of red roses, in the other a guitar.

"You're just in time," said the nurse. "She was just talking about you. Here, I'll get a vase for these." She took the flowers and left the room.

"Are you all right, honey?" Jim asked, his face filled with concern. He moved to the side of the bed and placed the guitar on a nearby chair. Then taking one of her hands, he squeezed it gently. "The doctor told me you're okay. It's just the small bone in your leg."

"Oh, Jim, I'm so sorry." She drew him toward her, wrapped her arms around his neck, and kissed him ardently.

Taking her hands, Jim sat down on the edge of the bed, his tired, worried face reflecting what had been a long night. "You gave us quite a scare. The police called...." He shook his head slowly, eyes downcast.

"Oh, honey, it was awful," she said, tears welling up. "I had a few drinks with the girls, was on my way home—only a half-mile from the house—somehow I went out of control. Next thing I knew I was upside down in that creek. I crawled back up to the road and—"

"Don't think about it, darling." He took her into his arms, embracing her gently. "It's all over. Everything's okay."

"But your car...." She shuddered. "It's—"

"Forget the car. It's nothing. The main thing is you're all right. Look." He turned, picking up the guitar. "Look what I brought. The clerk said it was the one you'd been looking at."

"Oh, Jim," she exclaimed, brightening. She took the instrument, stroking its glossy surface appreciatively. "It's just what I wanted. You're so wonderful." She placed the guitar aside and drew him close, hugging him tightly. "I love you so much, Jim. I'm so lucky to have you...." The rest of her words were lost in tears.

At that moment, the nurse reappeared in the doorway carrying the roses in a vase. She hesitated, then departed. With love blooming, who needed roses?

If Jim had finally found happiness in Mantua, it was no less so for his new wife. Blanche adored her husband. Years later when commenting about their marriage she spoke of it as the most enjoyable period of her life:

> He was wonderful to Teresa and me. Such a gentleman. After our marriage Jim got the job as bookkeeper at White Construction. He'd do the books on Saturdays, then we'd travel or party. I think he may have been doctoring the books. At any rate he was well taken care of. After all, he was family. We had enough money.
>
> We bought the house on Samuel Drive. Jim took good care of it—although he almost lost it in an all-night poker game during a trip to Akron. We always ate dinner together. No smoking at the table, though. He was immaculate in his grooming. Showered and shaved every morning.
>
> Jim liked to play tennis and chess. He was a good painter, too, and he had some expensive painting equipment—brushes, easels. He painted van Gogh-like things: landscapes, portraits. He once did a self-portrait. Sports car racing was his favorite

pastime. It was in his blood, somehow. At one time we had two sports cars, a Fiat and a gold 280Z, which he raced. He loved racing—mostly at Nelson Ledges. He once was in a race there with Paul Newman.

When Jim wasn't racing on the weekends, we'd travel. Trips to Kentucky, Tennessee, North Carolina. Jim was used to traveling from his days in the Air Force. Just look at all those souvenirs there with his belongings. From all over the world. Was he familiar with the Cleveland area? Yes, of course, he went there often. He mentioned his trips to Cleveland in his three-year diary.

His sister Stella? She was rich and arrogant. Lived in a five-bedroom house with a tennis court and Olympic pool. We used to go to her place for family outings.

Was Jim ever violent? Not really. He could handle himself, of course. Once he put a man, "Uncle Bob", up against a wall and straightened him out about me. But he could usually handle things like that with a few words.

Yes, Jim told me all about the shooting at Lake Placid. He said he was playing cards with some policemen and another policeman came in shooting; that he shot one of the officers in self-defense. I don't believe that stuff in his confession. Jim was trained to defend himself and would do whatever it took to survive.

He'd seen the red Lotus sports car in a local dealership and literally begged me for several weeks to let him buy it. It was a lot of money. I had a bad feeling about the car, but he'd been so good to me that I had to let him do it.

Jim wanted to get out of Mantua. He loved the woods. He was building a house for us in the mountains in Gatlinburg, Tennessee. It was half finished when it happened that Sunday morning.

◆ ◆ ◆

79

"Bye, honey." Jim kissed his wife and started for the door. Suddenly, he paused, turned and went toward the bedroom.

"Where you going?" asked Blanche.

"Forgot something." He entered the bedroom and walked to the dresser, where he picked up a sophisticated stopwatch used to measure precise timing during sports car racing. Walking from the bedroom, he put the lanyard attached to it around his neck so that the watch hung down on his chest.

"Why are you taking that?" asked Blanche, frowning, her eyes on the timepiece. Her husband's passion for speed was always a concern.

"Don't worry, honey, it's okay." This was his standard answer when he deemed no explanation necessary. "Be home soon." Another quick kiss, not as warm.

"Be careful." She drew her fingers lanquidly through her hair, looking off over her shoulder with a trace of uneasiness.

Jim emerged from the house, his eyes coming to rest on his latest acquisition parked in the driveway, the sleek Lotus Europa. For him, it personified everything he wanted in a high-performance racing car. He had spent the previous afternoon tinkering with the engine and applying a coat of wax to the chassis. He took satisfaction from the lustrous red finish glistening in the sunlight. It was Sunday morning, a good time to travel. He was on his way to pick up Teresa, who had spent the previous night with Rich and Carol Smith, friends who lived in nearby Warren.

Approaching the vehicle he stomped his feet to remove any dirt from his shoes. Then, opening the door, he slid behind the wheel, savoring the rich aroma of new leather as he settled into the soft seat. He turned the ignition key and the finely tuned engine roared instantly to life, then quieted down to a deep, resonant purr. Jim thrilled to the feel of harnessed power. For him, the car was more than a mechanical object. He sensed its power, speed, personality. Dormant all night, it was straining to be unleashed. Jim knew the feeling—prison, parole. He depressed the accelerator lightly and watched the rpm needle leap to 2500.

He slipped the lanyard from his head and placed the stopwatch on the console next to him. From the glove compartment he took out his sunglasses, adjusting them over his eyes. Easing the shift into reverse, he slowly backed from the driveway out onto Samuel Drive. Within a few minutes he was turning onto Route 88 headed east, toward West Farmington.

There was little traffic, most of the residents of Portage County confining their Sunday morning to church or home. Route 88 was a two-lane asphalt highway with long stretches of white lines that restricted passing on hills and curves. An occasional sign warned of hazardous areas. This was not to say that there were not straight passages where a car might pick up considerable speed without undue risk. But for the most part, it was a rural road where drivers were well advised to keep their wits about them, and not just because of the bends and dips in the road. It was not altogether unlikely to come over the rise of a hill and to find oneself sharing the road with a stray horse or cow, or even a stalled tractor. It was, in short, an unpredictable route where things could happen—even to a skilled sports car driver.

But caution was not on Jim's mind the morning of May 5, 1974. He knew the road well, having traveled it many times. And his spirits were high with plans to attend a sports car race later that afternoon. The day was bright and clear, the morning sun reflecting off the car's brilliant red hood. Before him lay a pastoral landscape of rolling meadows, fresh hay, and wildflowers. Now and then a stand of trees hugged the road, their sharply defined shadows stretching across the pavement, flickering through his windshield.

Rounding a slight curve, he saw before him a long stretch of straight open road. Gently, he pressed down on the accelerator. The speedometer jumped to 60 mph, the engine effortlessly gathering power. Then 70 ... 80. The car had taken over now, 90 ... 95.... A whirl of flashing trees, telephone poles. Suddenly, a rise in the road, a slight curve, the car partly off the road, the right rear wheel spinning in dirt on the shoulder. Then, inconceivably to those familiar with

Jim's driving skills, the car was out of control. Nervelessly, he steadied it, almost bringing it back. Too late, though. Tires screeching, the Lotus spun and slammed into a steel guardrail on the opposite side of the road—at over 90 miles per hour, according to an estimate by the Ohio State Patrol. With a shattering crash the guardrail pierced the passenger door like a gigantic lance, penetrating the car and emerging through the door on the driver's side. Jim Call, consummate survivor of countless life-threatening escapades, was now the victim of a Sunday morning auto accident. Truly dead.

◆ ◆ ◆

80

John Schlacht heard the crash. He had just returned home from his nearby horse barn when the squeal of tires and then the horrific sound of shattering glass and metal reverberated through the house. Rushing to a front window, he looked down across the meadow to Route 88 some 200 yards away, and saw a sports car impaled on the steel guardrail. Shouting to his wife to call for help, he raced to his truck parked in the driveway. Within seconds Schlacht was at the scene:

It was bad.... Guardrail went straight through both doors. Must've been traveling at a tremendous speed to do that. The car was heading east on Route 88 when it went out of control. It hit the guardrail on the other side of the road, broadside on the passenger door. The guardrail wasn't bent down to the roadbed the way they are now. The end just stuck out straight. It went through both doors. I looked in through the driver's door—or what was left of it. There was only one person, the driver. He was pinned behind the wheel by the rail. It was obvious he was dead. Must've been killed instantly. But surprisingly, there was no blood. Nothing. He was just sitting there, head back against the seat, eyes closed. The strangest part of it, though, was his right hand. It'd been severed at the wrist. It was just lying there in his lap ... almost like it wasn't his.

◆　◆　◆

Jim Call's accident site
Route 88, Portage County, Ohio

81

Blanche Call was notified of her husband's death by a telephone call from the Ohio State Highway Patrol.

"I was devastated," she said later. "He was so good to Teresa and me. He'd been through a lot, you know, with prison and all his troubles. Never talked about it, though. I guess he just wanted to forget it all. I must say, if he had to go, that's the way he would've wanted it. Real fast, in his car. He loved speed. And he loved that car. More than anything."

A funeral was arranged and Jim was buried beside his mother in Mantua's Hillside Cemetery. It was a serene location beneath a cluster of tall spruce trees. His grave was marked by a large headstone. Next to the headstone was a bronze emblem of the American eagle, designating a veteran of World War II, which was underway when he enlisted in 1943.

For Jim, such confinement, however peaceful, may not have been his choice. After such a rampageous life he may have preferred a less restrained disposition of his corporeal remains. It is doubtful that one who had spent much of his life in the heavens would find it proper to be lingering underground suppressed by a block of granite. He would have preferred some other way. Cremation, perhaps. A spiral of smoke. Yes, more fitting for an aviator. One last flight. "Lo! the bird is on the wing."

◆ ◆ ◆

James Arlon Call burial site—1998

EPILOGUE

Meridian, Mississippi
Spring 2001

Some thousand miles south of Ohio's Hillside Cemetery is another burial ground—Magnolia Cemetery, the final resting place for many Meridians. A quaint small-town graveyard, it retains much of the dignity of the Old South. In some ways it is similar to Hillside. Both cemeteries are set in rural areas on rolling hills that afford lovely views. Both reflect the care of their respective communities in landscaping and well-tended graves.

In other ways the two are quite different. Magnolia is replete with fragrant magnolia trees that cover the landscape in a profusion of color, whereas Hillside is dominated by clusters of brooding maples as well as dark, hardy conifers—trees found in the wild, such as spruce and rugged northern pine.

There are other differences. Hillside with its shaded grounds and northern weather is more somber. Particularly with nightfall when living things depart and the restless wind bemoans the plight of those who remain. Adding to this sense of unrest is a thin mist which sometimes collects in the lower areas. Here, in the vapors, wraithlike forms emerge from the graves and attempt to slip past a stony brigade of winged mercenaries that stand guard over the bone-white tombstones. Such efforts at escape quickly fade, for these are the final cells from which flight is hopeless.

Magnolia Cemetery, bathed in southern sunshine, suggests more relaxed surroundings, more settled inhabitants. Row after row of eternal occupants neatly interred in small pockets of earth convey a sense of order and repose. An inscription on a simple gravestone near a small pond at the crest of the hill seems to reflect the mood. Tilted on the base of the marker is the image of a book carved in granite. Engraved thereon is a quatrain from *The Rubaiyat of Omar Khayyám:*

THE MOVING FINGER WRITES; AND HAVING WRIT,
MOVES ON: NOR ALL THY PIETY NOR WIT
SHALL LURE IT BACK TO CANCEL HALF A LINE,
NOR ALL THY TEARS WASH OUT A WORD OF IT.

—THE END—

Muriel Call burial site—1998

ADDENDUM OUTLINE

THE CASE AGAINST MAJOR CALL

I CRIME SCENE EVIDENCE

(1) Murder Weapons

(2) Assailant's Wound

(3) Leather Fragment

(4) Unexplained Evidence

(5) Blood Images on Pillow

II WITNESSES

(1) Dr. Sheppard's Description of Intruder

(2) Witnesses Outside the Sheppard Residence

(3) Positive Identification of Subject
by Richard and Betty Jean Knitter

(4) Positive Identification of Subject by Dr. Gervase Flick

III DISCREPANCIES IN SUBJECT'S ALIBI

(1) Subject's Whereabouts Prior to Sheppard Homicide

(2) Subject's Flight Following Sheppard Homicide

IV SUMMARY

V CONCLUSION

ADDENDUM

The foregoing narrative includes passages which describe Major Call's role in the Sheppard homicide. Some of the evidence that links him to this crime does not lend itself to full analysis in the text. Because of the notoriety of the Sheppard case and its significance in our criminal justice system, a compendium of the evidence incriminating Major Call is added here as a supplement to the main narrative.

The conclusions presented in this addendum are based on a far-reaching search for evidence undertaken by research and investigative personnel retained by British American Publishing. The search included an extensive review of Major Call's own written and oral histories, records of law enforcement organizations throughout the country—including local, state, and federal agencies—together with personnel files of the United States Air Force, trial records, contemporary press accounts and archival documents. Numerous interviews, many of which were tape recorded and transcribed, were conducted with individuals knowledgeable about Major Call's life. Those interviewed include relatives (next of kin and otherwise), friends and associates (both civilian and military), government officials, and members of the legal profession who participated in the prosecution and defense of Call's crimes. Other individuals chose to furnish information on a confidential basis. From this research the following thesis was developed regarding Major Call's involvement in the Sheppard homicide.

THE CASE AGAINST MAJOR CALL

There is strong evidence to support the charge that James Call (hereinafter referred to as the subject) murdered Marilyn Sheppard. An analysis of the evidence, with exhibits, appears at the conclusion of this supplement. From this data, as well as the evidence presented in the preceding narrative, the following theory was constructed regarding the subject's motives and actions:

The subject was present in the environs of Cleveland when the murder was committed. He was in a state of profound psychological distress at this time because of the death of his wife, gambling debts, and career setbacks. Military and civilian associates described him as emotionally distraught, resentful, bitter about recent events in his life, and prone to violence and crime. During a meeting in Chicago with his closest friend a few weeks prior to the Sheppard homicide, he related how he had embarked on a life of crime. He stated that he had recently robbed a man in a hotel at gunpoint and described how the encounter had provided him with a tremendous "rush" or thrill. The meeting so unnerved his friend that he immediately notified the FBI that the subject was AWOL, armed and dangerous. Another friend, a military associate, stated at the time that the subject "was disposed to commit criminal acts and to feel justified in doing same."

The subject's propensity for crime and violence was evident from later admissions to police that he continuously committed acts of burglary, assault, and armed robbery during the time frame immediately before and after the Sheppard murder. The only break in his crime spree, according to the subject, were the days prior to the Sheppard homicide when he professed to have been alone on the Appalachian Trail—an assertion he was unable to support with a single verifiable presence. He acknowledged that a few weeks prior to this he was in Cleveland, a city with which he was very familiar.

The subject's involvement in violent crime at the time is further revealed by a signed statement he furnished to the New York State Police (NYSP) on November 19, 1954, in which he gave his reasons for shooting three police officers in Lake Placid, New York on August 5, 1954, one month after the Sheppard murder. He stated in part:

> I knew that I had committed many crimes and transgressions and knew that I was wanted. I had decided that if I were cornered at any time, I would shoot my way out if possible and if I could not do this, I decided that I would turn the gun on myself. For this reason, I carried a 9mm Luger or a 32 automatic pistol fully loaded....

This statement is significant in that it manifests the subject's state of mind during the days immediately following the Sheppard homicide: an admission that he was fleeing from crimes of such an egregious nature that he was prepared to kill police officers and himself rather than surrender.

There is broad explicit evidence linking the subject to the Sheppard murder. Elements of the crime conform to the subject's modus operandi. He repeatedly forced entry to dwellings with a crowbar, and then proceeded directly to upstairs bedrooms in an effort to secure cash, wallets, or jewelry. He wore gloves and never left fingerprints. Unlike most intruders who are fearful of awakening inhabitants, the subject seemed unconcerned about such risks, often using violence against those who defied him. Following his apprehension, he readily admitted to officials and the NYSP that he was prepared to kill anyone who stood in his way. Many individuals who were knowledgeable about the subject's record and penchant for violence, such as his son Jeff, confirmed that the subject would have no compunctions about killing anyone who resisted him. Most of his victims did not resist. One exception was Fred Wertheim, who was held up in Lake Placid. He yelled for help. The subject stated afterwards that if he had been able to free his Luger, which was entangled in the lining of his pocket, he would have shot Wertheim on the spot. Another victim who cried for help was Marilyn Sheppard. She paid the ultimate price.

The subject's propensity to commit crimes of burglary, armed robbery, and violence has been recorded by police agencies in many parts of the country. To place him at the scene of the Sheppard murder, we turn to the evidence developed by forensic scientists who examined the Sheppard crime scene, and to the testimony of witnesses who observed a suspicious-looking person resembling Call near the victim's residence both before and after the murder.

I CRIME SCENE EVIDENCE

The most credible and cogent evaluation of the crime scene evidence was done by Dr. Paul Leland Kirk, regarded by peers as a "giant in the field of forensic science." Dr. Henry Lee, world-renowned forensic scientist, commented on Dr. Kirk's work in connection with the Sheppard case in his book entitled *Famous Crimes Revisited*. He stated that during the second trial of Sam Sheppard:

> Dr. Kirk made his points convincingly over more than five hours of direct examination.... And while his testimony was

crucial to the defense, it was not well-received by the law enforcement and forensic communities. Many likened his support for the defense to an act of treason, breaching a silent code among forensic scientists of the day. Kirk's application for membership in the criminalistics section of the American Academy of Forensic Science (AAFS) was rejected. But standards have changed. Now, most experts in the field, in admiration of his courage and pioneering contributions, consider Professor Kirk the father of modern forensic science. And ironically, the AAFS's Distinguished Criminalist Award has been renamed the Kirk Award. (Dr. Henry Lee & Dr. Jerry Labriola, *Famous Crimes Revisited*, Page 139)

Dr. Kirk's curriculum vitae is included here to clarify his credentials and extensive experience. (**See Exhibit A**)

Dr. Kirk conducted a thorough examination and investigation of the physical and technical evidence in the Sheppard homicide and summarized his conclusions to the Ohio Court of Common Pleas in a sworn affidavit dated April 26, 1955. His analysis describes the Sheppard homicide, and serves as the groundwork for the case against Major Call. It is important to note that Dr. Kirk expressed profound disagreement with the case presented against Dr. Sheppard by the Cleveland authorities. His affidavit stated in part:

> Careful appraisal of the technical evidence presented by the prosecution shows it to be completely worthless as proof of the guilt (or innocence) of the defendant. Only the autopsy and pathology findings are really pertinent to the case. (Affidavit of Paul Leland Kirk, *State v. Sheppard*, No. 64571, April 26, 1955, Page 4)

The following material implicating the subject in the Sheppard homicide contains excerpts from Dr. Kirk's thesis describing the nature of the crime.

(1) <u>Murder Weapons</u>

DR. KIRK:

From the known and demonstrable facts of the case, a reconstruction of the murder is possible. A limited amount of inference is unavoidable, but in the main, the facts are clear, and the conclusions inescapable....

The probable absence of serious outcry [from the victim] may well have been because her mouth was covered with the attacker's hand....

At some point in the activities of the attacker, the victim obtained a firm grip on him with her teeth. His defensive reaction of jerking away was violent enough to break two or three of her teeth....

Presumably inflamed by the resistance and pain, the attacker utilized some available weapon to strike the victim down....

The weapon was almost certainly not over a foot in length, and had on it an edge, quite blunt but protruding. This edge was almost certainly crosswise to the axis of the weapon....

It is still clear that the injuring edge of the weapon was more or less angular, or possibly rounded with a small radius. This is necessary to produce the injuries as described in testimony, which are not sharply cut, but were parted through to the bone, and beyond. A small bar type instrument could have produced this effect, but only if bent at a sharp angle from its axis....

A larger cylindrical instrument like a piece of pipe flared on the end is more reasonable, and consistent with the type of injury and the reconstruction of its mode of application.... [emphasis added]

If the weapon was carried into the room to be used as it eventually was used, a wide variety of possibilities exist. If it were acquired at the time it was needed, it would have to have been present in the bedroom prior to the murder which is improbable. A third possibility exists viz. *that it was an object carried for another purpose, but serving as a murder weapon when needed....* [emphasis added]

With the available limited information, it is not possible to infer an exact weapon, but certain of its characteristics are quite definite and can be safely assumed. (Affidavit of Paul Leland Kirk, *State v. Sheppard*, No. 64571, April 26, 1955, Page 17)

In connection with Dr. Kirk's observation that the murder weapon could have been an object carried for another purpose, it is noted that Henry E. Dombrowski, a detective of the Cleveland Police Department who investigated the Sheppard homicide, furnished the following written statement to his superiors on July 23, 1954, regarding a tool mark on a door in the Sheppard basement:

A plasticine impression was made of what appears to be a freshly made tool mark in a door at the foot of the basement stairs. This door leads to a crawl space at the front of the house. Mark appears to have been made by a chisel or wedge-like tool of more than 7/8" in width which is the length of the impression, however this does not show both edges of the tool.

Professor James Chapman, a noted criminalist from New York who became closely involved with the Sheppard case, stated that the tool described by Dombrowski resembled a prybar, which he said was often used by burglars during the fifties. He stated that the prybar was about 12 to 18 inches long, much like a small crowbar, one end being flat and the other end having two claws. He claimed that Dombrowski's description of the tool mark appropriately portrayed a prybar or crowbar.

In addition to the foregoing, small fragments resembling nail polish were recovered near the victim during the crime scene investigation. Upon examination Dr. Kirk concluded that rather than being nail polish, the fragments were chips of red lacquer:

DR. KIRK:
The relative opacity of the materials found on the floor as compared with nail polish raised a strong presumption that the material actually is not nail polish, but is a red lacquer such as is used to coat small objects, and which is available

commercially in many stores, *and could conceivably be chips from the weapon.* [emphasis added] (Affidavit of Paul Leland Kirk, *State v. Sheppard*, No. 64571, April 26, 1955, Page 16)

In subsequent comments about the case following the Sheppard trial, Dr. Kirk alluded to prosecution testimony given by Mary Cowan, a medical technologist in the Cuyahoga County Coroner's Laboratory, regarding microscopic red scrapings removed from under the victim's fingernails.

DR. KIRK:

Where would Marilyn Sheppard chip off red lacquer with her fingernails except from the weapon that was beating her to death. The [Cleveland] Plain Dealer of Wednesday, July 7, contained the statement, "The material, resembling a chip of paint, was found near the foot of the bed on which Marilyn's body was found. Gerber said it was possible to have come from the murder weapon." (Paul L. Kirk and Alys McColl, *The Dr. Sam Sheppard Case,* Chapter 17, Pages 6-7)

Correlative Evidence Implicating Subject with Murder Weapons

It is a reasonable conclusion that the "cylindrical instrument like a piece of pipe flared at the end," "certainly not over a foot in length" described by Dr. Kirk as the murder weapon, and the "crowbar" mentioned by Professor Chapman as the bar used to force a door at the Sheppard dwelling, are one and the same, and that it was, indeed, as Dr. Kirk stated, "carried for another purpose, but serving as a murder weapon when needed." Microscopic red scrapings believed to be lacquer from under the victim's battered fingernails indicate that she had grasped at the weapon, attempting to ward off the blows.

Following the shootout with police officers at Lake Placid one month after the Sheppard homicide, authorities confiscated belongings of the subject which included a crowbar complete with chipping red paint. The crowbar conformed in remarkable detail to the instrument described by Kirk and Chapman. It was listed in the NYSP Scientific Laboratory report dated October 4, 1954 as:

Item 78. Crow bar
This evidence is a 12" crowbar, labeled "ATHA". *Particles of white and red paint adhering.* [emphasis added]

The Stanley Tool Company described the crowbar as a "Stanley-Atha Goose Neck Ripping Bar, Number 112," which was 12 inches in length and had red claw ends. (See Exhibit B)
In addition to numerous crescent-shaped wounds on the victim's head believed by Dr. Kirk to have been inflicted by a pipe-like object, two rosette-shaped wounds appeared on her right forehead. An analysis of the wounds showed a resemblance to the toggles on the receiver of the Luger carried by the subject. Evidence indicates that the victim initially may have been struck with the Luger, which was then dropped on the bed. The subject thereupon struck the victim repeatedly with the crowbar. James Ebert, Chief Scientist, Ebert and Associates, Albuquerque, New Mexico, stated that, "After an extensive review of the crime scene evidence, the autopsy photographs, and photographs of the death mask of Marilyn Sheppard, it is my opinion that the crowbar found with Major Call's belongings cannot be excluded as the murder weapon." (See Exhibit C)

(2) Assailant's Wound

Dr. Kirk concluded that the assailant was bitten by the victim, probably on the hand or finger.

DR. KIRK:
Two points are highly significant in the explanation:
1. The teeth were found outside her mouth, not inside, or in her throat as would be expected if broken by an external blow; and
2. The medial incisor fractured at an angle that is consistent only with a pull outward, not a blow inward.... It seems very clear that the teeth were clamped on something that was forcibly withdrawn with removal of the fragments completely from the mouth. The only reasonable article would be the attacker's hand, possibly placed over the mouth to

prevent an outcry—which is consistent with defendant's story and the fact that nobody heard such an outcry.... *It is entirely reasonable and highly probable that she bit her attacker's hand. It is equally certain that a bite of this ferocity would have left distinct injury to such a bitten member, and that blood would have been shed.* [emphasis added] This is not pure speculation but a reasoned approach to the established facts, and it must represent at least a close approximation to the truth.... (Affidavit of Paul Leland Kirk, *State v. Sheppard*, No. 64571, April 26, 1955, Pages 12-13)

Many years after the trial, Cleveland authorities claimed the victim did not bite her assailant, an assertion which has little credibility in the light of the evidence. Dr. Adelson, who performed the original autopsy, testified at Dr. Sheppard's criminal trials in 1954 and 1966 stating that it was possible the victim's teeth had been broken by something being pulled from her mouth. Dr. Kirk addressed this issue directly when later writing about the case:

DR. KIRK:

As stated, the teeth from the bed were: (1) the entire visible portion of the right medial incisor, cleanly broken at the gum line, and (2) a part of the left incisor, roughly half as large, also broken at the gum line. This tooth had split down the middle....

In the photographs of Marilyn's face no injuries were visible below the temple and the bridge of her nose. Except for the crusted abrasion or bruised scrape (inside the mouth) described by Dr. Adelson, there were no injuries around her mouth. (**See Exhibit D**) Teeth do not break by themselves. *A blow to the victim's chin would have bruised it.* [emphasis added] An exterior blow to the mouth would have left an abrasion on the outside, as well as the inside of the lower lip.

There is one other possibility. If the victim's mouth were open, could a direct blow to the teeth have broken them? Such a blow would not explain the abrasion <u>inside</u> the mouth; also, the teeth would have been driven back into the throat....

Depending on the direction of the force applied, teeth always break off at an angle that slopes either inside, toward the tongue; or outside, toward the lips. The slope indicates the direction of the force. The broken edge is always (a) higher on the side opposite the force; (b) lower on the side to which force was applied.

Both teeth had broken cleanly—one showed only a single cross-break; the other had split lengthwise as well. Further application of the principles outlined showed that a force from a relatively soft object had produced the break. The break slanted upward on the side next to the lips. Here was positive proof that the teeth had been broken by pull exerted from the inside out. They could not have been broken by an outside force. (Paul L. Kirk and Alys McColl, *The Dr. Sam Sheppard Case*, Chapter 20, Pages 5-7)

During a civil trial in 2000, Cleveland authorities defending an action for wrongful imprisonment brought by the estate of Dr. Sheppard introduced evidence based on an examination of the exhumed remains of the victim, contending that a likely cause of the fractures to the maxillary right central incisor and all the additional tooth fractures were caused by "a blow of great force to the mandible which would have driven the mandible into the maxilla."

Had Dr. Kirk had an opportunity to review these reports he would have been quick to point out their deficiencies, not the least of which would have been that the examination was conducted on a forty-five-year-old cadaver in a severely deteriorated condition whose skull remnants were filled with plaster of Paris. Further, he would have cited the meticulous autopsy conducted on the victim in 1954, which reflected no wounds whatsoever to the mandible region. Surely a "blow of great force to the mandible" as it was described in the forensic odontologist's report, would have caused wounds or bruises. There were none.

Contrary to the conclusions reached as a result of an examination of the victim's remains forty-five years after the fact, Dr. Kirk detailed very specific evidence found at the crime scene to confirm his contrary opinion that the victim had, indeed, bitten her assailant. He further documented his findings by means of an analysis of the blood spatter in the room. He concluded that a spot of blood from the victim's assailant was apparent on the wardrobe door on the east wall of the room. The blood type of this spot was determined to be different from the blood of Marilyn and Sam Sheppard. Thus there exists irrefutable evidence of a third person in the room at the time of the homicide—a person who had an open wound.

> DR. KIRK:
> One very large blood spot was present on the wardrobe door.... It measured about one inch in diameter at its largest dimension. It was essentially round, showed no beading, and had impinged almost exactly perpendicular to the door, i.e., horizontally and at right angles to the door. <u>This spot could not have come from impact spatter.</u> It is highly improbable that it could have been thrown off a weapon, since so much blood would not have adhered during the back swing for so long a distance, and then separated suddenly at just the right moment to deposit as it did. This spot requires an explanation different from the majority of the spots on the doors. *It almost certainly came from a bleeding hand,* [emphasis added] and most probably occurred at a time different from the time that hand was wielding a weapon. The bleeding hand could only have belonged to the attacker....
> Blood shed from the hand after being bitten could have placed the large blood spot on the wardrobe door, and in fact flowing blood from a wound is about the only reasonable manner in which this spot could have been placed.... *It is the opinion of this examiner that the murderer had a definitely injured hand or finger on July 4, 1954.* [emphasis added] (Affidavit of Paul Leland Kirk, *State v. Sheppard*, No. 64571, April 26, 1955, Pages 9-11, 13)

Correlative Evidence Implicating Subject with Victim's Bite

The evidence shows that as the subject attempted to stifle the victim's yells with his left hand, she bit him severely on the left index finger. Following the Lake Placid shootout, investigators found a fresh fingertip bandage on the top of the stairs where the subject had supported a wounded officer he had taken hostage, using his left hand to hold the officer by his belt. A later examination of subject's fingerprints (taken at the time of his apprehension on November 20, 1954) by an odontologist revealed an injury to his left index finger, which upon enlargement was found to be *"consistent with a bite mark."* [emphasis added] An examination of his earlier Air Force fingerprints shows no previous injury to this member. (See Exhibit E)

---

(3) Leather Fragment

A further corroboration of the bitten finger is perceived in Dr. Kirk's and Coroner Gerber's comments about a small piece of brown leather found near the victim's bed.

DR. KIRK:

A leather fragment, approximately triangular in shape and measuring about 1/4 x 1/4 x 3/8 inches on the sides was examined in the Prosecutor's office. It appeared to be leather rather than a synthetic substitute. It also appeared to have been torn off recently, as indicated by the fresh appearance of the torn surface. (Affidavit of Paul Leland Kirk, *State v. Sheppard*, No. 64571, April 26, 1955, Page 16)

Coroner Gerber described the leather in trial testimony as follows:

Microscopic examination confirms impression that the brown material is leather. One side has a glossy appearance as if stained and dressed. Although this appears to be similar to the top side of the belt submitted with Dr. Sam Sheppard's trousers, there seems to be a slight difference in color and porosity. No defect was found on the belt.

Correlative Evidence Implicating Subject
with Leather Fragment

As a flyer, the subject was issued Air Force B-3, thin, high-quality leather flying gloves which had a glossy appearance, stained and dressed on the outside as described in Dr. Gerber's testimony. He often wore such gloves during off-duty hours. The absence of fingerprints at his numerous crime scenes is indicative that gloves were worn. One of the subject's robbery victims, John Lester Carney of Cranberry Lake, New York, stated the subject was concerned about leaving fingerprints, meticulously wiping his prints from silverware he had used while eating. It is noteworthy that investigators of the Sheppard homicide reported that there was evidence of an attempt to remove fingerprints from the Sheppard premises. It is plausible that the subject, having sustained the bite wound would have removed his Air Force gloves and afterwards, concerned about prints, would have wiped off the objects in the Sheppard house cited by investigators.

An inventory of subject's clothing and equipment was conducted by Air Force personnel immediately following his desertion, and his B-3 flying gloves were determined to be missing. Microscopic examination of the leather fragment by forensic scientists and leather experts shows it to be similar to the material used in the manufacture of Air Force B-3 gloves during the fifties. Further examination by odontologists revealed that the torn edge of the leather fragment had features of a bite mark, and that the bite mark was consistent with the bite mark found on subject's fingerprint. The examination revealed that the bite marks on the leather and the fingerprint were within a millimeter of the size of the victim's left front tooth, leading forensic scientists to conclude that the victim's tooth could not be excluded as the source of the marks on the leather fragment and subject's finger. (See Exhibit F)

---

(4) Unexplained Evidence

In addition to the fragment of leather, an unexplained piece of aluminum foil and matches were found at the scene. In a nearby commode was an unfiltered Lucky Strike cigarette butt. This was significant to the investigation in that the victim, four months pregnant, had given up smoking. Her previous smoking had been confined to filter tips. Dr. Sheppard smoked only pipes. In his den he kept a rack of pipes, including an uncommon kind called a "meerschaum."

During his trial Dr. Sheppard testified that his medical bag had been ransacked:

> I found there was a box of emergency morphine ampules missing. We call them "ampins". They are little ampules that have a needle on the end so that they may be broken and injected very rapidly for emergency medication. I was unable to find a bottle of Demerol which I commonly keep at the bottom of my bag.

Correlative Evidence Implicating Subject with Items in Sheppard Residence

The subject, a compulsive smoker, repeatedly stole cartons of cigarettes, and wooden matches, during his burglaries. He wrapped the matches in aluminum foil to prevent moisture damage—a habit derived from his survival training. His smoking addiction was manifest during stressful times. Of the numerous photos taken following his apprehension, there are few that show him without a cigarette—even police mug shots. Among his confiscated belongings following the Lake Placid shootout were cartons of cigarettes, wooden matches in aluminum foil, and two pipes. One of the pipes was the uncommon kind kept by Dr. Sheppard in his den—a *meerschaum*. With regard to the missing morphine, it is logical that such analgesics would be sought by the subject after sustaining his wound. He was trained in the use of morphine, standard issue for first-aid kits on Air Force planes. (**See Exhibit G**)

(5) <u>Blood Images on Pillow</u>

During the course of Dr. Sheppard's trial, one of the strongest contentions offered by Coroner Gerber was that the outline of the murder weapon was present in the bloodstains on the victim's pillow. He testified that during his examination of the pillow he discovered an "impression of a two-bladed instrument" which he was unable to identify, but which he believed was "some sort of surgical instrument." Dr. Kirk commented on the pillowcase in his report.

DR. KIRK:

The pillow from the victim's bed indicates far more than was stated or implied in the [trial] testimony regarding it. Solid regions of bloodstain are present on both sides of the pillowcase. One of these can be explained by contact with the pool of blood on the bed which seems to have spread far enough to be soaked up from the sheet. Blood spatter from the blows themselves show that the side opposite to the alleged instrument mark was upward during the beating. That it was earlier in contact with liquid blood in quantity is shown definitely by the large bloody area on that side which could not have been placed during the beating had the pillow remained as it was found. It is certain that the pillow was either used to prevent outcry earlier, or that the victim attempted to shield herself by holding the pillow on her face or head. In either case, the pillow had to be moved at a subsequent time.... (Affidavit of Paul Leland Kirk, *State v. Sheppard*, No. 64571, April 26, 1955, Page 16)

Correlative Evidence Implicating Subject's Weapon with Images on Pillow

Most experts would agree that identifying images in bloodstains can be an uncertain process, as evidenced by Dr. Gerber's so-called "surgical instrument." Nevertheless, mention must be made of what appears to be a blood outline of a Luger found on the victim's pillow. If, indeed, it were a Luger that caused the image, one may deduce that the subject's Luger was on the bed in a pool of blood, the pillow resting on top of it. The Luger would have formed a blockade of sorts, preventing that portion of the underside of the pillow over the Luger from coming in contact with the blood, thereby leaving the outline of the Luger on the pillow. The image does not reflect the entire Luger, but the pistol grip, trigger guard, receiver, and other identifying features are apparent. When crime scene photographs of the pillow are enlarged to actual size, the subject's Luger can be superimposed on the imprint with remarkable conformity. Although it cannot be stated with certitude that this image is the subject's Luger, extensive analysis shows strong similarities. Forensic experts, including representatives of the

New York State Police, as well as Professor James Chapman, identified six artifacts on the imprint matching that of a German Luger. Although this striking image may fall short of the proverbial "smoking gun," it is worthy of presentation and more credible than the so-called "surgical instrument" never identified but used by the prosecution to convict Sam Sheppard. (See Exhibit H)

II WITNESSES

Following are witness accounts which connect the subject to the Sheppard homicide:

(1) Dr. Sheppard's Description of Intruder

What happened on Lake Road following the discovery of his wife's body was described repeatedly by Dr. Sheppard at his trial. He stated that after being struck from behind upstairs, he regained consciousness and rushed downstairs to find the living room in disarray. He testified that he saw the rear door open and a "form progressing rapidly toward the lake." As best he could tell, it was a tall dark-complexioned man whose hair had a "sort of bushy appearance." He pursued the intruder, who he said was *"limping slightly,"* [emphasis added] down the wooden steps leading to the beach, where "I lunged and grasped him in some manner from the back, either body or leg. It was something solid." A struggle ensued and he found himself "twisting or choking, and this terminated my consciousness."

Correlative Evidence Implicating Subject with Intruder

The subject was limping during this period, having sustained a knee injury in an automobile accident several weeks prior to the homicide. According to Coroner Gerber, an examination of the beach below the Sheppard residence following the homicide showed footprints indicative of a limping person. Witnesses who later observed the subject during his trek in the Adirondacks confirmed that he was limping. Otherwise, he was athletic (playing halfback on his Air Force football team), "combat tough" from his survival training, and thoroughly schooled in "defensive tactics." His Air Force records reflect that he was active in many athletic endeavors and repeatedly received an excellent rating in his efficiency reports for physical activity and endurance. In a later interview his son Jeff described the subject's physical attributes: "Jim was one tough road warrior. He pumped a lot of iron. He could handle himself with anyone. No one fooled with him in prison." (See Exhibit I)

—————————————

(2) Witnesses Outside the Sheppard Residence

In addition to Dr. Sheppard, several other witnesses, including Mr. and Mrs. Leo Stawicki, Mr. and Mrs. Richard Knitter, Alfred Adams, and Donald Tripp, reported to Cleveland police that they had observed a bushy-haired man answering the subject's description near the Sheppard residence during the time Marilyn Sheppard was murdered. *Mr. and Mrs. Knitter positively identified the person they had seen as the subject.*

William Lawko, a Cleveland attorney, stated that one of his clients had told him confidentially that he had seen a figure running on the beach behind the Sheppard house around the time of the murder, but had declined to furnish the information to authorities inasmuch as he was married and in a compromising situation with another woman at the time.

Another witness, Mrs. Beatrice Wolfe, declared that while traveling east on a bus near Bay Village shortly after the murder she observed a nervous man with dark bushy hair board her bus. She said that he remained on board heading east when she left the bus in Cleveland. Mrs. John Lesnak, a resident of Mantua, Ohio (where the subject was staying at the time), reported she had seen a suspicious figure bearing this description at Colliers convenience store and bus stop in Mantua during this period, and was so concerned that she contacted the Bay Village Police Department.

Correlative Evidence Implicating Subject with Person Observed Near Sheppard Residence

The descriptions given by all of the witnesses conformed to the subject. Moreover, in other crimes in which the subject was involved, witnesses gave descriptions similar to the "bushy-haired" individual offered by the witnesses in the Sheppard case. Associates described the subject's hair as unmanageable and standing up when disheveled. Photographs of the subject show protruding wisps of hair. A bottle of Vitalis hair grooming oil was recovered with his belongings (an unusual item for one hiding in the woods) and is indicative of the unruly nature of his hair.

The composite drawing made from descriptions furnished by the Sheppard witnesses bears a marked resemblance to the subject. Later, eyewitnesses who observed him during his flight in Lake Placid a few weeks after the Sheppard murder offered descriptions from which a Lake Placid artist made another composite drawing. Although these drawings by two different artists may appear dissimilar, an analysis of the technical aspects of the renderings reflects great similarities. Bearing in mind that the two artists had never seen the subject and were attempting to depict features that were described by some twenty different witnesses, the resulting two drawings are remarkably similar: long black hair combed straight back (or standing up when in the wind), high forehead, wide piercing eyes, slightly elongated nose, firm jaw, and rather small ears. Indeed, a self-portrait by Call himself reflects features quite similar to those rendered by the artists. (See Exhibit J)

---

(3) <u>Positive Identification of Subject</u>
     <u>by Richard and Betty Jean Knitter</u>

The positive identification of the subject by Richard and Betty Jean Knitter is of paramount importance in that these two witnesses had the best look at the suspicious person outside the Sheppard residence the night of the murder. It was from their description that the police artist rendered the original composite which was distributed in the wake of the murder. The Knitters' identification of Major Call takes on great significance in light of the credibility of this couple. Throughout the years, the Knitters have remained firm about what they saw that night. "I will never forget his face," Mr. Knitter said. "He had a look of horror and helplessness. We slowed down thinking he needed help, but as we drew close and saw that face, we decided to keep going.

I remarked to my wife, 'How would you like to meet that guy in the dark?' The next day, when we heard about the Sheppard murder, we were certain we had seen the killer. We received tremendous unwanted publicity and were concerned about our personal safety. It has caused us great anguish through the years."

The Knitters stated they had reviewed hundreds of photographs, and had been subjected to enormous pressure to identify the man they had seen that night through their car window. They said that they had been subpoenaed to all three Sheppard trials. They declared that they had never seen any likeness in the numerous photographs that they had been shown previously, and had refused to identify anyone. Mr. Knitter firmly stated on many occasions that the man's face was etched in his mind and that he would never forget it.

Correlative Evidence Implicating Subject with Person Observed Near Sheppard Residence

On April 6, 2000, Richard and Betty Jean Knitter were shown an array of photographs which included pictures of Major Call and Richard Eberling, the Sheppard's window washer, who became a suspect in the case. They positively identified Major Call as the individual they had seen, Mr. Knitter stating, "That's the man we saw through our car window that night." In a follow-up interview five days later on April 11, 2000, Mr. Knitter adamantly reaffirmed his previous identification stating, "Yes, I'm sure it was F" [referring to the photograph of Major Call that had been labeled F]. (See Exhibit K)

---

(4) Positive Identification of Subject by Dr. Gervase Flick

Another detailed and significant statement regarding the subject came from Dr. Gervase Flick, a respected doctor and lawyer who also had been in the Air Force, serving with distinction as a captain in Vietnam. Dr. Flick, then a medical student, picked up a hitchhiker carrying a suitcase, heading east from Cleveland shortly after the murder. According to Dr. Flick, the individual had straight black hair combed back, and answered the description of the man observed near the Sheppard residence. Dr. Flick said that the hitchhiker seemed knowledgeable about the murder although it had happened only a few hours before, stating that he had heard about it on the radio during his previous ride. The man acted strangely, repeatedly changing stations on the radio as though listening for something. Dr. Flick stated the hitchhiker was limping, and that he used wooden matches to light his cigarettes. When Dr. Flick commented about a dark substance on the man's shoes, the individual replied that during his previous ride the car had struck a dog and that he had acquired blood on his shoes as he kicked the animal off the road. When asked about his limp, he said that he had injured his leg while kicking the dog from the road. Dr. Flick submitted a detailed statement of his ride with the man. Later, upon viewing photographs of Major Call, he identified him as the hitchhiker.

Correlative Evidence Implicating Subject with Hitchhiker

Dr. Flick's detailed statement of his encounter with the hitchhiker is a significant confirmation of evidence incriminating the subject. The fact that Dr. Flick's contact with the hitchhiker occurred only a few hours after the homicide in a location where the subject might reasonably be expected to be during his flight, and that the person fit the description offered by the nine witnesses, is telling in itself. However, when these facts are added to the other observations in the doctor's statement, (viz., the hitchhiker's suitcase, bloody shoes, limp, wooden matches, and knowledge of the crime, and Dr. Flick's positive identification of the subject), the doctor's testimony is that of a star witness, rendering a compelling indictment of the subject. (See Exhibit L)

III DISCREPANCIES IN SUBJECT'S ALIBI

(1) Subject's Whereabouts Prior to Sheppard Homicide

In his comments to the NYSP following his apprehension, the subject claimed that during the days immediately preceding the Sheppard murder he was alone on the Appalachian Trail. He said that after robbing John F. O'Connor, a Springfield cab driver, on June 13,

1954, he went to an Army Navy store in Springfield where he used his victim's check and identification to buy "camping equipment including a sleeping bag, etc." for a trip up the trail. He said that he then jumped his hotel bill, leaving behind personal items such as a Samsonite bag, and headed for the Appalachian Trail.

Correlative Evidence Reflecting Discrepancies in Subject's Statements

The evidence reflects discrepancies in the above statements made by the subject to the NYSP. The comments almost certainly were intended as an alibi to cover his whereabouts at the time of the Sheppard homicide. It is unrealistic that a person of the subject's reputed brilliance would assault, kidnap, and rob a cab driver, and then immediately use his victim's identification and personal check to buy camping equipment in the vicinity of the crime for a trip up the nearby Appalachian Trail—unless, of course, it was done for purposes of disinformation.

It is also unlikely that the subject would have undertaken such a difficult trek laden down with the quantity of personal items—including dress clothes—that he had with him upon his arrival in Lake Placid. He deposited clothes, including the expensive suit he had purchased while on leave in Asia (it bore the tailor's trademark and address in Kowloon, Hong Kong), with a dry cleaner in Saranac Lake shortly after his arrival. He left other garments, some bearing Tucson labels, at a nearby laundry. Evidence shows that, rather than undertaking a solitary trip on the Appalachian Trail, the subject was in reality continuing his crime spree, which by this time had become ingrained, including numerous burglaries and armed robberies such as the Liberty Package Store holdup. (See Exhibit M)

---

(2) Subject's Flight Following Sheppard Homicide

NYSP officials in charge of the Lake Placid homicide repeatedly stated they believed the subject was hiding out after committing a crime they described as "something big." Officials in both Reno and New York stated they intended to interrogate the subject about the

Sheppard murder even though Dr. Sam Sheppard had already been indicted. The subject submitted a signed statement following his apprehension in which he said that he was fleeing from crimes he had committed. He stated that if cornered by police he was prepared to shoot his way out and, if unsuccessful, to kill himself. These statements reflected his feelings during the period immediately after the Sheppard murder. Following his apprehension, the subject continued to reveal his flight mentality. In one incident he considered grabbing an officer's pistol and shooting his way to freedom, stating to the officer, "I wouldn't do that again, your revolver sticking out of its holster right in front of me. I was tempted to grab it and let you all have it." Life-long friend Robert Sylvester described the subject after he went AWOL, stating that he admitted he would shoot someone "if they caught him and were trying to make him 'go back'.... His mind seemed clear and functioning well enough, but the rationality of what he was saying was alarming. Every shread [sic] of logic was gone." (See Exhibit N)

IV SUMMARY

The evidence implicating the subject in the Sheppard homicide may be summarized as follows: The subject was reported to be in the Cleveland area at the time of the murder. He was emotionally distraught during this period, bitter over recent events in his life, and disposed to commit violent crimes. Indeed, he confessed to numerous felonies which included burglaries, armed robberies and murder—many of which were committed within one month of the Sheppard homicide. He readily admitted to police officers on several occasions that he would kill anyone who stood in his way while he was engaged in crime. In a signed statement he declared that he was hiding out from unspecified crimes immediately after the Sheppard murder. He indicated that the crimes were of such an egregious nature that if cornered by police he would shoot his way out. If unsuccessful, he was prepared to turn the gun on himself.

Elements of the Sheppard crime bore marked similarities to the subject's modus operandi: a forced entry with a prybar; an intruder in the bedroom; theft of cash, wallets and jewelry; acts of extreme violence against those who resisted. Investigators discovered no fingerprints, also characteristic of the subject's crimes because he wore his Air Force gloves.

With regard to the crime scene, forensic experts described the murder weapon as "... almost certainly not over a foot in length ... a cylindrical instrument like a piece of pipe flared at the end ... an object [possibly] carried for another purpose but serving as a murder weapon when needed...." Forensic experts, as well as the coroner, stated that chips of red lacquer found next to the victim possibly came from the murder weapon. One criminalist described the tool used to force entry through the basement door as a "prybar or crowbar commonly used by burglars during the fifties." A crowbar conforming in remarkable detail to all of these descriptions, including the chipping red lacquer, was found among the subject's belongings by the NYSP after the murder.

Dr. Kirk determined that the assailant had been severely bitten by the victim on the hand or finger and stated, "... the murderer had a definitely injured hand or finger on July 4, 1954." The subject's fingerprints taken at the time of his apprehension four months after the murder show a wound on his left forefinger described by a forensic expert as "consistent with a bite mark." The subject's Air Force fingerprints taken prior to the murder show no injury to this member. Further indications of a bitten finger are found in the leather fragment discovered near the victim, which appeared to have been recently torn and resembled a fragment of the leather flying gloves known to be worn by the subject. Forensic analysis determined that the leather fragment was similar to the leather used to make Air Force B-3 gloves during the fifties. The torn portion of the fragment was found to be consistent with the bite mark on the subject's fingerprint and the victim's front tooth.

An unexplained piece of aluminum foil and matches were found at the murder scene, as well as a cigarette butt in a nearby commode. Neither of the Sheppards smoked unfiltered cigarettes. Dr. Sheppard smoked pipes, including the expensive, uncommon meerschaum, and had a rack of pipes in his den. The subject, on the other hand, was a compulsive smoker and used wooden matches that he carried in aluminum foil. Among his confiscated belongings subsequent to the murder were wooden matches in aluminum foil and two pipes: a briar and the unusual meerschaum.

Crime scene photographs of the victim's pillow enlarged to its actual size reveal the outline of a German Luger which conforms to the size and shape of the pistol carried by the subject during his criminal acts. Two rosette-shaped wounds on the victim's forehead resemble the toggles on the receiver of the subject's Luger.

Dr. Sheppard stated that a box of morphine ampules and a bottle of Demerol had been stolen from his medical bag. The subject was thoroughly trained by the Air Force in the use of morphine and very likely would have sought a remedy for the pain of his wounded finger.

Dr. Sheppard described the intruder with whom he had grappled at the murder scene as a "man with dark bushy hair" who was "limping slightly." The description fits the subject, who had injured his knee and was limping at the time. During his other crimes the subject often was described as a "dark bushy-haired man."

No fewer than nine individual witnesses observed a bushy-haired figure, whose description conformed to the subject, near the Sheppard residence around the time of the murder. Mr. and Mrs. Richard Knitter executed signed statements positively identifying the subject as the person they saw outside the residence at the time of the murder. An analysis of the composite drawing made from descriptions offered by these witnesses reveals a strong resemblance to the subject. One of the witnesses, a resident of Mantua, Ohio, where the subject was residing, reported that she had seen a suspicious individual bearing this description in Mantua during this period. Dr. Gervase Flick, a respected doctor, lawyer and author, positively identified the subject as the limping hitchhiker with bloody shoes whom he picked up heading east out of Cleveland on July 4, 1954, a short time after the murder. Several eyewitnesses who observed the subject during his flight in Lake Placid a few weeks after the murder offered descriptions from which a second composite picture was made. The picture reflected strong similarities to the composite drawing that was previously done in Cleveland.

Questions about the subject's participation in the Sheppard homicide are not of recent origin. Indeed, at the time of the subject's apprehension in November 1954, authorities in both Reno and New York were sufficiently suspicious about his possible involvement in the Bay Village murder that they saw fit to interrogate him about the crime. They elected not to pursue the issue inasmuch as the Cleveland authorities were already in court convicting Dr. Sheppard of the murder.

V CONCLUSION

One may reasonably conclude from the foregoing evidence that Major Call committed the Sheppard murder. The elements required for proof of guilt are present: motive, modus operandi, crime scene evidence, murder weapons, witnesses, flight. In essence, the Sheppard homicide was a burglary that went awry. By his own admission Major Call was prepared to kill any person who stood in his way. Tragically, on July 4, 1954, that person was Marilyn Sheppard.

Note: The purpose of this addendum is to focus on items of substantive evidence which do not lend themselves to analysis in the preceding narrative. The addendum does not include all of the particulars of the case which were used in passages of the narrative to describe Major Call's involvement in the Sheppard homicide.

OPINIONS FROM PROMINENT LAW ENFORCEMENT OFFICIALS

"When I began my law enforcement as a young New York State Trooper in January of 1962 my Sergeants and Senior Troopers were still discussing their roles in the difficult 1954 manhunt for Major Call. Now nearly forty years later my interest in this infamous case has been rekindled upon reading Bernard Conners' book, a fascinating account of Call's tortured life. In addition to accurately describing the efforts of the New York State Police, the work captures the essence of a paradoxical character whose wartime heroism and devotion to family contrasted shockingly with his violent criminal activities. Conners presents the life of this dangerous criminal in a riveting account, and in addition, appears to offer a credible solution to one of the more notorious crimes of the 20th century."

THOMAS A. CONSTANTINE
Former Superintendent, New York State Police
Former Head, US Drug Enforcement Administration

"Major James A. Call was the subject of an intensive investigation by the New York State Police for many crimes committed in New York state, including the murder of a police officer. During the past few years author Bernard Conners has submitted evidence to the New York State Police Forensic Investigation Center which professes to implicate Call in other crimes including the Marilyn Sheppard murder. After careful review of this material, it is my opinion that there are numerous evidentiary items implicating Call in the Sheppard case. Based on an examination of this evidence it is my opinion that Major Call's involvement in this crime cannot be excluded."

W. MARK DALE
Director, New York State Police Forensic Investigation Center

"An extraordinary synthesis of evidence including eye witnesses, circumstantial evidence and forensic examinations that lead me to believe that the individual who committed a notorious murder is identified in this book. I have seen people convicted with far less evidence. Reaching back almost fifty years, it gives a compelling story about a tragedy for the American Criminal Justice system."

PAUL V. DALY
Former Deputy Assistant Director (Investigations), FBI
Former Assistant Administrator, US Drug Enforcement Administration

"Close to a half century after Dr. Sam Sheppard was charged and tried for the murder of his wife Marilyn in their Cleveland home, the controversial case continues to fascinate the nation. This book, one of the best written on the subject, sets forth a theory that will hold the reader spellbound from start to finish."

NEWMAN FLANAGAN
Former Longtime District Attorney, Suffolk County, Boston, Massachusetts
Executive Director, National District Attorney's Association

"This is the best book I have read in a very long time. It grabs your attention on the first page and never lets go. It is on the one hand a real human-interest story of how a war hero turns into a violent predator. However, it goes much deeper than that as the author also makes a very compelling case that the subject of this book is the person responsible for one of the most publicized and debated crimes of all time. I had not heard the story of Major Call before reading this book but now I shall never forget it."

LARRY A. POTTS
Former Deputy Director, FBI

Southern Tier Law Enforcement Academy
459 Philo Road — Building 1
Elmira Heights, New York 14903
TEL: (607) 734-1656--FAX: (607) 795-5347
E-Mail: STLEANY@aol.com

ruary 12, 2001

Bernard F. Conners
ish American Publishing, Ltd.
·itish American Boulevard
am, NY 12110

Physical & Forensic Evidence: Marilyn Reese Sheppard Homicide
Major James Arlon Call

r Mr. Conners:

After analyzing the physical and forensic evidence pertaining to Major James Call
ject) I am pleased to submit the following report:

ther Fragment Recovered at Crime Scene

I microscopically examined the leather fragment found at the crime scene and compared
ith a B-3 glove of the type issued to Major Call by the United States Air Force. I further
sulted with a leather expert who confirmed that the leather fragment was consistent with the
s characteristics of the leather used to manufacture the Air Force B-3 glove. It is my opinion
a B-3 glove cannot be excluded as the source of the leather fragment found at the crime
e.

gerprints and Bite Mark

A forensic odontologist described a mark on the subject's left forefinger which appeared
is fingerprints taken subsequent to the Sheppard homicide as consistent with a bite mark. I
mined sets of the subject's rolled fingerprints taken by the US Air Force before the homicide,
compared them microscopically with those taken by the New York State Police after the
icide. The Air Force prints taken prior to the homicide show no injury to this finger.

tim's Dentition

I examined exhumation photographs of the victim's dentition which showed a fractured
illary incisor. I compared the torn edge of the leather fragment with the bite mark on the
ject's forefinger and the victim's tooth. Microscopic analysis and computer enhanced

imagery of the leather, tooth and bite mark reveal corresponding individual characteris consistent with a bite mark. Odontologists' reports confirm the fact that there is ample evide to support a finding that the fracture to the victim's tooth was due to her having bitten on finger of her assailant, and that in an attempt to remove it her tooth was fractured.

Blood Spot on Wardrobe Door

Criminalist Dr. Paul L. Kirk described a large blood spot on the wardrobe door at crime scene. Dr. Kirk stated that the victim probably bit her assailant on the hand or finger, his bleeding wound deposited this blood on the door. The microscopic comparison of victim's fractured maxillary incisor, the fragment of leather, the bite mark on the subject's forefinger and Dr. Kirk's theory cannot exclude a lacerated finger from the assailant as source of blood on the wardrobe door.

German Luger

Utilizing computer enhanced imagery, I compared the subject's Luger with the bl image on the victim's pillowcase and found artifacts that are consistent with the phys characteristics of a German Luger.

Evidence of Forced Door and Murder Weapon

The tool mark on a basement door of the Sheppard residence and the plastic impression taken by the Cleveland Police Department are indicative of a forced door utilizin crowbar. The size and shape of the crowbar recovered from the subject by the New York S Police conform to the size and shape of the murder weapon identified by forensic scientists. red lacquer paint chips found at the murder scene are compatible with the red lacquer paint ch on the subject's crowbar.

Witnesses

Major Call was identified as being in the Cleveland area at the time of the murder. was familiar with the area from his days at Hiram College and his many visits to his siste nearby Mantua, Ohio. The similar descriptions from ten witnesses is a key point against M Call. The most striking accounts are from Mr. and Mrs. Richard Knitter and Dr. Gervase Fl who identified Major Call from a photographic array utilizing contemporary standards.

Psychological Profile

Following is a brief psychological profile which supports the foregoing evide implicating the subject in the Sheppard homicide:

Major James Call was on the fast track for promotion in the US Air Force. He described as brilliant, often promoted before his peers, and volunteered for dangerous con missions over North Korea. He was a product of the US Military survival schools of escape evasion. He perfected his skills as a survivor, and was able to function in extre circumstances. He always remained composed and focused, and was taught to kill with

2

sitation.   His masteries of these skills became apparent when he shot three police officers, ing one of them, and evaded the manhunt of thousands of police officers and civilians in the irondack Mountains for more than 100 days.

Major Call was devastated by the death of his wife. His behavior changed and his achant for gambling intensified. He deserted the Air Force and began a life of crime. Armed beries, assaults and burglaries ensued. He added to his cash of weapons and survivor gear. s mental condition deteriorated precipitously.

He visited his best friend in Chicago, at which time he was armed with three handguns. s friend was so alarmed with the changes he saw in Major Call and the danger he posed to ers, that he reported him to the FBI.

Major Call often forced his way into buildings and residences with a crowbar.   He nfronted his victims with a weapon and used physical or deadly force to neutralize them. llowing his apprehension, he readily admitted to authorities that he was prepared to kill yone who stood in his way. Cognizant of leaving fingerprints, he wore his B-3 flying gloves. ssessing a top-secret clearance, he realized his prints were on file with the military and the I.

Major Call was mission oriented. He planned his criminal activities as methodically as planned missions to North Korea. After targeting an area, he would burglarize many homes ickly, then flee the vicinity before the local police could effectively react.   In many of his rglaries he exhibited a brazen disregard for the presence of his victims.

nclusion

After a careful review of the totality of evidence developed in this case, it is my fessional opinion that there are reasonable grounds to indict and convict Major James Call for murder of Marilyn Reese Sheppard.

Very Truly Yours,

James L. Chapman

---

es L. Chapman is Professor Emeritus, former Director of the Criminal Justice Program, and Former Director of Crime Laboratory of the State University of New York at Corning.   Currently, he is Executive Director of the thern Tier Law Enforcement Academy, New York State Zone 12.   Prior to his career in education, he was olved with law enforcement and served in the United States Marine Corps.   In 1980 Professor Chapman was ed by the Sheppard family to evaluate physical evidence and documents pertaining to Marilyn Sheppard's nicide.   Since that time, he has been involved extensively with many aspects of the investigation.   He has erviewed many of the principals in the case, and reviewed extensive material, including crime scene evidence, opsy and exhumation photographs.   He was listed among the expert witnesses for the third trial in 1999, and eared as one of the experts who participated in Nova's comprehensive television program regarding the eppard case in 1999.

3

EXHIBITS

INDEX OF EXHIBITS

ibit A
urriculum Vitae of Dr. Paul Leland Kirk, April 26, 1955
ibit B
.tha Crowbar circa 1954
JYSP Laboratory Report—Item 78, Crow bar
ibit C
ubject's German Luger—Serial No. 8782T
ictim's Wounds
.eport of Autopsy
.rime Scene, Autopsy and Reconstruction Photographs
ibit D
hotograph of victim with absence of wounds on lower face
xcerpts from autopsy report highlighting mouth and teeth injuries
ibit E
omparison of subject's fingerprints before and after Sheppard homicide
JYSP Laboratory Report—Item 20, fingertip bandage

ibit F
hotograph enlargement of fingerprint with bite mark
hotograph enlargement of leather fragment
hotograph enlargement of damaged teeth
ite mark corresponding to teeth and leather fragment

- Professional opinions regarding dentition
- Air Force Leather B-3 Glove
- Photograph of subject wearing Air Force gloves
- NYSP Report—John Lester Carney

Exhibit G
- Inventory of subject's belongings confiscated by NYSP
- Mug Shot, Reno, Nevada, November 1954—subject with cigarette
- Additional photographs of subject with cigarette

Exhibit H
- Subject's Luger superimposed over imprint on victim's pillow
- Presentation and comparison of Luger and pillow imprint

Exhibit I
- Air Force record of subject's physical abilities
- Subject's statement to NYSP regarding knee injury
- Witness account of subject's limp
- Newspaper account of subject's limp
- Photograph of subject on Air Force football team

Exhibit J
- Photographs of subject with composite drawings
- NYSP Report—Vitalis hair oil

Exhibit K
- Positive identification of subject by Mr. & Mrs. Richard Knitter
- Identification of Picture F
- Identification of Picture A
- Pictures A & F compared with police composite
- Statement from Mr. & Mrs. Richard Knitter

Exhibit L
- Statement from Dr. Gervase Flick, Vero Beach, Florida, November 1997

hibit M

NYSP report regarding clothing deposited at dry cleaners

Statements from owners of dry cleaner and laundry establishments

Clipping and police report concerning liquor store robbery, June 5, 1954

hibit N

Clippings concerning subject's flight and interrogation regarding

he Sheppard homicide

Subject's statement regarding flight

Clipping reflecting subject's propensity for violent escape

Correspondence from friend reflecting subject's propensity for criminal violence

EXHIBIT A—Curriculum Vitae of Dr. Paul Leland Kirk, April 26, 1955

STATE OF OHIO)		IN THE COURT OF COMMON PLEAS
) SS:		Criminal Branch
CUYAHOGA COUNTY)		

No. 64571

STATE OF OHIO,)	
)	
PLAINTIFF)	
)	
vs.)	AFFIDAVIT of PAUL LELAND KIRK
)	
SAMUEL H. SHEPPARD)	
)	
DEFENDANT)	

PAUL LELAND KIRK, of lawful age, being duly sworn, states that he resides at 1064 Cresto Road, Berkeley, California; that he was graduated with the highest honors from Ohio Stat University in 1924 with a degree of Bachelor of Arts in Chemistry; that in 1925 he was awarded a degree of Master of Science in Chemistry by the University of Pittsburgh; that in 1927 he received a degree of Doctor of Philosophy in Biochemistry from the University of California; that he was an assistant in Chemistry at the University of Pittsburgh dur ing 1924 and 1925; taught biochemistry at the University of California 1926 and 1927; wa research Assistant in Biochemistry at the University of California in 1927 and 1928; Research Associate at the University of California 1928 and 1929; Instructor in Micro chemistry in the Biochemistry Division from 1929 to 1933; Assistant Professor of Bioche istry at the University of California from 1933 to 1939; Associate Professor of Biochem istry from 1939 to 1945; on leave to the Radiation Laboratory directed by Ernest O. Lawrence from 1942 to 1943. This was the first organization devoted to atomic energy research; from there he was transferred to the Metallurgical Laboratory of the Universit of Chicago, in 1943 to 1944, which was a branch of the Manhattan Project, concerned with the development of plutonium; Technical Specialist, Hanford Engineering Works, Richland, Washington, 1944 and 1945, in charge of Microchemical, Research and Development in con nection with the manufacture of the atomic bomb fuel, plutonium, (explosive) used at Nagasaki, Japan; Professor of Biochemistry and Advisor in Criminalistics from 1945 to 1948; Professor of Biochemistry and Criminalistics in the University of California from 1948 to 1954; Professor of Criminalistics, School of Criminology, at the University of California from 1954 to the present time; member of the Medical School Faculty of the University of California from 1927 to 1950; Associate Professor in Physiology, Hopkins Marine Station (Stanford University), 1935; Investigative work in Criminalistics in 1935 for the Berkeley Police Department in California, and investigation for the District Attorney of Alameda County, California, who was Hon. Earl Warren, now Chief Justice of the United States Supreme Court; Continual Investigative work in Criminalistics for various public bodies and individuals until 1942, when the work was discontinued due to services required in the Atomic Energy Research Project; from 1945 continuous investi gative work for district attorneys in Alameda and San Francisco Counties and other counties throughout the northern part of the State of California, this investigative work being principally on behalf of agencies of the State.

Affiant further states that prior to World War II he was placed in charge of the trainin program in Criminalistics of the University of California and wrote the curriculum; that after the War he renewed his activities in criminalistics; that he was consultant to num erous agencies, including the State Crime Commission of California, the Army, Atomic Energy Commission, and numerous industrial concerns with investigative problems, and private individuals.

- 1 -

fiant further states that he has been accepted as an expert witness in Criminalistics for
rious Federal and State Courts, including the Federal and State Courts of California, Fed-
al Court of Nevada, Federal Court of Oregon, State Court of Arizona, Federal Court of Idaho
d the State Court of Louisiana.

fiant states that Criminalistics is the application of the techniques and principles of the
sic sciences, particularly chemistry and physics, to the examination and interpretation of
ysical evidence; that he is in charge of the Criminalistics portion of the School of Crim-
ology of the University of California, which school is concerned with the training of
lice laboratory technicians, crime laboratory technicians, and the scientific investigation
crime; that the persons entering and studying in said School come from all parts of the
ited States and from all over the world; that many of the State Crime Laboratories are
affed with graduates of said School, which gives a degree of Bachelor of Arts and Bachelor
Science, and Master of Criminology.

fiant has been the author of at least 150 original papers in scientific literature and
ny of said papers are on Criminalistics; that he is the author of "Quantitative Ultra-
croanalysis", 1950, publisher, John Wiley & Company; "Density and Refractive Index" -
neir Application to Criminal Identification", 1951, publisher, Charles C. Thomas Company;
riminal Investigation", 1953, publisher, Interscience Publishing Company. This work has
ternational circulation among state and governmental agencies in the United States and
reign countries, and is a guide to the use of physical evidence by persons engaged in
w enforcement.

fiant is Associate Editor for Police Science of the Journal of Criminal Law, Criminology
d Police Science, which is the official publication of the International Association of
son Investigators, the Illinois Academy of Criminology, the Society for the Advancement
Criminology; Associate Editor of Mikrochimica Acta, which is an international journal
microchemistry, published in German, English, French and Italian.

fiant is Vice President of the Microchemical Commission of the International Union of
re & Applied Chemistry; a member of the National Research Council Committee on Analytical
emistry; a member of the American Chemical Society Committee on Weights and Balances, a
mber of the Belgian Royal Academy, the American Chemical Society, the American Association
r the Advancement of Science; the American Society of Biological Chemists, and the Society
r the Advancement of Criminology.

EXHIBIT B

- Atha Crowbar circa 1954

- NYSP Laboratory Report—Item 78, Crow bar

STANLEY TOOLS

STANLEY-ATHA RIPPING BARS AND CHISELS

These tools are drop-forged from high grade hexagon tool steel and will not easily bend or break. The~ attractively finished.

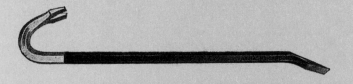

GOOSE NECK RIPPING BARS

No.		Weight	
112	½ in. x 12 in.	1	lbs.
118	⅝ in. x 18 in.	2	lbs.
124	¾ in. x 24 in.	3¾	lbs.
130	¾ in. x 30 in.	4½	lbs.
136	¾ in. x 36 in.	5¼	lbs.

Red Claw Ends

(Courtesy of Stanley Tools, Inc., New Britain, Connecticut)

P Laboratory Report—Item 78, Crow bar

I.

173077

STATE OF NEW YORK

ALBIN S. JOHNSON
SUPERINTENDENT
GEORGE M. SEARLE
DEPUTY

FRANCIS S. McGARVEY
CHIEF INSPECTOR

SCIENTIFIC LABORATORY
8 NOLAN ROAD
ALBANY 8
PHONE 8-3578

NEW YORK STATE TROOPERS
EXECUTIVE DEPARTMENT
DIVISION OF STATE POLICE

WILLIAM E. KIRWAN
DIRECTOR

October 4, 1954

SUBJECT: Supplemental Report
Investigation of Death of Richard Pelkey
Lab case 19-F-69

TO: Inspector R. J. McDowell, New York State Police,
District "B", Malone, New York

1. **EVIDENCE**

Additional evidence brought to Laboratory on
September 30, 1954 by Tpr. Harris, District "B", BCI.

69. Rubberized sheet.
70. Blue sweater.
71. Swim trunks.
72. Blue trousers.
73. Rubberized pants.
74. Sport shirt.
75. White handkerchief.
76. Red sport shirt.
77. Screwdriver.
78. Crow bar.
79. Two pipes.

2. **HISTORY OF CASE**

Refer original report dated August 25, 1954.

3. **EXAMINATION OF EVIDENCE**

69. Rubberized sheet.

This evidence is a khaki colored rubberized
rain covering, with hood for head, snap fastener. This
is the top portion of a 2-piece outfit.

Examination does not show presence of blood or
any significant evidence.

70. Blue sweater.

This evidence is a man's blue wool slip-over
sweater, manufacturer's label "Bloomingdale's size 40".

This sweater was apparently worn over a red woolen
garment, as particles of red wool were found adhering
inside.

Nothing else significant observed present.

NYSP Laboratory Report

Lab case 19-F-69   *173077*

71. Swim trunks.

This evidence is a man's blue nylon bathing trunks, manufacturer's label "Saks 5th Ave., size 34".

A 5¢ piece was found in the pocket.

Nothing else significant.

72. Blue trousers.

This evidence is men's blue cotton trousers, no manufacturer's label. Left leg torn full length up on the inside seam. Waist measures 33½"; length from waist to bottom, 37½".

73. Rubberized pants.

This evidence is rubberized pants rain covering, which may be the bottom half of Evid. #69. This evidence is green in color, while Evid. #69 is khaki colored.

Bottom portion of left leg is torn off.

Nothing significant present.

74. Sport shirt.

This evidence is a blue and green checked sport shirt, manufacturer's label "Saks Fifth Ave, size 18".

Nothing significant observed present.

75. Handkerchief.

This evidence is a man's white handkerchief, 17" square, embroidered with initial "D".

Nothing else significant.

76. Red sport shirt.

This evidence is a red wool sport shirt, manufacturer's label "The Camp Shop".

Nothing significant.

77. Screwdriver.

This evidence is a wooden handled screwdriver, overall length 7-3/8", blade 2½" x 6/15". Identified as a "United" product.

Nothing significant.

Lab case 19-F-69

//3071

78. Crow bar.

This evidence is a 12" crowbar, labeled "ATHA".
Particles of white and red paint adhering.

Nothing else significant.

79. Two pipes.

Evidence consists of two tobacco pipes, one
labeled "Sterncrest Imported Briar".

Teeth marks indicate that both pipes were used
by the same person.

Nothing else significant.

With regard to Evid. #69 - 79, inclusive, described
above, examination did not show presence of any blood
stains on any of the evidence.

Re: examination of evidences -

66-B. Blue dungarees.

Waist measurement of these blue dungarees is 34".
The leg measurements are: 35½" left leg, and 37" right leg.

Bottoms of both legs are very frayed and considerably worn.

60. Khaki colored sleeping bag.

The zipper on the evidence sleeping bag is identified as 113" zipper fastener, manufactured by the
Murrlen Fastener Co., 241 W. 36th St., New York City.

Contact with the Murrlen Co. indicates that they
shipped 113" fasteners to the Empire Sporting Goods
Manufacturing Co., 92 Bleecker St., New York City,
attention Mr. Melvin Rausch.

62. Guest Check pad.

Several distributors of hotel, restaurant and
janitor supplies were contacted, relative to distribution
of the evidence Guest Check pad, with the following results:

Kopel Supply Co., Utica, N.Y. - no accounts in the Lake
Placid area.

Riverside Wholesale Distributors, Burlington, Vt. -
possibilities: Angelo's Restaurant and Andy's Restaurant,
both in Plattsburgh, N. Y.

NYSP Laboratory Report

Lab case 19-F-69

173677

G. F. Blackmer & Son, Saratoga Springs, N.Y. -
possibilities: McCauley's Restaurant, Ticonderoga.
Red Diner, North Creek.

Gladwin Restaurant Supply Co., Utica -
possibilities: Arena Grill)
Dollar Diner)
Grand View Lodge) All in Lake
The Lodge) Placid.
Majestic Restaurant)
The Spot)

Holland House)
LaFave's Restaurant) In Tupper Lake.
Roy's Restaurant)

Miss Saranac Diner, Saranac Lake.

White Face Inn, White Face.

G. T. Brigham Co., Pittsfield, Mass. -
possibilities: Hoosick Falls, N. Y.

J. B. Paper Co., Inc., Pittsfield, Mass. - do not supply
the Lake Placid area.

4. DISPOSITION OF EVIDENCES

In view of the many pieces of evidence submitted in
the subject investigation, we respectfully advise the
allocation of the following pieces of evidence:

26. 9 mm Luger, serial No. 5754 - returned to
Dr. Perkins.

27. P-35 Radom pistol, serial M6322 - returned to
Dr. Perkins.

28. 1 of the 2 combat boots submitted - returned to
Tpr. Harris on August 12, 1954.

49. White shirt - turned over to Sgt. Hardy on
Sept. 16, 1954.

50. Tan trench coat - turned over to Sgt. Hardy on
Sept. 16, 1954.

65. Playing cards - 27 of the evidence playing cards
turned over to Inspector McDowell, via Registered
Mail on Sept. 23, 1954.

The Laboratory is in possession of all other evidences
mentioned in Laboratory reports.

Respectfully submitted,

Orig: Insp. McDowell
Cy: Chief Inspector
District Attorney
WEK:r

William E. Kirwan, Director

EXHIBIT C

HIBIT C

The reader is forewarned that Exhibits C and D contain graphic photographs from the crime scene and autopsy. Although the photos are explicit, in view of the fact that substantive evidence implicating the subject derives from these reports, it is felt the material must be included.

EXHIBIT C

- Subject's German Luger—Serial No. 8782T
- Victim's Wounds
- Report of Autopsy
- Crime scene, Autopsy and Reconstruction Photographs

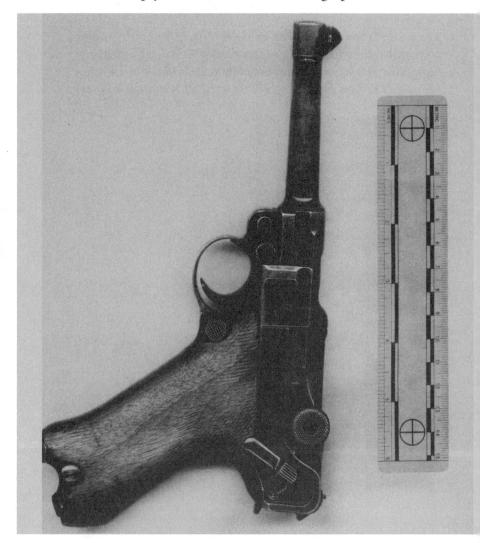

EXHIBIT C

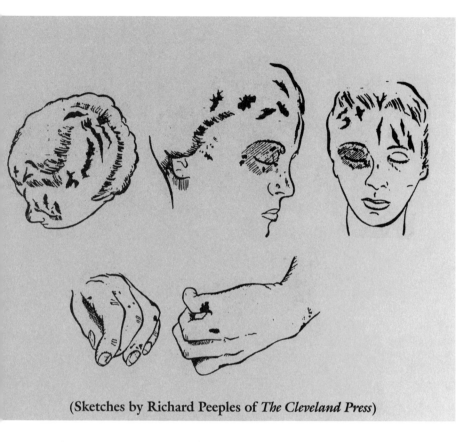

(Sketches by Richard Peeples of *The Cleveland Press*)

Report of Autopsy shows a total of 35 wounds to the victim's head, arms, and hands.

wounds: left and right forehead, top and back of the head

ounds: eyes, nose, and near the ear

ounds: two broken teeth and abrasion on buccal surface of lip

ound: bruise on the shoulder

ounds: forearms and hands

409

Victim's Wounds

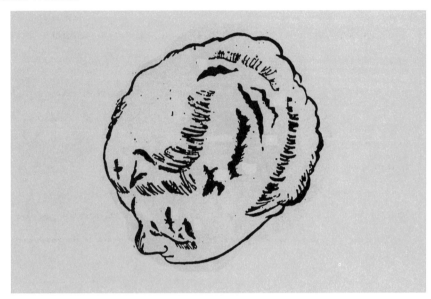

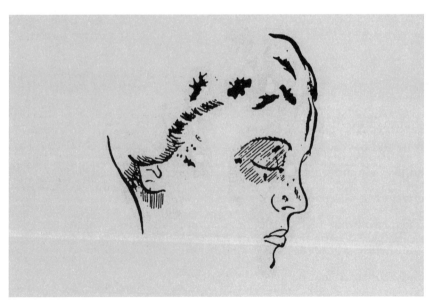

(Sketches by Richard Peeples of *The Cleveland Press*)

ort of Autopsy

CORONER'S OFFICE, CUYAHOGA COUNTY, OHIO

THE STATE OF OHIO }
CUYAHOGA COUNTY } ss: REPORT OF AUTOPSY

                              CASE No. 76629 AUTOPSY No. M-7280

I, _____ S. R. Gerber _____ M.D., Coroner of Cuyahoga County, Ohio,

Certify that at __12:30 A.M. P.M.__ on the __4th__ day of __July__, 19 54

in accordance with Section 2855-6 of the General Code of the State of Ohio, made or

caused to be made a post-mortem examination on the body of_____

__Marilyn Reese Sheppard__ of No. 28924 Westlake Rd., Bay Village. Ohio, and that

the following is a true and correct report of said examination to the best of my knowledge
and belief:—

SEX __Female__   AGE __31__   COLOR __White__

COMPLEXION __Medium__ EYES __Hazel__   NATIVITY __American__

WEIGHT __125#__   TEETH __Good__   OCCUPATION __Housewife__

HEIGHT __67"__   HAIR __Brown__   MARITAL STATUS __Married__

MARKS AND WOUNDS:

1. There is a contused abraded laceration measuring 1 x ½" in the left frontal
    region, centered 2½" from the midline. It extends from the supra-orbital
    margin cephalad. The injury extends down to the underlying bone.

2. There is a contused crescentic laceration measuring 1 x ¼" in the left frontal
    region, centered 2" from the midline. The lowermost point of the laceration
    is located 1½" above the supra-orbital margin. The laceration extends down
    to the underlying bone.

3. There is a contused gaping laceration measuring 1¼ x 3/8" in the left frontal
    region, centered 1" from the midline. It extends from the supra-orbital
    ridge cephalad. The underlying bone is visible in the depths of the wound.

4. There is a linear laceration measuring 2 x ¼" in the midfrontal region.
    The injury originates at the glabella and extends cephalad. The laceration
    extends through the soft tissue to the underlying bone.

    (Cont'd - other side)

<u>CAUSE OF DEATH:</u> The death of the decedent was the result of:— MULTIPLE IMPACTS
TO HEAD AND FACE WITH COMMINUTED FRACTURES OF SKULL AND
SEPARATION OF FRONTAL SUTURE, BILATERAL SUBDURAL HEMORRHAGES,
DIFFUSE BILATERAL SUBARACHNOID HEMORRHAGES, AND CONTUSIONS
OF BRAIN.

                    HOMICIDE BY ASSAULT.

                         S. R. Gerber M.D.
                    Cuyahoga County Coroner

Report of Autopsy

Decedent said to have been assaulted and found by husband apparently dead on her bed at home, 28924 Westlake Road, Bay Village, at about 5:30 A.M., 7-4-54. She was conveyed to the Coroner's Office where she was officially pronounced dead following arrival at 8:00 A.M., 7-4-54. (Dr. Gerber)

* · * * · * * · * * · * ¬ * · * · * * * · * * · * * *

MARKS AND WOUNDS - Cont'd

5. There is a ragged cresentic laceration measuring ½ x ¼" in the right frontal region centered 1" from the midline and 2½" above the supra-orbital ridge. The laceration is located immediately below the hair line. The edges of the laceration are abraded over a zone measuring up to 1/8" in width. The laceration extends down to the underlying bone.

6. There is a contused laceration measuring 1 x ¼" in the right frontal region centered 2" from the midline and 1½" above the supra-orbital ridge. The laceration runs from lateral and posterior medially and anteriorly. The laceration extends down to the underlying bone.

Comminuted fractures of the frontal bone are visible and palpable in the depths of the lacerations described above.

7. There is a gaping contused elliptical laceration measuring 1 x ¼" in the right frontal region, centered 2" above the right supra-orbital ridge and 3" from the midline. The underlying bone is exposed.

8. There is a ragged contused laceration measuring 1 x ½" in the right parietal region, centered 4" from the midline and 4" from the right external auditory meatus. The laceration extends down to the underlying bone.

9. There is a ragged contused laceration measuring ½ x ¼" in the right occiput, centered 3½" from the midline and 5" from the right external auditory meatus. The laceration extends only partially through the scalp.

10. There is a ragged contused laceration measuring 1½ x ½" in the mid-fronto-parietal region, centered 3" above the glabella. The posterior aspect of the wound forks to produce a Y each of whose arms measure ½".

11. There is a ragged contused laceration in the left parietal region measuring 2" in length. The wound extends from the midline to the left, originating at a point 6½" from the left auditory meatus.

12. There is a ragged cruciate contused laceration measuring 1½ x 1" in the left temporal region, centered 3" from the left lateral canthus and 4½" from the left external auditory meatus. The laceration extends down to the underlying bone. Fractures are visible and palpable in the depths of the laceration.

13. There is a ragged contused laceration measuring 2½ x 1½" in the left parietal region, centered 3" from the midline and 4½" from the left external auditory meatus. The injury extends from anterior and lateral posteriorly and medially. The anterior aspect of the injury is separated from the preceeding injury (#12) by a bridge of skin which measures from ½ to ½".

14. There is a contused cresentic laceration measuring 2¼ x ½" in the left parietal region, centered 3½" from the midline and 5½" from the left external auditory meatus. It is separated from the preceeding injury (#13) by a bridge of skin measuring ½" in width. The bridge of skin separates the posterior extremity of the preceeding injury from the present laceration.

15. There is a ragged cresentic laceration in the left parietal region centered 3" from the midline and 6" from the left external auditory meatus. The laceration measures 1½ x ¼" and is separated from the preceeding injury (#14) by a bridge of skin measuring up to ½" in width. The underlying bone is exposed.

EXHIBIT C

MARKS AND WOUNDS - Cont'd

16. There is a laceration measuring 5/16 x 1/8" in the right pre-auricular region over the temporo-mandibular joint. It is centered 1 3/4" from the right external auditory meatus.

17. The right upper and lower eyelids are swollen and discolored a dark purplish brown.

18. There is an area of crusted abrasion in the mid-right upper lid measuring $\frac{1}{4}$ x $\frac{1}{2}$".

19. There is an area of crusted abrasion measuring $\frac{1}{2}$ x $\frac{1}{4}$" in the mid-right lower lid.

20. There is swelling and purple-brown discoloration of the left upper and lower eyelids. The discoloration and swelling are less marked than on the right.

21. There is a fracture of the nasal bone with crepitus on manipulation.

22. There is a contused abrasion measuring $\frac{1}{4}$ x 1/8" over the bridge of the nose with the long axis of the abrasion following the long axis of the nose.

23. There is a contused abrasion measuring 1 x $\frac{1}{4}$" on the left mid-infra-orbital margin.

24. There is a crusted abrasion measuring 1 x $\frac{1}{2}$" on the buccal surface of the mucosa of the lower lip.

25. There is a complete fracture of the upper right medial incisor at the junction of the proximal and middle third of the tooth. The fracture is recent and the fractured surface is sharp. The distal fragment of the tooth is not present within the mouth.

26. There is a chip defect on the occlusal-frontal surface of the upper left medial incisor. The defect measures 3/16 x 1/8", and the edges are sharp.

27. There is an area of purple brown contusion measuring 2" in diameter over the superior aspect of the right shoulder. The discoloration is faint.

28. There is a contused abrasion measuring $\frac{1}{4}$" over the right radius centered 7$\frac{1}{2}$" proximal to the tip of the right thumb.

29. There is an area of contused abrasion measuring 2 x 3/4" on the lateral aspect of the dorsum of the right wrist.

30. There is a dried abrasion measuring 3/4 x $\frac{1}{4}$" over the base of the right thumb on the palmar aspect.

31. There is an abrasion measuring $\frac{1}{4}$ x $\frac{1}{4}$" over the dorsum of the proximal phalanx of the right index finger immediately distal to the metacarpophalangeal joint.

32. There is an area of crusted abrasion measuring $\frac{1}{4}$ x 1/8" over the metacarpophalangeal joint on the dorsum of the right 4th finger.

33. There is hyper-mobility and crepitus on the right 5th finger at the metacarpophalangeal joint.

34. There is a contused abrasion measuring 1$\frac{1}{2}$ x $\frac{1}{4}$" over the left ulna centered 10" proximal to the tip of the left middle finger.

35. There is partial avulsion of the fingernail of the left 4th finger with the root of the nail exposed.

413

Report of Autopsy

ANATOMIC DIAGNOSES

1. Multiple impacts to head and face with:
   a) Comminuted fractures of skull and separation of frontal suture.
   b) Bilateral subdural hemorrhages.
   c) Diffuse bilateral subarachnoid hemorrhages.
   d) Contusions of brain.
   e) Multiple contused lacerations of forehead and scalp.
   f) Fractures of upper medial incisor teeth.
   g) Fracture of nose.
2. Multiple abrasions and contusions. Partial avulsion of 4th left fingernail
3. Aspiration of blood.
4. Intra-uterine pregnancy - circa 4 months.
5. Adenomata of thyroid.

LABORATORY FINDINGS

   Blood: alcohol--0.00%; barbiturates--negative.
   Blood : type: O Rh negative type MS

EXHIBIT C

ne Scene Photograph

Reconstruction of Victim's Wounds

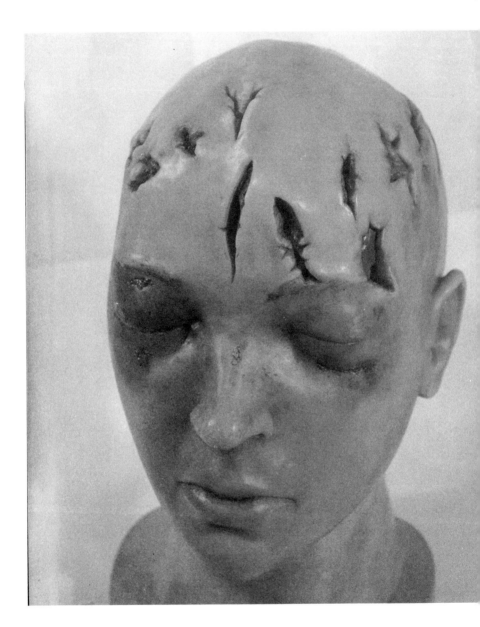

HIBIT D

1otograph of victim

cerpts from Autopsy report

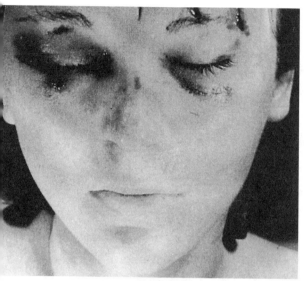

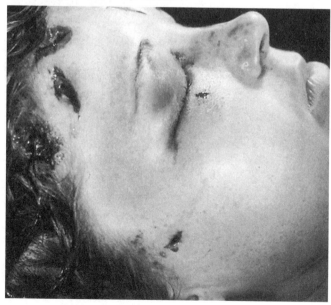

absence of wounds
wer face

Excerpts from autopsy report highlighting mouth and teeth injuries
(for entire report see Exhibit C)

CORONER'S OFFICE, CUYAHOGA COUNTY, OHIO

THE STATE OF OHIO
CUYAHOGA COUNTY } ss: REPORT OF AUTOPSY

CASE No. 76629   AUTOPSY No. M-7280

I, _____ S. R. Gerber _____ M.D. Coroner of Cuyahoga County, Ohio,

Certify that at __12:30__ A.M./P.M. on the __4th__ day of __July__ 19 54

in accordance with Section 2855-6 of the General Code of the State of Ohio, made or

caused to be made a post-mortem examination on the body of _____

__Marilyn Reese Sheppard__ of No. _28924 Westlake Rd., Bay Village Ohio_, and that

the following is a true and correct report of said examination to the best of my knowledge

and belief:—

SEX __Female__   AGE __31__   COLOR __White__

COMPLEXION _Medium_   EYES __Hazel__   NATIVITY __American__

WEIGHT __125#__   TEETH __Good__   OCCUPATION __Housewife__

HEIGHT __67"__   HAIR __Brown__   MARITAL STATUS __Married__

MARKS AND WOUNDS - Cont'd

24. There is a crusted abrasion measuring 1 x ½" on the buccal surface of the mucosa of the lower lip.

25. There is a complete fracture of the upper right medial incisor at the junction of the proximal and middle third of the tooth. The fracture is recent and the fractured surface is sharp. The distal fragment of the tooth is not present within the mouth.

26. There is a chip defect on the occlusal-frontal surface of the upper left medial incisor. The defect measures 3/16 x 1/8", and the edges are sharp.

HIBIT E

Comparison of subject's fingerprints before and after Sheppard homicide

YSP Laboratory Report—Item 20, fingertip bandage

t forefinger rolled
y 20, 1943
or to Sheppard homicide

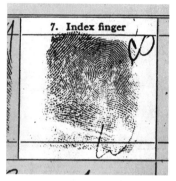

Left forefinger rolled
September 14, 1948
Prior to Sheppard homicide

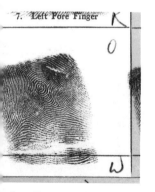

t forefinger rolled
tember 20, 1954
er Sheppard homicide

Enlargements

419

Induction, May 20, 1943

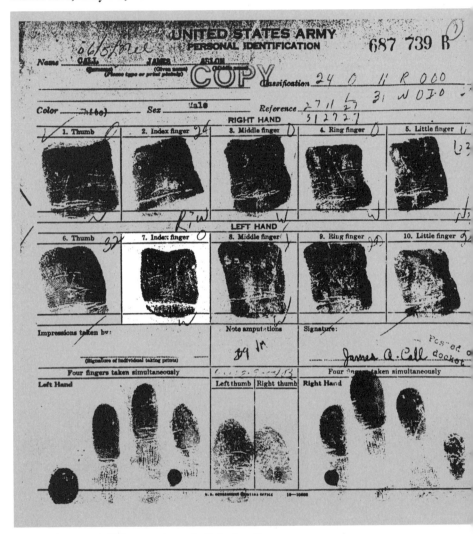

Note absence of bite mark on left index finger.

C, September 14, 1948

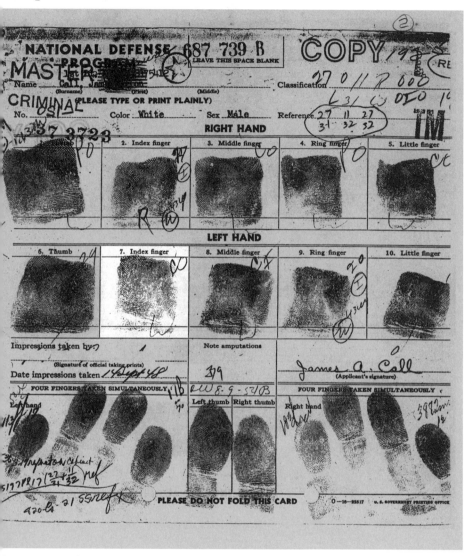

te absence of bite mark on left index finger

Reno Police, November 9, 1954

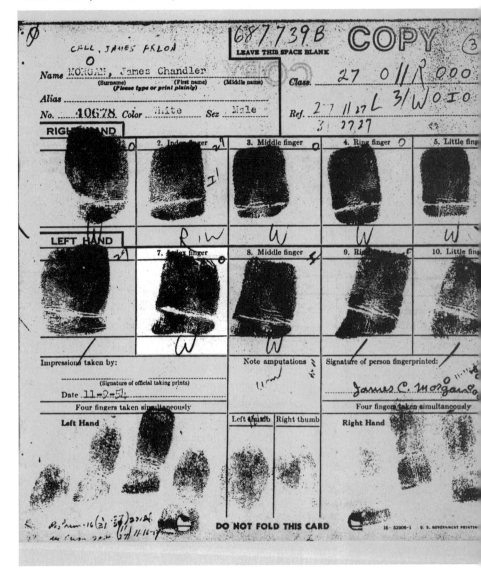

Note presence of bite mark on left index finger.

SP, November 20, 1954

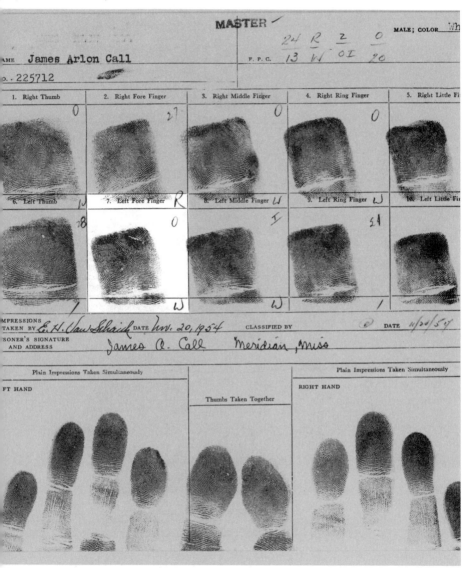

te presence of bite mark on left index finger.

NYSP, November 18, 1954

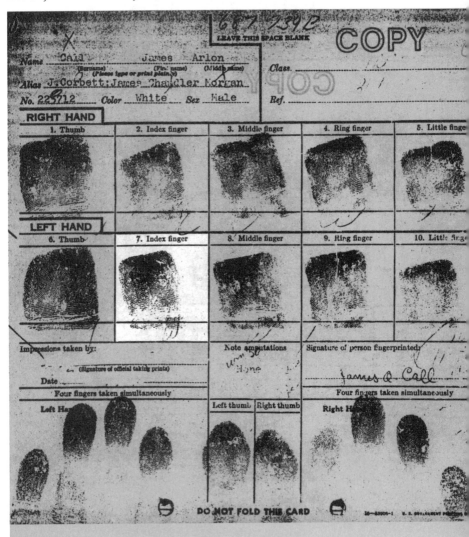

Note presence of bite mark on left index finger.

mparison of subject's fingerprints before and after the Sheppard homicide

Fingerprints taken before the Sheppard homicide.
Note absence of bite mark on left index finger.

luction, 1943

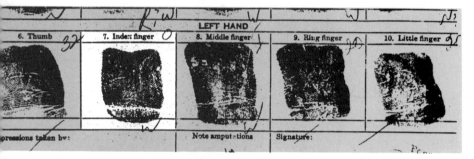

C, 1948

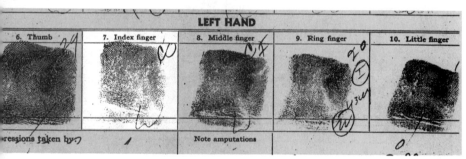

Fingerprints taken after the Sheppard homicide.
Note presence of bite mark on left index finger.

Reno Police, November 9, 1954

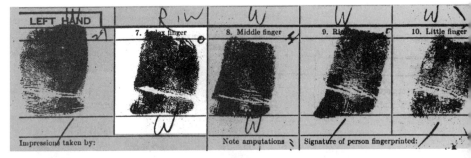

NYSP, November 18, 1954

NYSP, November 20, 1954

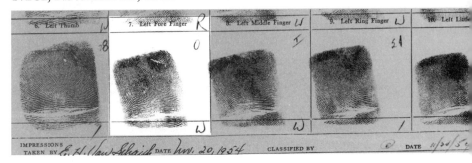

SP Laboratory Report—Item 20, fingertip bandage

173077

STATE OF NEW YORK

DN
ERINTENDENT
RLE
    DEPUTY

FRANCIS S. McGARVEY
    CHIEF INSPECTOR

SCIENTIFIC LABORATORY
8 NOLAN ROAD
ALBANY 5
PHONE 8-3578

NEW YORK STATE TROOPERS
EXECUTIVE DEPARTMENT
DIVISION OF STATE POLICE

WILLIAM E. KIRWAN
DIRECTOR

August 25, 1954

UBJECT: Investigation of Death of Richard Pelkey
              Lab case 19-F-69

O: Inspector R. J. McDowell, New York State Police,
        District "B", Malone, New York.

        EVIDENCE

           Refer examination.

---

b case 19-F-69   173077

presence of blood were negative.

    20. No envelope marked #20 submitted.

    21. Envelope marked "#21 - 1100 Aug 5-54 Blaisdell
          & Harris".

          Evidence envelope contains a finger tip bandage.
Test for presence of blood was negative. Nothing significant identified present.

    22. No envelope marked #22 submitted.

    23. Large envelope marked "#23 - Pair white shorts
          found under mattress in camp. H. E. Blaisdell,
          H. T. Muller 0800 Aug 5-54".

          Evidence white shorts are identified as men's
white boxer type shorts containing a stencil "J Sanforized
26008 40".

EXHIBIT F

- Photograph enlargement of fingerprint with bite mark
- Photograph enlargement of leather fragment
- Photograph enlargement of damaged teeth
- Bite mark corresponding to teeth and leather fragment
- Professional opinions regarding dentition
- Air Force Leather B-3 Glove
- Photograph of subject wearing Air Force gloves
- NYSP Report—John Lester Carney

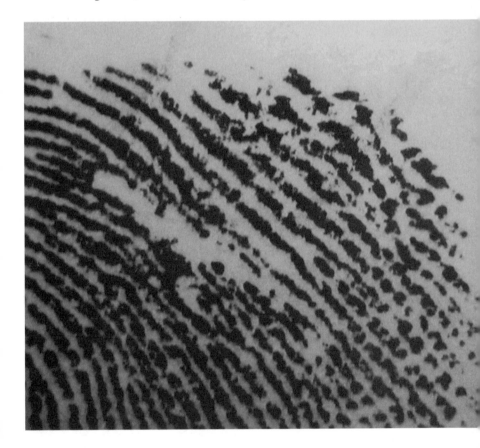

tograph enlargement of leather fragment

Photograph enlargement of damaged teeth

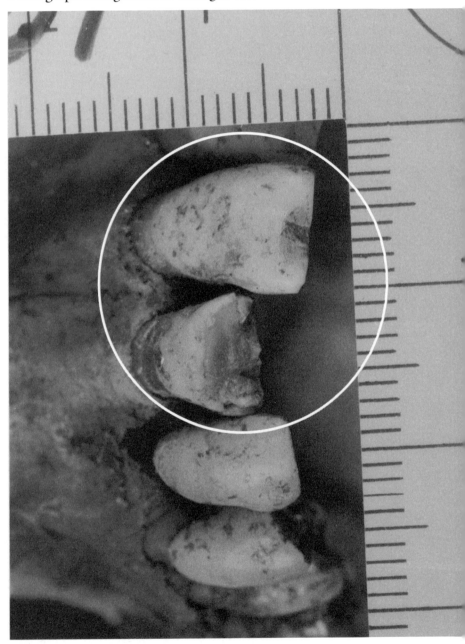

mark corresponding to teeth and leather fragment

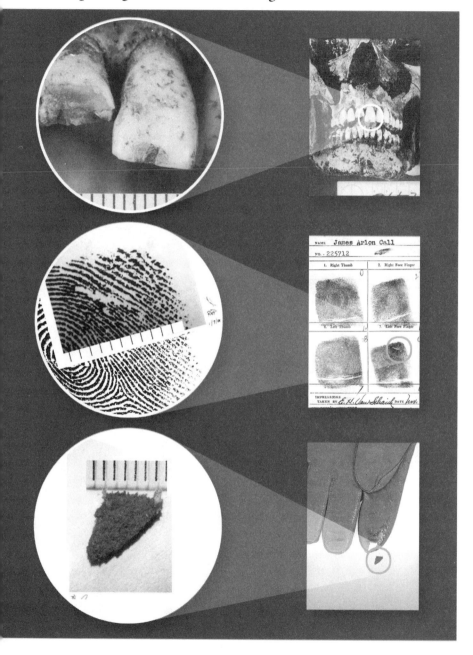

Approximate location of leather fragment

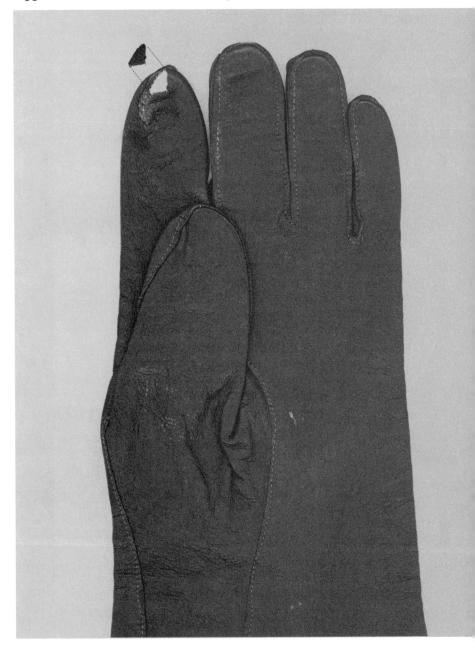

fessional opinions regarding dentition

STATE UNIVERSITY OF NEW YORK

STONY BROOK

HEALTH SCIENCES CENTER

School of Dental Medicine
Department of Dental Medicine
Health Law

September 12, 2000

Mr. Bernard F. Conners
Chairman, British American
4 British American Boulevard
Latham, New York 12110

Re: Marilyn Reese Sheppard Homicide

Dear Mr Conners;

The opinions expressed below are based upon a review of the evidence forwarded to me by your office. It included post mortem photographs of the above captioned along with the coroner's autopsy report of July 4, 1954, and the photographs taken following her exhumation on October 5, 1999.

As to the theory that the fractures to the upper central incisor teeth were the result of the victim being stuck on the face, there is no evidence present on the photographs of the victim taken immediately after the discovery of the murder of any injury to the face inferior to the zygoma. Had she received an external blow to the mandible with enough force to fracture her upper central incisor there would have been some evidence of a blow – but there was none. In addition, if there had been a blow to the mandible the force would have been directed to the occlusal surfaces of the molars, not to the incisor teeth, assuming her occlusion was normal, which was indicated on a report by her dentist. The photographs of the occlusal surfaces of her posterior teeth show no evidence of an injury. My conclusion is that the fractures of the central incisor teeth were not as a result of the victim being struck on the face, or on the mandible.

It is my considered opinion that there is ample evidence to support a finding that the fracture to the upper right cental incisor tooth was due to her having bitten down on the finger of her assailant, and in an attempt to remove it her tooth was fractured. The biting force supplied by the jaw muscles can result in excessive pressure placed on any foreign body, such as a finger, placed between the upper and lower teeth, and an attempt to remove the finger clamped between the teeth would require considerable strength; enough to fracture a tooth. The portion of the tooth remaining in the maxilla was greater on the lingual surface than on the labial surface that indicates the force was directed outward. Finding the tooth fragment outside the oral cavity further supports the outward-thrust theory, although this evidence is not conclusive, it is suggestive. The abrasion on the buccal surface of the mucosa of the lower lip of the victim could have been the result of the assailant's struggle to remove his finger from the victim's mouth.

If I can be of any additional assistance relative to the dental injuries in the murder of Marilyn Sheppard, please do not hesitate to contact me.

Sincerely,

Burton R. Pollack

Professional opinions regarding dentition

CHRISTOPHER J. LYONS, D.M.D.

Mercycare Medical Campus Center, Suite 102
319 South Manning Boulevard
Albany, New York 12208
(518) 438-4401

July 11, 2000

Bernard F. Conners, Chairman
British American
4 British American Boulevard
Latham, New York 12110

Re: Marilyn Reese Sheppard Homicide

Dear Mr. Connors:

Upon review of extensive evidence and photographs concerning the Marilyn Reese Sheppard homicide, it is my professional opinion that the fractures of the anterior incisors were caused by an outward force consistent with Ms. Sheppard biting something that was simultaneously being retracted from her mouth.

The angle of the fracture on tooth # 8 and #9 shows a straight edge on the palatal side and a bevel on the facial surface extending gingivally, an indication of an outward force.

Strong evidence suggests that Ms. Sheppard may have bitten her assailant's finger causing a laceration. Evidence does not support a blow to the face or mandible which would cause such fractures. There were no signs of injuries to the submandibular areas.

It is my opinion therefore, that the dental injuries which were limited to the maxillary and mandibular anterior teeth, are indicative of Ms. Sheppard biting into an object with extreme force which was simultaneously being retracted from her mouth.

Sincerely,

Christopher J. Lyons, D.M.D.

Force Leather B-3 Glove

Photograph of subject wearing Air Force gloves during earlier period

SP Report—John Lester Carney

tness account shows subject was concerned about leaving fingerprints

Gouverneur, New York.
September 21, 1954.

7.   (Sept. 15-54) Teletype alarm was dispatched from
SP Tupper Lake, N.Y., with all facts about this hold up mentioned as an added info to the File 12, for any connection
regarding the unknown man wanted for the shooting of the Lake
Placid policemen.
          Numerous troopers, Sheriff deputies, and SGT HORTON
& TPR. RUSSELL TROMBLY came to scene with bloodhounds in en-
deaver to apprehend and trace directions in which this unknown
subject may have gone off in the woods. Proved unproductive.
Road blocks set up in area roads, proved unproductive. Direct-
tion in which unknown subject left camp could not be ascertained.

8.   (Sept. 16-54) Interviewed numerous hunters and wood-
mens in area relative to complainant's story about being held
up, and their opinion as to him telling the truth. Most every
man interviewed stated that they would back MR. CARNEY up in
any such statement, that he was not known to tell any false
stories, and had never lied to them. Stated that if he said he
was held up, that as far as they were concerned it was the truth.

9.   (Sept. 18-54) Re-Interviewed complainant, JOHN LESTER
CARNEY at his camp, Cranberry Lake, N.Y., where he stated he was
held up. MR. CARNEY gave the same story of this incident as he
had told on Sept. 15-54 the day he was held up for the food. Further was pretty well put out as he stated regarding the articles in the Post-Standard Newspaper concerning the troopers not
believing his story about the held-up. Was advised that the articles he read was not giving to any newspapers by the troopers,
and was probably made up by the newspaper reporter who had been
to the camp, the night of the hold-up.
          MR. CARNEY further advised that he knew how serious it
would be for him or anyone else to make a false report of a held-
up and describe a man as he did who looked similar to sketch of
guns man wanted for Lake Placid Shooting. Further stated that he
was telling the truth and what he had stated before was the truth.
Would not change his story, only added something that came to
his mind a few days later. Further remembered that this unknown
subject, after finishing eating, had taken both the knife and
fork, and held them with his hand in a vertical position, and
cleaned them off by running his right hand down each article,
from top to bottom, using his thumb and index finger, to wipe
the knife and fork dry, then let both articles fall on table,
after running his fingers down them, which would wipe off any
prints he may have left on the knife and fork. Could add nothing to further assist in investigation.
          Pending.

                              J. A. CONNOR   TPR.   BCI
                              J. H. ANDRE   TPR.   UNIF

EXHIBIT G

- Inventory of subject's belongings confiscated by NYSP
- Reno Police Department mug shot—subject with cigarette
- Additional photographs of subject with cigarette

```
39-9 MM Cartridges
1-Pair of eye glasses in brown leather case
1-White shirt, Arrow, Laundry mark 6-6
1-Tan lightweight raincoat, Saks Fifth Ave.
    dry cleaning mark, CR 21/15
                          R44
1-Olive colored waterproff cloth, marking
    Alan V Davies
1-Pair of olive colored rain trousers
1-Olive rain jumper
1-Olive colored sleeping bag, red plaid lining
2-Olive colored pillow slips
1-Green plastic covered pillow with white border
1-US Army type canteen with canvas cover
1-Flask canteen with brown canvas cover marked "Palco"
1-Blue leather belt, size 34, make "Textan"
    full grain cowhide
1-Pair brown leather Aviator boots, zipper pocket
    in right boot
1-Brown paper bag containing two tomatoes
1-Brown composition notebook, number 2532 "Alladdin"
1-Copy of "The Rubaiyat of Omar Khayam"
1-Yellow rough paper scratch pad, 8" by 13"
1-Checkbook containing 4 blank checks, National
    City Bank of New York
1-Hunting knife, leather and bone handle, brown
    leather sheath
1-Screw driver, red handle
1-Box of Jack Fronst light brown cane sugar
1-Yellow plastic tobacco pouch containing small
    amount of tobacco
1-Copy of "The Prophet"
```

entory of subject's belongings confiscated by NYSP

(29)

```
1 - hullof White toilet paper
1 - Deck of cards, playing, tied with dirty string
1 - Book of guest checks, number 15501 to 15550 inc.
1 - Black leather garrison belt with buckle
1 - Piece of white cloth
2 - Pipes, one meerschaum and one briar, yellow
    cloth "Sterncrest 14K, pipe bag
6 - Socks, wool, one white, one gray, four faded tan
1 - Shell roadmap, East Central states
1 - soiled white handkerchief
1 - Blue handkerchief
1 - 2oz. can of Ann Page black pepper
1 - Can of GI foot powder
1 - Plastic bag containing stainless steel combina-
    tion knife, fork and spoon
2 - Pair Sun Glasses, one in brown plastic imitation
    snake skin case, marked USL
1 - Metal can opener
5 - Packages of Camel cigarettes, two packages of
    Chesterfields, one package of Old golds, one
    package of Herbert Tareytons
4 - El-Roi-Tan cigars (5)
2 - Packages of Diamond safety matches (Boxes)
1 - Package of Wrigleys Spearmint Chewing Gum
1 - Nail file
1 - Pair of tweezers
1 - Piece of candle, two inches long
1 - Large salt shaker
1 - Brown leather toilet article Kit, containing:
    two tooth brushes, one red and one white; one
    Stavo deodorant for men; one can of Colgates
    Ammoniated tooth powder; one bottle of Vitalis
    hair oil; one can Barbasol brushless shave cream;
    one Gillette razor; one box of Bayer aspirin;
    one bottle Merthiolate; one bottle of yellow
    fluid with dropper; one blue mechanical pencil;
    one Schaffer's maroon fountain pen; one pair of
    scissors; one switchblade knife; "Edgemaster;
    one tube of Chapstick; one rubber eraser; and
    $6.85 in silver.
1 - Utica Club cardboard container, containing 3
    bottles of 7 UP, and one bottle of Coca-Cola
1 - Wooden hand mirror - brown wood back
1 - Bottle containing 9 Capsules
1 - Bottle containing Brown fluid
1 - Zippo cigarette lighter
1 - Brown leather Utility case "La Cross" with a
    zipper around three sides, containing 11 Cundrums,
    one toe nail clippers, one nail clipper and one
    small mirror.
```

36.   The evidence as listed above was transported to the
Tupper Lake Station by assignment. Inspector Dillon contacted
Chief Inspector F.S. Mc Garvey at Troop "B" Headquarters, Malone,
N.Y. The Chief Inspector directed that the pistol and other
evidence be transported to the Scientific Laboratory, Albany, N.Y.

Mug Shot, Reno, Nevada, November 1954—subject with cigarette

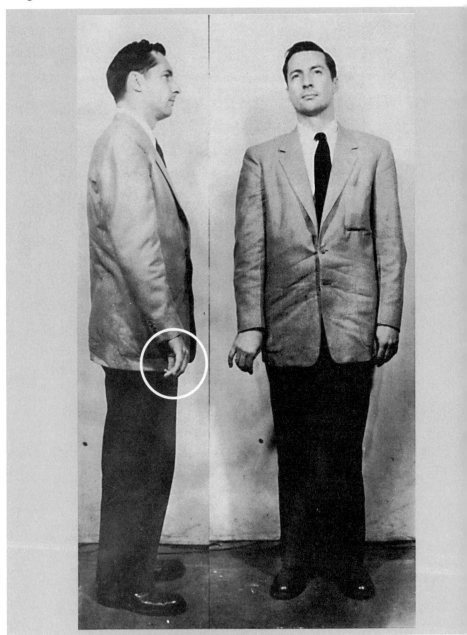

litional photographs of subject with cigarette

Additional photographs of subject with cigarette

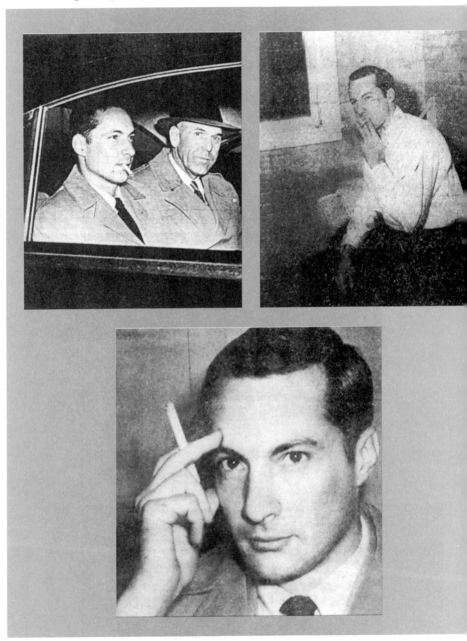

EXHIBIT H

Subject's Luger superimposed over imprint on victim's pillow

Presentation and comparison of Luger and pillow imprint

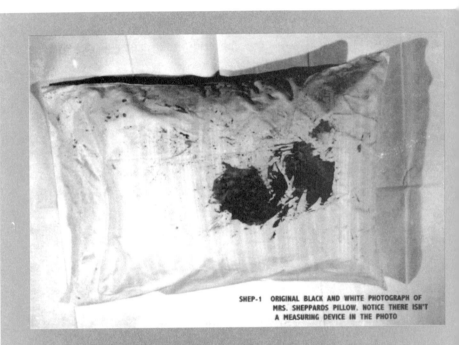

SHEP-1 ORIGINAL BLACK AND WHITE PHOTOGRAPH OF MRS. SHEPPARDS PILLOW. NOTICE THERE ISN'T A MEASURING DEVICE IN THE PHOTO

SHEP - 2 TWO COLOR PHOTOGRAPHS, WITH A MEASURING DEVICE IN EACH, TAKEN OF IMAGES PURPORTED TO BE OF A SURGICAL TYPE INSTRUMENT WHICH LEFT A RELIEF IMAGE IN THE BLOOD ON THE PILLOW. NOTE: THE IMAGE ON THE RIGHT WILL BE USED TO ' BRING INTO SCALE ' THE BLACK AND WHITE PHOTOGRAPH OF THE WHOLE PILLOW, AS WELL AS BRINGING INTO SCALE THE LUGER. (FOR THE PURPOSES OF COMPARISONS).

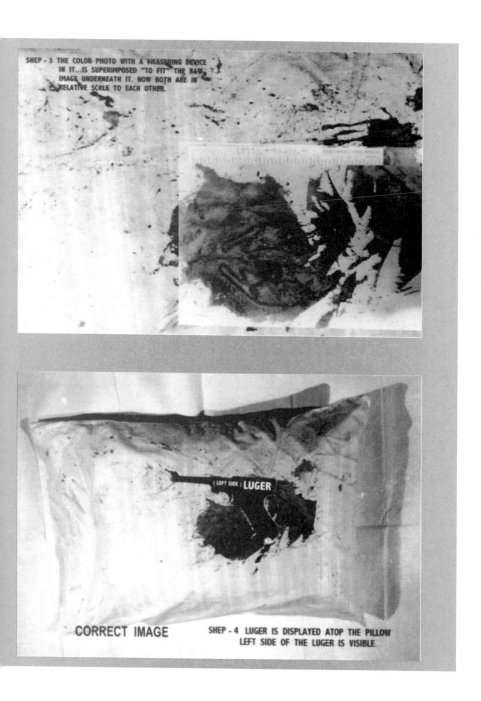

SHEP - 3 THE COLOR PHOTO WITH A MEASURING DEVICE IN IT...IS SUPERIMPOSED "TO FIT" THE B&W IMAGE UNDERNEATH IT. NOW BOTH ARE IN RELATIVE SCALE TO EACH OTHER.

(LEFT SIDE) LUGER

CORRECT IMAGE

SHEP - 4 LUGER IS DISPLAYED ATOP THE PILLOW LEFT SIDE OF THE LUGER IS VISIBLE.

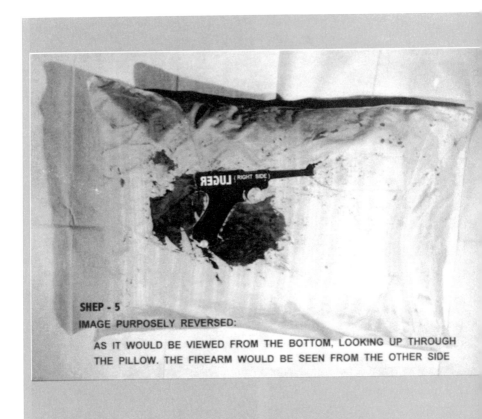

SHEP - 5

IMAGE PURPOSELY REVERSED:

AS IT WOULD BE VIEWED FROM THE BOTTOM, LOOKING UP THROUGH
THE PILLOW. THE FIREARM WOULD BE SEEN FROM THE OTHER SIDE

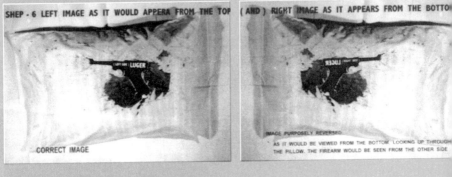

SHEP - 6 LEFT IMAGE AS IT WOULD APPERA FROM THE TOP

CORRECT IMAGE

(AND) RIGHT IMAGE AS IT APPEARS FROM THE BOTTO

IMAGE PURPOSELY REVERSED

AS IT WOULD BE VIEWED FROM THE BOTTOM, LOOKING UP THROUGH
THE PILLOW. THE FIREARM WOULD BE SEEN FROM THE OTHER SIDE

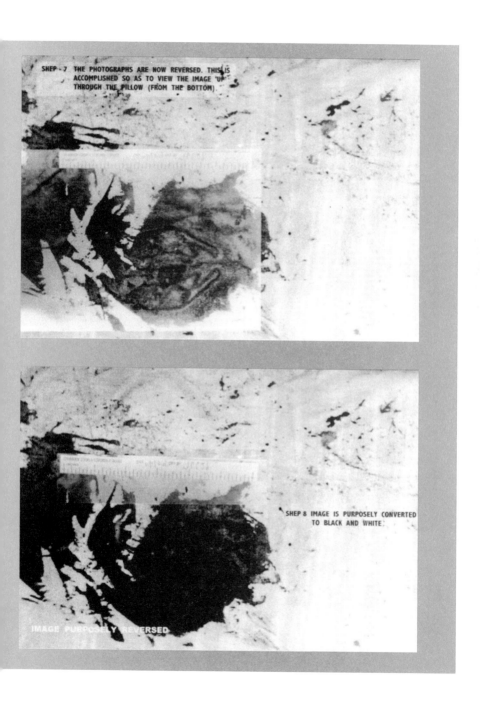

SHEP - 7 THE PHOTOGRAPHS ARE NOW REVERSED. THIS IS ACCOMPLISHED SO AS TO VIEW THE IMAGE 'UP' THROUGH THE PILLOW (FROM THE BOTTOM).

SHEP 8 IMAGE IS PURPOSELY CONVERTED TO BLACK AND WHITE.

IMAGE PURPOSELY REVERSED

SHEP - 9

THE LEFT SIDE AND THE RIGHT SIDE OF A LUGER ARE DIFFERENT

NOTE: ACTUAL RIGHT SIDE OF LUGER WITH MEASURING DEVICE

SHEP - 10 IMAGE OF LUGER IS CONVERTED TO BLACK AND WHITE, AND SUPERIMPOSED OVER IMAGE OF PILLOW WITH MEASURING DEVICES ALIGNED, BRINGING ALL IMAGES INTO 'SCALE' WITH EACH OTHER.

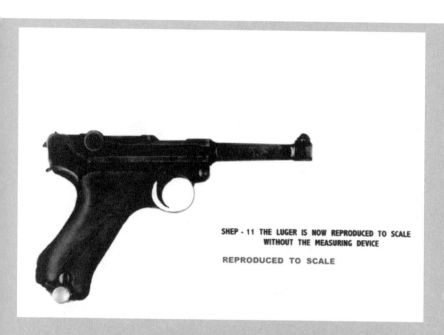

SHEP - 11 THE LUGER IS NOW REPRODUCED TO SCALE
WITHOUT THE MEASURING DEVICE

REPRODUCED TO SCALE

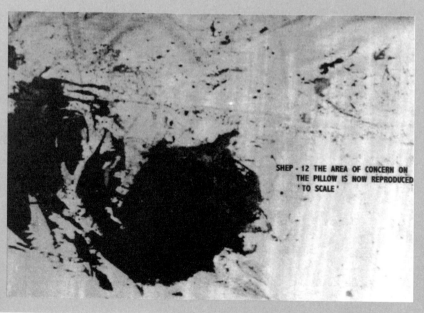

SHEP - 12 THE AREA OF CONCERN ON
THE PILLOW IS NOW REPRODUCED
'TO SCALE'

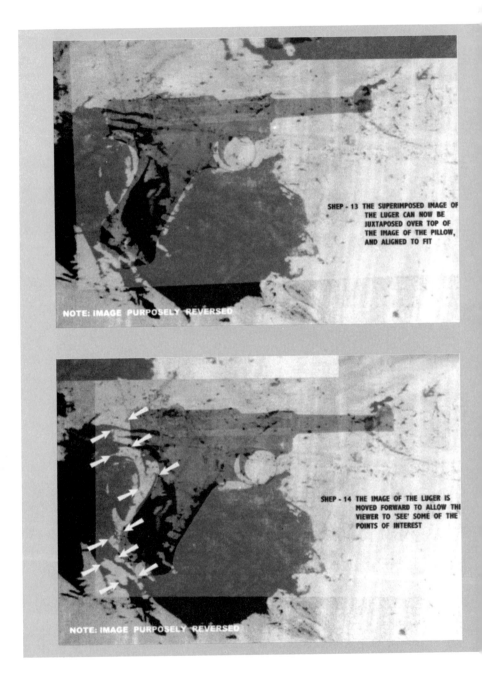

SHEP - 13 THE SUPERIMPOSED IMAGE OF THE LUGER CAN NOW BE JUXTAPOSED OVER TOP OF THE IMAGE OF THE PILLOW, AND ALIGNED TO FIT

NOTE: IMAGE PURPOSELY REVERSED

SHEP - 14 THE IMAGE OF THE LUGER IS MOVED FORWARD TO ALLOW THE VIEWER TO 'SEE' SOME OF THE POINTS OF INTEREST

NOTE: IMAGE PURPOSELY REVERSED

nsparency of Luger over blood image,
:t measurements used for both images

NOTE: IMAGE PURPOSELY REVERSED

EXHIBIT I

- Air Force record of subject's physical abilities
- Subject's statement to NYSP regarding knee injury
- Witness account of subject's limp
- Newspaper account of subject's limp
- Photograph of subject on Air Force football team

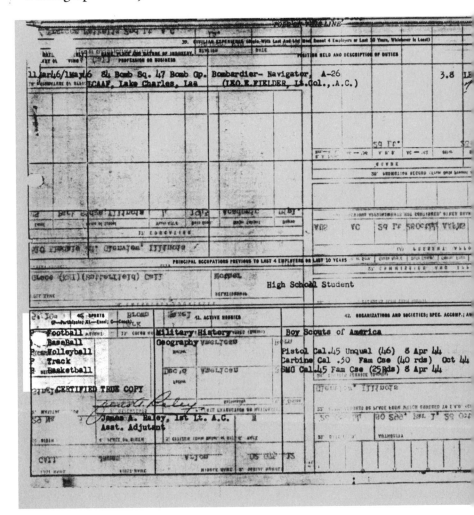

— EXHIBIT I —

ject's statement to NYSP regarding knee injury, November 19, 1954

November, 1953. He then went to Barkdale AirForce Base, 76th Bombadis
Wing, 51th Squadron, concentrated on B 47's taking special training
for high altitude flying. January, 1954 he went to Stead Air Force
Base, Reno, Nevada and took a special cource in outdoor survival,
prisoner of war training, and how to resist interrogation. His survival training consisted of being taken 60 or 70 miles out in the
mountains at 8 below aero with a 60 pound pack and surviving your way
back. He had a pleurisy attach. He was in Reno for about three weeks
He went back to Bardale, then to Sacramento, California in February or
March, 1954. At this time he was getting jumpy and pretty well fed
up with Army life. He then went to high speed navigation school at
Sacramento. He has 3500 to 3600 flying hours. He then lost all
interest and went to Reno, Carson, City, Lake Taho and other places.
He likes to gamble crap as it helps him to forget. He got in over
his head and he put out many bad checks. At this time things were
mounting up. He was also finanching his car at the time. He said he
had gambled for the past twelve to fourteen years and very heavily
for the past six. He had an automobile accident in LasVagas with his
Jaguar and banged up one knee. He hit his head a little on the wheel.
The car was a mess. He stayed at Las Vagas requesting an extension
on travel time while the car was being fixed. He went broke and
wrote more bad checks. Things looked black but he didn't give up.
He took the car from the garage before properly fixed and went to
Barkdale, then to Meridian and got his summer uniforms, saw Jeffrey
in May of 1954, then went back to Barkdale. At this time he saw
everything closing in on him and everything was blowing up in his face
He was in way over his head and as far down in despair as one could get
He had no interest in women or anything. He was much dissatisfied with
the Air Force. Everything came to a head at once. He was not man
enough to take it. It was a matter of pride to him and he couldn't

Witness account of subject's limp

Gouverneur, New York.
September 21, 1954.

2. (Con't.)
After leaving the camp, complainant stated from where he was
sitting he could not see which was this subject had gone.
Stated he looked to his left and from where he was sitting in
the chair could see out a window on left side of camp, but(North)
stated that he did not see this subject go that way. Further
some trees were in way obstructing his view. Further advised
that he waited a few minutes, and then went to his telephone (Star
Lake exchange # 8603) and at first called the State Troopers
at Star Lake,N.Y. Did not get any answer, then called the
operator at Gouverneur,N.Y., and asked for the Sheriff's Office
at Canton,N.Y. Further advised that he gave this complaint
to one of the Deputy Sheriff's, of him being held up at gun
point. A dial telephone system is in effect at complainant's
home,same partly hidden in pantry as upon entry into the camp
from Tooley Pond road, front door of camp, same on a table on
left side, and person entering camp would have to look close
to notice the telephone. Further advised that he could not tell
which way this unknown man left, only that he went out the front
door of camp, which is in a east direction, and leads onto the
Tooley Pond road, which direction if north and south from Cranberry Lake, to De Grasse,N.Y.
Complainant described unknown man as being about
40 years of age, 5-7-8, in height, normal weight about 150 lbs.,
had long black hair and in need of a haircut, dark large eyebrows,
believed to have dark eyes, could not observe his teeth, hadabout
10 days to 2 weeks growth of beard, further that he noticed a
slight limp in subject's walk when he went out the front door, coul
not state whether he was wearing shoes or boots, did not have on
any hat, had dark sort of suit coat, dark shirt under the suit
coat, and dark trousers, all these clothing were wrinkled and
seemed that subject had been in rain, as he observed the back of
the coat when subject left the camp, back was all wrinkled in rear,
same believed by him due to wet weather. The trousers part came
down to the shoe line, and they were also badly wrinkled. Believed
that subject looked like an "ITALIAN", or from that type of race.
Further subject had a dark complexion. Was very sure that gun held
in subject's hand was a revlever, because while this weapon was
laying on the table while this subject was eating, he noticed that
he could see the ends of the cartridge easing's protruding in rear
of the cylinder of the gun. Further believed it had about a five
inch barrell, and the weapon had wooden grips. Could not tell
exactly what color the grips were, but was sure they were wooden.

3.   (Sept. 15-54) Complainant was further questioned by
TROOP COMMANDER, CAPT. H.T.MULLER, Troop "B", Malone,N.Y., and
gave nearly same account of incident as he had given writer.
Further complainant was also questioned by TPR. T.J.
BURNS,BCI- SP Canton,N.Y., to see if there was any change in the
story he gave writer and CAPT. MULLER, but complainant gave about
the same account as to what occurred, and stuck to his story. Complainant is 80 Yrs. of age, but very active, cuts wood and works

— EXHIBIT I —

ewspaper account of subject's limp, August 5, 1954

SEARCH WIDEN

SCENE OF THE SHOOTING: An unidentified State Trooper is shown standing guard at the front the one-story frame-constructed Perkins' camp. In the foreground are thermos jugs of coffee brought the men who had been on duty since 1 o'clock this morning.

Three Lake Placid men are in bad conditio gun wounds and the car ber who shot them is a The fugitive may be ed.

The shootings occurre ly after 12.30 o'clock thi ing at the Summer h Dr. James Perkins, a of Watervliet, in the Troy area. The Perki tage is on West Valley at the outskirts of Lake and within sight of a b dential section.

The wounded:

PATROLMAN J. BEF FELL. He received tw in the abdomen and is tical condition in Place orial Hospital. He was o on by Dr. Edwin James George Hart and Dr. M. Bergamini, all of th tal staff.

SGT. DOMINIC VAI He was shot twice. On went through his arm a tered a bone; the secon into his chest, punctu lung. The same three operated on the serge condition this afternoo cribed as "serious".

PATROLMAN RICE PELKEY. He has a wound and a shot thro leg. He is in the Saran General Hospital where operated on by Dr. W Woodruff and Dr. Carl His condition is descr "fair."

There is a 13-state alarm out for the des Road blocks have been up on practically ever way and road in the dacks. The three-squ area of woods around t king cottage is being

AVE YOU SEEN THIS MAN?

The desperado sought in today's Lake Placid shooting described as 5 feet, 8 inches tall, weighing 140 to 150 nds, with black bushy hair and a thin moustache. He is ut 35 years old. One report is that he walks with a slight p.

When last seen, the suspect was wearing a tan trench t and blue jeans, with a sheaf knife in the belt. He was less.

At the time of shooting he was reported armed with a 22 e and 9mm semi-automatic pistol, possibly a Luger or P-38. may still be armed.

If you see him, call the police BUT STAY AWAY FROM M. There is no question that the man is desperate—and dan ous.

FIRST SUSPECT IS TAKEN HERE

The first suspect in the Lake Placid shooting was picked up in Saranac Lake by the local police. He was taken off the train from Utica when it arrived at 7:40 o'clock this morning.

One witness of the pick-up described the suspect as 6 feet tall and dark haired. He was said to be "well-built." He wore a rain-coat and no hat. This witness said he didn't know whether or not the man had a moustache.

(Adirondack Daily Enterprise)

Photograph of subject on Air Force football team

Friday, November 17, 1950

THE DESERT AIRMAN

Undefeated . . .

The mighty 65th Bomb Squadron has rolled up 47 points in subduing three straight American League opponents. The 65th squad, as it stacks up from end to end, is Jack O'Reagan, Kurt Thurmond, Jerry Spray, Albert Stage, and Denny Long; in the backfield is Tom Athanassion, right half; Otis Moore, quarterback; and Jim Call, left half.

(The Desert Airman)

HIBIT J

hotographs of subject with composite drawings

YSP Report—Vitalis hair oil

ice photo circa 1954
truding wisps of hair

Police photo circa 1954
Protruding wisps of hair

Air Force circa 1952

circa 1955
ort hair standing up

High School Senior
circa 1943

Air Force circa 1950

omposite drawing
Sheppard case,
July 1954

Self portrait by Call
circa 1944

NYSP composite
Call manhunt
August 1954

457

Hair oil found at Brunette camp used by subject to control unruly hair

Excerpt from NYSP Report
September 15, 1954
Saranac Lake BCI Case Q-60

(29)

1 - Roll of White toilet paper
1 - Deck of cards, playing, tied with dirty string
1 - Book of guest checks, number 15501 to 15550 ins.
1 - Black leather garrison belt with buckle
1 - Piece of white cloth
2 - Pipes, one meerschaum and one briar, yellow cloth "Sterncrest 14K, pipe bag
6 - Socks, wool, one white, one gray, four faded tan
1 - Shell roadmap, East Central states
1 - soiled white handkerchief
1 - Blue handkerchief
1 - 2oz. can of Ann Page black pepper
1 - Can of GI foot powder
1 - Plastic bag containing stainless steel combination knife, fork and spoon
2 - Pair Sun Glasses, one in brown plastic imitation snake skin case, marked USL
1 - Metal can opener
5 - Packages of Camel cigarettes, two packages of Chesterfields, one package of Old golds, one package of Herbert Tareytons
4 - El-Roi-Tan cigars (5)
2 - Packages of Diamond safety matches (Boxes)
1 - Package of Wrigleys Spearmint Chewing Gum
1 - Nail file
1 - Pair of tweezers
1 - Piece of candle, two inches long
1 - Large salt shaker
1 - Brown leather toilet article Kit, containing: two tooth brushes, one red and one white; one Stavo deodorant for men; one can of Colgates Ammoniated tooth powder; one bottle of Vitalis hair oil; one can Barbasol brushless shave cream; one Gillette razor; one box of Bayer aspirin; one bottle Merthiolate; one bottle of yellow fluid with dropper; one blue mechanical pencil; one Schaffer's maroon fountain pen; one pair of scissors; one switchblade knife; "Edgemaster; one tube of Chapstick; one rubber eraser; and $6.85 in silver.
1 - Utica Club cardboard container, containing 3 bottles of 7 UP, and one bottle of Coca-Cola
1 - Wooden hand mirror - brown wood back
1 - Bottle containing 9 Capsules
1 - B ottle containing Brown fluid
1 - Zippo cigarette lighter
1 - Brown leather Utility case "La Cross" with a zipper around three sides, containing 11 Cundrums, one toe nail clippers, one nail clipper and one small mirror.

36.   The evidence as listed above was transported to the Tupper Lake Station by assignment. Inspector Dillon contacted Chief Inspector F.S. Mc Garvey at Troop "B" Headquarters, Malone, N.Y. The Chief Inspector directed that the pistol and other evidence be transported to the Scientific Laboratory, Albany, N.Y.

HIBIT K—Positive identification of subject by Mr. & Mrs. Richard Knitter

dentification of Picture F

dentification of Picture A

ictures A & F compared with police composite

tatement from Mr. and Mrs. Richard Knitter

Picture F

✓   Positive Identification

___   Very Strong Resemblance

___   Strong Resemblance

___   Moderate Resemblance, Exclusions: _____

x _Richard E Knitter_

x _Betty Knitter_

Witnessed by: x _Lisa Lombardo 4/4/00_

Identification of picture A

Picture A

____ Positive Identification

____ Very Strong Resemblance

_✓_ Strong Resemblance

____ Moderate Resemblance, Exclusions: _____
_____

x _Richard E Knitter_

x _Betty Knitter_

Witnessed by: x _Lisa Lombardo 4/4/00_

ures A & F compared with police composite

Statement from Mr. and Mrs. Richard Knitter

It was July 3, 1954 when we went to the Cleveland Palace to see Gone with the Wind. We couldn't get tickets to the early show so we got tickets for the late show. We came out of the show at about 2:00 am and proceeded to Bearden's in Rocky River for a sandwich. We took our time and then we drove west on Lake Road to go home. We came to Huntington Park where it narrows down to a brick road to allow 2-lane traffic. As we were approaching Huntington Park our lights picked up an object on the side of the road. When we got to it, we slowed down and it enabled us to see the look of disbelief, frantic, shock on the man's face. He was wearing a white shirt, dark pants and his hair was in disarray, bushy, standing up. He was about 30 years old, his weight was about 180 pounds, and he was 5 foot 9. I said to my wife then, "How would you like to meet that man in the dark?" and she said, "Keep going, don't stop." So I proceeded home. We just looked at the man, we didn't think much of it, we didn't even talk about it, we just went home.

The next morning my wife's girlfriend called her and said, "what did you think of the murder?" My wife then replied, "what murder?" The girl said Mrs. Sheppard was murdered last night. My wife then said, "Gee, that's funny. We saw a man on the side of the road near Huntington Park." The girl then said, "Maybe you should take that information to the Police Department in Bay Village." We said, "I don't know" because of different things. We didn't want to get involved. Then the girl's father who was the Police Chief of Sheffield Lake talked to us and said that he felt we should report that we did see someone around that area. We then after a few days said that we would go to the Bay Village Police and report what we saw. We didn't realize at the time what we were getting into.

The police of Bay Village had a sketch artist come in and from what we described, the way he looked, clothes he wore, his height, weight and his facial expressions he was able to make a picture of the "bushy-haired man."

We went to see where Sam Sheppard lived since we did not know and realized it was where the place was that the man was standing because his house was roped off to indicate the crime scene. The next day we were called to Bay Village police to go through the mug shots. We went through approximately 50-60 pictures and didn't find the man that matched up. At a later time we reviewed photos that an officer brought for us to review. We were unable to match up the man at that time.

After the inquest at the Bay Village school, we were subpoenaed to appear in court on December 9, 1954 by clerk Leonard F. Fuerst.

The press harassed us by following us and trying to force us to say it was Sam. They maneuvered all kinds of ways to trick us to open the door, putting their foot in the door to gain entrance. At the time if we had known, we would have called the police and gotten these reporters arrested but we didn't know our rights. It went on for several days. The reporters were at our house with their cameras and we just never gave them a chance to enter. They wanted us to say that it was Sam Sheppard who killed his wife, but we didn't. This went on for several years. The bothering and the harassment continued on for years. It was then after a period of 19 years we moved to Lorain to get away from all the harassment. We lived there for 2 years before anyone recognized that we were involved with the Sheppard case. We said we were, but not to tell anybody. On February 14, 2000 we appeared at the Justice Center in Cleveland for the third trial.

After all the years and all the pictures that we have reviewed, the picture of Major Call is the closest resemblance to the man that we saw as the "bushy-haired man." We were surprised when we saw the pictures and they were so much alike that that it was amazing.

September 12 2000	Richard E. Knitter
Date	Signature

September 12, 2000	Betty J. Knitter
Date	Signature

September 12, 2000	Lynette R. Moon
Date	Witness

EXHIBIT L

- Statement from Dr. Gervase Flick, Vero Beach, Florida, November 1997 (corrections made by Dr. Flick)

Flick left home ~~about~~ *shortly after* 11:00, driving eastward through Cleveland. The weather was

unremarkable, except that it was somewhat cool for the 4th of July . Sometime about a ~~half~~

hour after he had left home, ~~just past Ashtabula~~ *Fed Route 20 in Astabula,* he stopped to pick up a hitchiker. The man

was in his late twenties, early thirties, had straight black hair combed back and was wearing

dark blue trousers (darker than jeans), a short coat and carried a small two suit suitcase.
 (see list of laundry that Call left in cleaners in Saranac Lake)

Gerry's impression was that the man did not look like a bum or an itinerant, but was pleasant

and well spoken. He indicated that he was going to New York (city or state?) and that he was

going to catch a train from Erie,Pa.

As the man got in the car , Gerry noticed that the man's shoes, which he thinks might have

been brown loafers,were very soiled and Gerry was concerned about the carpeting in his

father's new car. The man indicated that the stains were blood ,now dried, and that he would be

careful not to get it on the carpet. He indicated that he had hitchiked a ride earlier, an*d* that the

driver had run over a dog, and that he had gotten out of the car and kicked the dog ~~out~~ *off* of the *side*

road.

Gerry says the man did not say much, but did inquire if Gerry had heard anything on the

radio about a murder in Bay Village. Gerry had not been playing the radio until then, but turned

it on and got nothing but country and western music. The hitchiker either did not like the music

or was agitated by the lack of news. The hitchiker seemed to know alot about the murder,

including the fact that a wrench had been used as the murder weapon,but this did not strike ~~as~~ *Ger*

unusual at that time.

— EXHIBIT L —

At one time the hitchiker started to light up a cigarette, definately using a wooden match with *2 one of a packet of*

is left hand and Gerry askedhimnot to smoke in his father's new car.. The hitchiker accepted

his without comment. *and ground out the cigarette in the ashtray along with the used + unused match.*

Prior to reaching Erie, Gerry suggested that they stop for coffee. At the restruant the man sat *The man got out of the car and walked a delicate limp to the*
o the right of Gerry and held his cup with his left hand. While lifting his cup he bumped into *restraut when Gerry*

Flicks left arm and spilled a considerable amount of coffee down Flick's leg. Flick was quite

concened about the stain on his only trousers. *question about the limp. He asked later that he had the pts nockickle when he kicked the door*

NOTE*** I did not ask Flick if the man appeared to limp, was wounded on the right hand or

or if his blue trousers had a tear in the leg.

Gerry Flick dropped the man at a filling station outside of Erie, Pa.and proceeded to ~~Syracuse~~ *Brock to continue comparctive anatomy*

or the weekend, before returning home and ~~then on~~ to more summer courses at ~~Western~~ *at NWMSC now Truman*

~~Reserve College in Cleveland.~~ *and just prior to beginning additional courses at the 2nd semester at Western Reserve in Cleveland*

Several weeks later Gerry returned home and his mother showed him ~~clippings~~ *whole newspaper* of the

Sheppard murder. Only then did it strike him that the man he had picked up hitchiking on the

4th of July might have been the man whom Sam Sheppard had encountered earlier in the day.

The man matched the description that Dr.Sam had given of his assailant, and several others

had reported a seeing a man of similiar description near the Sheppard home that evening. One

woman even reported to the police that a man of that description had boarded an interstate bus

near the Sheppard house ealy that morning and that he remained on board after she got off in

Cleveland. However, what struck Flick as very alarming was the fact that the man seemed

to know a great deal about the murder, despite the fact that it had not as yet been in the papers

or on the radio, *at the time he picked him.*

EXHIBIT M

- **NYSP** report regarding clothing deposited at dry cleaners
- **Statements** from owners of dry cleaner and laundry establishments
- **Clipping** and police report concerning liquor store robbery, June 5, 1954

New York State Troopers
Bureau of Criminal Investigation
Troop "B", Malone, New York

December 21, 1954

Saranac Lake BCI
Case   Q-60

Subject: RICHARD ELMER PELKEY   (DECEASED)
Lake Placid, New York

DOMINIC JOSEPH VALENZE
Lake Placid, New York

JAMES BERNARD FELL
Lake Placid, New York

Murder - Lake Placid - New York - Essex County

TO   :   Inspector R.J. Mc Dowell, BCI, Malone, New York.

SUPPLEMENTAL REPORT TO ORIGINAL REPORT DATED SEPTEMBER 1, 1954

74.   December 6, 1954, the undersigned acting on the instructions of Captain H.T. MULLER, Troop Commander, Troop "B", Malone, N.Y., caused an investigation to be conducted at the BERKELEY DRY CLEANER'S, 27 Broadway, Saranac Lake, N.Y., to ascertain if JAMES A. CALL, left a suit of clothing there to be dry cleaned. CALL is alleged to have used the name CORBETT at the time he left the suit there.

75.   December 6, 1954, interviewed Mrs. LUELLA JEWTRAW, age 54, 76 Algonquin St., Saranac Lake, N.Y., an employee at the dry cleaners advised that on July 7, 1954, a person whom she can not identify as CALL, did leave a suit there to be dry cleaned. She added that this person gave the name of CORBETT and the suit in question was still at the dry cleaning store.

76.   Suit in question was turned over to the undersigned by Mrs. JAWTRAW. Suit is described as being TAN in color, MANS two piece and bore a label over the left inside coat pocket showing that the suit was purchased or made by ORIENTAL'S - TAILORS OF DISTINCTION - No. 63 Nathan Road, Kowloon, N.K. Suit held as evidence in this case and will be transported to S.P. Malone for safe keeping.

SP report regarding clothing deposited at dry cleaners

77. A sworn statement was obtained from Mrs. JAWTRAW and is attached to this report.

78. December 6, 1954, an investigation was also conducted at the TROY LAUNDRY INC., Sumner Lane, Saranac Lake, N.Y. where CALL left laundry to be cleaned, using the name of CORBETT when leaving the dirty laundry there to be cleaned. Interviewed

MANUEL BENERO, age 66, 34 Virginia St., Saranac Lake, N.Y., an employee of the TROY LAUNDRY INC. He advised that some time before July 22, 1954, maybe a day or two before that date, a person whom he can not identify as being CALL, using the name of P.A. CORBETT did come to the Laundry Office and left a bundle of laundry to be cleaned, advising at that time he would call for the laundry when it was finished, adding that the laundry was still at the office, the person who left it there failed to callfor it. The laundry in question was turned over to the undersigned by Mr. BENERO and a sworn statement was obtained showing an itemized list of the clothing left there to be cleaned. Statement is attached.

79. The laundry in question is being held as evidence in this case, tagged and will be transported to S.P. Malone for safe keeping.

Cpl. P.A. Keane   BCI

Statement from dry cleaner, December 6, 1954

State of New York
County of Franklin
Village of Saranac Lake

I, Luella Jewtraw being duly sworn deposes and says:

That I am 54 years of age, and I reside at 76 Algonquin St., Saranac Lake, N.Y. I am employed as a clerk by the Berkeley Dry Cleaners, 27 Broadway, Saranac Lake, N.Y., having been employed there for the past three and a half years.

On July 7, 1954, I don't know what time it was, but it was during business hours, between 8:00 A.M. and 6:00 P.M., a person came into the Dry Cleaning Store at 27 Broadway, Saranac Lake N.Y. and requested that a light tan suit which he was carrying be dry cleaned. This person also requested that the suit be ready by the following Friday and he would call for it.

I accepted the suit and this person told me his name was CORBETT, and I made out a ticket for the garment. the ticket was dated 7-7-54 in the name of CORBETT, for one suit, dry cleaned and the cost of same was to be $1.25. Also on the ticket I showed that the garment was desired for the following Friday, sure. This ticket is numbered 4745.

On December 6, 1954, I was shown a photograph of one JAMES A. CALL and was asked by Cpl. F.A. Keane of the State Police, Saranac Lake Sub-Station, if he was the person who left the suit to be dry cleaned. After viewing the photographs I can not say that I can identify CALL as the person from whom I took the garment from, as during the summer months we do a large amount of business with strangers who come to this area on vacatio

Also on December 6, 1954, I turned this two piece light tan suit over to Cpl. F.A. Keane, he requesting me to do so. This suit bore a label over the left inside coat pocket showing that the suit was purchased or made by ORIENTAL'S --- TAILORS OF DISTINCTION --- No. 63 NATHAN ROAD, KOWLOON, H.K.

I have read the above statement and I swear that it is true to the best of my knowledge and belief.

Luella Jewtraw

Sworn to before me this 6th
day of December, 1954.

Edmund S. Ayer

NOTARY PUBLIC
State of New York

468

tement from laundry establishment, December 21, 1954

State of New York
Village of Saranac Lake
County of Franklin

    I, MANUEL BENERO, being duly sworn deposes and says:

        That I am 66 years of age, married and reside at 34 Virginia St., Saranac Lake, N.Y., and for the past 11 years I have been employed at the Troy Laundry Inc., Sumner Lane, Saranac Lake, N.Y.

        That sometime before July 22, 1954, a day or two before that date a person came to the Laundry and left some clothing to be cleaned, giving the name P.A. CORBETT and advising that he could call for the laundry when it was cleaned. The laundry which this so called P.A. CORBETT left is as follows:-

1- White Nylon Shirt - Trade name RICHMAN BROS
1- Yellow Sport Shirt - Trade name - VAUGHN - AT - SATHER - GATE
                              OAKLAND - BERKELEY - SACRAMENTO
1- Blue and Grey Sport Shirt
1 White Sport Shirt - Tradesman AERTEX - Size 40
1- Blue Denim Work Suit - Jacket & Pants, Trade name - LEE
1- Grey T Shirt - Trade name - STEINFELD, Tuscon, Arizona.
1- Blue T Shirt - "
1- White sweat shirt
3- White T shirts
1- White pillow case
1- Yellow Cannon Towel
6- Mens White handkerchiefs
4- Shorts - white - Jockey make
1- Pair of mens Green Shorts
1- Pair of mens Red - White - Blue striped shorts.

        On December 6, 1954, I was shown a photograph of one JAMES CALL and was asked by Cpl. P.A. Keane if he was the person who left the above laundry to be cleaned. After viewing the photograph I can not say that I can identify CALL as the person who was in the Troy Laundry and left a bundle of laundry to be cleaned, as during the summer months we do always amount of business with strangers who come to this area on vacations.

        On December 6, 1954, I turned over to Cpl. P.A. Keane the bundle of laundry which contained the aforementioned items of clothing which were left at the Laundry by a person who gave the name P.A. CORBETT.

        I have read the above statement and I swear that it is true to the best of my knowledge.

                          Manuel Benero

Sworn to before me this 21st
day of December, 1954

Clipping concerning liquor store robbery, June 5, 1954

Hancock Liquor Store Owner Slugged, Robbed by Gunman

Edward H. Freehoffer, 55-year-old proprietor of the Liberty package store on Route 20 in Hancock, was nursing a painfully battered head today after being slugged unconscious by a young gunman who held up his store shortly before 10 Saturday night.

Police in eight states have been alerted to be on the lookout for the lone bandit who is still at large. He is described as a dark-complexioned man in his 20s, about 5 feet, 10 inches tall with black hair and a small mustache. He was wearing a light-colored suit.

Mr. Freehoffer said he was alone in the store when the gunman entered, brandished a pistol and announced, "This is a stickup!"

Demanded Liquor, Too

He said the bandit told him to empty the contents of the cash register into a paper bag and to hand the bag over the counter. When that was done, the gunman demanded "a couple of quarts of liquor and I gave them to him, too," the proprietor related.

Mr. Freehoffer, standing next to the shelves with the counter between himself and the gunman, was ordered to turn around to face the shelves. The bandit then leaned over the counter and struck Freehoffer a hard blow on the head with the butt of the gun. Stunned, the proprietor slumped behind the counter and the gunman fled.

"It all happened so quick there's very little I can tell," Mr. Freehoffer told an Eagle reporter. "It only took a matter of a minute or two and it was all over with."

"He just came in and told me it was a stickup, conked me over the head and that was it . . . I've got a couple of nice holes in the top of my head where he hit me."

Treated by Doctor

"I wasn't knocked out for too long, maybe a minute or two, that's all. I went next door (to Ida & John's restaurant) and they did everything, called the state police and a doctor who came and treated me."

Mrs. John Connors, co-proprietor of Ida John's, said Mr. Freehoffer was in very bad shape when he staggered into the restaurant for help. She said he was covered with blood and still dazed from the blow on the head.

Pittsfield State Troopers Stanley Bower and James E. Molloy launched an investigation of the robbery as soon as they arrived in response to the call from the restaurant.

Clues were scarce since Mr. Freehoffer did not see the bandit very long and could only give a description of him based on the short time the man was in the store. He said he did not see the car the gunman was driving, nor could he state whether the man even had a car.

$100 Believed Stolen

Sgt. John Loughlin said the amount of money stolen was in the vicinity of $100, but that was only an approximate figure.

The Liberty package store is located at the foot of Lebanon Mountain only two or three miles from the New York State line. Two years ago the store was broken into by thieves who stole a quantity of liquor.

The armed holdup was the first perpetrated in the Pittsfield area for more than a year. It was the first in many years in which someone was injured.

(The Berkshire Evening Eagle)

ce report concerning liquor store robbery, November 26, 1954

```
2748    FILE 13   SP PITTSFIELD MASS    NOV 26-54 REPLY
TO      SP MALONE NY                                          173077

MESA 5528 FILE DATE GA - RE JAMES ARLON CALL WITH ALIASES-
SUBJECT ANSWERING HIS DESCRIPTION WANTED BY THIS DEPARTMENT IN CONNECTION
WITH THE HOLD-UP OF THE LIBERTY PACKAGE STORE ON RTE 20 IN HANCOCK MASS-
ABOUT 4 MILES WEST OF PITTSFIELD MASS- ABOUT $100 AND TWO FIFTHS OF
CORBY WHISKEY WAS TAKEN- SUBJECT HIT PROPRIETOR OVER THE HEAD THREE
TIMES WITH A GUN- THIS HOLD-UP TOOK PLACE ABOUT 10PM ON 6-5-54-
DESCRIPTION OF MAN WE HAVE IS SIMILAR IN THE DESCRIPTION YOU HAVE OF CALL
OUR SUSPECT ALSO DESCRIBED AS SPEAKING VERY GOOD ENGLISH- WORE A SMALL
MOUSTACHE- AND THOUGHT TO BE OF FRENCH EXTRACTION-
PLEASE ADVISE IF YOU HAVE KNOWLEDGE IF CALL COULD HAVE BEEN IN THE
PITTSFIELD AREA ON THE ABOVE MENTIONED DATE- WETHER HE FITS OUR DESCRIPT
PROVIDED ABOVE - ALSO WETHER OR NOT HE IS AVAILABLE TO BE QUESTIONED BY
OUTSIDE DEPARTMENTS- IF SO WILL BRING VICTIM TO ESSEX COUNTY JAIL YOUR
STATE FOR POSSIBLE IDENTIFICATION-

AUTH SGT JJ LOUGHLIN    TPR RUSZCZYK 2019
RP H RHW 2117
                                          Superintendent
                                          Deputy Superintendent
                                          Chief Inspector
```

EXHIBIT N

- Clippings concerning subject's flight and interrogation regarding Sheppard homicide
- Subject's statement regarding flight
- Clipping reflecting subject's propensity for violent escape
- Correspondence from friend reflecting subject's propensity for criminal viole

| The Adirondack Daily Enterprise circa November, 1954 | The Nevada State Journal November 16, 1954 | The Post-Standard November 17, 1954 |

OUR EYEWITNESSES AT HAND

"We've got enough evidence against our prisoner," Capt. Muller told The Enterprise. "Aside from his fingerprints that match some of those we found at the scene of the shooting, we've got eyewitnesses."

The captain was referring to Lake Placid Police Sgt. Dominic Valenze and Patrolman J. Bernard Fell who were seriously—almost fatally—wounded by the the desperado. Sgt. Valenze and Patrolman Fell have said they are certain they can identify the man who shot them and Patrolman Pelkey.

Capt. Muller said he was convinced that his prisoner Call had been hiding out in the Adirondacks before the shootings.

"I'll find out if it's the last thing I do," he said. "It was something big he was hiding from."

He declined to speculate what it might have been.

Capt. Muller told The Enterprise that Call claimed he could remember nothing of his activities during the past few months.

Unaware of Charge

Call was unaware last night that he had been charged with the murder. But a whirlwind of official activity was clearing up the past he says he cannot remember before he was in St. Louis a short time ago.

Yesterday Call agreed to pose for newspaper photographers, who were warned not to discuss developments in the case before him.

Neatly dressed, but unshaven, Call smiled tightly at the cameramen, then asked Sergeant Gregory, "Who are these guys?"

When he was told they were newspaper photographers he murmured, "I hate them," and settled down to posing.

Sheppard Case Mentioned

As if Call's definite linkage with the New York murder was not fantastic enough, last night there were persistent reports that he may be questioned as the "bushy-haired" burglar who Dr. Samuel Sheppard is claiming at his trial in Cleveland, Ohio, killed his pretty wife, Marilyn.

When Call was booked as James Chandler Morgan last Tuesday he gave his home address as Lakewood, Ohio. Lakewood is near the resort town where Mrs. Sheppard was killed in the bedroom of her lakefront home.

Dr. Sheppard, on trial for the murder, claims the murder was committed by a young, bushy-haired burglar. Dr. Sheppard says the same burglar slugged him over the head as he attempted to save his wife.

LOOT IS FOUND

Loot from these burglaries we found in his hotel room he where he had been living si Oct. 26, and Capt. Muller said portion of the loot found in Ca room had been taken from t Lake Placid area in the days p ceding and following Pelke murder.

Call was to be questioned abo a $100,000 jewel theft at the La Placid Club, a swanky reso three days before the Pelkey m der. And it was possible that t fast-moving Call would be ask about any possible connecti with the murder of Marilyn She pard, a Bay Village, Ohio socialit who was killed July 4. Her hu band, Dr. Samuel Sheppard, is trial in Cleveland for the murd but has claimed a "bushy-haire burglar did it

Call gave Lakewood, Ohio, ne Bay Village, as an address whe he checked into his Reno hotel.

Call learned for the first ti yesterday what all the fuss w about. The first inkling of wh was happening was Monday wh press photographers asked and received permission to pho graph the man. Call balked first, but obeyed Gregory wh asked to pose. Tuesday, aft questioning Call for almost fo hours, police hurried the m back to his cell without permitti photographers or newspaper

ppings concerning subject's flight and interrogation regarding
ppard's homicide

: Post-Standard
vember 17, 1954

The Post-Standard
November 20, 1954

a sudden. I want time to clear
the cobwebs up, to light up the
ark corners in my mind."
Capt. Muller said a first degree
murder warrant against Call was
eing mailed from New York
tate.

TALKED NICELY

The state police captain said
Call's attitude seemed friendly,
and that he "talked very nicely,"
ut insisted he couldn't remember
anything.

"He told us he couldn't even
remember if he had any relatives
r who they were," Capt. Muller
elated.

Capt. Muller said Call also
would be questioned about a
$100,000 jewel robbery at Lake
Placid three days prior to the
Aug. 5 shooting in which 22-
year-old Patrolman Richard
Pelkey was wounded fatally.

The "one thing" Capt. Muller
ould like to determine, he said,
as the reason for Call's alleged
resence in the Adirondacks at the
ime of the shooting.

"That's the one question I'd like
find out," he declared. "I will
find out if it's the last thing I do."

FLOOR SQUEAKED

Call was arrested by Reno police
bout nine ho   r a squeak-
ng floor disci   presence as
n intruder in   o home. Po-
ce said   oose   boards made

Troopers Wednesday ended a
104-day long manhunt for the
person who shot and fatally
wounded Patrolman Richard
Pelkey, and wounded Patrolman
J. Bernard Fell and Sgt. Dominick
Valene. Pelkey died a week after
the shooting in a lonely cabin
just outside of Lake Placid.

A fourth policeman was unhurt
in the shooting that followed investigation of a cabin that was
reportedly being burglarized.

State police said that Call's
details of the shooting itself and
his reason for being in the
Adirondack resort village were
not immediately apparent. Further questioning was expected
to unveil it.

TRAINED BY ARMY

Call, troopers pointed, had been
trained by the Air Force to survive lone drops into forest land
in military survival tests. He had
put that knowledge to work in
eluding state police and civilian
posses that had numbered as high
es 500 men.

The stolid Air Force officer was
brought here early today shortly
after being returned from Reno
Nev. where he had been arrested
on burglary charges. He was ex-
tradited on a murder warrant.

Earlier last night, troopers had
indicated that Call "was beginning" to talk after the questioning that had started before noon.

Subject's statement regarding flight

I further state that on being discovered in this camp, I had but one purpose in mind and that was to get out of the camp at any cost as I did not want to be apprehended . I knew that I had committed many crimes and transgressions and knew that I was wanted. I had decided that if I were cornered at any time, I would shoot my way out if possible and if I could not do this, I decided that I would turn the gun on myself. For this reason, I carried a 9 mm Luger and a 32 automatic pistol fully loaded.

I state therefore that the reason for this shooting affair at the Dr. Perkins camp was the result of my decision to make every effort to avoid apprehension and arrest at the camp.

I have read the above statement typed on three pages by Sgt. H.E. Blaisdell, at the Hawthorne State Police Barracks, from the story I have told him and Captain H.T. Muller and Corporals F.A. Keane and P.J. Harris of the State Police and I swear that it is all true, each and every part.

I again state that at no time have I been abused in any manner by any persons whatsoever and I have given this statement absolutely of my own free will, and with no promises being made to me whatsoever, and with full knowledge that I was wanted on a Homicide charge as a result of this shooting.

Subscribed and sworn to before me this 20th day of November 1954

James A. Call

Dorothea E. Fischer

DOROTHEA E. FISCHER
NOTARY PUBLIC, State of New York
Qualified in Westchester County
No. 60-6304200
Term Expires March 30, 1956

H. Blaisdell
F. A. Keane
P. J. Harris

ping reflecting subject's propensity for violent escape

RANDOM TALES

By ROGER TUBBY

Major Call and the troopers

"Dutch" Mueller, commander of Troop B of the New York State Police, invited me to accompany him and three or four other troopers and recently captured murderer Major Call of the Air Force into the woods near the Saranac Lake club golf course.

Call had gunned down Lake Placid policemen, killing one of them, when they found him in the basement of a vacant house. He'd been breaking into homes and camps that summer after being AWOL, absent without leave.

He'd flown several missions in the Korean war and then, returned to the States. He had taken off from his base in Alabama and roamed into New England and the Adirondacks.

After the shooting he'd escaped, lived for some time in a lean-to near the golf course, and eventually made his way out of the Adirondacks despite the biggest and longest man-hunt in our history.

Vanity did him in. Arrested in Reno, Nevada, on a minor charge the police emptied his wallet. Among the papers in it was a newspaper clipping about the shooting and his escape. An alert reporter notice it, phoned Capt. Mueller, and said, "I think we've got your man."

Brought back in handcuffs, eventually jailed but released after several years and killed in a traffic accident, Major Call seemed a sensitive, slight, intelligent man, well-read in the classics. I interviewed him in his re-trial cell in Elizabethtown.

The Troopers, Call and I went out along the railroad track from Lake Placid. To get to his lean-to (where he'd cached stolen food and a radio on which he got police and other reports), we had to cross a small stream on a log. Call's wrists were unshackled so he could balance himself on the log, a Trooper walking before him, another behind.

On the other side Call said calmly to the Trooper who had been ahead of him: "I wouldn't do that again, your revolver sticking out of its holster right in front of me. I was tempted to grab it and let you all have it."

After all, he thought he faced a life sentence. Maybe a second shoot-out and death seemed preferable.

(The Adirondack Daily Enterprise)

Correspondence from friend reflecting subject's propensity for criminal viole

```
                              Robert L. Sylvester
                              425 Neal Court
                              Schaumburg, 60193, Il
```

Dear Mr. Conners,

    I must apologogize for not talking to you on the phone yesterday morning. My hearing is not good, but not so bad that I can't carry on a telephone conversation. The fact is, simply put, I didn't want to because I was surprised and not willing at first to discuss a particularly disquieting situation with a stranger I felt could not be unbiased.

    On further reflection I decided to write. Perhaps there is something here you may not already know- something that might clarify a point in a twisted, uncomphrehensible and tragic life.

    Bear with me. I am not a typist.

    I first met James A. Call in the seventh grade of Lowell Elementary School. My parents had moved into Oak Park that summer, and when school started I was the "new kid" in the class. I was big and Jim was small. He seemed somewhat of a loner and so was I. We soon became fast friends because of a great number of similar intrests. I can still recall the late summer evenings Jim and I would spend in my parents back yard with our BB guns shooting at the toy soldiers we had hidden in fortified places, or the nights we used to spend lying on the roof studying the stars, or the fun at the beach, or the Boy Scouts, or the long bicycle rides.

    In highschool we were inseprable, we joined the chess club, and later got jobs as ushers at the Lake theater. I believe we were in our junior year when war finally came to the United States.

    We joined the Air Force together thinking we would be together in the service, but our birthdays were in different months so Jim went several months before I did. Mr. and Mrs. Call became good friends with my parents, and later, patients of my father. My folks always treated Jim like a mamber of the family, and always included him whenever we went out to dinner or a show. Every week my father would write me a letter while I was in the service, and he would always include money. He did the same for Jim.

Of course Jim and I corresponded all the time, and even played a war game by mail. We even traded hats- his Air Force, and my infantry. His is still hanging on the wall in my house.

During the war whenever Jim got a delay in route or a furlough, he would visit my folks. Our house was his second home. He was the brother I never had and I was the brother he never had.

With the war ending I began my academic career. Jim said he didn't think he had the money to go to college, although everyone said with the GI bill he could make it. He decided to stay in. He was an officer and making a very good salary, and wouldn't change his mind even when my father said he would help him financially until he got a degree.

We continued to correspond by mail until we each bought a tape recorder and then sent tapes back and fourth, and again, whenever he could, Jim would come and visit.

When Mr. Call- George Call retired, the Calls sold their house in Glenview and moved to Tucson where Jim was more-or-less permanently stationed at the Davis Monthan Air Base. He had met a girl out there and wanted to marry . He asked me to be his best man, and of course I accepted. I flew out to Tucson, and as soon as I got there we left by car for Meridian Miss. because, while Jim had a furlough, Harry Truman committed us to Korea that day, and the air base was put on alert and he could have had it cancelled.

This was when I first met Muriel, a very pretty and likable young girl but unfortunately not in the greatest of health because of a severe bronchial asthma. Before the wedding I was told Jim and his parents had some sort of misunderstanding because neither of them attended. It seemed strange, but I never questioned Jim about it, feeling it was really no business of mine.

I believe it was a year later. Jim and Muriel had their first child. My folks were driving to Los Angeles to see my dad's brother, and of course, stopped in Tucson to see the Calls. Jim and Muriel seemed like a happy couple at that time, although Muriel did complain a little about the caliber of some of the other officers wives. Both seemed happily adjusted to married life in the military. Mr. and Mrs. Call said they saw very little of Jim Muriel or the baby, but passed it off as the fault of the military life Jim was leading.

We continued to correspond, and I began to understand just how sick Muriel was with her second pregnancy. Then, I was told of the blood transfusions, the Rh problem, and her death.

I flew to Meridian for the funeral and I regocnized the change in Jim right away- beside the fact that he was grief stricken, he drank, constantly from morning to night, sipping a little now and then until he averaged almost a fifth of Scotch a day. He never exhibited drunkenness or showed intoxication in any way. I was shocked, and when I spoke to him about it, he passed it off lightly.

Then he told me he had given the care of his son to the Johns- that he felt Robie could give him much more than he or his family could. I knew this hurt Mrs. Call because she spoke of it many times.

Jim couldn't make my wedding. The next time I heard from him he called on the phone and told me to meet him, that he was in Chicago. When I did, he told me he was AWOL. I couldn't believe it. I thought he was kidding. It made no sense at all. He said he owed five thousand dollars to someone. I told him I would lend him the money if he would go back. He said he owed me too much already. He said he was going to Lake Placid, and I remembered he had mentioned being in New York state when he was much smaller. He said he still owed money on his car, and if I wanted it, he would give it to me if I kept up the payments. It was crazy. At that time, recently married, and with a car I was paying off, another car was out of the question. Then he told me how he was going to live. He wouldn't be able to get a regular job because he was AWOL and would be found because of his social security. He was going to become a thief. I laughed, but he was serious. He would steal to make a living. Then I found out he was armed. Did he plan to use the gun in armed robbery? Did he intend to shoot someone if they wouldn't give him their money? No, he would never shoot anybody- only if they caught him and were trying to make him 'go back'.

I really did not know what to do. His mind seemed clear and functioning well enough, but the rationality of what he was saying was alarming. Every shread of logic was gone.

The next day I went to the FBI and reported him as being AWOL, armed, and possibly dangerous. Nothing whatever was done. Months later two agents came to our apartment and asked my wife a few questions. Too little too late.

It was sometime later- months later, I think, when I received a phone call from Jim. He was in Chicago and wanted to see me. He said he had a lot to tell. I wish I had heard what it was. I told him I couldn't. I was working all day at the hospital and evenings

at my fathers clinic. I did not fail to see him because I was afraid
of him in case he found out I had turned him in, because I told him
that was what I was going to do. I just couldn't make connections
that day.

After Jim was apprehended I learned a great deal about the life
he had been leading- of his addiction to drink and gambling- of how
he got money from his parents who could ill afford it- how he passed
bad checks and eventually became a thief. All too well I remember
the shock, disappointment and anger my family experienced upon
learning what Jim had done- and the tears of his mother, and
particularly his father who was so proud of Jim that he refused to
believe the truth.

We corresponded throughout the trial and Jims years in prison.
He said once he was defending himself, that he only wanted to get
away and hide like an animal. He also spoke of becoming aquainted
with Willie Sutton who mentioned him in his book "Where the Money Is"

I was asked at one time to write a letter to someone doing a
review of his case for possible parole. They wanted to know my
relationship to him and what I knew and how I felt. I told them
just the way I saw it.

When Jim was paroled and hired by [...] (his sister) husband,
he was in Ohio. We met at a park half way between Mantua and Chicago.
I was happy to see him, but he wasn't the same person I grew up
with. He was quiet and somewhat withdrawn.

Before we met again, he wrote about the shame he felt for what
he had done, and how much he owed the Johns for bringing up his son,
and how he could never repay them. Perhaps this embarassment might
have led to a seeming aloofness. I don't know. He never mentioned it
again.

We met his wife and stepdaughter once, and for a time had the
feeling things were looking up for Jim, but then came the accident.

In retrospect I can only say I don't know what inner failings
chemical inbalance, or cerebral insult could have caused the change
from the person I grew up with- the person my family loved, to the
inept criminal he turned out to be. No one does. My father, a
physician, could only speculate on what could have so utterly destroyed
his moral fiber.

There are many incongruities and questions without answers. Jim was thrifty to the point of being cheap. He bought a Crosley automobile which was going to save him a lot of money in gasoline, but found out sadly that it couldn't make it to Tucson before breaking down and needing a new engine. Jim next bought a very expensive Jaguar XK120 sports car.

Jim was always extremely fond of children, always finding time to play ball or teach them football, or build things with them- this was at a time when the average highschool kid didn't know younger kids existed. I remember many times having to wait for him to finish playing baseball with a bunch of little kids, and how it always rankled me. I find it almost impossible to believe he was distant or aloof with his own son.

So, to sum it all up, all I can say is he was my friend and we shared a lot together, and I miss him and I suppose I always will.

Truly Yours,

Robert Sylvester

AFTERWORD

This book is predicated on a mass of research material that has been compiled over a period of almost fifty years, much of which is quoted extensively in the preceding text. In consonance with these facts the author uses a dramatized narrative style which professes to express what individuals were saying and thinking under various circumstances. It would be impossible, of course, to resurrect precisely the unrecorded thoughts and statements of characters involved in events that took place fifty years ago. But where reasonable extrapolations may be made from the record, the writer has offered an imaginative reconstruction of thoughts and discourse which derives from factual data. The addendum contains evidence to support in toto the conclusions reached in the narrative.

ACKNOWLEDGMENTS AND SUPPLEMENTAL SOURCE NOTES

The sources for much of the material in this book are apparent in the course of the main narrative account of Call's story while other sources (witnesses and relevant documents) can be found in the addendum and exhibits section. Following are supplemental notes that pertain to individual passages. Documentation for this material, where available, includes the names of those who provided information or material, as well as how and when information and material were obtained. In some instances general time periods in which certain events took place have been used when precise dates were unobtainable.

The author would like to express his appreciation to the individuals and organizations who graciously furnished information and materials for this book, in particular, current and former members of the New York State Police, the New York State Department of Correctional Services, the Federal Bureau of Investigation, the National Personnel Records Center, the Lake Placid Police Department and the Cuyahoga County, Ohio, Prosecutor's Office. On many occasions these contributions were made at the expense of considerable time and effort on the part of those who supplied the material and the author is grateful for their assistance.

Prologue

Information contained herein derives in part from the records of the United States Air Force (USAF), the New York State Police (NYSP), and the Lake Placid Police Department (LPPD), as well as interviews conducted with personnel from these agencies. These contacts included personal interviews in July 1961 by George W. Warburton with Daniel Manning, the District Attorney who prosecuted Call; Captain Harold Muller and Sergeant Harry Blaisdell, NYSP, who were in charge of the crime scene investigation and ensuing manhunt; Captain Platt Harris and Trooper Russell Trombly, NYSP; Trooper Robert Fowler, NYSP, whose personal scrapbook Warburton reviewed; Patrolman John Fagan, LPPD, who was involved in the shootout, and Chief Lawrence McDonald, LPPD. Subsequent taped and transcribed in-person interviews were conducted by Neil Drew, an investigative journalist, with the following individuals who either participated in the investigation or had first-hand knowledge of the matter: Dr. James J. Perkins, owner of the premises in which the confrontation occurred, August 5 and 6, 1980; Harry Blaisdell, September 7, 8, 9, 1978; E. Stewart Jones, Major Call's attorney, January 16, 1979; Red Robinson, NYSP Trooper, January 17, 1979; Paul Willette, Lake Placid resident, June 9, 1980; Daniel Manning, Call Prosecutor, January 19, 1981; Harold Soden, Assistant Prosecutor, January 26, 1981; Russell Trombly, NYSP Trooper, February 19, 1981; Fred Teeple, NYSP Captain, March 2, 1981; and Edward Van Schaick, NYSP Trooper, March 4, 1981. Surviving officers of the shootout, John Fagan and Bernard Fell, were interviewed by Drew in untaped interviews during this period.

Numerous interviews were conducted by the author during the late 1990s with many of the aforementioned persons as well as personnel from the USAF, the NYSP, and the LPPD, and with other Lake Placid residents who were familiar with the crime. These personal interviews included Michael Saulpaugh, Chief of Police LPPD; the widows of Officer Bernard Fell and Patrolman John Fagan; and the daughter of Captain Harold Muller, Pam Muller-Smith, who furnished her father's personal files on the case. The author, accompanied by Colonel Bruce Arnold and Major William Warburton (no relation to George Warburton) of the NYSP, inspected the crime scene on August 28, 1998, at which time the then-current owner, Samuel Murray, provided further data. Major Call's gun battle with the four Lake Placid officers received wide coverage in the print media, from which additional information was secured. Laura M. Viscome of the *Lake Placid News* and the North Elba Historical Society was particularly helpful, providing substantial background information to the author by telephone in 1998 and 1999, and in a letter dated December 10, 1998. Other news sources who furnished information to George Warburton in August 1966 were Evelyn Outcalt, *Adirondack Daily Enterprise,* and Marge Lamy, *Lake Placid News.*

Part I

The background material regarding Major Call's personal and military life described in Part I was obtained from a wide range of sources, including records of the Federal Bureau of Investigation (FBI), the USAF, the NYSP, and the LPPD. Files of the NYSP reflect an extensive background investigation of Call conducted after his apprehension in 1954; this material included interviews with Call's friends and associates in both military and civilian life.

On February 12 and 13, 1955, NYSP personnel, including Harry Blaisdell, traveled to Meridian, Mississippi, and interviewed the following persons who professed to be well-acquainted with Major Call's family: Lester Williamson, District Attorney; William Rush Mosby, Sheriff; and A. William Creel, City Detective. During their trip the NYSP team interviewed the following friends and associates of Major Call at the 376th Bomb Wing, 514th Squadron, Barksdale Air Force Base (AFB), Shreveport, Louisiana, on February 14 and 15, 1955: Lt. Colonel O. A. Weddle, Call's commanding officer at Barksdale; Colonel Edward E. Matthews, who attended Survival School with Call; Lieutenant Calvin C. Gaskins, a close friend who also attended Survival School with Call; Major Samuel T. Battalio, Call's immediate superior at Kadena AFB, Okinawa, who flew missions with Call and wrote several of Call's efficiency reports; Lieutenant R. L. Kaiser, Chaplain, Barksdale AFB, who conferred with Call regarding his personal problems; and Major Vernon B. Kelly, Call's immediate superior at Kadena AFB. The NYSP contacted several other persons in Louisiana including: J. N. Birdswell, Vice President, Bossier Bank & Trust Company, who reported on Call's banking activities, transactions involving his car, and bounced checks from gambling casinos in Las Vegas and elsewhere; and Steve Barange, proprietor of Tom's Restaurant in Shreveport, who knew Call as a friend and frequent patron. The author contacted some of Call's former military associates by telephone, including Colonel (formerly Lieutenant) Gaskins on February 23, 1998, and May 27, 1998, and Colonel (formerly Major) Battalio on October 28, 1998, and May 5, 1999, and corroborated much of the data previously reported.

Additional information regarding the private life of Major Call and his wife, Muriel John Call, came from meetings between the author and Call's friends and relatives in Meridian, Mississippi, on November 11 and 12, 1998, as well as numerous follow-up telephone interviews during 1999, 2000, and 2001. Major Call's son, Jeffrey Call, was particularly helpful and graciously furnished considerable background data, as did Camille Mitchell, a family friend. Major Call's granddaughter, Muriel Call, was interviewed by telephone by George Warburton on June 7, 1999, and by the author on June 15, 1999; she furnished further information to the author by e-mail on March 1, 2000. Blanche Call, Major Call's second wife, and his stepdaughter, Teresa Solano, were interviewed by telephone by Warburton on March 1, 1999, April 22, 1999, May 12, 1999, and May 27, 1999. They were interviewed in person by Warburton at their residence in California on June 11, 12, 13, 1999, at which time they furnished considerable information regarding Call's private life, including portions of his personal diary and other memorabilia.

Robert Sylvester, Call's life-long friend, was interviewed at his residence in Chicago, Illinois, on February 1, 2000, and April 3, 2000, by Lisa Lombardo, Managing Editor, British American Publishing, and her husband, US Navy Lieutenant Daniel Lombardo, who accompanied her on the first interview. In addition to furnishing data about Call's lifestyle and criminal activities, Mr. Sylvester submitted a comprehensive letter postmarked January 22, 2000, chronicling many of Call's experiences throughout his life.

Major Call's USAF Service Records from May 20, 1943, through May 13, 1954, revealed a detailed, indeed almost encyclopedic, description of the flyer's life during this period. His efficiency reports offered significant insight into his physical, emotional, and intellectual abilities. Specific information regarding Call's Korean combat missions was obtained from his USAF records, as well as Call's statements to friends and associates and the NYSP. James J. LeCleir, Major General, USAF (Ret.), confirmed certain technical matters regarding the Korean combat missions during interviews in 1999 and by letter dated May 20, 1999. Warburton received written material from the following: D. Menard (MSGT Ret.), US Air Force Museum, December 9, 1998; The Emil Buehler National Aviation Library, July 10, 1998; The Empire State Aeroscience Museum, September 14, 2000.

Ms. Jody Elmer, long-time Tucson resident, confirmed background material regarding Tucson in the 1950s to the author by telephone in 2000 and by letter dated April 26, 2001. Lester L. Amann, President, AMRIC Associates, Ltd., conducted background investigation during 1998, 1999, and 2000 and furnished considerable information to the author by telephone and in writing. Hiram College, Hiram, Ohio, supplied historical data by facsimile on September 23, 1999. Other sources of material were records of the

State of Mississippi; Lauderdale County, Florida; the Tucson Arizona Police Department by report dated November 30, 1954; the Ohio Department of Health; the Newberry Library, Chicago, Illinois; the City of Tucson Economic Development Agency; the Metropolitan Tucson Convention and Visitor's Bureau; the Arizona Historical Society; the Tucson Chamber of Commerce; the Tucson Film Board; Squadron/Signal Publications, Inc.; and Maine Township High School, Park Ridge, Illinois, which provided James Call's 1943 high school yearbook.

Part II

Material appearing in Part II was obtained from Major Call's USAF Service Record, the files of the FBI and the NYSP, and interviews with family members, friends, and Air Force associates, as well as from many of the sources mentioned previously. His military efficiency reports reflected the marked changes in his behavior and decline in performance. Fellow officers mentioned in Part I, including Major Battalio, Colonel Mathews, Lieutenant Gaskins, Major Kelly, and Lieutenant Kaiser, all attested to Call's decline. Robert Sylvester, Call's friend, described Call's mental deterioration and headlong plunge into crime in the letter to the author mentioned in Part I. In a report dated August 1, 1963, the FBI confirmed Sylvester's appearance at their Chicago office in June 1954 to report Call's criminal activities. Major Call's collapse following his wife's death was described by his mother-in-law, Mrs. Robbie John, in statements to the press in 1954 and 1955.

Information regarding the Survival School at Stead AFB was obtained on February 14 and 15, 1955, from Colonel Mathews and Lieutenant Gaskins, who attended the school with Call, as well as statements made by Call to the NYSP in November 1954. Lieutenant Gaskins was interviewed by telephone by the author on February 23, 1998, and again on May 27, 1998, and supplied considerable information regarding Call's personal and professional life. Lieutenant Robert McGeehan, USAF (Ret.), who had attended the Survival School (but not with Call), was interviewed in person at his residence in Vero Beach, Florida, by the author on February 23, 1998, at which time he described the severe combat-like training which prevailed at Stead. Additional information regarding the curriculum at the Survival School was obtained from retired Sergeant Donald Wertz, formerly an instructor at the school, who was interviewed on the phone by George Warburton on April 7, 1998. Major Call's military decorations and awards are described in a report dated May 6, 1998, from the National Personnel Records Center, St. Louis, Missouri, and from his USAF Service Record covering the period May 20, 1943, through May 13, 1954.

Part III

This segment relating to the activities of Major Call during the seven-week period following his AWOL from the service up to the time of the Sheppard murder was based on the following: Call's friend Robert Sylvester furnished information, by the letter and interviews mentioned previously, about their three-day meeting in Chicago when Call told him he had deserted from the service and had embarked on a life of crime. Sylvester described, among other things, Call's mental condition, the problems his friend was having with his damaged car, the thrill he experienced from his crimes, and the weapons he was carrying. Files of the NYSP show that Call was interrogated repeatedly by Muller and Blaisdell, NYSP, regarding his whereabouts during this seven-week period. Call offered information that confirmed his presence only at the locations of crimes for which police had hard evidence of his involvement. Captain Muller stated several times to the press that Call "was hiding out from something big."

Information regarding Call's crimes was also obtained from the files of the Massachusetts State Police (MSP), Chief Paul Meara of the Springfield Police Department, and Emilie Piper of Pittsfield, Massachusetts, who conducted background checks in Massachusetts in 1999 and on February 2, 2000, at the request of Warburton. Specific information regarding Call's robbery of the Springfield cab driver, John O'Connor, was provided by Detectives Henry F. Dolphin and Frank A. Saccavino of the Chicopee, Massachusetts, Police Department to Harry Blaisdell on November 27, 1954, and by correspondence from Inspector R. J. McDowell to Inspector B. E. Denman of the BCI on December 13, 1954. Additional material for Part III was obtained by the author's telephone interviews with the following: Howard Commander, President of the Lebanon Valley Speedway, New Lebanon, New York, March 2000 and April 12, 2001; John Conners, owner of the Liberty Package Store, and Ida and John's Restaurant, Hancock, New York, January 27 and 31, 2000; and Mrs. James E. Molloy, spouse of Trooper J. E. Molloy, MSP, February 2000. Information was also obtained from the NYSP Report dated November 26, 1954, from the Pittsfield, Massachusetts, Police Department to the NYSP, the Reed Memorial Library in Ravenna, Ohio, and from the following Massachusetts newspapers: *The Berkshire Evening Eagle*, *The North Adams Transcript*, and *The Union-News*.

Part IV

Accounts of the importance of Omar Khayyám's *Rubaiyat* to Jim and Muriel Call came from their families, his Air Force associates, and files of the NYSP. Following his apprehension in November 1954, Call stated that *The Rubaiyat* volume inscribed "Mubby" found among his possessions was very precious to him and that he had carried the book with him throughout the manhunt. Bill Leone, of the William K. Sanford Library, Colonie, New York, provided background information regarding *The Rubaiyat* to the author by telephone and in person in 1998 and 1999.

Information regarding the Lake Placid Club jewel robbery on August 1, 1954, came from tape-recorded interviews made by Neil Drew with Harry Blaisdell on September 7, 8, 9, 1978, and with Dr. James Perkins, camp owner, on August 5 and 6, 1980, and from Drew's correspondence regarding his investigation of the jewel robbery to the author, dated April 24, 1999. The author interviewed by telephone the jewel theft victim's daughter, Nancy Roe Conway, on April 28, 1999. T. Matthew De Waelsche, Librarian, San Antonio Public Library, furnished written information on March 18, 1999. Evidence of a hole dug in the crawlspace beneath the Perkins' camp, where the jewels may have been stashed, was discovered by NYSP Troop Commander Major William Warburton and the author on August 28, 1998.

Accounts of the Perkins' camp shootout and the ensuing manhunt were obtained from numerous sources mentioned previously in the Prologue, including the files of the USAF, the LPPD, the FBI, the

Essex County Sheriff's Office, the NYSP, and the NYSP Bureau of Criminal Investigations Report 173077, as well as many New York State newspapers, including: *The Times Union, The Post-Standard, The New York Herald-Tribune, The New York Daily Mirror, The New York Times, The Press-Republican, The Adirondack Daily Enterprise, The Malone Telegram, The Watertown Daily Times,* and *The Warrensburg-Lake George News.* Periodicals reviewed include: *True,* The Man's Magazine, "Wilderness Wager with Death" by Norman Carlisle, April 1965; *Argosy,* "The Hide and Seek Killer" by A. Breen, December 1965; *Sunday News,* Justice Story, "The Phantom Burglar of the Adirondacks" by Ruth Reynolds, December 23, 1956; *Master Detective,* "Manhunt for an AWOL Major" by Leonard Bennett, February 1960; *True Detective,* "Murder Manhunt and the AWOL Major" by Seymour J. Ettman, March 1955; *Real Detective,* "The Manhunt 102 Days Long" by Tom Conway, April 1955.

Files of the NYSP contain reports from interviews with Call dated November 19 and 21, 1954, and a signed statement dated November 20, 1954, by Call in which he recounts the August 4, 1954, shootout in explicit detail. Files of the NYSP, the LPPD, and minutes of the Essex County Grand Jury proceedings contain detailed accounts regarding the shootout from the surviving officers and those who were first at the scene.

Information regarding Call's gambling and social activities, including his affairs with women during this period, was obtained from the above files, as well as from several personally recorded interviews conducted by Neil Drew. These interviews included the following NYSP personnel: Sgt. Harry Blaisdell, September 7, 8, 9, 1978; Trooper Red Robinson, January 17, 1979; Captain Fred Teeple, March 2, 1981; and Trooper Edward Van Schaick, March 4, 1981. Other individuals who gave personally recorded statements were: Raymond Brunette, Essex County Highway Superintendent, September 30, 1978; E. Stewart Jones, Major Call's attorney, January 16, 1979; Officer Reg Cormier, Saranac Lake Police Department, December 1978; Paul Willette, Lake Placid resident, June 9, 1980; Daniel Manning, Essex County District Attorney, January 19, 1981; Harold Soden, New York State Supreme Court Justice, Ret., a former District Attorney who assisted with the Call prosecution, January 26, 1981; Russell Trombly, Sheriff of Clinton County, former NYSP expert woodsman involved in the manhunt,

February 19, 1981; and Irene Montayne, Call burglary victim, Sloansville, New York, March 11, 1981.

The author conducted many interviews during the late 1990s with former NYSP Troopers and Lake Placid residents who either worked on the Call manhunt or were knowledgeable about the case. Some who furnished valuable information are: Kenneth O'Dell, former NYSP Troop Commander, interviewed in person by the author, accompanied by Colonel Bruce Arnold and W. Mark Dale, Director, NYSP Forensic Investigation Center, on June 3, 1998 (Mr. O'Dell later furnished substantial material by mail on February 5, 1999); NYSP Trooper Russ Slingerland on July 6, 1998, accompanied the author to various sites involved in the manhunt. Warren Surdam, NYSP, was interviewed in person in 1998. Other NYSP troopers who were interviewed by telephone by the author were: Harold Osborne in 1998; Fred Wright, who spent considerable time with Call following his apprehension, on May 6, 1998 (Mr. Wright later furnished specific information by mail); and Blake Muthig in 1998. Art Devlin, owner of the Olympic Motel and long-time resident of Lake Placid, provided the author with considerable background on the case during in-person and telephone interviews during the late 1990s; Ms. Gail Johnson, daughter of Harry Blaisdell, permitted the author to review her father's personal records regarding the Call case in September 1998, as did Harold Muller's daughter, Pam Muller-Smith, in October 2000. In 1966 George Warburton conducted many interviews with local residents and personally visited the sites where Call had committed some of his crimes, including burglaries of the following houses: Clarence Davies, "Sunny Cove"; Charles Walker, "Bear Club Road"; Francis Brewster, "Seventh Heaven"; and Dr. James Perkins' camp, where the shootout occurred.

Part V

The accounts in Part V relating to Call's activities in Manhattan and on Long Island are based on information from the files of the New York City Police Department (NYCPD), the Nassau County Long Island Police Department (NCPD), the Old Westbury Long Island Police Department (OWPD), the Reno Nevada Police Department (RPD), and the NYSP. Although Call was suspected of several crimes in all of these areas because of his MO and his presence in specific locations, he admitted only to those offenses for which authorities had irrefutable evidence of his guilt. The following police reports served to confirm his crimes while he was on Long Island: OWPD Detective Division Report dated October 21, 1954, and report #1707-3-54 dated November 27, 1954; NCPD Alarm 20107 dated October 21, 1954; and NYSP Report regarding Montayne car and E. Gerry dated November 25, 1954. NYSP records show that the vehicle Call stole in Sloansville, New York, was recovered in New York City on October 14, 1954, by the NYCPD, and reflected the subsequent investigation involving Call undertaken by the NYCPD. The Montayne account of Major Call's burglaries and car theft in Sloansville are based on Neil Drew's recorded interviews with Harry Blaisdell on September 7, 8, 9, 1978, and with Irene Montayne at her residence on March 11, 1981.

The passages in Part V pertaining to Call's experiences in Reno, Nevada, came from files of the USAF, the RPD, the NYSP, and the LPPD. Details regarding Call's burglaries of the Loomis, Mapes, Linnecke, and Thatcher residences in Reno are covered in RPD files and summarized in the RPD Follow Up Report dated November 11, 1954, as well as in reports dated November 9, 11, 15, 22, 23, 24, 1954. Call admitted to the Reno offenses in a signed statement to the RPD dated November 10, 1954.

The NYSP and RPD files contain much information regarding the apprehension of Major Call, his subsequent interrogations by Chief of Police L. R. Greeson, Detectives William Gregory and Beverly Waller, and his extradition to New York (Case #91276, Reno Nevada PD). Warburton confirmed much of the foregoing information during his visit to Reno in May 1997. Bradley Drake, Reno resident, furnished Warburton with detailed written material on October 1, 2000, about Call's activities in Reno, including photographs of four residences burglarized by Call. The following newspapers offered considerable coverage of the Reno proceedings: *The Nevada State Journal* and *The Reno Evening Gazette*.

Part VI

The account of the Sheppard homicide and its aftermath in this section derives from prodigious research beginning with interviews conducted by George Warburton in 1961. After reviewing archives of the Sheppard murder and the Lake Placid shootout in Cleveland and New York State newspapers in the microfiche of the Library of Congress, Warburton contacted many individuals who were knowledgeable about the case. The following were interviewed by him in person in the environs of Lake Placid during 1961: Daniel Manning, Call prosecutor, and Harold Muller and Harry Blaisdell, NYSP. The following persons were interviewed in person by Warburton in Bay Village, Ohio, in August 1966 (prior to Sheppard's second trial): F. Lee Bailey, Sheppard's defense attorney, and Dr. Richard Sheppard, the defendant's brother. The background material regarding the Sheppard case was developed from a multitude of sources, including a review of portions of the transcripts of the three trials (1954, 1966, 2000). Other materials reviewed include the following: Pre-trial, trial, and post-trial notes of Sheppard's Defense Attorney William Corrigan, Western Reserve Historical Society; Report of Autopsy, Case No. 76629, Autopsy No. M-7280 by S. R. Gerber, MD; Trace Evidence Report by Mary Cowan, Cuyahoga County Coroner's Laboratories, Trace Evidence Department, in re: Marilyn Sheppard, Case # 76629, Autopsy M 7280; X-Ray Report, Cuyahoga County Coroner's Office, Case No. 76629, X-Ray File Number 254-2383; Affidavit of Paul Leland Kirk, *State v. Sheppard*, No. 64571, April 26, 1955. Also reviewed were reports from the following experts which were part of the most recent Sheppard trial in 2000: Barton P. Epstein, Criminalist and Terry L. Laber, Forensic Serologist, Laber & Epstein, Forensic Serology & Microscopy; Mitchell M. Holland, Ph.D., Scientific Laboratory Director, AFDIL; Thomas D. Holland, Ph.D., Behavioral Criminology International; Lowell J. Levine, DDS; Gregg O. McCrary, Supervisor Special Agent, Federal Bureau of Investigation (Ret.), National Center for the Analysis of Violent Crime; Mohammad A. Tahir, Ph.D., Indianapolis-Marion County Forensic Services Agency; Robert J. White, MD, Ph.D., Professor, Neurological Surgery, Case Western Reserve University School of Medicine.

Carmen Marino, Assistant County Prosecutor, Cuyahoga County, was interviewed in person by Warburton and the author in April 1998 and on June 15, 1998, and by telephone by the author on March 24, 1999. Under the supervision of Marino's associate, David Zimmerman, the author and Warburton were permitted to review the records and evidence of the Sheppard case, which included police reports, exhibits, physical evidence, autopsy photographs and scientific reports from expert witnesses. Interviews were conducted in Cleveland in 1998 by the author and Warburton with witnesses, forensic scientists, reporters, attorneys, and law enforcement officials. Lieutenant (Ret.) Edward Lewis and Lieutenant (Ret.) James Thompkins of the Bay Village Police Department were interviewed over the phone by Warburton in 1997. Fred Drenkhan, the first police officer to arrive at the Sheppard crime scene, who later became the Bay Village Police Chief, was interviewed in person by Warburton and the author on April 26, 1998.

Sheppard's attorney, Terry Gilbert, was interviewed in person by the author and Warburton in April 1998, and by Warburton in person in August 2000, and by telephone by the author on April 20, 2001. Dr. Stephen Sheppard, Dr. Sam Sheppard's brother, was contacted periodically from 1997 to 2000 by telephone and letter by Warburton. Sam Reese Sheppard, Dr. Sam Sheppard's son, met with Warburton and Lisa Lombardo on June 17, 1999 in Oakland, California and has been contacted periodically by Warburton by letter and telephone since 1999. Don Lowers of AMSEC was contacted by Warburton periodically from 1996 to 1998 by telephone and in person in June 1997 and October 1998. Paul V. Daly, a former FBI official, was contacted during the late 1990s both in person and by telephone and graciously offered his counsel on the Call case on numerous occasions. The following telephone interviews were conducted by Warburton: Chief Booker, Mantua Police Department, on July 6 and 7, 1998; Karen Cornelius, daughter of Captain David Kerr, Cleveland Police Department, on April 15, 2000; Michael Grabowski, former Cleveland Police Department investigator, in July 1998; Vincent J. Kremperger, Lakewood Police Department, in July 1998; Pat Shannon, Records Access Officer, Lakewood Police Department, several calls in July 1999; Jerome Poelking, Cleveland Police Department, in July 1998; Harry Deal, Cleveland resident, on April 21, 1999; Mary Cowan, former Lab Technician, Bay Village Coroner's Office, in April 1999; Mohammad Tahir, Ph.D., Indianapolis-Marion County Forensic Services Agency, on December 5, 1998; James Wentzel and Dr. Elizabeth Balraj, Cuyahoga County Coroner's Office, by telephone and in person in August 2000; Ronnie Kuntz, the first newspaper photographer at the Sheppard crime scene, in 1999 and 2000; Russell Sherman, F. Lee Bailey's assistant at the second trial, on September 1, 1998; Robert B. Cummings, by phone in January 2000 and by letter dated January 26, 2000; Leah Montgomery Berton, former reporter, *The Plain Dealer*, on February 2, 2000; Cindy Leise, reporter, *The Chronicle Telegram*, 1999; James Neff, author and former *Plain Dealer* reporter, at various times in the late 1990s; Doris O'Donnell, former *Cleveland Press* reporter, in 2000; Bill Tanner, former *Cleveland Press* reporter, on April 27, 1999, and via email on August 20, 1999, and in 2000; and James F. McCarty, reporter, *The Plain Dealer*, by telephone in 1998 and in person by Warburton and the author in May 1998.

Dr. Gervase Flick was interviewed by telephone by Warburton in the spring of 1997, and interviewed in person by him several times in November 1997. Dr. Flick was interviewed by telephone by the author in February 1998. Attorney William Lawko, was interviewed by telephone by the author on March 31, 1999. David Lesnak, son of Mrs. John Lesnak, was interviewed by telephone by Major Warburton on June 18, 1998. Mrs. Joyce Nichol, Mrs. Lesnak's daughter, was interviewed by telephone by the author on August 23, 1999. Mr. and Mrs. Richard Knitter were interviewed by telephone by the author on January 20, 2000, and in person by Lisa Lombardo in a tape-recorded meeting on April 4, 2000. The Knitters were subsequently interviewed in person by the author on September 11 and 12, 2000. Donald H. Tripp was interviewed by telephone by Warburton on April 22, 1999, and by the author on November 24, 1999. A review of Attorney William Corrigan's pre-trial, trial, and post-trial notes was done by Warburton at the Western Reserve Historical Society in August 2000.

The following forensic scientists familiar with the Sheppard homicide were interviewed on several occasions by the author: Peter De Forest, D. Crim., in person and by telephone on several occasions from July 1, 1998, to 2001; Barton P. Epstein via telephone, e-mail and facsimile in 2000; Lowell J. Levine, DDS, forensic odontologist, in person on November 12, 1999, and by telephone on May 11, 2000. Dr. Burton Pollack, forensic odontologist, was interviewed by telephone on several occasions in 2000 and 2001 and submitted a written opinion on September 12, 2000; Christopher Lyons, DMD, was interviewed in person and by telephone in 1999 and 2000 and submitted a written opinion on July 11, 2000; Anthony M. Piscitelli, forensic scientist/trace evidence, NYSP Forensic Investigation Center, was interviewed in person by the author in 2000. Professor James Chapman, criminalist, who submitted a written opinion on February 12, 2001, was interviewed in person and by telephone by the author on many occasions from 1999 through 2001. David Ackebauer, leather expert, Ackebauer Laboratories, Fulton, New York, was personally contacted by Professor Chapman and the author on December 27, 1999, to conduct tests to compare the B-3A glove with the leather fragment found at the crime scene. Fay Parrella, leather expert, Gloversville, New York, was interviewed by telephone by the author in 2000, as was Steve Palenik on December 16, 1999. James L. Ebert, Chief Scientist, Ebert & Associates, submitted pillow-image analyses to James Chapman on January 5, 1981, January 2, 1982, April 19, 1982, May 1, 2001, and was contacted by telephone on June 4, 2001. Dan Nippus, Criminalist, Indian River Community College, was interviewed in person by Warburton on June 4, 1999. W. Mark Dale, Director, NYSP Forensic Investigation Center, offered unofficial comments regarding evidence implicating Call in the Sheppard homicide by personal letter to the author dated February 5, 2001.

Research was conducted by Warburton and the author with the assistance of the following individuals and organizations: The Western Reserve Historical Society, 1998 and 2000; Robert Swanson, President, Fulton Industries, Inc., by telephone by Warburton in August 2000 and Kim Griggs, Vice President of Sales, Fulton Industries, Inc., by written correspondence dated December 21, 2000; Peter Gray, President, Gray Security, Inc., was contacted by Warburton by telephone and letter in March 1999 and by the author by telephone and letter on April 6, 1999; Herman Schaub, The Society of Air Racing Historians, June 27, 1997; *Golden Pylons*, newsletter of the Society of Air Racing Historians, July-August 1997. David Bunsey, President, Cleveland Sports Car Club, was contacted by telephone by the author on March 16, 2001. Hurd Robenstine of the Portage County Historical Society was interviewed by telephone by the author on May 4, 1998, October 1999, and December 2000. The Collectors' Armory, Alexandria, VA, was visited by Warburton in 1997, as was the National Rifle Association,

Fairfax, VA, on June 17, 1997. Carl Stoutenberg, Stanley Tools, New Britain, Connecticut, was contacted by telephone and mail by the author and supplied written material in March 1999. W. Mark Dale and Herb Buckley, NYSP Forensic Investigation Center, were interviewed in person by the author on several occasions from 1998 to 2001. Rusty Bloxom, Librarian, The Mighty Eighth Air Force Heritage Museum, Savannah, Georgia, was interviewed in person by Warburton in September 1998 and contributed information in a letter dated May 29, 1997. Professor Charlie Strom, New York University, furnished information regarding meerschaum pipes via email on March 9, 1999. The following were interviewed by telephone by Warburton: Buck Rigg, The Mighty Eighth Air Force Heritage Museum, (supra), in July 1998; the United States Air Force Museum, Wright-Patterson AFB, Dayton, Ohio, in 1998.

The following books have been reviewed for background information by the author and British American Publishing personnel: *The Years Were Good* by Louis B. Seltzer; *The Sheppard Murder Case* by Paul Holmes; *My Brothers' Keeper* by Stephen Sheppard and Paul Holmes; *Retrial: Murder and Dr. Sam Sheppard* by Paul Holmes; *Endure and Conquer: My 12-Year Fight for Vindication* by Dr. Sam Sheppard; *Crime and Science: The New Frontier in Criminology* by Jurgen Thorwald; *Murder One* by Dorothy Kilgallen; *The Defense Never Rests* by F. Lee Bailey; *Dr. Sam: An American Tragedy* by Jack Harrison Pollack; *Mockery of Justice: The True Story of the Sheppard Murder Case* by Cynthia L. Cooper and Sam Reese Sheppard; *Famous Crimes Revisited* by Dr. Henry Lee and Dr. Jerry Labriola; *Survival* by Xavier Maniguet; *How to Survive on Land and Sea* by Frank C. Craighead, Jr., et al.; *The U. S. Armed Forces Survival Manual,* edited by John Boswell; *Leathercraft By Hand* by Jan Faulkner; *Imaginative Leatherwork* by Jeanne Argent; *The Leatherworking Handbook* by Valerie Michael; *Leather* by Donald J. Willcox, et al.; *Brendan's Leather Book* by Brendan Smith.

Documentaries regarding the Sheppard case which were reviewed include the following: *The Killer's Trail: Murder Mystery of the Century* by NOVA/WGBH Educational Foundation; *The Sam Sheppard Story* by American Justice/A&E Television Networks; *The Sam Sheppard Murder Case: E! True Hollywood Story* by E! Entertainment Television, Inc. Portions of other television and film programs reviewed include:

The Fugitive television series (ABC, 1963-1967; CBS, 2000-2001); *The Fugitive* (Warner Brothers, 1993); *My Father's Shadow: the Sam Sheppard Story* (CBS).

Newspapers reviewed include the following: *The Plain Dealer*; *The Cleveland Press*; *The Beacon Journal*; *The Post-Standard*; *The New York Times*; *The Adirondack Daily Enterprise*; *The Times Union*; *The Knickerbocker News*; *The Press-Republican*; *The Nevada State Journal*; *The Reno Evening Gazette*; *The Record-Courier*.

Part VII

The source of much of the information concerning Major Call's crimes and apprehension in Reno, Nevada, appears in Part V of these source notes—e.g., the files of the Reno PD, the USAF, the FBI, and the NYSP, and interviews conducted with personnel of these agencies. Neil Drew's recorded interviews with Harry Blaisdell on September 7, 8, 9, 1978, confirmed much of this data, as did Blaisdell's personal papers, including a hand-written diary of the Call events provided by Blaisdell's daughter, Gail Johnson. The circumstances surrounding Call's return to Lake Placid and his subsequent arraignment and incarceration in Essex County, New York, came from the minutes of the Essex County Grand Jury held January 1955, at which the following persons gave sworn testimony as to their knowledge of events involving Call: Arthur Adams, Jr., Ambulance Driver, page 109; Dr. Herbert Bergman, page 126; Sgt. Harry E. Blaisdell, NYSP, pages 142, 171, 177, 179, 183, 226; Fred Bolckmann, page 23; Raymond Borden, LPPD, page 41; Raymond E. Brunette, Town Hwy. Supt., page 118; William E. Cashin, page 204; Reginald Clark, Ambulance Driver, page 91; Inspector Martin F. Dillon, NYSP, page 140; John L. Fagan, LPPD, page 79; James Bernard Fell, LPPD, page 64; Cpl. P. J. Harris, NYSP, pages 159, 234; Tpr. Andrew Hart, NYSP, pages 180, 211; Dr. George G. Hart, page 97; Dr. Edwin M. Jamison, page 101; Spencer J. Johnston, page 4; Cpl. F. A. Keane, NYSP, page 235; Tpr. D. H. Maring, NYSP, page 164; Lawrence MacDonald, LPPD, page 236; Tpr. W. J. McDonald, NYSP, page 181; Inspector R. J. McDowell, NYSP, pages 135, 142, 163, 178; Patrick W. McKeown, page 176; Dr. Carl G. Merkel, page 152; Captain H. T. Muller, NYSP, page 232; Tpr. K. D. O'Dell, NYSP, page 130; Sgt. H.

M. Osborne, NYSP, page 165; Ruth Pelkey, Officer Pelkey's widow, page 237; Tpr. L. J. Robinson, NYSP, page 198; Sgt. F. J. Sayres, page 174; Lt. James C. Smith, page 171; Charles H. Stephen, page 103; Sgt. Dominic Valenze, LPPD, pages 46, 184, 241; Cpl. Edward H. Van Schaick, NYSP, pages 24, 186, 200; Donald Edgar Whalley, page 114; Tpr. Robert Wilson, NYSP, page 225.

In addition to the foregoing minutes, information was obtained from work papers used in preparation for the grand jury proceedings, secured from the District Attorney's office. Neil Drew's recorded interviews with the following individuals corroborated much of this data: E. Stewart Jones, January 16, 1979; Daniel Manning, January 19, 1981; Harold Soden, January 26, 1981; and Raymond Brunette, September 30, 1978. Adding to the description of this period was Robert Sylvester's letter postmarked January 22, 2000, and the author's subsequent telephone interviews with Sylvester, as well as Lisa Lombardo's interviews in person with Sylvester on February 1, 2000, and April 3, 2000. The author, accompanied by Colonel Arnold and Major Warburton of the NYSP, reviewed records of the Essex County Courthouse and personally interviewed the sheriff and prison guards at the Essex County Jail, as well as Ron Briggs, Essex County District Attorney, on August 28, 1998. Maxine Smith's son, John Smith*, furnished information regarding his mother's interest in Call by telephone to Lisa Lombardo in November and December 1999, by letter on January 28, 2000, and by e-mail on November 8, 9, 17, 1999. Onondaga County Public Library furnished news articles and photographs regarding Call's apprehension, by letter dated October 29, 1999. Shirley Morgan, Saranac Lake Free Library, contributed written material by letter dated June 30, 1997. New York State newspapers mentioned in Part IV provided extensive coverage from which further information was secured regarding Call's incarceration and court proceedings in Essex County.

Part VIII

Passages describing Call's incarceration at Attica and Clinton Prison, Dannemora, are based in part on information from the

---

*fictitious name

records of the following agencies: the New York State Department of Correctional Services (NYSDCS), the New York State Division of Parole; the NYSP; and the FBI. In addition, many interviews were conducted with those knowledgeable about Call's prison time. Neil Drew held recorded and in-person interviews with the following: Jack LaGree, Dannemora Prison Guard, July 4, 1980; Daniel Manning, District Attorney, January 19, 1981; Harry Blaisdell, September 7, 8, 9, 1978. The author conducted interviews in person and by telephone with Jack LaGree, Jr., Dannemora Prison Guard (son of Jack LaGree) in 2000 and 2001. Terrance B. Gilroy, Dannemora Town Historian, was interviewed in person and by telephone and submitted written material in October and November 1998. Glenn S. Goord, Commissioner, NYSDCS, was contacted in person by the author on April 17, 1998, and arranged meetings with the following associates, who furnished background information regarding the Clinton Correctional Facility and Attica Prison: James Flateau, Donna Roy, and Linda Foglia.

Other interviews conducted by the author regarding Call's incarceration are as follows: Eleanor Mayette and Judith Harris, Dannemora Free Library, by telephone and by letter, October 1998; Jerry Burke, member, NYS Board of Parole, by telephone, October 1998; Diane Petrashune, Clinton Correctional Facility, by telephone and by letter, October 1998; Thomas P. Grant, Special Assistant to the Chairman, NYS Department of Parole, by letter, April 24, 1998, and by telephone, May 12, 1998. Specific information regarding Call's stay in Clinton Prison at Dannemora and Attica was obtained from the following prison records: John R. Cain, Head Clerk, Interdepartmental Communication, Clinton Prison, dated November 9, 1955; Call's November 7, 1955, letter to his sister and to various government agencies in November 1955; and Warden's Record Card, May 11, 1955, May 15, 1955, September 10, 1966, and February 16, 1968. Call's son, Jeff Call, furnished some limited information regarding Call's prison time during the author's visit to Meridian, Mississippi, on November 11 and 12, 1998, and in subsequent telephone calls during 1999, 2000, and 2001. Records obtained from the FBI on January 19, 2000, contain seventy pages of information detailing an investigation of Call conducted by the Bureau while Call was in prison, including reports dated April 19, 1955, April 10, 1956,

April 19, 1956, April 20, 1956, April 27, 1956, April 30, 1956, July 14, 1956, July 15, 1956, July 16, 1956, and March 7, 1958.

Additional communications were received from the following: Daniel A. Senkowski, Superintendent, Clinton Correctional Facility, by letter to Warburton on June 3, 1996; John E. Haas, Archivist, Ohio Historical Society, by letter to British American on November 19, 1998. Correspondence between Call, prison officials, the FBI, his family, Robert Sylvester, Maxine Smith, and others appearing in Parts III, VII, VIII, and Exhibit N was obtained from prison records, the FBI, and the NYSP, as well as family, friends, and associates of Call. The letter from Muriel Call to her mother appearing in Part I is a reasonable extrapolation based on information received from the foregoing sources. The reference to Willie Sutton during Call's imprisonment at Attica was obtained from Willie Sutton's biography *Where The Money Was* by Willie Sutton with Edward Linn.

Following are newspapers, magazines, and periodicals from which information was obtained pertaining to NYS prisons at the time Call was incarcerated: *The Saturday Evening Post,* "Inside Dannemora" by Hal Burton, December 29, 1956; *The Press-Republican,* August 6, 1953, September 13-18, 1987, and August 2, 1992; NYSDCS— *Manual on Orientation of Inmates in Correctional Institutions.*

Part IX

Much of the material in the concluding passages of the book dealing with Major Call's life in Mantua, Ohio, is based on public records and contacts with Call's family and his business and social friends and acquaintances, as well as personal visits made by George Warburton and the author in April 1998 to various sites in Mantua that were connected with events in Call's life. Records of the following organizations were reviewed by Warburton and the author: The Portage County Historical Society; Portage County Court House; Portage County Probate Court; Portage County Recorders' Office; LaBrae High School (formerly Leavittsburg High School); Ohio State Board of Parole; Ohio State Highway Patrol; Mantua Police Department; Portage County Sheriff's Office; and *The Record-Courier.*

The following individuals provided additional information: John McGill, Nelson Ledges Race Course, furnished written information to Warburton dated May 19, 1998; employees of the White* Contracting Company were interviewed by Warburton, including Paul White, in person in June 1998, Hal White, in person on April 29, 1998, and Barry White, by telephone in 1998. The following were interviewed in person by the author and Warburton in April 1998: Doris and Hollis Dye, Blanche Call's sister and brother-in-law; Lt. Alan Moore, Ohio State Highway Patrol; Geraldine Stamm, Town Clerk, Mantua, Ohio. Stella White*, Call's sister, was contacted by telephone by Warburton in August 1966, July 1988, and on April 10, 1998, and by telephone by the author in July 1998 and on April 20, 2001. Additional interviews by Warburton were conducted with: Harry Booker, Chief, Mantua Police Department, by telephone on July 6 and 7, 1998; Linda Rickard, owner, Sher-Lin's Little Store, Mantua, in person in April 1998; Dean of F&S Automotive by phone in April 2000; Sgt. Kevin Kaiser, Oceanside, California, Police Department, by telephone on December 28, 1998; William Funtig, Blanche Call's former boyfriend, in person on December 29, 1998; Robert Klose, Blanche Call's brother, by telephone in May 1998; Ken Schiemann, Blanche Call's brother-in-law, by telephone in 1999. Call's second wife, Blanche Call, and his stepdaughter, Teresa Solano, were interviewed numerous times by telephone by Warburton in 1999 and 2000, and in person by him at their residence in California in June 1999, at which time they furnished a broad range of information regarding Call's life. Subsequent to these interviews they continued to furnish a considerable amount of information by telephone and mail. Mrs. Furman Jenkins, wife of Blanche Call's former husband, was interviewed by telephone by Lisa Lombardo of British American Publishing on October 30, 1998.

Following are additional telephone interviews conducted by the author: Hurd W. Robenstine, Portage County Historical Society, October 1999 and December 2000; Frank Buell, long-time resident of Mantua, October 7, 1999; Loris Troyer, former editor, *The Record-Courier*, April 1998 and May 2, 2000. Harold Crew, Call's former parole officer was interviewed by telephone by Warburton on June 28,

---

*fictitious name

1999, and by telephone by the author on July 27, 1999, and June 8, 2000. In April 1998, Warburton and the author personally observed and photographed the location of Major Call's fatal car crash in Trumbull County, Ohio, at which time they personally interviewed John Schlacht, nearby resident who had been the first person to arrive at the scene of Call's accident. Schlacht was contacted again on the telephone by the author in 1999. Warburton and the author visited Call's gravesite in Hillside Cemetery, Mantua Village, Ohio, in April 1998, at which time photographs were taken of the cemetery and Major Call's tombstone. Carolyn Hummel, Chairman of the Hillside Cemetery Board, was interviewed by telephone by the author on September 19, 2000. Pam Wilson, State Automobile Mutual Insurance Company, assisted Warburton in the research of Call's car accident and death, in July 1998. Other agencies and individuals providing information on Major Call's death in Mantua, Ohio, are: Ohio Department of Health, December 8, 1998 (Death Certificate copy date) and Pat Carney and Cindy Shomo, Title Professionals, Inc., of Warren and Ravenna, Ohio, who furnished documents regarding Call's estate by mail on July 29, 1998.

Epilogue

Material describing the Hillside Cemetery in Mantua Village, Ohio, is based on George Warburton's and the author's visit to Hillside Cemetery in April 1998, and the author's telephone interview with Carolyn Hummel on September 19, 2000. Material pertaining to the Magnolia Cemetery in Meridian, Mississippi, was obtained by the author from Janie Reeder, Family Counselor, Magnolia Cemetery, by telephone and facsimile on November 9, 1998, and from Sherry Middleton, Magnolia Cemetery, who was contacted by telephone by the author on September 14, 2000. The author, accompanied by Major Call's son, Jeff Call, visited Muriel Call's gravesite on November 12, 1998, at which time the author was permitted to take the photograph of the gravestone which appears in this book.

In concluding these acknowledgements the author would like to make special mention of Major Call's son, Jeff Call. During the past four years Jeff gave unstintingly of his time and provided much information, both while the author was visiting Jeff in Meridian, Mississippi, as well as subsequent contacts. Throughout countless interviews he remained gracious and cooperative, never attempting to influence the author's portrayal of his father. Indeed, he appeared remarkably candid. On one occasion when the author remarked that he did not think the book was going to do Jeff or his family any good, Jeff replied that he understood this and, in fact, had declined to cooperate when contacted about a book on the subject twenty years previously. He stated that he finally decided a story was inevitable and had come to grips with it. "Jim walked close to the line his whole life," he said. "The book's probably only the tip of the iceberg." When asked if he thought his father would kill people he replied, "Hell, that's a no brainer. That's a given. If you stood in Jim's way he'd kill you."

Jeff never requested any special consideration or changes in the text other than one. At the conclusion of the work the author read to Jeff a closing scene in the epilogue in which Jeff was visiting his mother's grave with a close family member. Jeff requested that there be no mention of the relative in the book, and since the scene was not material, it was deleted.

Now in his early forties, Jeff Call is a respected businessman in Meridian, Mississippi. As was Major Call, he is handsome, charming and quick-witted.

SCHEMATIC
TIMELINE

MAJOR CALL—MARILYN SHEPPARD CASE

The diagram that appears on the inside back cover illustrates salient points dealing with the criminal activities of Major Call (subject) for the six-month period commencing with his AWOL from the Air Force on May 13, 1954, until his apprehension in Reno, Nevada, on November 9, 1954. Starting with the left side of the chart, icons are used to illustrate how the subject, reacting to pressures in the military, went AWOL and committed many crimes which culminated in the murder of Marilyn Sheppard. These graphic symbols show the correlation between the subject's modus operandi and the Sheppard crime scene evidence. They further depict the flight of the subject from Cleveland and Mantua, Ohio, after the Sheppard homicide to Lake Placid where he committed numerous burglaries and armed robberies. Here he shot three police officers and evaded authorities during a one hundred day manhunt in the Adirondack Mountains. The timeline concludes with the subject's apprehension and confessions following numerous burglaries in Reno, Nevada. This schematic rendering offers a comprehensive picture of the magnitude and severity of the subject's crimes during this six-month period.